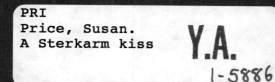

A
STERKARM
KISS

Also by Susan Price

A
STERKARM
KISS

†††

S U S A N P R I C E

An Imprint of HarperCollins*Publishers*

Eos is an imprint of HarperCollins Publishers.

Library of Congress Cataloging-in-Publication Data
Price, Susan.
    A Sterkarm kiss / Susan Price. – 1st U.S. ed.
        p.   cm.
    Sequel to: The Sterkarm handshake.
    Summary: The Time Tube has opened again between the sixteenth and twenty-first
centuries, and a wedding is arranged between the Sterkarms and the Grannams, catching
Andrea up in the disastrous consequences.
    ISBN 0-06-072197-9 – 0-06-072198-7 (lib. bdg.)
    [1. Time travel–Fiction. 2. Science Fiction.]   I. Title.
PZ7.P9317Sr2004   2003025836
[Fic] – dc22

1 2 3 4 5 6 7 8 9 10
❖

First American Edition, 2004
Published in the United Kingdom in 2003 by Scholastic Press

For David Simpson, a Scottish Treasure

CONTENTS

A
STERKARM
KISS

I

21ST SIDE:
DOWN AT THE PUB

†††

P er? Hite thee Per?"
The young man seated at the table looked up—and it *was* Per. From the bar she'd doubted, but looking into that strikingly pretty face, with the large eyes, so pale a blue they were almost silver, there could be no doubt at all. Especially when the younger boy who sat beside him was so much like him, and could only be Per's cousin Ingram. Except that it was impossible for either of them to be there.

Per stared at her, startled, and then his eyes gave that silver flash she remembered so well, as if a small bulb had lit behind them. He jumped up, still staring. *"Yi hite Per Toorkildsson Sterkarm—oh vah air thee hite?"*—I'm called Per Toorkildsson Sterkarm—and what art *thou* called?

It was afternoon. The bar was almost empty and almost silent. Per's throaty yell shocked a couple on the other side of the room, and they looked around. The Sterkarms had always shouted where other people murmured—it came from habitually conversing across valleys. That loud voice, and its bronchial hoarseness, would have made her absolutely sure, even if she hadn't been before. Besides, who else in this entire world could have understood what she said, and answered her in the same thick dialect? Who else would stare at her—big fat Andy—with such obvious admiration and place such flirting stress on *"thee"*? It was Per, it could only be Per. But as certainly as she knew it was him, she knew it couldn't be. I am going mad, she thought. She'd read somewhere that hallucinations always seemed perfectly real to those who experienced them.

It was the start of her afternoon shift, and she'd been checking that there were plenty of chips and peanuts, when she'd felt her attention pulled to the seat in the corner by the door. Something she'd glimpsed there, subliminally, was hammering for her fuller attention. She'd looked, and had seen Per.

The shock had jolted her. She'd thought she was over the phase of seeing him everywhere, had done with following tall, fair-haired young men through the streets convinced, against all sense, that it was Per. Don't say it was starting again. Take a better look, she ordered herself. You'll see that it's not him.

She'd leaned over the bar to get a good look, to make it plain to herself that it wasn't Per and couldn't be him. He was dressed in jeans and sneakers, for God's sake, with a zip-up jacket and a baseball cap. Sitting beside him was a thin young man with close-cropped hair, dressed in a gray suit and wearing spectacles with fine gold frames.

Ah—but sitting on the other side of the table, also dressed in jeans and sneakers, was a slightly smaller, younger version of Per, a boy of about fourteen. Ingram Gobbyson, the cousin who admired and ran after Per, and wished they could be brothers.

It could not be Per and Ingram. Could not be.

But the way they sat, the way their hair grew—it *was* them.

Andrea felt scared and sick. To hallucinate so vividly, while stone sober, in the daylit afternoon—it couldn't be good.

There was only one way to settle it. She had to go right up to the man, look into his face at close quarters, speak to him. . . . Her heart had thumped wildly as she'd approached him. Now he stood looking down at her, smiling. Her heart hammered and raced, half stifling her. Heat flushed her face, her vision blurred, and she thought that she would faint. Turning, she ran for the quiet room behind the bar.

Near the bar she collided with someone. A big man. An expanse of smooth dark suit filled her blurring vision. Looking up, she saw a rather pink and fleshy but still handsome face. It smirked at her with full red lips from beneath a quiff of very dark hair. She gaped at the man in confusion, recognizing the face and feeling dread at recognizing it, but unable to remember, at that distracted moment, where she had seen it before.

"Andrea!" said the smirking lips, and the whole face creased into what was meant to be a winning smile, though it retained much of its habitual sneer. "You don't look a day older or a pound lighter!"

James Windsor. Meeting James Windsor, under any circumstances, would have spoiled her day. To meet him seconds after meeting Per where Per could not possibly be was sinister and frightening. She couldn't breathe; her knees shook. The edges of her vision were brightening to white—"Let me by!" She shoved past him and hurried, as best she could, through the open gate of the bar and into the little stockroom.

There, among dingy cartons of chips and peanuts, she collapsed onto a stool, gasped in a deep breath, and leaned forward, putting her head between her knees.

It had been a normal, settled day in what had become her normal, settled life. A casual glance across the bar had torn all that to pieces and thrown it into a wind, to whirl about her. To see Per again, when she had just been recovering from—

And it was not possible! The Tube had been closed down. Per was in his own world, he was five hundred years dead. He could not be here in the 21st, hanging out in pubs with James Windsor.

And Windsor. Per had put a lance through him, and he'd ended up in a hospital bed with half his guts missing. Even if it was possible—which it was not—why would he be in company with—?

She realized something else, which made her sit up straight, something almost as surprising as seeing Per at all. Per hadn't known who she was. She'd spoken to him, she'd stood right in front of him, and he'd looked at her without knowing her and had asked what her name was.

That was impossible. She'd known his shock of roughly cut fair hair, the slope of his shoulders, the slant of his neck. She'd have known his voice, instantly. At a distance she'd have known his walk. She'd have known him in the dark. But to him she'd been a stranger.

The Tube was up and working again.

It was the only explanation. They'd said they were closing it, but it must be up again, it must be. And they'd gone back to a time before contact had been made with the Sterkarms. So Per had never met her and didn't know her.

Per hadn't looked any younger, though.

Of course, if the Tube had gone back to a time ten minutes before contact had been made with the Sterkarms previously . . .

She put her face into her hands again, her head aching as her brain tied itself in knots. She didn't understand. She knew only that if James Windsor was involved, it had to be bad news.

A clump of heavy shoes made her look up. Her boss, the landlord, was intruding on her hidey-hole. "Aren't you supposed to be–?" He broke off. "You all right, Petal?"

Andrea opened her mouth to say, automatically, like the good sort she was, that she was fine–but then changed her mind. "I've had a bit of a shock." Her voice wavered convincingly.

"Oh." Her boss stood awkwardly, just inside the door. "Well. Sit there for a bit, if you like. We ain't what you could call busy. Have a cup of coffee."

"Thanks. I'll be okay in a minute."

"Bloke gave me this for you anyway." He held out a small card to her. "Posh sort." Andrea looked at the card but made no attempt to take it. "Go on then–I don't want it."

She took the card. It gave Windsor's name, his telephone number, his cell number, his fax, and his e-mail. On the back he'd written: *Want a better job? Call me.*

She knew immediately that calling him would be a big mistake, and that she would do it the first chance she had.

At the table in the corner by the door, there was some consternation.

"She spoke English!" Per said to both Gareth and Ingram.

"She did," Gareth agreed, and stared across the bar. James Windsor was speaking to the broad-beamed barmaid. A barmaid who could speak an obscure 16th-century northern dialect of English, so thick it was almost another language—and a language, moreover, not even from this dimension. It was, to say the least, surprising.

"She was beautiful!" young Ingram said enthusiastically.

"Aye," Per agreed, and cupped his hands. "Lovely big tits!"

They both laughed, and Gareth sighed, feeling depressed. The Sterkarms often had that effect on him. They were as unthinking and crude as any 21st-century yobs. Somehow he had expected better from the 16th century. They didn't even have good taste. The woman wasn't beautiful. She was fat.

"She came right up and asked thy name!" Ingram said. "Looked thee right in the face and asked thy name!"

Leaning back, adopting a knowing air for his young cousin's benefit, Per said, "The Elf-Mays are like that—forward and free."

Giggling, Ingram leaned across the table and poked his cousin. "She wants thee for her prick!"

Per glanced across the bar, in time to see the Elf-May push past Elf-Windsor and run away into a back room. "Nay," he said, to hide his disappointment. "She's frit it's too big for her!" They both laughed again. Inwardly, Gareth groaned. Soon he would be back 16th side, hemmed in on all sides by people like this.

James Windsor came up, smiling. "Shall we go?" It was an order, framed as a question.

"Elf-Windsor wishes to leave now," Gareth said to Per and Ingram.

Per hesitated for no more than an eye's blink. He would have liked to stay longer—the alehouse was palatial, with thick cloth on the floor and glass in the windows and polished wood and brass everywhere. And then there was the serving may. He would have liked another look at her, and a chance to see if Ingram was right—but this wasn't the tower, where any woman was fair game for him. He was a guest in Elf-Land, and if Elf-Windsor wished to leave, then as a polite guest he had to leave. So he said to Ingram, "Another ride in the cart!" Ingram rose readily at that, a smile on his face, and both of them made for the doors.

Falling in beside James Windsor, Gareth said, "That barmaid. She spoke to Per—in Sterkarm."

"She used to work for me," Windsor said. "She was rather good." He omitted to mention that the rough dictionary and tapes from which Gareth had initially learned his "Sterkarm" had been made by Andrea. "I'm thinking of asking her to come back to her old job. You didn't think we'd come all this way just to give the Merc a run?"

"Ah," Gareth said, and wondered if the fat barmaid could be a rival for promotion. Surely not.

Outside the alehouse several Elf-Carts were at rest and waiting. They were of many bright colors—the colors of Elf-Land were brilliant, even garish, and sometimes hurt the eyes. Per led Ingram past them all to the gleaming black cart that was Windsor's. As they stood beside it, waiting for the others, he drew his fingers along its smooth, glassy surface. Dimly, as though in a black mirror, they could see themselves reflected in the cart's side.

"I like the red carts," Ingram said, pointing to a scarlet cart on the other side of the pound.

"'Car,'" Per corrected him. "They call them 'cars.'"

The car gave a shrill electronic squeal as Windsor came nearer— it had picked up the signal from the coder in one of his pockets, identified him as its owner, turned off its alarm, and unlocked its doors. Both Windsor and Gareth smiled to see the two Sterkarms jump at the noise.

But then Per opened the driver's door and got into the driver's seat. Ingram laughed aloud, looking from his cousin to the approaching Elves, thrilled by his cousin's daring but a little apprehensive at what the powerful Elf-Windsor might do.

Gareth looked to see how Windsor was taking it too, and was surprised to see Windsor watching the Sterkarms with a strange expression that was almost tender. Windsor was remembering how Per's feet had crumpled the hood of another, similar Merc, and how the lance point had come through the windshield, crazing it, shattering it. That hadn't been this Per, of course. Except that it had.

"He's quick to learn," Windsor said. "Smarter than a Labrador. You could teach him all sorts of tricks."

Per, in the driver's seat, had his hands on the wheel. He pressed the pedals with his feet and pulled at the gear lever, knowing that they had something to do with making the cart go.

Windsor, stooping to look into the car, said, "Okay, okay."

Per, instead of getting out of the car, simply moved over into the passenger seat, thereby ensuring that he sat in the front, next to the driver. Windsor got behind the wheel, and Gareth, opening the back door, ushered Ingram inside before climbing in beside him.

Per had already fastened his seat belt—snapping the belt together seemed to have something to do with the magic that made the car go—and was looking eagerly toward the ignition, wanting the ride to begin. In the back, Gareth had to help Ingram fasten his belt. It was the boy's first visit to Elf-Land—he'd been brought along only because Per had asked for him to come.

Windsor didn't fasten his own belt. Instead, he turned and said to Gareth, "We'll give them the gewgaws now, I think. Will you do the honors?" When Gareth looked blank, he said, "The trunk?"

Gareth climbed out of the car again, resentfully. It had begun to rain slightly. He opened the trunk and took out the two shopping bags, handing them to Windsor through his now opened door.

As Gareth climbed back inside, Windsor handed the bags to Per and Ingram. They were much struck by the material the bags were made of, their smoothness, bright colors, and perfect lettering. The rustling, crinkling noise they made was appreciated too. After a few moments Windsor lost patience, took the bags back, and gave the Sterkarms the velvet boxes from inside. "Open them."

Two watches were found inside: large, chunky, shiny gold things. Per immediately slipped his on over his wrist, showing Ingram how to do it and pointing out the watches that Windsor and Gareth were wearing.

"Gareth will teach you how to use them, eh, Gareth?" Windsor said.

"Oh—aye." Gareth translated what Windsor had said, and promised to teach them how to tell time. A perfect waste of his time, he thought, since the Sterkarms had absolutely no use for watches. They got up at first light and went to bed when it was dark. In between, they herded cattle, robbed one another, and fought. What did it matter to them if it was eleven in the morning or three in the afternoon? Still, he supposed, there was nothing else for him to do once he was back 16th side.

"Toosand takh!" Ingram said. A thousand thanks.

"There are packs of aspirin in there too," Windsor said. "Enough to keep you going for a while."

Gareth translated. Per and Ingram were impressed and excited to see how many boxes of "wee white pills" they were getting. Windsor had supplied the very cheapest and nastiest-tasting aspirin, but it didn't matter. The Sterkarms had nothing to match it for painkilling properties.

"And a couple of rather special T-shirts," Windsor said, and taking one from the bag, he spread it out. Both Per and Ingram exclaimed. The T-shirts were of cheap black cotton. On the chest, in red, was an upraised arm—a left arm—holding a dagger. The arm and dagger were enclosed within the red outline of a shield. It was the Sterkarms' badge, their name in picture form—"strong arm."

Per and Ingram were thrilled. Per undid his seat belt, shrugged off his jacket, dragged off the white T-shirt he was wearing, and put on the new one. Ingram quickly followed suit.

Windsor laughed as he fastened his belt. He pressed the starter button, and the car began to purr. He said, *"Kvenna,* eh? *Stoor kvenna?"*

Per wasn't listening, too interested in his gifts and the steering of the car out of the parking lot. Even when Windsor repeated himself, he was puzzled. "Woman, eh?" Windsor had said. "Big woman?" But despite being a powerful Elf-Man, Windsor spoke terrible English, and you had to make allowances. Looking over the back of his seat at Ingram, Per said, "He means the Elf-May in the alehouse."

"Hoon var smookt!" Ingram said.

Gareth translated for Windsor. "She was beautiful."

Gareth spoke unenthusiastically, but Ingram's tone had been very different. Windsor laughed. "You like her, eh?"

Gareth repeated the question in the Sterkarms' dialect, and Per and Ingram answered together, *"Ya!"* and laughed.

"Big way!" Per added, trying out some of the Elvish he'd picked up.

Windsor turned the large car onto the main road and picked up speed. The Sterkarms were distracted by the scenery flying past, by the car's faint vibration, like the breathing and heartbeat of a living thing. Ingram, especially, was as scared as he was excited.

"Ask them if they'd like her," Windsor said.

"I've already asked them that."

Irritated and contemptuous, Windsor said, "No. Ask them if they'd like to screw her."

Gareth was silent for a moment. He wanted to ask, What? Am I a pimp now? But he knew that Windsor would only order him to do his job. "I'm not sure how to ask that."

"I thought you were a translator? Ask them!"

It took a few seconds to get their attention away from the car and its speed, but then Gareth said, "The woman in the alehouse–er–" He felt his face reddening and was furious with himself. "Would you–er. Like to lie with her?"

They stared at him. Had they understood? Blushing even more, Gareth put one hand in the crook of his elbow and jerked his arm upward in an unmistakable gesture.

Per laughed. *"Ya!"* Ingram just laughed.

2

21ST SIDE:
TAKING THE POSITION

††††

S unlight streamed through the large windows into the room, shining on the polished wood of desk and floor, glinting in the mirrors. The warmth strengthened the scent of the roses in a bowl on a side table and made their petals fall.

Andrea sat on the couch under the window, feet neatly together, hands folded in her lap, waiting, as she'd been waiting for nearly fifteen minutes. In front of her was a low table holding a spread of glossy magazines. On the other side of the room, at her work station, sat Windsor's plump, pleasant, middle-aged secretary.

Sighing, Andrea turned her head and looked out at the wide lawns and mature trees of the grounds. She knew them well, having worked here, at Dilsmead Hall, before—in the days when she'd commuted five hundred years in the Time Tube, as other people commute five miles on the tube.

This is a mistake, she thought. I know it's a mistake. Worse—if I take this position, it'll be a disaster, because it has to be a setup. Windsor must already have decided to give her the job, or why would he have gone to the trouble to find out where she was working and come visiting? Windsor wouldn't have dropped in on her for old time's sake. So it was a scam. Beware, beware!

Just get up, she told herself. Walk out. Go home. Get a life.

She remained on the couch.

Catching her eye, the secretary smiled and said, "I'm sure Mr. Windsor won't be much longer." A buzzer sounded, and with another smile she said, "There you are! You can go in now."

Oh, thank you so much, Andrea thought as she stood. I am now graciously allowed to enter Windsor's presence. She crossed to the door of the inner office, thinking, I should march in there, tell him where he can stick his job and his head, and walk out.

She teetered on the edge of doing it.

She did refuse to knock before opening the door. Grasping the door's brass handle, she firmly turned it and strode in.

"Andrea!" Windsor said, rising from behind his desk and coming to meet her, as if her appearance was a complete surprise and he hadn't deliberately been keeping her waiting. She noticed that he still had the big, framed photo on his wall—the one of the Sterkarm tower against a stormy sky. As if he owned the tower—as if it was his country home. "Let's use my cozy corner," he said, ushering her to one side of the room.

The "cozy corner" had a couch and three easy chairs arranged around a low, smoked-glass coffee table. Whenever she'd spoken with Windsor in his office before, she'd had to take one of the low chairs directly in front of his big desk, where she'd felt—as she'd been meant to feel—exposed and clumsy. Obviously, today she was to be charmed. She refused to be charmed.

"Beryl will bring us some coffee and cookies soon. Or cake? Would you prefer cake? Or both?" Windsor gave his supposedly charming smile, which Andrea would have called a smirk. Even when he tried to be charming, he couldn't resist a jibe.

"Just coffee, thank you."

"Sure? We don't want you fainting on the train home."

Andrea looked at him, at his thick, dark, oiled hair; at his fleshy face, above all at his smirk; and the detestation she felt for him rose up in her so strongly that it was difficult to keep her face from showing it, and perhaps she didn't entirely succeed. She remembered all the good reasons she had for detesting him, and thought: Why am I meekly going along with this? "Cut the crap," she said. "What's this about?"

"Andrea! That's not like you!"

"When you came into the pub that day—was that Per with you? Was it?" It was the question she'd traveled two hundred miles or more to ask, and she saw a flicker—just a flicker—of consternation in Windsor's face. The conversation wasn't going the way he'd planned. Good.

The door opened and Beryl came in, carrying their coffee and cookies on a tray. The few seconds she was in the room, asking if everything was all right and if there was anything they needed, gave Windsor time to collect himself.

"So how have you been?" he asked, pouring coffee as the door closed behind Beryl. "I haven't been too well myself. I'm still not one hundred percent—probably overdoing it, but once a workaholic, always a workaholic."

Andrea set her teeth and refused to say the polite, solicitous things her upbringing prompted her to say.

"They grew me a new piece of gut, you know—amazing work. I had an incredibly good team of surgeons, and tiptop aftercare. One of the best hospitals in the country. Shockingly expensive, but worth every penny and more. Still, it's not something you shrug off, a lance in the guts."

"Was it Per?"

Windsor smirked. "You mean, who stuck the lance in my gut?"

"You know what I mean."

"My, Andrea, you've become very prickly." He leaned back in his chair, smiling, and crossed his legs. His trouser leg hitched up a little, but only enough to show a black sock, damn him. "In answer to your question, I can only say, yes—and no."

"And does that mean anything?"

"Working as a barmaid is obviously very bad for the temper. I mean yes, it was Per, but not Per as you know him."

Andrea stood. "I've had enough of this. I'm going."

"Back to working in a pub?"

"The great advantage of working in a pub," Andrea said, looking down at him, "is that every day I meet a far better class of person than you."

Windsor raised his thick, dark brows. "Oh dear. Andrea, sit down. Please, sit down. I'll explain. The Tube is up and running again."

"I guessed that much," Andrea said, still standing. "Why? It was supposed to be economically unviable. It was closed down."

"Just because something's closed down, Andrea, it doesn't mean that it has to stay closed down."

"It was closed because the Sterkarms slapped your greedy snouts away from the trough. So why is it suddenly open again?"

Windsor didn't like being spoken to like that, but he hardly showed it—which made Andrea even more suspicious. "Please sit down again, Andrea. It was that crowd of unimaginative penny stackers in Accounts who got it closed, with their usual short-sightedness. It stayed closed for just as long as it took the company to digest Accounts' figures and realize how many billions they'd have thrown away on research and development if it stayed closed, with about as much chance of getting any of it back as a paraplegic has of playing for Manchester University." He smiled, congratulating himself on being daring enough to say things like that. "So the Board gritted its collective teeth and decided to push on until there is a return. This is real business, you see, Andrea—Big Business. It's not managing your building-society account—or the books at the Rose and Crown. Besides, what's a few billion against loss of face? And properly considered, our problems last time were more a failure of security than anything. I said so, in my report."

Andrea blinked and thought through her memory of events. She had the impression that, all along, Windsor had consistently underestimated the Sterkarms' treachery, intelligence, and ferocity. Despite being warned many times. "It was a failure of *security*?"

"Bryce. You remember Bryce?"

Andrea did. She'd liked the man. Ex-army and Head of Security at Dilsmead Hall. He'd been killed. By the Sterkarms. Skewered by a lance, actually, and then beheaded, on the neat gravel path that ran behind the building. "So you're blaming it all on Bryce," she said. "Because he isn't here to say otherwise."

"That's very cynical, Andrea."

"It's very true, you mean? Bryce did a good job, as far as he was allowed to. And he was still trying to do a good job when—"

"I'm not deaf, Andrea. Don't shout at me."

"I'm not shouting. Bryce was killed. And not just Bryce. I've been wondering ever since—just how the hell did you cover that up?"

Windsor sighed. "We paid compensation, of course. What's the big deal? Thousands of people are killed every day in car crashes—who ever worries about that? Bryce was killed in an industrial accident. Shit happens. Everybody who works for us signs waiver forms. You did yourself."

"But he was beheaded," Andrea said. "Didn't his family ask questions?"

"What if they did? It only needs a soap-opera wedding, a Hollywood couple getting divorced, a politician caught with his pants down—and then who cares about some drone being beheaded north of Watford? Get real, Andrea."

She sat quietly for a few moments. Discussing ethics with Windsor was a waste of time and breath. "It was Per in the pub. I knew it was. But he was wearing jeans."

"Did you expect me to take him into a pub without his jeans?"

Andrea grimaced impatiently and didn't bother to answer. "He didn't know me."

"No," Windsor agreed. "He wouldn't."

"You've taken the Tube further back in time," she said. "To *before* we arrived the last time."

"Very good! But you don't quite win the weekend break and luxury hamper."

"What then? How could Per not recognize me?"

"The dimensions," Windsor said. "Did you ever master the theory? Sixteenth side isn't *our* past. It's the past of another dimension."

Andrea sat down, the better to think. Her brows came together as she fought to concentrate. Something tickled at the back of her mind, some connection, but she was too distracted to see what it meant. Abstractedly, she picked up a cookie and bit it, and as the chocolate melted in her mouth, the connections snapped together.

"You've gone into yet another dimension!" she said. "It was Per—but from another dimension—a dimension where we've never been. Per—but a Per I've never met."

Windsor smirked. "*Now* you get the cigar."

Andrea remembered how Per—this unknown Per—had stared at her in the pub, admiring her. "But it's close—this dimension? It's close to the one we did go into?"

"There's no essential difference. Except on our side. We've tried hard to be pally with the Sterkarms this time, not to upset them. Give them what they want. Aspirins. Jeans. It seems to be working."

Andrea was only half listening. A snatch of words and melody ran through her head—one of the many, many songs she'd learned when she'd lived with the Sterkarms.

Oh, see you my tall love, with his cheeks like roses?

Screw the job, she thought. Who cared about the job? What mattered was that she was being given a chance to meet Per again for the first time.

Oh, his hair it shines like gold,
His eyes like crystal stones—

He wouldn't know her, but she would know him. She would be the beautiful Elf-May again, knowing more than mere mortal women know. She had here what people had always longed for but had never before had—the chance to go back to the best, most exciting part of their lives and live it again.

From the midst of a whirl of feeling, she tried to reason. "But why am I here?"

"I need you to do your old job—a bit of diplomacy and liaising, a lot of translating. Observing, educating. You always were the best."

Beware of flattery, Andrea thought, especially when it comes from James Windsor. "I broke the terms of my contract. I fraternized with the 16th siders. You wouldn't have brought Per 21st side if it hadn't been for me. He wouldn't have burned down the Elf-House—I mean the office. You wouldn't have had a lance stuck in you."

Windsor had been nodding ruefully as she spoke. "All true, yes. You were a sad disappointment to us all. But you're still the best." It was easy for him to sound sincere because what he said was the truth. If he had other motives for asking Andrea to work for him again, he didn't have to think of them at that moment. "We've found others who could do the job. Universities are full of brain boxes who pick up languages faster than you can scarf a bar of chocolate, but still can't get work. We gave them your notes and tapes—I might be able to get those freed to you, by the way. You could finally write that book." Andrea stared at him without smiling or responding. "Just a thought. What was I saying? Oh, the brain boxes. Trouble with them is they can't take living over there. After a few days they're running back to the Tube whining that they want to come home because there are no showers or flush lavatories, and there's bugs and fleas, the food's awful, and the people are nasty and rough. Whereas you seemed to thrive on it."

It sounded plausible, but Andrea was suspicious of the implied compliment. Windsor had never been given to complimenting people. (Per, she was thinking, with another part of her mind. Grab the chance. Meet Per again for the first time.) "You," she said. "You want. You can—work with Per again? How can you?"

Windsor spread his hands. "Well," he said. "I nearly died."

"I heard that you were very ill."

"And you never even sent me a card. But—when you come that close to death . . . you change. I know it's a cliché, but it really is true."

Windsor sounded so sincere that Andrea didn't believe a word. And even as she studied his face, and doubted him, something at the back of her mind yammered, I get to meet Per again! I'm going to see Per again!

"And I need work," Windsor said. "And here is work for me to do. I look at it this way—it might have been Per Sterkarm who rammed a spear through me, but it wasn't *this* Per Sterkarm. No point in bearing a grudge against this one. And I'm managing things differently this time. I've learned from past mistakes. There's no reason there should ever be any unpleasantness with *these* Sterkarms."

"But—you know what they're like." Andrea shook her head. "God knows *you* know what they're like. How can you think of trying to do business with them again?"

"I'm shocked, Andrea. I thought you were their friend."

"They were good to me personally," she said. "I couldn't help but like them. But nobody could say they're easy to deal with."

"For a pattern of behavior to be changed," Windsor said, "it needs only one side to change. And *I've* changed. I really think I have. I'm more patient. I'm more relaxed. I don't mind if things take a little longer, if I don't win every point. Instead of demanding that they stop raiding, I'm taking a more pragmatic approach. Making it worth twenty times more to them to keep the peace than to raid."

Andrea spent a few seconds trying to imagine how that could be done, and failed. "How?"

"Money, of course. And gifts. We pay them and bribe them to keep the peace. We're paying them to end the feuds. In fact, at the moment I'm negotiating a truce between the Sterkarms and the Grannams."

"The *Grannams*?" When she'd lived among the Sterkarms, she'd come to think of the Grannams as almost horned, hoofed, and tailed. They'd feuded with the Sterkarms for so long that it had become a given of life, without needing a reason or origin. Scores of murders and maimings had been committed on both sides, for which each family blamed the other. Making peace between them was at least as difficult as bringing peace to Northern Ireland or the Middle East.

"I'm filling their sword hands with gold," Windsor said. "Loading their sword arms with jeans, and T-shirts, and stout boots, and aspirin. Every time they remember another killing, another raid, I pay them blood money for it—so much that even they have to admit the score is settled. I'm promising them ongoing payments as long as peace lasts."

"And, of course, what they think is a fortune is chicken feed to you."

Windsor gave a stately nod, almost a bow. "Admittedly."

Andrea shook her head. "It'll never work."

"It is working."

"And you," Andrea said, staring at him. "You can still see Per—even this Per—and be with him—without. I mean, you don't—go through it all again? It must have been frightening. You don't—?"

"Suffer flashbacks?" Windsor said. "Post-traumatic stress disorder? You read too many magazines, Andrea."

"But surely—?"

"It happened," Windsor said. "It was bad, but it's over. I lived. What's that calendar motto—'If it doesn't kill you, it makes you stronger'? So I'm stronger, and I get on with the job. Simple as that. Not all of us need lifelong counseling every time we trip on a pavement."

"And you don't want revenge? At all? That's not why you're doing this?"

"Oh, you barmaids do love your drama. *I'm* not doing anything. It was the Board's decision to open the Tube again. It's business, not revenge."

"You could have asked for a transfer," Andrea said. "Or got another job."

"I thought about it," Windsor said with apparent frankness. "But I thought it would be more likely to cause me problems than facing up to things. And my experience is valuable to the company—there aren't many people who have experience of working 16th side with the Sterkarms. Which brings us back to you. We had our differences, I know, but you were very good at your job. You'd mastered the language, you researched their customs, you got on with them—you understood them. We need you. How about it? Can we bring you back on board?"

"I don't know. . . ." It was all Andrea could do to speak. She felt that she was melting in heat. Another snatch of song returned to her, one that moved to a slow, almost sad tune that rippled like the little river that ran through Bedesdale:

For there's sweeter rest
On a truelove's breast
Than any other where.

Per, was all she could think. Per, Per, Per. I'll see him again, be with him again. Back to all the squalor and hardship of the 16th—but she knew that, she was prepared for it, could face it. It would mean being with Per again. But still, a small voice struggled to be heard: This will be a disaster. Say no. Escape.

"More money, of course," Windsor said. "And we'll help you find a place up here, a nice little apartment—or a house. We'll help you with moving. Can you drive? I could maybe wangle you a company car for when you're this side. Get yourself a little MPV and you could—"

"Get a what?"

Windsor sighed heavily. "An M–P–V. A multipurpose vehicle. You can drive it here, 21st side, but press a button and you can drive it off road in the 16th, too. Get yourself one of them and take it through. Things have changed over there. We're not being so purist this time."

"I don't know," Andrea said, trying, despite herself, to save herself. "I have to think it over. It would mean giving up my job—"

"As a barmaid?"

"I have to talk it over with my partner."

Windsor looked surprised and was about to speak, but swallowed whatever jibe he'd been about to make on the unlikelihood of her having a partner. "Take all the time you need," he said, displaying his new, patient, caring nature. She rose, and he rose with her. "I'll call you tomorrow," he said.

3

21ST SIDE—16TH SIDE:
THE ELF-PALACE

†††

ndrea parked her little blue MPV in the parking lot at the side of Dilsmead Hall and locked it up. She'd taken it on the principle of screwing as much out of FUP as she could, but as driving 16th side was even more nervewracking than 21st side, she was quite happy to leave it here and accept a lift from Windsor. Shouldering her rucksack, she walked to the rear of the Hall, where the Time Tube stood.

The Time Tube—a huge concrete tube, as its nickname implied—was where it had always been, behind Dilsmead Hall, on the lawn, close beside the gravel path. There was the shed that housed the cold-fusion power plant, about which Andrea understood nothing, and there was the long prefab office, raised on stilts, that housed the controls and the many monitoring computers. The building, painted an ugly beige, was grubby and mundane. You would never have suspected it of holding such technology.

A large white van was parked on the gravel nearby. Lettering on its side, to Andrea's surprise, proclaimed it to be from a catering company. In front of it was parked a big, dirty truck that looked as if it was used for heavier business. Around these vehicles, and the office, stood a crowd of waiting people. Despite her curiosity about them, Andrea passed the gathering by, crunching along the gravel path to get a look at the Tube itself. She wanted to see if it had changed.

It was far more impressive than the shabby office. The vast concrete tube was supported in a cradle of steel girders, all painted a flat blue. A ramp rose from the gravel path to the mouth of the Tube, which was screened by dangling strips of plastic. Vehicles would drive up the ramp and stop on the platform outside the Tube's mouth. When the green light beside the Tube gave them the signal, they would drive slowly into the Tube as its shrill sound mounted and passed beyond hearing. And somewhere around the middle of the Tube, they passed into another dimension and another time. Half of the Tube punched through into that other dimension and vanished from the 21st. It was said to have "traveled" while the other half "stayed at home." Utterly miraculous and, at the same time, just technology, like the cell phone in her bag.

She left the path and went onto the lawn, to look at the Tube from the side. Its whole length was "at home," and she could clearly see the division between the half that remained always in the 21st and the half that "traveled." The stationary half was gray with 21st-century dirt and stained with rust, while the traveling half was unmarked and white.

The last time she had stood here, there had been a battle going on. Well, all right, a skirmish. Whatever you called it, people had been killed. She remembered the huge, sweating, thundering horses, the crunching and thumping of hooves and feet on the gravel, the frantic, panicky running to and fro, the threatening yells and terrified wails, the hacking, the blood. Bryce, the Head of Security, had been beheaded in that skirmish. With a gulp she turned quickly to look behind her, and was only slightly relieved to find the path empty and no threat nearby. Windsor might claim that he never had flash-backs, but for a few moments, feeling increasingly queasy, she wondered if she had the nerve to go through with this. . . .

Snap out of it, she told herself. Have you come this far—all the misery of parting with Mick and packing and moving and finding a new place—to chicken out now? And unless you go through the Tube, you'll never see Per again. He just doesn't *do* the 21st.

That wasn't what she'd said to Mick. She'd talked to him about work. How fascinated she was with research, with the past—she'd told him about the Tube, though swearing him to secrecy. "I had to sign a paper saying I wouldn't tell anyone about it, so if you tell anyone, you'll drop me in it." Mick wouldn't tell anyone if she asked him not to, she was sure of that. "How many people get this chance?" she'd said to him. "I can't let it slip. I've got to go."

"It's dangerous," he'd said.

"So's crossing the road." He'd looked glum. "I've been there before. I know the risks. I'll be careful. But I've got to go."

"Well," he'd said, in the end. "If it makes you happy."

He always said that. And meant it. A great feeling of love for him rose up in her as she stood outside the Tube's office, bringing tears to her eyes. Lovely Mick. Few people would see him as a great catch. He was older than her by nearly fifteen years, and he looked it. He was a bit chubby and had great shaggy eyebrows and thinning hair on his head, but he was gentle, loving, protective, and didn't seem to be aware that she was fat. Most of the time she felt fond of him, but now and again—as now—she was shocked to discover how deeply she adored him. Never did she want to hurt him, but—on the other end of the Tube was Per.

She felt that she needed to brace herself by doing something ordinary and bureaucratic. Walking back along the path, she pushed through the people standing around the office steps and went inside. In a tiny anteroom a receptionist sat at a desk. Behind her was the doorway leading to the room, crowded with more computers, where technicians and scientists controlled the Tube.

"I'm Andrea Mitchell. I'm booked to go through the Tube."

"Do you have your pass?"

Andrea had forgotten that she would need it, and had to take off her rucksack and search through its pockets until she found the bit of paper. The receptionist studied it, and looked at her computer screen, while Andrea marveled yet again at the mix of breathtaking technology and plodding bureaucratic ineptitude that made up the Time Tube project. It had always been the same. Bryce—when he'd been alive—had frequently raged against the penny-pinching accountancy that wouldn't pay to repair broken security cameras or train guards, and then had blamed him for failures of security.

"That's fine," the receptionist said. "Enjoy your trip."

There were toilets off this entrance hall, and Andrea went in—after all, it would be five hundred years before she had a chance to go again, and then it would be in nowhere near as much comfort. Afterward she checked her face in the mirror. One of the pockets of her rucksack held a small makeup kit, and she carefully applied just a trace of lipstick and kohl. Dotting a little lipstick on her cheekbones, she rubbed it in to create a slight, becoming flush. For a moment she studied herself, then pulled out the pins and ties that held her hair up. It fell down about her face and onto her shoulders in heavy, light-brown waves.

She grimaced at herself, then gathered her hair up in her hands, holding it on top of her head, trying to decide whether she looked better with it up or down. It looked slightly better up, she thought, but 16th side only unmarried women wore their hair uncovered and loose. As soon as a woman married, she pinned up her hair and covered it with a cap. When she met Per again, her loose hair would be a signal. She put the pins and ties in her pocket.

Wandering outside, she found that things were moving, with people shouting good-byes and hastily clambering into vehicles. Quickly she slipped the weight of the rucksack from her shoulders again and took a cell phone from one of its side pockets. Sixteenth side it wouldn't be any use to her, but she'd brought it for this moment. Switching it on, she keyed in a text message. "Going thru. Luv U. C U. Andy." As she sent the message to Mick, she looked up. A large, square MPV, in a metallic racing green, was coming up the drive. She knew immediately that Windsor was behind the wheel.

Windsor saw her and smiled. Good old reliable big fat Andrea: He'd known she would be waiting. Drawing the jeep up alongside her with a spray of gravel, he leaned over and opened the passenger door. "Get in!"

She did, noticing that two big men were seated silently in the long back. "Hello," she said to them, and smiled. They looked at her, but neither smiled or spoke.

"Never mind them," Windsor said. "They're just muscle."

Andrea supposed that after his previous experiences with the Sterkarms, you couldn't blame him for taking bodyguards with him this time. She fastened her seat belt, half expecting some jibe about it needing to be extended before it would fit around her.

Instead, peering at her, he said, "Are you wearing makeup?"

"No!" she said. She felt like asking him why he was dressed in a light-gray suit with an embroidered yellow waistcoat and a lavender tie—but that would show more interest in him than he deserved.

"You're looking well," he said, and moved the car slowly forward. She was wearing makeup, he was sure of it—and he didn't need three guesses to know whose benefit it was for. All to the good: If she was actually making an effort to catch young Sterkarm's eye, he was all the more likely to notice her, and young Sterkarm was known to have a weakness for big room darkeners like Andrea.

The truck was ahead of them on the ramp, the catering van behind them. Windsor switched the radio on. "Good old Handel." He liked to know the exact moment when the Tube transferred him from the 21st century, and at that moment the radio would cut out. It gave him some slight feeling of control, and helped him overcome the unease that he felt now whenever he used the Tube. Deliberately he moved his mind from consideration of what might go wrong to the objectives he had to achieve.

Oh God! Andrea thought as the MPV slowly crept forward. We're going through! We're going into the Tube. Her heart hammered. How could she have agreed to go back there? As if life wasn't difficult enough in the 21st century. She wondered whether Windsor would listen to her if she demanded that he stop and let her out.

He'll have to stop at the top of the ramp, she thought. I'll get out then. But he didn't stop. The plastic strips slapped against the windshield as they drove straight through.

Andrea couldn't find her voice to say that she wanted to get out, and in any case she was afraid to get out now that they were in the Tube. She had no understanding of how it worked, and feared radiation, atom dismemberment, or possibly being whizzed back to the

Age of Dinosaurs. Evil magic.

The inside of the Tube looked like a section of an underground walkway. There was a road of some sort under the wheels—possibly made of rubber—and the walls were covered with white tiles, though with many inspection hatches. Terrified, she stared at the back of the truck ahead.

The truck lifted up the plastic strips at the other end of the Tube, went through, and the strips fell back into place. Their car still moved forward slowly, and Andrea found herself sitting with every muscle braced hard. When the music from the radio stopped in mid note, replaced by static, she clenched her teeth, and her hands gripped the edge of the seat. I'm growing cowardly in my old age, she thought. I used to buzz backward and forward through the Tube without a care. True, the first time she'd ever used it, she'd been awestruck, but after that, she'd soon grown used to it, and had used it as casually as she might have used an elevator or an escalator. But now she could remember all too well what had come of that casualness. Casualties.

She looked at Windsor. He was staring ahead, drumming his fingers on the wheel, and making a hissing noise between his teeth in time to some tune in his head. Perhaps he's telling the truth, she thought; and he really has recovered completely. Well, was it so surprising? The man always had been as sensitive as a brick.

The plastic strips scratched over the car's hood, windshield, and roof as the car proceeded. Whatever the Tube did, she realized, it had already done it. Somewhere about the midway mark, when the music had stopped, they'd been translated from the 21st to the 16th century. They'd left their own dimension, whatever that meant. Anyone looking at the Tube, back in the good old 21st, had seen their half of it vanish.

The car nosed through the plastic strips and emerged on the platform beside the office, 16th side. In front of them was the 16th century.

Space. That was her first impression. The world opened out. The wide hills, and the wider sky, spread out before her—and there were hills beyond the hills she could see, and hills beyond those. She wound down the window, and a small breeze, cool, damp, and carrying the scent of thyme, touched her face. She could sense the miles and miles and miles of emptiness it had traveled over.

And silence. A deep silence, so deep it muffled her ears. A silence that she could almost gather up in her arms and fold in great, thick, velvety layers. All the petty din that the 21st century called silence fell away. There was no longer any drone of traffic noise, not even in the distance. No constant, almost disregarded hum of electrical equipment. No piped music, no radios, no cell phones, no car alarms, no planes flying overhead. This was true silence.

And color. Here there were no scarlets, no Day-Glo yellows or electric pinks. Everything was green, gray, buff, brown. But before visiting the 16th, she'd never realized how many subtle tints of green there were. And here they were again, on the hillsides, in the trees, together with soft golds and russets. The cloud-filled sky was full of grays, violets, and gentle blues. It was like being given new eyes, because the air was so clean here that every delicate tint of every color was more distinct, and everything was pin sharp. You could see farther, in more detail, than in the 21st. The heather was flowering, pink and mauve among the greens and fawns of the grass. There were harebells, bluer than the sky, and yellow stonecrop, and white and red campion, and many other flowers that she couldn't name. She felt a thrill of homecoming as she experienced, again, what she had always loved about the 16th. Why had she been so nervous about going through the Tube again? It was less frightening than flying, and it brought you—not to another airport in another crowded, dirty city, but here.

Then, with a sharp sense of bafflement, she realized that she had never seen these hills before. They were in the wrong place, and were the wrong shape, to be the Bedesdale hills! What had gone wrong? Was a Tyrannosaurus Rex going to be the next thing they saw? When she looked at Windsor, he seemed quite relaxed. And beside the ramp the MPV rested on, there was the usual ugly, prefabricated office.

Ahead of them, the truck had reached the bottom of the ramp and was turning, to drive around the office. Windsor steered the MPV to follow.

"This isn't Bedesdale," Andrea said.

"Should it be?" Windsor asked.

"I thought—"

"That we were going to have tea with your friends, the Sterkarms? Well, we are—but the Grannams have graciously agreed to join us."

"What?" Andrea said.

"Oh, did I forget to mention that?" He thumped his hand on the steering wheel. "Damn! I bet I forgot to mention that it's a wedding, too, didn't I?"

Andrea almost choked. "A wedding?"

"Silly me. You could have bought yourself a new outfit and a big hat. It's all part of the new deal—we're promoting cuddling and snoogling of all kinds between Sterkarms and Grannams. We're paying for the wedding, heaping the happy couple with gifts—just doing everything we can to promote happiness and harmony, really."

"I can't believe it," Andrea said. "Who's getting married?"

"Look at that," Windsor said. They'd rounded the corner of the office. The truck ahead of them was driving toward the steel-link fence, and Andrea glimpsed buildings beyond the fence. Shining buildings. They didn't look like anything the 16th siders would build. She stared ahead, trying to make out more.

Gates in the fence opened automatically to let the truck ahead of them through. The MPV followed, onto a rough, rutted track. Despite its superb suspension it lurched and swayed.

The truck turned aside, and Andrea had a clear view of what lay ahead. Her eyes and mouth opened. A few yards from the steel fence of the FUP compound, a large inflatable building had been erected—unmistakably a 21st-century building, the kind put up for posh weddings. It had a central dome surrounded by four smaller domes at the corners, and it was made from silver fabric with a metallic sheen. "Architectural" detail had been added, in white and gold, especially around the arched door. On either side, painted silver, were the generators that kept it inflated. Strange, shining buttresses of filigree metal sprang from its roof to the ground—scaffolding that would support the weight of the building if the generators should fail and it deflated. To Andrea's eye the whole thing had an oddly Eastern appearance, but with a slight shock she realized how utterly bizarre and alien it would look to the 16th siders. Its strange shape, its unknown, glittering fabric, its weird beauty, the fact that it had appeared, in an hour, where previously there had been nothing—it would seem to them a truly eldritch palace.

They drove past the inflatable and into a shantytown of huts built around it—the sort of hut that the Sterkarms could build in a morning from thin timber and mud, thatched with heather. Many 16th siders—mostly women and children, but some men—were bustling around these huts, and from the smell of roasting meat and the sight of fires and pits, Andrea soon realized what they were doing. A feast was being prepared. She looked at their faces, hoping to recognize someone, and failing in that looked for some sign—some flag or badge—that would tell her whether they were Sterkarms or Grannams. There was nothing. Reluctantly she asked Windsor, "Who are they?"

"God knows," he said. "Who cares? Little people."

Gritting her teeth, Andrea asked, "Little Sterkarm people, or little Grannam people?"

"One or the other. The Sterkarms have sent people to set up this shantytown on one side of us, and the Grannams are camping on the other side—all because they won't eat our filthy Elvish food."

Andrea looked out at the people busying themselves around the cooking huts. "Has there been any trouble?"

"I really don't know. I have other things to think of."

One of the security guards leaned forward from the back and said, grinning, "Hell an' all from the kiddies—running around, knocking lumps off one another. Bit of hair pulling from the women, but the men have just been strutting around and glowering at each other."

"Happy now, Andrea?" Windsor asked.

Andrea ignored him and looked out the window. Behind the first inflatable building was another. In fact, as Andrea soon realized, there were several, a small town of them. Lots of 21st siders, in jeans, fleeces, and sneakers, were hurrying in and out. Windsor drew up the MPV in front of a long, low, prefabricated office.

As they got out, a young man came toward them from the doorway. He was dressed in jeans, sneakers, and, over his shirt, a casual jacket emblazoned with the emblem of FUP. He carried a clipboard and, on his head, wore a tiny, fragile headset, with a wire-thin arm holding a tiny mike in front of his mouth. Andrea thought he looked faintly familiar. She'd seen his thin, worried face with its wire-frame spectacles and scattering of red pimples somewhere before, but couldn't place where.

"Gareth!" Windsor said, greeting the young man with outstretched hand. "I've brought you some help. This is Andrea Mitchell."

As he shook hands with Andrea, Gareth said, in a decidedly cool manner, "Pleased to meet you."

"Any sign of either party?" Windsor asked.

"They won't take us by surprise," Gareth said. "We've got people watching for them. Do you want to look over what's been done?"

"Lead on," Windsor said, and followed as Gareth walked toward the first and largest inflatable. The bodyguards fell in behind them. Andrea took a quick look around at the blue moorland sky and at the cooking fires burning outside the 16th-century kitchen huts, then hurriedly followed the bodyguards.

The inflatable building, with its shimmering, silvery sides, dwarfed them as they walked beside it. In its sides were set round windows, and arched windows, with real, shining glass. Those windows would deeply impress the 16th siders with the Elves' wealth.

The entrance, when they reached it, was arched and screened by a curtain of shimmering silver beads. As they pushed through them, there was a musical chiming. Very eldritch, Andrea thought.

Inside, the building was far bigger than she'd expected, and its domed roof much higher—it was hard not to be reminded of a cathedral. The biggest, central dome was translucent, letting in a soft, pearly light, which made the building's silvery fabric shine and gleam.

A floor of polished wooden planking had been laid. Overhead hung circular frames smothered and dripping with artificial greenery and flowers—white and pink roses. More trellises and frames, decorated with flowers and leaves, hid much of the wall area. White and pink roses everywhere, with an occasional touch of yellow or pale blue. Andrea reached out and touched the petals and leaves of the nearest garland. She had to rub them between her fingers several times before she could decide that they were, as she'd suspected, artificial, though highly realistic. The very artificiality of the flowers would strike the 16th siders as wonderful. Who but the Elves could make such things, or supply them so lavishly?

In one of the corner domes a bar had been set up, and in another a sound system. Down either side of the main floor were long tables, covered with white cloths. The tables were decked with more flowers—real flowers, because their scent hung in the air—and set with shining glass, china, and cutlery. At the tables were long rows of chairs. It was all very pretty, but not particularly grand to 21st-century eyes. The chairs, for instance, were cheap ones of white molded plastic.

But here, 16th side, all but the richest stood to eat. An individual chair was a status symbol. Table coverings were a rarity, and people ate and drank from wooden plates and cups, or even slices of stale bread, though the better off might have plates of pewter or heavy earthenware. Smooth, glazed china was unheard of, and most of the 16th siders would never have seen a glass or a fork. Or a spoon made of anything except wood or horn. They carried their own sharp eating knives at their belts. These tables, with their cloths, china, glasses, metal knives and forks, with a chair for everyone— they were unspeakably lavish and luxurious.

Beyond the long tables, at the far end of the inflatable, stood something almost like an altar, decked with more flowers and supporting a large silver cross. Behind the table was a floral picture, showing two coats of arms. Andrea recognized them both. There was the Sterkarm badge: a red arm holding in its fist a dagger, on a black shield. The shield was made of dark-blue, almost black irises and the red arm of roses. Beside it was the Grannam badge: a red boar on a green shield. More roses for the boar, and a variety of green flowers and leaves for the background.

None of this would have come cheap in the 21st, so for once FUP weren't taking the 16th siders' goods and rewarding them with something that had cost them virtually nothing. But who exactly were the couple being married? Perhaps she'd met the Sterkarm during her previous stay in the 16th. She'd been told that she'd be sent a file to study, bringing her up-to-date on everything that FUP had been doing 16th side, but despite phone calls and e-mails, the file had never arrived. It had always been "in the post, with you tomorrow." Now she was going to have to rely on her previous experience to wing it.

It should be a memorable occasion. Ordinary weddings were bad enough, notoriously descending into rows between the families, but the Sterkarms and the Grannams had been feuding for generations, and their hatred for each other wasn't usually expressed by snubbing one another in the street or refusing to let their children play together.

Gareth was nervously eyeing Windsor, waiting for his approval. Andrea felt sorry for him. "It all looks beautiful," she said truthfully. It looked beautiful even if you were used to such things. To 16th siders, she could only imagine that it would seem beyond beautiful. Unearthly. Magical.

"What about when they arrive?" Windsor asked. "Are we all set to make them welcome?"

"Over here," Gareth said, and led them back down the hall to the entrance. A table had been set up just inside the door, crammed with many shiny little gift bags in brilliant metallic purples, reds, greens, and golds. "I thought wine and nibbles would be a waste of time," Gareth explained nervously, "since most of them won't touch our food. So I've made up these goodie bags instead. They've all got a packet of aspirins, and then things like a book of needles, bar of fancy soap, lacy hanky, little bottle of scent, a shiny brooch. . . . Things like that."

"How do you tell which are for men and which for women?" Windsor asked, since the bags seemed to be arranged in no order.

"Doesn't matter," Gareth said. "Everybody likes scent and lacy hankies over here."

"Excellent," Windsor said. "Andrea should play hostess. It'll help to introduce her. Okay, Andrea?"

Andrea's heart speeded up. "Oh! Yes! No problem." She caught another annoyed look from Gareth. What was his problem? She had enough of her own: She still didn't know quite what was going on. Should her greeting be lighthearted or solemn? "Er—whom, exactly, shall I be greeting?"

They both looked at her.

"Oh dear, fancy Miss Swotty-Drawers not doing her homework," Windsor said. "Didn't you read your file?"

Andrea opened her mouth to apologize, then changed her mind and was about to explain that the file had never arrived, and then realized that, whatever she said, Windsor would only twist it. Never apologize, never explain. She stared at Windsor but said nothing.

Gareth smiled. "I can take Miss Mitchell around, if you like, and bring her up to speed," he said to Windsor.

Windsor said, "Oh fine, go on, go on." He turned and left on business of his own.

Alone with Andrea, Gareth gave her another look over. He had been quick to bid for Brownie points with Windsor by offering to baby-sit her, but it wasn't a job he really wanted. She was on the large side, and all that long, loose hair made her untidy. There was too much of her in every way for Gareth's liking. He hadn't liked the crack Windsor had made as he'd introduced her either. "I've brought you some help." As if he needed help, especially from an ex-barmaid. And future concubine. "I'll show you around the complex," he said.

There was a lot to see. A second inflatable, just as large, had been erected behind the first. Music chimed as they pushed through the screen of silver beads. Inside was another wooden floor, and more bowers of artificial flowers, but all the seats were around the walls. "This is just for the dancing," Gareth said.

Behind this inflatable were two blocks of chemical toilets. "For us. The 16th siders make their own arrangements." Here, too, was the prefab office, the catering van for the 21st-side workers, and the prefab that housed Security. The cooking huts of the 16th siders had been put up at the edges of the encampment. At the back of the camp, on either side, were two more, smaller inflatables, standing apart from all the other buildings, and from each other.

"They're the dormitories," Gareth said. "One for the Sterkarms and one for the Grannams. We thought it would be pushing our luck to ask them to share. Where will you be staying?"

"Where I'm put, I suppose," Andrea said, surprised.

"There are a few beds for 21st people," Gareth said, "but I'm sleeping in the Grannam dormitory—I've been working with them. Would it be okay if you went in with the Sterkarms?"

"Of course. That's what I was expecting."

"Come on, then. I'll show you where it is." He led the way toward one of the inflatable dormitories, threading through parked vans and slight timber shacks. Sixteenth-siders stared at them, the Elves, as they went by.

The dormitory had a door. Inside was another wooden floor, and curtains in bright brocades, hung to make small private areas. Mattresses and sleeping bags lay on the floor. There were even beds. Gareth led the way all the way through the building to a door at the far end—a white door, its paneling picked out in gold. Andrea followed him through it.

On the other side was a domed room, all white, pink, pale blue, and silver. There were candles, and roses, and ribbons, and wreaths and garlands. On the floor were white fluffy rugs and white cushions decorated with silver fringes. There were couches and armchairs, with lots of curves and gilding, and white-and-rose cushions. Little white tables were scattered about, supporting small bowls of chocolates and bonbons wrapped in blue, silver, and pink foil. Since the 16th siders wouldn't touch Elvish food, Andrea supposed the sweets were just there for interior decoration. She helped herself to a chocolate so they wouldn't be wasted.

"This is only the anteroom," Gareth said with a touch of pride, and led her to the back of the room, where they mounted three shallow white steps and drew back a brocaded curtain of rose and silver.

Behind the curtain was a huge double bed with rose-colored covers. Garlands of roses twined the bed's posts, and it dripped with lace and was heaped with heart-shaped pink cushions and white pillows. Hung around it were diaphanous white curtains—which wouldn't be appreciated by the 16th siders, Andrea thought, who liked their bed curtains thick enough to keep out drafts. "Of course," she said, looking around. "This is the bridal suite."

Gareth allowed himself a small smile. "Like it?" Obviously he thought that all women went gaga for a few posies and bows.

"Beautiful," she said, though she thought it overfussy and a little ridiculous, especially for the Sterkarms, whose taste was more robust. She imagined Toorkild or Sweet Milk wiping their noses—or worse—on the gauzy drapes. "Who is it who's getting married?" She might know the couple, from her former stay in the 16th.

Gareth opened his mouth to answer, but his headset crackled, and he started for the door at a run. "Come on! They're here!"

Andrea followed eagerly, bridal suites forgotten. The Sterkarms were here. Soon she would see Per.

Outside, the paths between the inflatables were full of people, all heading in the same direction. There were men in the uniform of FUP security and people from catering; there were 16th sider women and children, and people in Elvish clothes with headsets.

They reached the edge of the encampment, the shantytown of wooden huts and cooking fires. The air was thick with the smell of roasting meat. And now they could hear the sound of horses' hooves and music. Someone was playing a jig on the pipes. They passed between the kitchen shacks, and then they could see, coming along a moorland path, a long procession.

A string of horses and riders. The horses were all the strong, barrel-bodied, thick-necked little hobs of the border, all of them black or dark brown, with manes and tails trailing the ground. Ribbons were plaited into the manes and tails; garlands of leaves and flowers were hung around the horses' necks. All the riders were wearing bright clothes, with plumed hats and flashing brooches.

On the leading horse sat a bagpiper, pumping his elbow and blowing for all he was worth. The rider beside him carried a spear from which flew a green-and-red banner. Andrea's heart dropped with disappointment. The device on the banner couldn't easily be seen, but if the colors were green and red, then this party must be the Grannams, not the Sterkarms. Around her, people cheered, 21st siders and 16th siders together, in welcome and appreciation of the fine sight the riders made. Andrea joined in, but her cheer was halfhearted.

Following the banner were men carrying lances, holding them upright, steadied on the toes of their right boots. From the heads of the lances fluttered little pennants of red and green. Behind them came men and women in finery, each woman riding sidesaddle, or pillion, behind a man. Even Andrea started to smile with the old sense of privilege—how lucky she was to see this! Then she remembered that she had to form part of the welcoming committee. She looked around for Gareth and, moving to his side, shouted in his ear. "Fill me in! Who are they?"

The procession swept past them, hooves thumping on the ground, and the crowd followed it, running alongside. Gareth waved to Andrea to follow him, and they fell back from the crowd and made their way, through by now almost deserted alleyways between the shacks, back to the biggest of the inflatables, the dining hall.

"The head man is Richard Grannam," Gareth instructed her as they hurried along. "He lives at Brackenhill Tower, so call him Lord Brackenhill if you want to get in his good books."

"Richard Grannam, Lord Brackenhill," Andrea repeated, trying to drive it into her memory.

"His sister'll be with him—he's a widower and she's a widow, so she keeps house for him. Her name's Christina Crosar, but you'd better call her Mistress Crosar—even her brother does. And she calls him Master Grannam and Lord Brackenhill."

The Grannams, so far, didn't sound much like the Sterkarms.

"You should know the bride, of course!" Gareth said. "Joan Grannam, old Richard's daughter. She's the best of them."

Oh, really? Andrea thought, as she hurried, panting a little, to keep up with him. She concluded that Joan Grannam was attractive. "And who's the groom?" she asked. But they'd reached the inflatable, and Gareth wasn't listening. The wedding ride was drawing rein in front of the building, and the crowd was gathering on either side to watch. Following Gareth, Andrea dived through the chiming silver beads that hung across the doorway.

Windsor was waiting just inside, his bodyguards discreetly in the background, among the artificial flowers. "The Skye Boat Song" was playing over the speakers, sung by a woman with an upper-crust English accent and a soprano so sharp it made Andrea wince. Presumably whoever was in charge of the music thought that was what the Grannams would like, despite the fact that the song had been written long after their time.

Gareth drew back the chiming curtain of beads and fastened it in place. Looking through the doorway, Andrea could see the Grannams dismounting and grooms leading away the horses. A man and a woman detached themselves from the bustle and came toward the inflatable, stopping at a little distance from it and gazing at it, while the rest of the procession formed up behind them.

Gareth, with the slightest nod of the head toward this man and woman, whispered, "Lord Brackenhill. Mistress Crosar."

There was, Andrea saw, a sword hanging at Lord Brackenhill's side. And several more swords to be seen among his followers. At the back of the crowd men were leaning lances together, like wigwam frames. She said to Windsor, "You're not going to let them in armed?"

He raised his brows. "Why not?"

"They'd be insulted," Gareth said irritably, "if we asked them to hand over their weapons." He resented her implication that he'd organized things badly.

"The Sterkarms and the Grannams?" Andrea said. "Armed? Drinking? There'll be murder done."

"They're big boys," Windsor said. "They can look after themselves."

And now the Grannam party was advancing toward the door. They walked slowly, with dignity, but even so could not prevent their eyes from darting about when they entered the building and saw the abundance of flowers and the twinkling white lights. There was astonishment on many faces, though those at the head of the procession suppressed it quickly.

Richard Grannam, Lord Brackenhill himself, was a tall, lean, and expensively dressed man. His long horse face, weathered to a dark brown with roughened, reddened cheeks, was set in a grim expression, with deep grooves making a permanent frown on his forehead. He had a neatly trimmed gray beard, but the hair on his head was hidden by a floppy blue beret, trimmed with a feather. A cloak of thick green cloth was thrown back on his shoulders to show its fur lining, and his russet jacket had ornamental slashes on the chest and sleeves, to show the quality of the linen shirt he wore underneath. His breeches, also russet, were loose and baggy, to show how much material he could afford to use, and below them he wore wide, black leather riding boots. He was one who rode, not one who walked. His sword hung from an embroidered baldric slung across his shoulder. The men immediately behind him, his private guard, all wore weapons. The piper, finding himself in disharmonious competition with the squalling soprano, stopped playing.

Windsor, smiling blandly, held out his hand in greeting.

Lord Brackenhill wore embroidered gauntlets and clasped hands with Windsor without removing them. Nor did he smile. *"Dey glayder migh a sae thu,"* he said.

"It gladdens me to see you," Andrea translated automatically, as if she'd never left 16th side and never stopped doing her job. Richard Grannam, Lord Brackenhill, didn't make any attempt to look glad, though he had used the respectful "you" rather than the familiar "thee," so he at least acknowledged Windsor as an equal, if not a superior.

"*Dey glayder migh,*" Windsor said, and Andrea was surprised that he had bothered to learn even so much of the 16th-side dialect.

Mistress Crosar, who stood beside her brother, was almost as tall, but a little heavier set. Her hair was hidden completely under a cap. Beneath it her face was also long and horsy, but though it was a little touched by the sun, it was neither as brown nor as weathered as his. Her cloak was blue, and as she made a slight curtsey to Windsor, it parted and showed a black dress beneath. She glanced at Andrea disapprovingly, looked Windsor right in the eye, and spoke to him. She didn't smile.

"She says that she is delighted to meet you again, and that they owe you thanks," Andrea said. Mistress Crosar seemed neither delighted nor thankful.

Windsor repeated his *"Dey glayder migh,"* and Andrea thought it was time to offer gifts. So she held out a shiny gold bag to Lord Brackenhill and, hastily snatching a shiny red bag from the table, offered it to Mistress Crosar with a big smile. "You are well come," she said. "We hope you won't go early away, and this will make sure that you don't go away empty-handed."

Brackenhill and Mistress Crosar turned their eyes on her. With unsmiling faces they stared at her as she spoke. They seemed to be wondering who she was, and why she thought she had any right to speak to them. What did I say that was so bad? Andrea wondered. If these were the Grannams, no wonder the Sterkarms didn't like them.

When she finished speaking, Brackenhill deliberately shifted his eyes from her to Windsor, while Mistress Crosar continued to stare at her, as if unable to believe quite how lowly she was. Neither of them attempted to take the gift bags. Reaching a hand behind him, Brackenhill said, "May I present my daughter?"

Oh no! Andrea thought as her face flushed. She had jumped in and rudely interrupted the introductions. Hastily she translated what Brackenhill had said and watched as he drew forward one of the girls whom she had taken for a maid. It's understandable, she thought—the girl was wrapped in a black, hooded cloak and hung her head as if trying to disappear.

Joan Grannam, keeping her face lowered and her hood over her head, curtsied to Windsor, who bowed slightly in return. As the girl curtseyed, her cloak parted—it was velvet, Andrea now saw—and there was a glimpse of the splendid dress beneath, of a shining metallic scarlet, glittering with sequins. Twenty-first-century cloth and 21st-century, machine-made sequins, obviously a gift from Windsor. A gaudy frock by 21st-century taste, perhaps, but here, 16th side, there was nothing like it. People would walk twenty miles across moorland in the rain just to see that dress. It would be woven into fireside tales. Catskins, a local Cinderella, would from now on go to church in a dress like that.

As the girl rose from her curtsey, Mistress Crosar reached out and brushed the hood of the black cloak from the girl's head, in what might have been an affectionate gesture. The girl's hair was long and reddishly fair, partly bound into plaits and partly loose, to signify that she was still unmarried. For a moment Joan raised her head, glancing toward her aunt, and Andrea saw that she was tall, and very beautiful indeed. No wonder Gareth was smitten.

Joan's small round head perched, with lovely poise, on a long, graceful neck. Her face was an oval, with high cheekbones, large eyes, and a soft, naturally red mouth. She could have been no older than fifteen, at most, and her skin was absolutely unlined, unblemished, moist and shining.

"I am honored to meet you, Mistress Grannam," Andrea said, trying to make good her mistake. "May I congratulate you and wish you every good tiding for the day?"

Joan looked at her directly for a moment. Her eyes were clear, huge and white and blue. "Thanks shall you have," she murmured, before her cheeks turned a delicate foxglove pink, and she lowered her face again. With her height, her slenderness, and that lovely face, Andrea thought, the editors of 21st-side magazines would have fist fought for the right to put her on their covers.

"Be so kind," Andrea pressed. "Take a bag. There are gifts inside. Take the red one—to match your beautiful dress."

Joan Grannam looked up momentarily, took the offered bag, and looked at the floor again. But then Mistress Crosar took the other bag.

While Andrea turned to Gareth for more bags, Brackenhill turned to a man who stood beside him: a small, stocky man with a close-trimmed beard, dressed all in black except for a small frill of white shirt at his neck. "This," said Brackenhill, "is Father Nicholas, my priest."

Andrea quickly translated what Brackenhill had said for Windsor.

"It gladdens me, Father Nicholas," Windsor said, holding out his hand.

The priest ignored the proffered hand. Instead, he crossed himself and glowered. "I am here," he said, "to wed the couple, not to consort with Elves."

Andrea glanced at Lord Brackenhill and his sister, but they were blandly staring about at the tables and flowers, apparently content for their priest to be so blatantly rude to their hosts. Windsor was looking at her questioningly, and she saw no choice except to translate what the priest had said.

"Please yourself, God Botherer," Windsor said in his own language. Andrea offered a gift bag to the priest, who pointedly looked away. Lord Brackenhill, perhaps as a sign of graciousness to make up for his priest's boorishness, took the bag himself.

"Be so kind," Andrea said, "as to go in and—be at home. This is all for your comfort. Be so good."

Without another word, or a look, Brackenhill, his sister, his daughter, and his priest went on into the hall, looking about them at the long tables, the flowers and lights.

The Grannams who came behind them were not so reserved. They happily accepted their gift bags and peered into them, exclaiming in pleasure at the little gifts they found inside. They gaped at the tables, at the high roof, at the massed flowers. Whispering to one another, they felt the flowers and argued about whether they were real or not. Others fingered the glittery beads that made up the curtain. Andrea wondered how many of the decorations would be left when the guests departed.

She heard Gareth's headset crackle again. "The Sterkarms," he said to Windsor.

Andrea's heartbeat quickened. Per was here. She looked around and saw that the Grannam party was well into the hall, admiring the glass and china on the tables. Obviously, they were going to take no part in greeting the Sterkarms.

"Well then, Andrea," Windsor said. "Try not to screw it up this time."

But all Andrea could think was: I'll soon be seeing Per!

4

16TH SIDE:
THE WEDDING RIDE

†††

"Oh, the birds were a-singing in the bushes and trees,
And the song that they sang was 'She's easy to please!'"

"Tha'd better hope she will be, Per!"

"Best not drink too much!"

Standing in his stirrups for a moment, Per called back, "Ach, she's nobbut a Grannam! She'll think hersen lucky to get a Sterkarm man!"

There was laughter, and hooting. "Think thasen a man?"

In the first bright morning light the Sterkarm wedding ride trotted along a high moorland track, through bright-green pads of moss and grass, and pink-and-purple heather. On either side of the long column, at its head, and behind, rode armed men wearing helmets blackened with soot and carrying eight-foot lances. A wedding party, with guests dressed in their finest, was a good target for an attack. But brightly colored ribbons fluttered from the lances, and red cockades were bright on the helmets.

Behind the armed men rode two bagpipers, pumping their elbows and playing as they rode along. Toorkild Sterkarm rode behind the pipers, with his wife, Isobel, pillion behind him. Per rode beside him. Behind them came Toorkild's brother, Gobby Per, and riding beside him his eldest son, Little Toorkild, with his young wife pillion. Next came Gobby's youngest sons, Wat and Ingram, and then, behind them, various guests from other Sterkarm towers and bastle houses, some of them carrying children on their saddlebows, while others had youngsters riding beside them on ponies.

After them rode such officials of their households as had horses to ride: blacksmiths, head shepherds and cattlemen, and Sweet Milk, Toorkild's right-hand man. In a long raggle-taggle at the back came all those who hadn't horses: small farmers and their wives, maids, shepherds, some carrying children in their arms, or on their shoulders, or leading them by the hand. Gangs of children ran alongside the procession or chased one another through the ferns beside the paths.

The ride was itself a sight worth walking a few miles to see, and people stood waiting along the way. They pointed out Per Sterkarm, the May, not only because he was the bridegroom, but because of the Elvish clothes he wore. "He's been into Elf-Land, him—and come back to tell the tale."

Every horse in the procession had been combed and groomed, and the ground-brushing manes and tails plaited with ribbons and flowers. The guests were dressed in their brightest colors, and gold and amber jewelry flashed. Per's two big gazehounds, Swart and Cuddy, loped beside his horse, with wreaths of leaves and flowers twisted around their collars.

The pipers shifted into another tune:

"Oh, can you find the cuckoo's nest
That's hidden in the prickly bush, the prickly bush?
Oh, can you find the cuckoo's nest
That's hidden there?"

With cheers and laughter the ride took up the song and bellowed it out, though the sound was quickly lost in the vast moorland.

"Canst find the cuckoo's nest, Per?"

"Scared to put thy hand in that prickly bush?"

Per put back his head and laughed aloud, not because the ancient jokes were good, but because he was in a high mood. He turned his horse out of the procession and rode back along it. No sooner had he done so than Ingram, his youngest cousin, maneuvered his own horse out of the crowd and rode after him. His brothers, Wat and

Little Toorkild, looked at each other and smiled. Whatever Per did, Ingram had to do.

Per called out to the procession, "I've put a few cuckoos in a few nests! Shall I name my cuckoos?"

Clods were thrown at him. He kicked up Fowl, his thickset black hob, and rode all the way around the procession, with Ingram, laughing, close behind him, and back to his place at the ride's head. People cheered him as they went by, waving and—if they were women—blowing kisses. Everyone was in a good mood. Because of Per and his wedding day, they were all to enjoy a whole day of eating and drinking, and dancing and music, without work. Much of the food would be Grannam food, too. It would add extra relish to know they were emptying the Grannam larders.

Per could hardly keep a grin from his face. Marriage was not something he'd hankered for, but every man had to marry sooner or later—and this marriage brought with it such wealth and land that it would be worth it. The favor of the Elves, too, was part of the bargain—he would be famous as the Sterkarm who went into Elf-Land and married a Grannam! And, at the day's end, he'd be put to bed with the Grannam girl. Then he could truly show the Grannams who came on top.

Better still, Elf-Windsor might keep his promise and bring along the beautiful Elf-Maid. There was bound to be some time—either before or after he was bedded with his bride—when he could try for the Elf-Maid. She'd liked him when he'd met her in Elf-Land. Courting her on his wedding day would be difficult, but then, that would make it more fun. The Grannams wouldn't see the joke—but that was Grannams for you.

The ride wound its way down a hillside, and the Elf-Palace came into view. The ride slowed as people stared, and those on foot came crowding forward, to stand and jostle as they pointed and exclaimed. Two days before, there had been nothing there except empty hillside. Now, great, domed, bulbous, silvery buildings glittered against the soft greens and tawnies of the moor. Eerie, shimmering, they were like nothing anyone had ever seen before: so strange and beautiful, they even drew attention away from the Elf-Gate that stood near them behind its steel fence.

"Per! Per!" his mother called from her seat behind his father. "Be all the buildings like that in Elf-Land?"

Per shook his head. The buildings in Elf-Land had been massive, of expensive stone and brick, the work of giants. Their windows had been huge, with sheets of glass so large and pure and clear, they were like nothing, like air. They hadn't been anything like these. But the works of the Elves were beyond anything. He was struck with wonder that he should be lucky enough to live in the time when the Elves came.

Toorkild filled his big lungs and roared in a bellow that could have been heard on the other side of the valley. "Harken! When we get down there"—he threw out an arm and pointed to the silvery Elf-Buildings below—"there'll be Grannams! I want nobody messing with the Grannams!"

There was a silence from his people.

"No jeers, no starting fights! And keep away from their women!"

A great cough of laughter went up from the gathered people.

"Hear that, Per?"

"Keep away from the Grannam women!"

Toorkild cursed their stupidity and waved them all forward again. Armed riders and the pipers led the way down the hill with all the crowd of people on foot following. The pipers started a new tune:

"My hob is surefooted and swift,
My sword hangs down at my knee:
I never held back from a fight—
Come who dares and meddle with me!"

It was the Sterkarms' song, and the whole party took it up, shouting out its refrain, clapping its rhythm and cheering, announcing their coming as they rode down toward the Elves' camp. The armed men drew their pistols and fired their one shot into the air, with deafening, startling bangs that made the horses skip, the children cry, and the women squeal.

As they drew near the Elf-Palace, they came among the straggle of small kitchen huts built by the Sterkarm cooks, into the harsh smoke from the turf fires and the smell of cooking. Women and children came from the fires, clapping and cheering as the ride went by—and, ahead, they saw more people gathering before the largest of the glittering palaces. Elves, with their strange hairstyles and stranger clothes, stood among Sterkarms and Grannams too, and all laughed and cheered to see the ride come in.

The leaders of the ride reined their horses in. "No whiff of Richie Grannam!" Toorkild called out, and those near enough to hear him laughed. Richie Grannam would sell his daughter to a Sterkarm, in return for enough Elvish gold, but thought himself too good to greet the Sterkarms as they arrived.

A bustle of dismounting, and horses were given over to servants. Toorkild and Isobel took off their cloaks, handing them to servants, in order to display their best clothes to advantage, and Isobel shook out her skirts before going to Per, to comb his hair again with the comb from her belt. She made him bend his head down for the grooming and checked that his face wasn't smutched.

"Leave him, woman, leave him!" Toorkild said, offering her his arm. "Let's be doing!"

Isobel linked her arm through his, and they marched toward the entrance of the Elf-Palace, followed by Per. Their people, massed behind them, seeing them stroll forward so grandly, raised a cheer of pride, and cheered again when Per looked back at them over his shoulder and grinned.

As they drew nearer to the door—which was arched, like a church door, and decorated all around with fantastically whirling, delicate white-and-gold filigree—Per saw the beautiful Elf-May. She was standing close beside Elf-Windsor, holding a small, shining bag in either hand. In the slightly dimmed light just inside the doorway, she seemed to glow, more beautiful than ever. Her large eyes shone, her red lips were parted, her cheeks were flushed, and her pale-brown hair fell down over her shoulders in long waves. The tight

Elvish top she wore, the color of harebells, showed the fine, full curves of her figure and became her well. At the sight of her, Per smiled. He couldn't help it. Life was good, life was fine. He would be Per the May who had a Grannam for a wife and an Elf-May for a mistress.

Andrea, catching sight of the Sterkarms, wanted to jump up and down and wave. Her excitement was such, she could hardly breathe. But she had to remember that, except for Per, they had never seen her before in their lives and would think she was mad. So she clenched her fists around the strings of the little bags, drew in long, deep breaths, and remained outwardly calm. Toorkild, she thought, looked remarkably spruce: His beard and long hair must have been trimmed for the occasion. He was all decked out in blue, with a blue sash slung over one shoulder to support the sword he wore. Isobel, beside him, was small, plump, and pretty in russet, all her hair tucked away beneath an embroidered and beaded cap. They were gaping up at the inflatable, making no attempt to hide their astonishment and admiration.

And behind them, there was Per! He wore a bright-red baseball cap, with the word "Texan" printed across the front of it in white letters—a word which, even if he had been able to read it, would have meant nothing whatsoever to him. His jacket was black, of soft suede with a fur collar and a 21st-century zipper; and with it he wore a pair of dark-blue denim jeans. Over them were pulled his thigh-high riding boots. Andrea was disconcerted. In her favorite memories of him, she always saw him in 16th-century clothes—but then he smiled. Her arms and legs twitched as her muscles wanted to run to him. She calmed herself.

Now they were near. Andrea took a deep breath and stepped forward. "Master Toorkild Sterkarm! You are well come! Be so kind, take this gift from us! Mistress Isobel Sterkarm! We are gladdened to see you here! Take this small gift and, be so good, forgive its meanness!"

Isobel and Toorkild, startled to be greeted by name by a woman they had never seen before, looked quickly at each other, as if they feared her knowledge of them might be due to Elf-Work. But they thanked her and accepted the goodie bags before moving on, farther into the tent, toward Windsor. Andrea took no more notice of them. Per was in front of her. She couldn't say anything in greeting, but simply stared at him.

Per was surprised, and then amused, by her wide-eyed stare. Maybe it wasn't only a Grannam woman who'd be glad to get a Sterkarm man! But the pause was becoming awkward. To break it, he took the brightly shining little bag from her hand without its being offered and said, "I'm gladdened to see *you*, Mistress!"

She started, and said, "Well come! Well come!"

He winked at her, by way of letting her know that he'd be looking for her later, and moved on. A few paces away, among wreaths and garlands of flowers, Elf-Windsor was standing with his man beside him—the little Elf who turned Windsor's Elf-Words into English and the other way about.

"It's a good day!" Per said, holding out both his hands to Windsor, who had shown him many favors and given him many gifts. "Well come to my wedding and a thousand thanks shall you have!"

Andrea's head jerked round. She stood still, holding out a little gift bag but unable to give it to the Sterkarm who waited for it. Per's wedding? *Per's* wedding? She ought to have seen it. It was amazing enough that Lord Brackenhill should wed his daughter to a Sterkarm at all: He certainly wouldn't throw her away on a lesser one. Per was going to be married to that beautiful Grannam girl.

She felt a gentle tug at the bag in her hand and remembered her job. "Well come! Well come!" she said, and smiled as tears filled her eyes.

Per turned to Gareth. "My good man! Well come to you too! And"—Per glanced over his shoulder at the Elf-May—"a thousand thanks for decking the hall with such bonny flowers."

Windsor, not catching the last of this, inclined his head toward Gareth, who hesitated, though he well understood what Per meant by bonny flowers. "He says a thousand thanks for decorating the hall so beautifully."

Windsor nodded, shook hands, and said, *"Har ayn god dah"*–have a good day–before turning to the person behind Per–a craggy-faced, bearded, and wicked-looking individual whom he knew to be Gobby Per, the lad's uncle.

Andrea, struggling to greet the endless line of guests who came after Per, found herself peering at them through a blur of tears. Per's smile, his flirtatiousness, and even his tactful manners had brought back, so sharply, such memories of that other time with him that her heart was twisted. But how could he flirt with her like that on his wedding day–especially considering how it would annoy the Grannams? And wasn't it just like him, to flirt with her on his wedding day–especially when it would annoy the Grannams? And she was glad he had.

While turning away to pick up a gift bag, she took the opportunity to wipe tears from her eyes, and turning back, she recognized Sweet Milk–big, hulking, fearsome-looking Sweet Milk, who had been her good friend. He didn't know her now, but he smiled at her because he thought her pretty.

Well, she thought, if I can't have Per this time around, I can always have Sweet Milk. She gave him a wide smile and said, "A good day to thee, Master Beale! I am gladdened to see thee!"

His face–usually so expressionless–broke into an expression of utter shock that a woman who had never seen him before should know his name–not his nickname, which even Grannams knew, but his real name, which he'd almost forgotten himself. Alarmed, he snatched his goodie bag and went by into the tent.

Well, she thought, at least he'd remember her. Her eyes filled with tears again as she tried to greet the next person in line. Fool! she scolded herself. Fool! Now you're stuck here, 16th side, when you could have been at home with Mick. And for what? Once Per's married to that lovely girl, he won't have any time for you.

"That's right, lass," an old Sterkarm woman said to her. "Cry at a wedding, laugh at a funeral!"

"I'll cry at your wedding, Katrin!" Andrea said to her, and the old woman's smile turned to a wild-eyed fright. She hurried into the inflatable without even taking a bag. There might have been others waiting in line to be greeted, but Andrea couldn't see them. She couldn't see for tears.

5

16TH SIDE:
THE WEDDING

†††

Per looked about the hall with amazement and delight. He was fortunate, he was blessed, to be living when Elves came to Man's-Home. Barely a twelve-month since their Gate had opened on the hillside and they had driven out in their carts, bringing gifts—gifts that had never yet turned to dead leaves or dirt.

This palace, built for his wedding, was a piece of Elf-Land brought to Man's-Home. It wasn't made of wood or even brick. It was silvery and glittered faintly, but it wasn't silver or even metal. And here, inside!

The roof wasn't glass—how could glass be that shape?—but it let in light: the sort of light that would reach you through the petals of a white flower, if you were inside the flower.

Flowers were everywhere. Little round-headed bushes, growing in pots and covered with white flowers. Wreaths and garlands winding up poles and hanging in festoons. Pink and white roses, and even Elvish roses of blue and lavender. Candles as thick as his arm. Little white flickering lights, like stars, threaded through it all.

Long tables were covered with lacy cloths whiter than fresh snow, and decked with more flowers, and shining silver knives and spoons, and shining glasses. There were chairs enough for everyone to sit at the table, without having to share a bench. Even the small folk, the kitchen people, the shepherds—even they would have their own chairs. The Elves were treating them all like princes. Per had never in his life seen anything so beautiful, or so lavish. All the stories—which he had hardly bothered to believe before the Elves had walked out of the air—warned that the Elves were dangerous friends.

But it was hard to remember that when the Elves had brought them so much good.

Windsor came through the crowd, gesturing to Per to follow him. Per looked about, collected his cousins and his parents, and followed Windsor. They pushed their way through the crowds of gaping Sterkarms and Grannams, toward the farther end of the Elf-Palace. There was the altar, with splendid shields displaying the family badges—made of more flowers! And there, waiting, was the Grannam who called himself Lord Brackenhill, with women and soldiers gathered about him. And a priest!

Perhaps it was the sight of the priest—a rare sight in the border lands—that made Per, for the first time that day, feel alarm. Wed! Why was he getting wed?

He calmed himself by reflecting that it was only a wedding. He and his wife might get on, even though she was a Grannam, once she was away from her family. Who knew? And if they didn't, well, there was plenty of other company at the tower. Get a couple of sons on her, and after that he wouldn't have to see her much.

A girl stood before the altar. That would be his bride. His pulse quickened as he walked toward his first sight of her. Would he be bedded that night with a beauty or—?

He stepped into his place beside her. She didn't look up—indeed, she lowered her head still further in a properly modest way. That wasn't promising.

Richie Grannam nodded to him and to his parents, and the grim-faced Mistress Crosar inclined her head graciously. Both looked as if they'd bitten crab apples.

Toorkild and Isobel took up their positions on the opposite side of the altar and left Per and his bride standing before it.

The priest shrugged himself into a white vestment and, taking up his place, opened his Bible.

Joan Grannam saw the floor at her feet. A floor of neat, pale, polished wooden boards, laid by the Elves. She was afraid to look at anything else.

She had seen more floors in her life than any other thing. The wooden and stone floors at the tower, the trodden earth of paths, the grass of sheep meadows. If she raised her head and looked about, then her aunt nudged her sharply or pinched her and said, "Don't stare, like such a bold hussy!" Well-mannered, well-bred girls, said her aunt, showed their breeding and honored their parents and families by going about quietly, by standing neatly, with feet together and folded hands, and by keeping custody of their eyes. They did not run about like hoydens, or speak loudly, or squeal aloud with laughter. Still less did they stare people in the eye.

This evidently, Joan thought, did not apply to grown women. Her aunt, Mistress Crosar, was well-bred, but when she was giving her orders about the tower, she spoke loudly and not only looked boldly about her but scowled. True, she didn't run like a hoyden, but she strode. Joan had never said this aloud, though. If she had, her aunt would certainly have given her several blows and reported her impertinence to her father—which would have brought more punishment.

Joan could feel, beside her, the bulk of the Sterkarm she was to marry. She didn't dare to look at him—nor at his parents, more Sterkarms, who stood somewhere near. She had never seen any of them before but was too terrified to be curious. Curiosity, in her experience, only shortened the time before the arrival of the bad news or the bad time.

For weeks, ever since she'd been told about her marriage, she'd been almost overwhelmed with fear, even more afraid than usual, hardly able to eat, think, or sleep. The Elf-Man, Elf-Windsor, had been coming often to the tower and meeting with her father, but she had assumed that their business was about land or cattle. It had nothing to do with her, and she hadn't asked any questions. "None of thine affair, lass!" her aunt would have said, if she had, and would then have looked closely through all the work Joan had done that day, searching for faults. It was not wise, if you lived at Brackenhill, to draw Mistress Crosar's attention.

So it had been a shock when, before going to bed one evening, as she knelt before her father for his blessing, he'd said, "Joan, I've something to tell thee. Th'art to be wed."

The maids and serving men gathered near the fire caught the words, and a hush fell. They all listened.

A jolt of fear had gone through Joan like an arrow strike, but she'd kept still, her head down. With everyone watching and listening, the only privacy she had was to keep her feelings to herself. For a frantic eye blink of time, she'd searched through her mind for the right thing to say, something that her father and aunt would approve. "Thanks shall you have, sir."

"Is that all tha say?" her aunt demanded. "When thy father has gone to such trouble for thee? I should think tha'd be more grateful than that!"

Still kneeling, still keeping her head down, Joan said, "A thousand thanks shall you have, sir, a thousand thanks!" She was starting to cry and had to tighten the muscles of her throat to hide it so that no one would see or hear. No one must be able to whisper afterward, in kitchen corners and stables, "Didst see her tears?"

Sounding amused, her father said, "Dost not wish to know who th'art to wed?"

"If it please you, sir."

"Thy husband is to be Per Toorkildsson Sterkarm. The one they call the May."

The shock had been so great, she'd looked up and stared into her father's face. A Sterkarm? That ill-bred, brawling litter of upstarts? With their bragging badge, to which they had no right—that brood of thieves and murderers?

"No doubt tha'rt surprised," her father said, nodding. "It's a match I never thought to make myself. But the Elves wish it. I've thought on it much, and I reckon we can make no better bargain." He put his warm hand on her head. "God bless thee, child, and keep thee safe through the night."

Joan remained kneeling, her mind blank with confusion and fright, until her aunt said, "Art fixed there, lass? Away to bed!" And Joan left the hot, crowded, noisy hall and went up the cool, dark stairs to the family's private floor above. There her maid was waiting to undo her tight laces and let down her hair, and there Joan cried, while begging, "Don't tell, Christy, don't tell."

"I will no, I will no," Christy had said. "Everybody's sorry for you, mistress, everybody is. Wed to a Sterkarm!"

Of course, everyone had known before her.

She shared a little box bed with her aunt, and when Mistress Crosar came up, she had to pretend to be sleeping. But she lay awake all night, stifling any sound she made with the blankets. Her father slept across the chamber, in another box bed. She could not make a peep.

It was no surprise to her that she had to wed. Sons had to fight for the family, and perhaps be killed or maimed. Daughters had to wed for the family and face the dangers of childbirth. She had known this all her life, but it had always seemed something that would happen next year, or the year after, not now, not soon.

Sometimes she'd almost looked forward to her wedding, because it would mean escape from the rule of her father and aunt. She would be a woman, ruling her own household. She would stride then, like her aunt, and look up from the floor, and give orders in a loud, firm voice. How this change in her would come about she wasn't sure, but she had an idea that it was something that happened when you became a woman and married. You woke up changed, knowing what orders to give and how to give them so that they would be obeyed.

Then she would remember that she was still young, and wedlock would mean obeying a new family. They would be just as harsh as her own, but she would be less practiced in pleasing them. People would be angry with her all the time. Life would be miserable.

At worst, though, she had always imagined that this strange new family would be a decent family, perhaps the Yonnsons or Beaucloos. Not the Sterkarms. God have mercy, how could she live among Sterkarms? How could she eat with them, knowing how many of her family they'd murdered? How could she say, "Yes, mistress, no, mistress," to her mother-in-law, while knowing that she was one of the brood mares who'd spawned the thieves who'd plundered her family over and over again? How could her father and aunt expect this of her?

They expected it as they would have expected a brother of hers to fight. So, since she was a Grannam, she had to find in herself the courage that was her inheritance, and marry a Sterkarm and breed Sterkarms. . . .

She didn't know how she was going to do it.

She would have to please not only the Sterkarm family but a Sterkarm husband—in bed and out of it. She knew very well how a man pricked a woman, but she had never done it, or had even wanted to do it, since it rarely seemed to bring a woman any good. Besides, if she had been caught with a man, unwed, her aunt would have beaten her almost to death, she was sure. Now her husband would beat her for being unpracticed and disappointing him.

Why had God made life so hateful? she wondered. Her whole life had been punishments, and so it would continue, all her years, until her death. God was good, said her father's priest, and life a sacred gift from Him. Joan thought that God hated women. He made their life so hard. Once she was married, her husband would get her with child, and then she would be sick all the time, and tired. She'd seen enough big-bellied women at Brackenhill to know it was so. Their legs ached, their backs ached, they retched up their food, and at the end of their time they had to give birth. Joan felt a tightening of fear around her heart as she imagined herself suffering like that. She had seen births, she'd heard the women yelling. She knew it hurt. And women died. Her own mother had birthed five children: a brother older than Joan, who had died at two years; a stillborn child; Joan herself; another boy who'd died soon after birth; and the child whose birth had killed her.

A breeding woman lost a tooth with every child, it was said. Certainly, they lost their looks and much of their health and grew old quickly. What life was this?

But this was the courage that women had to have, instead of courage in battle. Joan was ashamed for being afraid. She was a

Grannam. She should be braver.

Everyone at the tower had been astonished at the beauty of the Elvish cloth Elf-Windsor had given them to make her wedding dress. It was a shouting scarlet, more vivid even than rowanberries or rosehips, and though scarlet, it had the shine of polished silver or gold. Its weave was so tight, it could hardly be seen. People couldn't stop themselves from stroking it again and again—it was as soft as thistledown and as smooth as oil. Even her aunt had said, "Well, the Elves have done thee proud, my lass."

Joan had touched it once and thought, "Red, like blood." She'd had to help stitch the dress, and she'd had to stand still while it was measured against her and pinned and tacked. But she couldn't make herself take an interest in what the dress looked like, or what it looked like on her. What did it matter? It would have been all the same if the dress had been made of gray sackcloth.

During the ride to the wedding, with the bagpiper playing, Joan saw little but her horse's ears. Her thoughts, in a numb, miserable way, ran through, again and again, the misery of her future.

"Try to smile—try!" her aunt shouted at her. Joan hadn't the spirit even to try.

Brought to the Elvish palace, made in moments by the magic of the Elves, she had given it one swift look before ducking her head again to avoid her aunt's criticism. The palace had been silver, shining—but really, what did it matter if she was wed in a hut?

They were standing now at the far end of the Elf-Palace, and everyone was crowded in behind them, trapping her. It was hot, and the board laced tightly to her breasts, to make her upright, dug into her. Her aunt gave her a sudden poke in the ribs, with so much force that she staggered slightly. She realized that the man beside her had spoken.

He said, "Wilt take my hand, honey?"

Wilt? *Honey?* She was shocked and angered to be addressed like a kitchen maid by a Sterkarm. Then she remembered that she had to get used to that. Once the wedding was made, the Sterkarms would be insulting her every moment of the day—and the night, too.

The Sterkarm was holding out his hand to her. A large, thin hand. Everyone was waiting.

She could refuse. She could walk away and say she would not, would never, marry a Sterkarm.

But people were standing almost at her back. She couldn't get out of the Elf-Palace. There was nowhere she could go if she did. And everyone would be so angry with her, more angry than they'd ever been. She'd be beaten, locked up, and beaten again until she agreed to the wedding.

So she might as well do it now. She put her hand into the Sterkarm's.

Per, seeing her reluctance, and feeling the chill dampness of the hand put into his, thought: God's arse, what a stick to be burdened with! She hadn't moved, or spoken, or looked at him, or even looked up from her feet. He had a terrible, itching desire to turn and see if he could spot the Elf-Maid in the crowd. But that would be unforgivable bad manners. There would be time later. For the time being, he had to think of the land and gold this Grannam stick would be bringing along with her.

"Place your hands on the Book," said the priest, "and make your vows."

Andrea had fought her way to the front of the crowd with Gareth, and they stood, raising themselves on tiptoe and leaning from side to side, trying to see. Andrea watched Per place his hand on the Bible and heard him say, "I, Per Toorkildsson Sterkarm, of Bedesdale, take thee, Joan Grannam, of Brackenhill, for my wife." His loud, hoarse voice effortlessly filled the hall, and every word hurt her like a slap.

Joan put her hand on the Bible, but her vow was inaudible except to those closest. While she was speaking, Per was fumbling at his waist, unbuckling a pouch. He then dropped the pouch onto the open pages of the Bible. It made an unmistakable sound: the chink of coins.

"You are now wed: man and wife," the priest said.

Andrea watched Per stoop to kiss his bride. She didn't lift her face to his. After a moment he had to stoop lower, and then touch her face to guide it toward his. He kissed her—and everyone in the hall broke into a loud, raucous, rolling cheer. The fiddlers and pipers started playing, in a cacophony of conflicting tunes—and balloons of every color fell from the roof, causing a slight panic until the 16th siders realized that they were harmless. Then there was much batting of balloons about, and shrieking and cheering, and such bedlam that Andrea couldn't imagine how enough order was going to be restored for the wedding feast to be served. In the end, it was only because Lord Brackenhill and Toorkild Sterkarm climbed on chairs and roared for order that any kind of quiet was achieved. But when the assembled Grannams and Sterkarms understood that food was to be served, there was a scramble for places at the tables.

Andrea wished that she had a glass of wine. Per—her Per—was married. To a girl far more beautiful than she.

But she couldn't look unhappy. She couldn't let Windsor see her misery. Lifting her head, she made herself look around the tent with a smile—and her eye fell on Sweet Milk, who was standing nearby, looking at her. He hadn't yet gone to claim a seat.

She gave him a big smile and shook a lock of her hair back over her shoulder. Sweet Milk gave a slow smile before lumbering off to table.

He was a fine big strapping broth of a lad, was Sweet Milk. A girl could do far worse.

6

16TH SIDE:
THE WEDDING DANCE

✝✝✝

Andrea got into bed, but she didn't undress and she didn't sleep.

She wasn't having to make do with a sleeping bag or a mattress because Isobel Sterkarm felt that, as an Elf and a guest, she ought to have the best they had to offer. So Isobel had assigned her a bed at the back of the dormitory, close to her own bed, and also near the entrance to the wedding suite.

She lay on her back, one hand under her head. The great silence of the moors at night leaned on the walls of the inflatable. There were none of the night noises of the 21st: no passing cars, no aircraft, no late homecomers slamming car doors. Around her the hall was quiet, lit dimly by one or two widely spaced Elf-Lamps, their light so faint that it was barely candlepower. One or two people were whispering, and one or two snoring, and there was the occasional rustle as someone turned over; but otherwise, it seemed, the whole Sterkarm clan was away with the fairies.

Of course, in that other hall a few yards away, in that big flouncy bed with the gauzy curtains and the heart-shaped pillows, there probably wasn't much sleeping going on. There were kisses and cuddles being exchanged that by rights . . .

Don't be a jealous bitch, she told herself, trying to stifle the pang she felt. After all, who was it lying here, hoping a cheating husband was going to come creeping out to join her?

Despite everything, it was pleasant lying there, in the almost dark and the almost silence, after the heat and noise and smell of the celebrations earlier. In the dancing hall the sound of fiddles playing a reel, super-amplified, had boomed and shrilled from the Elvish boxes at the back of the room; while 16th-sider fiddlers, pipers, and drummers, both Sterkarm and Grannam, had played with and against the phantom Elvish musicians. The bedlam of noise had been thickened by the din of feet pounding on the wooden floor, and laughter and shouting. It must have disturbed snoozing curlew and hunting foxes for miles around.

Whirling dancers, arms linked, had skipped the length of the hall, come together, parted, changed partners, whirled again, in a thick, foxy reek of sweat—horse sweat from their long ride as well as the dancers' own. Sterkarms danced on one side of the room, with other Sterkarms, and Grannams danced on the other, with Grannam partners.

It had been the same earlier still, at the wedding feast. Sterkarms had filled the tables on one side of the room, and Grannams the tables on the other. Sterkarm servants had gone among the Sterkarm tables with little wooden buckets of ale, ladling the drink into glasses, or had carried around wooden troughs piled with bread and sliced meat. Grannam servants had brought food and drink to the Grannams.

Only at the head table, where the bride and groom were seated with their parents, were the two sides together, and even there it was hardly friendly. Joan sat to Per's left, with her father and aunt beside her. Toorkild and Isobel sat beside Per. Between the bride and groom was a distinct gap, which was caused not only by their armed chairs. They leaned away from each other.

Toorkild Sterkarm and Richie Grannam had each risen, at different times, and called for toasts to the newlywed couple and to the alliance of two such great families. Everyone in the hall had responded—made happy by drink and food in unaccustomed amounts—and had yelled and cheered deafeningly, stamping their feet and pounding on the tables, so that the cutlery and glassware jingled. But no one had crossed the floor to sit, eat, and drink with the other side. It was a happy, excited company, but not a united one.

Andrea had been seated with the other Elves at a table near the head table, and her glass had been filled with wine from a clumsy green-glass bottle. She'd drunk it while watching Per and Joan. Per laughed, shouted responses to shouts and toasts from the body of the hall, and once stood to throw a bone at someone who taunted him. He often looked in her direction, whereupon she looked away and pretended she hadn't even noticed him. Joan Grannam—no, Joan Sterkarm—kept her head lowered and her eyes on the table-cloth. Occasionally she took a sip from her glass or ate something from her plate—usually when prompted by her father. Andrea had tried not to be glad that the newlyweds didn't seem to get along. It meant little. The following morning they might be the best of friends. She didn't want to think of that, either.

At the next table down, Sweet Milk was seated. Glancing around, Andrea caught him looking at her. He didn't look away but continued to stare. So she lifted one hand to brush back her hair, and smiled. His expression hardly changed, but as soon as they left the tables and started the dancing, she knew, Sweet Milk would come to her.

People were slow to leave the tables. Few people there, even the richest, got the opportunity to eat so much, and many had never drunk from clear, shining glasses or eaten from shining white-china plates laid on a white cloth. Seated like lords and ladies in their chairs, they chewed on greasy lamb while staring at the twinkling lights twined through the wreaths and garlands. They swigged beer and filled their mouths with cake—a great rarity and delicacy—while raising their eyes high to the silvery domes above them. Every shepherd felt himself a king, every kitchen maid felt herself a queen, and they were in no hurry to become mere shepherds and kitchen maids again.

So it had been midafternoon before Per rose and, taking his bride's hand, led her down the length of the hall to the door. Their families followed, and Windsor fell in behind them. Andrea and Gareth hurried to leave their seats and join the line behind him. Gradually everyone else followed, though even after the dancing had begun, there were still people hanging around the feast hall or drifting back there, snatching a little more meat, another glass of ale, another cake.

The dancing didn't start immediately. Almost everyone had stuffed themselves with food until they groaned, and even the slower, more stately dances didn't, at first, appeal. Windsor spoke to the DJ—Andrea supposed that he had to be called a DJ, since he was in charge of the sound system—and music started playing through the speakers: a selection of madrigals and other such courtly music. The 16th siders had been startled, at first, by the music suddenly sounding from the air, and a disturbance ran through the company. For a moment Andrea wondered if there was going to be a panic, but the people seemed to reconcile themselves to this Elf-Work and calmed down. "What can you expect, with Elves around," they seemed to say to themselves, "but music played by invisible spirits?" Not that there was much appreciation of the music. Fashionable court music—some of it decades later than the date it was being played here, at this wedding—was not to the taste of this remote, backward area. Edging through the crowd to Windsor, Andrea explained this and suggested that the 16th-side musicians be asked to play.

Windsor looked around the hall and saw the people's mood for himself. "See to it, then," he said.

She hunted out the musicians, who were drinking in the feast hall and sulking at being superseded by the Elves' phantoms. Once she'd promised them a bonus from the Elves—she was sure Windsor would agree to that, because they'd be thrilled with a few packets of cheap aspirins—they were happy to troop back to the dance hall—with a couple of buckets of ale—and play. She was amazed to see that Sterkarm musicians and Grannam musicians were willing to play together. Perhaps this alliance would work after all. Or maybe that was just musicians.

Once the jigs and reels were sounding through the hall, she thought she would earn herself a few Brownie points by congratulating the families on their new alliance. She was a little tipsy but still sober enough to approach the Grannams first. They considered themselves the superiors of everyone there, so it would flatter them if she seemed to agree. Lord Brackenhill and his sister were sitting on benches at the back of the dancing hall, under swags and wreaths of artificial flowers that glittered with white lights. "Lord Brackenhill, Mistress Crosar, please forgive me for coming up to you like this," Andrea began. Richard Grannam declined his head graciously and almost smiled—he had been drinking too, and had mellowed. Mistress Crosar cocked her head with a rather grim expression, as if to say that she would decide whether she minded or not when she'd heard what else Andrea had to say.

"It was such a lovely ceremony," Andrea twittered. "And such a beautiful bride!"

They both graciously nodded this time, and Mistress Crosar even smiled a little.

Unable to think of anything else to say, even after frantically searching her brains for several silent seconds, Andrea cried, "Enjoy the rest of the day!" and escaped. Where were the Sterkarms? It was the Sterkarms she really wanted to talk with.

Toorkild and Isobel were sitting together on a bench at the other side of the hall, holding hands. "Good day, Master Sterkarm, Mistress Sterkarm. My name is Andrea Mitchell—I'm Master Windsor's helper. What a lovely ceremony! And your son made such a handsome groom!" Didn't he just? she thought. Praise of their only son, she knew, was the way to Toorkild's and Isobel's hearts. She made a few other fatuous comments while watching their faces. It was strange, when she knew them so well, to see their faces reflect so little knowledge of her. They studied her carefully, a little wary, and much wondering, because she was an Elf.

"Where are you sleeping the night, Mistress Elf?" Isobel asked. That was so like Isobel in its concern—and so unlike the Isobel she knew in that she used the formal "you."

"I'm not sure," Andrea admitted. "But I'm sure I can find some-where!"

"Ach!" Isobel said and, leaning forward, gripped Andrea's hand. "You're to come to me at our hall, and I'll see you have somewhere!" She shook Andrea's arm in emphasis. "Come to me, now! I mean it!"

"I'll be sure to–thank you!" Andrea left them and, bracing herself, marched over to where Per and his new wife sat, side by side, but with a space between them. Per saw her approaching, and his face became alert. Joan was looking at the floor.

"All best wishes on your wedding!" Andrea said. She meant to say it to them both, but with Joan staring at the floor, it was difficult. Raising the glass in her hand, Andrea said, "Good health and good cheer to you! A child every year to you!" She watched Per's eyes drop from her face to her breasts, and lift again to her face, with a spark in them. For God's sake, she wanted to say, why did you have to go and get married?

Joan Grannam raised her head with a sort of flinch. A child every year? That was exactly what she dreaded. She looked at the person who wished it on her and saw the beautiful Elf-Woman who had greeted them on their arrival. Her rosy face was flushed, with more than heat; her large eyes were bright, her hair fell about her shoulders, and she was smiling at Per Sterkarm.

Joan glanced sideways at her husband–one of the few looks she had given him that day–and was held by the way he stared at the Elf-Woman.

"A thousand thanks shall you have, Lady, for your good wishes," he said, and smiled, and something in the smile, and the note of his voice, and the way he looked at her, hinted what form the thanks would take.

A little hot fire of insult and anger jumped up in Joan. Sterkarms! A faithful husband was far beyond her expectations, but it was only common courtesy to refrain from flirting with other women until the wedding day was over!

Andrea took another drink from her glass and smiled at Joan, who, to Andrea's surprise, didn't lower her eyes timidly but glared back at her.

"Thanks shall you have, Mistress Elf," Joan said. "But the dancing is begun and we keep you from the men."

Andrea's eyes widened in surprise. Blimey! she thought. The little bitch bites! After all that simpering and looking at the ground, too! Lifting her glass in farewell, she said gaily, "I'll see you around!" She spoke to them both but couldn't resist a quirk of the eyebrow in Per's direction. She twirled away, a little unsteadily, and thought: I'm drunk!

The music was persuading people to get up and dance. People were coming together to form sets. Per, watching, saw Sweet Milk go to Andrea and speak to her. Sweet Milk! Much as he loved his foster father, he'd like him to keep his big paws off *his* Elf-May. Turning to Joan, Per said, "Why didst say that? Thee insulted a guest." He wasn't going to address his wife as "you," however brief the wedlock.

Tears of rage and hurt came into Joan's eyes, but she fought to hold them back, and swallowed hard, to keep her voice steady. She was a Grannam woman, going into marriage as onto a battlefield. "That *Elf* insulted me." She left it to him to understand how the Elf had insulted her, and to take her part as a husband should, at least on his wedding day.

Per was faintly surprised. It seemed that his wife was not as quiet and meek as he'd feared. That was interesting, if not altogether pleasing. But he wasn't going to quarrel then and there. "We should join the dance," he said, and led her into a place in one of the sets. But, she saw, he was looking down the set, to where the Elf-Woman was facing the big man the Sterkarms called Sweet Milk.

The dancing was exhilarating and fast. The 16th siders were impressed by how well Andrea, an Elf, knew the steps, the turns and twists. They laughed their approval at her, whistled and cheered as she spun past them, clasping hands and whirling, her skirt and hair flying.

The grasp of Sweet Milk's hand was almost painful, and he lifted her off her feet at times, spinning her fast. They hardly spoke to each other during the dance, but then the noise was so much that they would have had to yell—and Andrea didn't think she had the breath. Anyway, as she remembered, Sweet Milk had never been one for talking much.

The dance ended, and some people made breathlessly for the benches at the side of the hall, while others came forward to dance. Toorkild came and took his daughter-in-law's hand from his son and led her into the new dance that was forming. That was like Toorkild, Andrea thought—he had a lot of good nature, really. When he wasn't raiding. But then she saw that Per, deprived of a partner, was making straight toward her. The room was full of Grannams, and his own in-laws. Nice one, Mr. Tact.

Sweet Milk was still standing beside her, and he was saying—very politely and formally using "you"—"Will you sit, mistress?" when Per came up.

"Will you dance, Lady?" Per asked. It was strange to hear him use "you"—but then, though she knew him so well, he hardly knew her.

Still a little out of breath, she nodded and held out her hand to him. But she looked at Sweet Milk, smiled, and said, "Maybe we'll dance again later."

Sweet Milk and Per looked at each other. Then Sweet Milk made her a slight, clumsy bow, stepped back, and walked away.

Per led her to a place at the farthest end of the dance, nearest the door. She thought it odd but supposed that he wanted to be as far from his parents and new in-laws as he could be. Once the dance started, she learned otherwise. Holding both her hands, he whirled her right out of the dance altogether and then pulled her out of the door and into the open air.

Two big, lean shapes sprang up from the grass outside the hall—Cuddy and Swart, Per's gazehounds. They looked like enormous shaggy grayhounds, except that their heads were more square. The nearest thing she knew like them among dogs of her own time were wolfhounds or deerhounds. Per said to them, "Down! Stay!"

Swart, the younger, male hound, named after his darker coat, immediately sank back to the ground; but Cuddy was more attached to Per. She had waited patiently for him outside the hall, and now she wanted to follow wherever he was going. "Stay, Cuddy! Stay!"

Reluctantly she sank down beside Swart.

With a yank on her arm, Per dragged Andrea on, giving her no chance to ask where they were going, towing her away from the Elf-Palace and into the small village of cooking shacks. A strong smell of smoke, burning turf, and roasting fat still hung thickly in the air. Andrea couldn't help but feel a small thrill, as she was dragged along by a hard grip on her hand. This was no imitation: This was Per.

They passed other couples who had left the dance and were now kissing, and almost fell over one couple lying full length on the ground, wrapped around each other. Per finally stopped where the shacks ended, and there was nothing beyond but open sky and moor. For a moment Andrea was struck, again, by the space and emptiness. Even the din of the amplified music behind them was now muffled by the sheer emptiness that surrounded this small encampment, by the deep silence that seeped from the hills.

"I thought we were going to dance!" she said.

Per grinned. "We can dance here, Lady."

"So we could," she said, and threw herself down in the grass and heather. Pointedly she left a little space between them. She was hot and there was a slight, cooling breeze, so she lifted her hair from her neck and saw his gaze shift downward from her face. "Will you not be missed?"

Ignoring her question, he sat beside her. "What are you called, Lady?"

"Andrea Mitchell."

"Entraya." Another thrill went through her as she heard him pronounce her name as the other Per always had—but no, this Per and her Per were the same. She felt suddenly dizzy as she wondered how many Andreas there were, all of them identical but all of them unaware of her or one another. And how many of them knew a Per? She didn't catch what Per said. "What?"

"May I call you Entraya?"

"I'd like that," she said.

He was leaning on his elbow beside her. "I am Per. Shall we be 'thee' to each other?"

He meant *Shall we drop formality and address each other as "thou," as friends and equals?* He was in a hurry. "I don't think I know you well enough," she said, a little piqued. *You'll have to work a bit harder than that, mate.* "Cuddy and Swart seem in good health," she said.

He sat up straight, astonished that she knew the names of his hounds. A wary look came into his eyes, but then he smiled and relaxed. "Elf-Work," he said. "We must ken each other better. We could take Cuddy and Swart out onto the moor and hunt for the bonny black hare."

Andrea smiled, looking away at the outline of the hills against the sky. She knew the words of the song:

I said, "Pretty fair maid, why dost wander so?
And canst tell me where the bonny black hare do go?"
Oh, the answer she gave me, her answer was, "No.
But under me apron they say it do grow."

"That would keep you away from your wedding for too long."

"For a long, long time," he agreed. She looked back at him to see him grinning even more widely.

"Don't you care what people will think?" she asked.

"We'll be quick, then–and they won't notice."

"I'm not tempted. What about your wife? She's very beautiful."

Without a moment's consideration, simply, flatly, he said, "No tits." His eyes dropped thoughtfully to Andrea's breasts. It was exactly what he thought, without calculation. His wife beautiful? No. No tits.

Andrea didn't know whether to laugh aloud, or be outraged, or be flattered. No! How could she be flattered? But she was–and delighted to be preferred above a skinny beauty like Mrs. Joan Sterkarm, when all her life she'd been called fat and overlooked. And yet a small part of her *was* outraged. A much larger part still wanted to laugh at the shameless honesty of Per's answer.

"Stay you here tonight?" he asked. "Or do you return?"

Do I return? she thought. She could resign, go home, back to Mick . . . but it would be interesting to see the wedding customs. She told herself. "I stay here. To see you bedded with your wife."

Leaning toward her, smiling, he asked, "Where will you sleep?"

He couldn't be planning what she thought he was planning, surely? She found herself smiling back, even leaning toward him. "Why do you want to know?"

He grinned. "We need to ken one another better, so we can be 'thee' to each other."

Andrea giggled. Why am I being coy? she thought. What did I come here for, if not for this? So what if he was married—it was an arranged marriage, made for land, money, and power. It didn't count. He and his wife didn't even know each other!

He doesn't know you, either, came a thought. You know him. You love him. He doesn't know or love you. Yet.

One night. One last night. Get him out of her system. Then she'd go home to Mick. With knowledge of 16th-century wedding customs.

She said, "I don't know where I'll be. Somewhere in one of the big halls. Your mother said she would find me a place in your hall."

"Aye. Sleep in the Sterkarm hall. Sleep near the door." He sat up, ready to get up, and looked at her attentively.

"All right," she said, and gave him her hand. He got to his feet and pulled her up too.

"I'll go this way," he said and, dropping her hand, made off into the cooking shacks at a run. She made her own way back, slowly, and went first to the feasting hall, where she helped herself to another glass of wine. When she went back to the dancing, Per was leading his wife into the figures of another dance.

"Will you dance, Lady?" She looked up, and there was a stranger—possibly a Grannam. But why not? She smiled and gave him her hand.

There had been a lot more dancing, and drinking and eating, and the evening light that came through the door and through the dome above had thickened into dusk before the fiddlers and the pipers began to play, once more, the tune called "Come to the Wedding." As they played, they bore down on Per and Joan, and people cheered and clapped and stamped. It was time that the wedded pair were put to bed.

7

16TH SIDE:
THE BEDDING CEREMONY

†††

Mistress Crosar put her mouth so close to Joan's ear that it tickled, and shouted, "Undo thy garters!"

Joan froze. They were at the back of the dancing hall, near the benches. People were everywhere. How could she pull up her skirts and undo her garters? Only vulgar, low-born girls, like the kitchen maids, pulled up their skirts without caring who saw. Besides, everyone would laugh at how skinny and bony her legs were.

"Oh, come here, lass!" her aunt said, and turned her around, tutting at how slow and clumsy Joan was in moving. Other women gathered around her. One of them was the Sterkarm woman, Isobel Allyot that was, whom she must now call mother. She could never do it. She'd choke. The women spread their skirts, blocking the view of other people, while her aunt pulled up Joan's magnificent scarlet dress of Elf-Cloth with a flurrying and rustling, and reached underneath to undo the garter strings. It was necessary to undo them because, very soon, the newlywed couple would be put to bed, and the bride's men would demand their right to take off her garters. It was better to have the garters already undone, and the strings dangling down where they could be easily reached.

Mistress Crosar slapped at Joan's leg, to turn her farther around, so she could reach the other garter. "There!" she said, throwing down the skirts and straightening.

"She didn't want them undone, that's what it was," said Isobel Sterkarm. "She wanted the men to reach right up her skirt." There was loud laughter from the Sterkarm women, either because they were really amused or because they wanted to curry favor with their mistress. The Grannam women, cocking an eye toward their own mistress, laughed less, and Mistress Crosar herself merely smiled. It wasn't her style of humor, but what could you expect from the Sterkarms? And such remarks were customary at a wedding–they were supposed to be lucky.

Joan told herself that if she could endure this, and the night to come, if she could only set her teeth and endure it all, it would pass, like everything else. Her new life as a married woman might not be a happy one, but habit would inure her to it, and in time it would be relatively calm. Even the dray horse became accustomed to the everyday rubbing of its harness, to its sores and aches. Only endure: All things pass.

Someone had told tales about the garters being untied, because now the bride's men came around Joan in an ebullient, noisy mob. She had known they would come, but still, their arrival was a shock. Men surrounded her: all beards and red, greasy faces, shining eyes and grinning teeth. They were drunk; shouting and laughing and shoving. She knew many of them–some by name, some by sight only. A few were uncles and cousins; many were neighbors. Not all were Grannams by name–if families lived in Grannam country and allied themselves to the Grannams, then they often called them-selves Grannam.

It was only a game–and yet when they caught at her arms with hard, gripping hands and pulled her this way and that, her body felt that it was being attacked, and her heart pounded so hard, she could hardly breathe. I am such a coward, she thought, but she hadn't expected them to come at her so quickly, to look so fierce, to bray and laugh with such harsh, loud voices; nor had she thought they would jerk her and shove her about, with so little care for her, as if she was a puppet, of no worth. Hands scrabbled at her skirts, touching and scratching her legs.

Sick and giddy, she struggled to pull down her skirts and fend them off. She'd forgotten that this was part of the ceremony–she could only think that she had to stop them pulling up her skirts and seeing her legs. They laughed all the more, and two of them held her arms. It was terrifying.

Two of the men straightened, yelling with triumph and flourishing her garters in the air. From the rest of the hall came a cheer, so loud that to Joan it seemed like a blow. She remembered the ceremony then, and forced a smile to her face, though tears spilled over her lashes. She was ashamed of her cowardice. She had let the Grannams down. They all saw my legs too, she thought. They'll laugh to one another about how bony they are, and tell everyone. . . . If she hadn't been on show, she would have wept. Because she was on show, her fierce smile stretched as wide and tight as a skull's.

The men were crowded away from her by women: all her brides-maids, all the important women of both families, married and unmarried, all laughing and crowing and reaching out to grab at her and pull her along. They were going to take her to the wedding chamber. Trying hard to seem brave, Joan forced a laugh and went with them, but at heart she felt hopeless. She did not want to go to the wedding chamber at all, yet it was the only place she could go.

The women dragged her into the middle of the dance hall and there, clumsily, they hoisted her in their arms and carried her, chanting and yelling, out of the light and heat of the hall and into the chill evening dusk.

Out in the air, the shrill of the fiddle and the laughter and shouting of the women seemed suddenly thin and weak. Bumped and jostled and breathless in their arms, Joan was carried along in a spangle of darkness and lantern light and into the Sterkarm dormitory. There it was light again, and she was carried the length of the hall, between the beds and bedding and decorations, and through the door at the back of the hall into the wedding suite.

In the white, pink, and gold anteroom, the air was stiflingly scented: expensive Elvish candles were burning, filling the air with perfumed smoke and a gauzy yellow light. Among the pretty couches and garlands, the panting women set Joan on her feet and then dragged her excitedly toward the curtain at the back of the hall. Someone snatched the curtain back, revealing the big bed.

Joan was thrown onto the bed, among the soft, heart-shaped pillows and rose petals. A scent of lavender and spices rose up—not a hint of straw from the mattress. And she bounced, the Elvish bed was so soft and springy.

"Th'art ever so lucky," someone said. "He's so handsome!"

"He is," Isobel Sterkarm agreed complacently. "He is handsome, my Per."

"A fine-looking young man," Mistress Crosar allowed politely. "But do you not think our Joan a beautiful lass, Mistress Sterkarm?"

"Oh, that she is, that she is," Isobel said. "No one could say she was not." Andrea, who had pressed in among the crowd of women, to see and hear as much of this ceremony as she could, tried not to smile. Isobel's tone lacked conviction. She guessed that Isobel was thinking: It'll be a long time before that skinny may gives me a grandson. Once she had the girl at the Bedesdale tower, Isobel would probably fatten her like a pig for Hogmanay.

A girl plumped herself beside Joan and began undoing the laces that held on her sleeve. Andrea, finding herself pushed close to the bed, knelt on it at Joan's other side and unlaced the other sleeve. Another young woman climbed onto the bed behind Joan, to unpin the wreath of flowers and ribbons from her hair. Leaning over Joan's shoulder, this woman said, "They call him the May—he's pretty as a may!"

Isobel laughed and said, "He's no may! Not my Per!"

"Let's hope not!" a Grannam girl said daringly, and there was a tiny pause, the tiniest of gasps, as everyone feared that Isobel would take offense—but Isobel only laughed. Everyone else burst into loud, relieved laughter, and they all beamed around at one another, exhilarated to find themselves all getting on so well, Grannams and Sterkarms together.

Joan, looking around, found that the woman close beside her, pulling the lace from her sleeve, was the Elf-May, the beautiful one her new husband had been making eyes at. As Andrea pulled the lace free, Joan said, "Keep that! Tie it around your arm, and you'll marry in a twelve-month."

Andrea looked up and met the girl's eyes. She thought again how very beautiful she was, but her cold glare was pure Grannam. "Thank you," she said, and rolling up the ribbon, she moved away.

Mistress Sterkarm herself bent to unfasten Joan's bodice. It was a relief to have it loosened, so that the board didn't press so hard against her breasts, but then she remembered why it was being removed, and felt sick. Behind her, she heard someone whisper what she herself was thinking: "He's a *Sterkarm.*"

Mistress Sterkarm must have heard, but she went on calmly pulling at the bodice laces and didn't show it by as much as a flicker of an eyelid.

"So?" said a whisper behind Joan. "He's a good-looking Sterkarm!"

"Careful!" Mistress Sterkarm said to the girls who were pulling off Joan's sleeves—perhaps she spoke more sharply because of what she'd overheard. "Don't pull off her gloves." The gloves had to be left on, by custom, for the bride's husband to remove. So when the sleeves were fully pulled off, the women anxiously tugged up the gloves again.

Ribbons and ribbon knots removed from Joan were being eagerly tied around sleeves and waists—they were pretty additions to a wardrobe and would be worn for weeks, both to show that their wearers were at the wedding and as good-luck charms to bring on another wedding. But every pin that pinned on a knot, or secured the skirt more firmly to the bodice, was carefully stuck into a pin-cushion wielded by Mistress Crosar. It was bad luck to keep a pin, and would ensure that the girl who kept it was not married for another long year.

Joan's bodice was pulled off, and her skirt tugged down, and she was left in her shift and stockings of fine wool. With much shrieking and laughter, the girls pulled down the bedclothes, despite kneeling on them, and tumbled Joan into the bed. Then there was a fight, with pushing and shoving, to see which of the girls would pull off her stockings. Joan cowered on the bed as they fell on top of her and, sweating, red-faced, heaved one another up again. Finding herself unencumbered for a moment, Joan hastily sat up, pulled off her own stockings, and tossed them to the end of the bed. With screams, the excited, drunken girls fell on them, as men playing football fell on one another in a heap while trying to gain possession of the ball. Drawing her legs back out of harm's way, Joan watched as the struggle rolled onto the floor. She had seen such fights before, at weddings she had attended as a guest, but while pretending to take part, she had always kept well back from the fight. She had never had any wish to win a bride's stocking.

The bundle of fighting girls broke apart at last, and two stood, their hair all awry, their faces scarlet, waving the stockings, too breathless to do more than pant. The other guests cheered for them though, and applauded. "Canny lasses!" Isobel shouted, holding her hands high as she clapped. "Canny lasses!"

"Fetch the groom!" someone shouted, and many voices took up the call. A little knot of girls separated themselves from the group and ran off to summon the men.

Mistress Crosar, guarding a glass of wine from pushes and shoves, moved her way through bouncing, excited girls to the bed. Seating herself on the bed's edge beside her niece, she handed her the glass. "Drink that, and never mind. Tha'll live to see the morn!"

Isobel Sterkarm sat down on the bed's other side. "Thine auntie's right. It's nowt but what every lass goes through."

The two women looked at each other across the bed. Mistress Crosar didn't care for being called "auntie" by Isobel Sterkarm, and she cared less for the woman using the familiar "thine," even though she reluctantly admitted that, as an in-law, she had that right. But for a moment she approved of the woman's good sense.

Joan took the wine and drank a big gulp, though her heart pounded and her breathing was tight. Still, her aunt and new mother were right. This had happened to Mistress Crosar herself, and to Isobel Sterkarm, and to their mothers, and grandmothers, and so on, back and back—to Grandmother Eve. They had all been brave, all the Grannam women, because they were Grannams. She had to be brave too.

* * *

Once Joan had been carried from the hall, there were many empty spaces on the Grannam side, and the Grannams fell quiet, watching and drinking as the Sterkarms grew noisier. Per's cousins, Little Toorkild, Ingram, and Wat, left their table and came to join him at the high table, together with many friends. Windsor, seated beside Toorkild, felt overwhelmed by the crush and the sharp, acrid smell of sweat, but he leaned back in his chair and smiled at everyone, pretending to feel at ease. His bodyguards, he told himself, weren't far away.

"If she's too strong for thee, Per, give us a shout!"

"Aye, we'll be listening—we'll run in and gi' thee a hand. Or something!"

Sweet Milk held up his glass and shouted, "Here's to Per's first son! Thy first grandson, Toorkild!"

Toorkild stood, almost falling back into his chair with his eagerness to stand, and, raising his glass, yelled, "My first grandson!"

Everyone roared and drank to that, even the Grannams. Per laughed, almost giddy with drink and good fortune. First the Grannam girl—wife, he had to remember she was his wife and a Sterkarm now—as if a Grannam could ever be a Sterkarm. But first his wife, and then the Elf-May. A full and happy day.

A knot of wild and excited girls came running in from the dark, with fluttering ribbons pinned to their breasts and their hair standing on end and flying everywhere. "The bride's in bed! She's waiting! Bring the groom!"

Per jumped onto his chair and, from there, to the tabletop. He waved his arms in the air, gave a cockerel crow, and dived, full-length, into the arms waiting to catch him. A tangle of shouting, struggling men moved down the hall, carrying Per among them. The girls danced around them, cheering them on. The older Sterkarm men, Toorkild, and his brother, Gobby Per, followed behind, and Windsor walked with them. He kept a smile on his face and tried to think of it as boisterous high spirits—but the combination of armed Sterkarms and high spirits made him nervous.

The procession grew as Grannams rose from tables and joined

them—even they were laughing and cheering. Per appeared above the knot of men, riding on their shoulders. They carried him out into the blue darkness of the evening, which smelled of damp earth and peat fires. The two big hounds, Cuddy and Swart, leaped up from where they'd been dozing and capered about the procession, jumping up and trying to reach Per. The men bawled about cuckoos' nests and the prickly bush all the way to the Sterkarms' dormitory, and even as they carried Per through the hall to the wedding suite.

Women peeped from behind the brocade curtain that hid the bed, giggled, and ducked out of sight again. The men set Per down in the midst of them and quickly undressed him, throwing aside his Elvish cap, pulling at the buttons of his Elvish shirt until it came undone. Some supported him while others yanked off his long boots, and then there was a fight—even more boisterous and noisy than the women's fight—for his woollen stockings. The hounds became so excited, frenziedly running about and howling as they tried to defend Per, that Sweet Milk and another man had to drag them outside by force and tether them to stakes. Inside the hall, by the time two men were victorious in claiming Per's stockings, there was a bruised eye and a bloodied nose among the company.

The undressing was completed by pulling down the strange fastening of Per's Elvish breeches and pulling them off, leaving him in his Elvish shirt.

"They're unco short, these Elvish sarks," Toorkild said. "Th'art only meant to show one lass what tha'rt made of!"

Per covered himself with cupped hands. His cousins swept back the curtain, and to squeals and cheers, Per was ushered to the bed, while the men chanted rhythmically in a way that reminded Windsor of 21st-century football supporters. Isobel started to cry, hugged her son, kissed him, and herself turned back the bedcovers so that he could get in beside Joan.

Andrea, watching, saw Per look at Joan with a big smile, but Joan was doing her usual thing of looking down. She stared at the cover of the bed and refused to look at anyone.

The men were giving deafening hunting whoops. Fiddlers and pipers were playing. And people started to scream, above the din, "The stockings! The stockings!" Andrea put her fingers in her ears. She could see Windsor standing among the men, looking pained.

The winners of the stockings, two men and two girls, now fought their way to the end of the bed, where one of each couple sat, their backs to the newlyweds. The girl looked over her shoulder, and everyone immediately yelled, "No looking! No looking!"

The girl threw her stocking, and it landed in the middle of the bed. Everyone groaned. Isobel snatched up the stocking and returned it to the girl. "Try again. Three goes!"

As the man threw his stocking, Per leaned forward, as if trying to catch it on his head—but the stocking fell onto the floor. The men booed, the women cheered. Andrea had no idea what was going on but was thrilled to be an observer.

The girl with the stocking tried another throw, tossing it harder this time. Joan, in the midst of all this noise, sat perfectly still, looking at the covers, as if she was alone. The stocking fell between her and Per, and Per threw it back to the girl so she could take her final turn.

This time the stocking landed on Joan's head—and the cheer that went up, together with the clapping, stamping, and whistling, was so loud that Andrea had no doubt that this was the point of the game. Joan plucked the stocking from her head and threw it aside, onto the floor.

Both of the men managed to throw their stockings onto Per's head—but then, he helped them considerably by moving to catch it. The second girl failed to toss her stocking onto Joan's head even after being given a fourth try, and everyone groaned with her in sympathy.

Then the game was over, and the uproarious noise subsided into chatter and laughter. Andrea sidled through the crowd until she was standing beside Isobel Sterkarm. "Be so kind, Mistress Sterkarm, will you tell me—why do they throw the stockings on their heads?"

Isobel turned toward her, her pretty face flushed and beaming. Her pale-blue eyes were exactly like Per's, and despite her happiness, she knuckled a tear from one. She dived at Andrea and enveloped her in a tight, warm hug, kissing her on the cheek. "Bless you, Mistress Elf—if you get a stocking on their heads, you'll soon be married yourself!"

A maid came through the curtain, carrying a large wooden bowl with handles on either side. At the sight of the bowl, the crowd gave another cheer. The maid gave it to Mistress Crosar, who took it solemnly and carried it to the bed. As she passed where Andrea stood beside Isobel, there was a whiff from the bowl's contents: something warm, milky, and spicy. There was a smell of alcohol, certainly, and cinnamon, and—nutmeg? Andrea wouldn't have minded a glass of it herself.

Mistress Crosar handed the bowl to Joan, who drank from it. Everyone watching clapped and shouted encouragement, and Andrea was quick to clap too.

Joan handed the bowl to Per, though without looking at him. Per took a big gulp, and there was enthusiastic applause, especially from the Sterkarms.

"That's it! Keep up thy strength!"

The crowd around the bed was thinning, Andrea noticed. People obviously knew that this was the end of the day's ceremony, and they were drifting away.

Per took another big gulp of the posset. The sooner it was all drunk, the sooner he and his wife would be left alone. He passed the drinking cup back to Joan, who took a tiny sip, then held the cup a long time before taking another tiny sip. She didn't want the posset to be finished at all.

"Come along now, come along," Mistress Crosar said. "Hurry up and drink it all."

Joan took the biggest gulp she could and handed the cup to her husband. There was no point in trying to put it off. She was a Grannam. She had to be brave.

Per finished the last of the posset and handed the cup to his new aunt-by-law. Only Mistress Crosar, Isobel Sterkarm, Andrea, and one or two other women were left by the bedside now. Isobel kissed Per on the forehead and both cheeks; and Mistress Crosar kissed Joan on the head, and they all withdrew.

Andrea, glancing back over her shoulder as she went through the curtain, saw Per wink at her.

8

16TH SIDE:
THE WEDDING NIGHT

†††

With a jump, Per woke from a doze. The room was too big, and reeked overpoweringly of flowers and spices, and sweet, scented smoke. Beneath him the bed bounced and wallowed if he shifted even slightly, and instead of the musty, homely whiff of hay, there was another gust of lavender and roses. Every sound, every smell, everything was strange.

The Elf-Chamber. His wedding. Remembering, he scrubbed one hand over his face. His head ached a little, and his mouth was dry.

Aye, his wedding night. Raising himself on one elbow, he looked over his shoulder. There was his bride, his Grannam bride, curled up under the covers, her bony, knobbly back turned to him. She slept, it seemed. Well, there was nothing he wanted to wake her for.

He shifted gently onto his back, fearing to disturb the Grannam woman—if he had to marry her a thousand times, she would never be a Sterkarm. Above him was the dark canopy of the bed. All was silence. Not a sound reached him from outside. Everyone must have eaten and drunk themselves into a stupor and fallen into bed.

He'd missed a few fights, most likely. Sterkarms settling scores among themselves at a time when they could blame it on the Grannams—and Grannams taking their chance to blame the mischief on the Sterkarms. There would have been a few skirmishes between the Grannams and the Sterkarms, too. Whatever his father and Richie—his father-in-law—said, there would be no preventing it. They would try to smooth things over by buying off the injured parties, and hope that only cheap blood had been shed.

The memory of the Elf-May rose from the forgetfulness of sleep, and he shifted eagerly, half sitting up, before remembering the sleeper beside him and stilling his movement. He studied the Grannam woman for a while. She slept on.

What a sweet wedding night. When they'd finished the posset and everyone had left them alone, he'd looked at her, and she, as ever, had looked at the bed covers. "I'm over here," he'd said, and then she'd looked at him with a frightened distaste.

He'd leaned over to kiss her, and she'd twitched her head aside, so that his kiss landed on her cheek. Sighing, he'd leaned back against the pillows, caught between annoyance and pity.

With any other girl he might have had more patience and taken more time—but this was a Grannam. And his wife. Hadn't they told her what was expected of her? Grannams had been reiving Sterkarm farms, driving off Sterkarm cattle, killing and raping Sterkarms for generations—were they now trying another way of robbing?

"What shalt tell 'em the morn?" he asked.

She'd given him a quick, guilty, wary glance from the corner of her eye. She knew as well as he did that their families would crowd into the chamber again the next morning, full of questions about their first night together, and making the filthiest possible jokes, for good luck. It would be a disgrace to her if she was still a virgin.

He'd pulled off his own shirt and thrown it on top of the bed-clothes and then reached for her gloved hands. She hadn't tried to stop him pulling the gloves off. "Now thy shift," he said, and pulled at it, tugging at it where it was trapped beneath her. She didn't help him, but he succeeded in dragging the shift off over her head. Then she'd slumped, drawing up her knees and folding herself over them.

The curtains around the bed were gauzy and let through the Elf-Light. He'd thrown back the covers and seen the sharp points of her shoulder blades and the knobs of her spine. He pulled her back on the pillows. Ribs showed across her chest, above her tiny breasts. More ribs showed below. Her thighs were like sticks. A skinned rabbit.

The Elf-May wouldn't be like that. She would be all warmth and softness, with no bones to stick in you—you could tell, even seeing her fully dressed. He would have to turn this skinny one around. There'd be a little more padding on her backside than on her front.

"Let me kiss thee," he'd said. "That's a start." He'd leaned toward her, and she'd held herself stiff with distaste—and even so, her chin retreated from him into her neck.

In the end it had been a struggle, like dancing with a wooden doll. But he'd done it. It had been pleasurable enough, as chores went, and they would be able to look their families in the face tomorrow and give plain answers. Now he'd done his duty, he deserved a reward. He remembered how the Elf-May had used her eyes when they'd been talking, the way she'd smiled. He'd bet it would be very different with her. Elf-Women were said to be eager and lickerish.

Carefully he sat up. His shirt had fallen onto the floor. Pushing back the covers, he slipped out of the bed. Joan didn't move.

The great thing about Elf-Clothes was that you didn't have to be laced into them. He went through the damask curtain into the main part of the hall, buttoning the shirt as he went. The Elf-Lights still burned. His Elf-Breeches were lying on the floor. Originally they'd been ankle-length, as the Elves wore their breeches, but he'd cut them off at the knee, to make it easier to wear his riding boots with them. The cloth was so stout and good, it had hardly frayed.

There was a spindly little chair—so delicate, it could only be of Elvish workmanship—and he sat on it to pull on his woolen stockings, and then struggled with his long leather boots, which reached above his knee.

He stood, listening. There were whispers and shiftings from the Sterkarm dormitory, but from the bed behind the curtain nothing. The Grannam woman was still asleep then. Walking quietly, Per went through into the dormitory—to find the Elf-May.

Joan knew that Per was awake and moving but kept still, her knees brought up almost to her chest, her arms folded tightly over her pinched, mauled breasts. Let him think her asleep. She prayed he might think her asleep.

A terrier catches a rat by the scruff of the neck and shakes it vigorously, choking it and rattling its bones, disjointing it. She felt that she knew, almost, what it was like to be the rat in the terrier's mouth: pounded, hammered, bruised. Her husband had gasped, sweated, grunted, as intent on his work as the terrier. She had kept quiet by clenching her fists, gritting her teeth, and enduring—and good God, it had gone on so long—for her family's honor. Why did people—why did *women*—speak of it as a pleasure? She could find no pleasure in being jolted, pounded, and rattled. Now she wanted only to attract no further attention. He might have put a child in me, she thought. A Sterkarm brat. Year after year, another Sterkarm brat, each one lugged in her guts for nine months and then brought forth in sorrow. Surely, God hated women.

When she felt her husband slip from the bed, a tiny hope flickered in her. Lying very still, not daring to move and hardly daring to breathe, she nevertheless listened hard and realized that he was dressing. Oh, thank You, God! He would hardly bother to dress if he only wanted to piss. There would be a chamber pot under the bed, or if the Elves had forgotten to put one there, he would do it in some corner. So he must mean to leave her—to join his friends, maybe. To sit up late, wasting candles, bragging and drinking and gambling. If she was lucky, he wouldn't come back until it was time to get into bed beside her before their morning visitors arrived. Even so little time free of his hot body, damp with sweat, seemed a blessing. And this was to be the rest of her life.

The curtain fell back into place behind him with a faint rustle. For a little while she heard him moving in the hall beyond the curtain, and then nothing more. He must have left the hall. Thank God, thank God. Let him never come back. Let him get into a fight and be killed. No one could blame her, and her family would still be paid her widow's portion. She would be a happy widow.

After the wedded couple had been put to bed, there was a little more drinking and dancing by the younger sort, but it was plain that everyone was tired. The 16th siders were people who rose in the morning as soon as it was light, or even before—at three or four in the morning in the summer, and only an hour or so later in the winter. They worked hard, most of them, all day, and fell into bed when it got dark, to save the waste of candles. This day of celebration had been, for them, a long, long day; and they were dozy with unaccustomed amounts of food, and fuddled with strong drink. They were ready for their beds, and most of the older people had already gone to them. Many were rounding up their sons and daughters and seeing them to bed too—and out of trouble, they hoped.

Andrea was not eager to lie awake in her bed, thinking of Per with his new bride—but found that she was not eager to go into the darkness at the edges of the camp with Sweet Milk, either. Not yet, anyway. But that was what Sweet Milk had determinedly on his mind. So she made her excuses and went to bed. And lay awake just as she'd feared she would.

She thought, from its direction, that the snoring she could hear came from Toorkild. Someone far off, near the hall door, was whispering and giggling. Otherwise all was quiet. From the wedding suite itself she could hear nothing. Well, she didn't want to.

Why had she come? That ridiculous notion she'd had—that she could live over again her first meeting with Per. This was nothing like her first meeting with him—how could it be? Then she had been introduced into the daily life of the Bedesdale tower as an honored guest and had slowly come to know everyone. Per had courted her. The first she'd known of his interest had been when she'd found his sheepskin cap at her place at table, filled with fresh mushrooms. The Sterkarms valued such fresh food highly, and this meant he had risen early to gather them—and then had given them to her instead of eating them himself.

But it was painful to remember such things here, now. This might be Per in everything—in looks, in temperament, in character, whatever that was—but everything else was different, and that difference changed them to each other. It had been a bad idea to come. She'd always known it. But still she'd come. Perhaps she could go to

Windsor tomorrow and plead that she couldn't hack it—say that she'd gone soft and no longer thrived on conditions 16th side. He'd have to understand.

Yeah. Right.

Probably she dozed—but woke again, thinking she hadn't slept. The morning—even the 16th siders' early morning—was hours away. Then someone was bending over her. It gave her a horrible shock. She hadn't been aware that she'd been sleeping, and hadn't heard this man's approach. A little, strangled squeak of alarm burst out of her.

"Whisht." It was Per. "Meet me outside." And he walked away, a tall, upright, dark shape in the dimness.

She got out of bed, not even thinking about what she was doing. After all, she'd intended to do this, against all her better judgment, for five hundred years.

She had to tread carefully as she made her way down the hall, eyes stretched wide in the dim light, careful not to step on any of the people lying wrapped in bedding on the floor, trying not to stumble on yielding mattresses. If anyone was awake to see her pass by, they were keeping it to themselves.

She could hear Per's voice before she reached the door. He wasn't speaking loudly—well, not for a Sterkarm—but he sounded annoyed.

Outside, most of the lighting had been turned off, or dimmed, and it was very dark. And cold. She shivered quite violently at the first touch of the cold wind after the warm fug of the hall. The Elf-Lamp over the hall door still burned faintly, and by its light she could see Per talking to two men, while Swart and Cuddy strained at their leashes, trying to reach him.

"And be wakeful!" Per said to the men as he reached out a hand to her. She put her hand into his, and without another word he led her away from the light into the darkness.

"What was the matter?" she asked in a whisper.

"Guards!" he said in disgust. "Drunk!" Then he laughed. "The Grannams' guards will be drunk too!"

They were passing along the side of the dormitory hall, going toward the edge of the encampment. As the cold, damp wind touched her again, she became aware of the wide, empty moorland stretching away in the darkness—wild and dangerous country, with not a single metaled road anywhere. Nothing but sheep tracks and horse rides. Not a single telephone that worked. No policemen.

A shriek from the darkness made her start, gripping Per's hand and pulling at his arm. She gasped with fright but then heard his soft laugh. "Owl," he said, and yanked on her arm, bringing her stumbling forward to fall on the soft, springy turf. A second later he threw himself down beside her. She said, "Oh!" in surprise, and then he was kissing her, and his hand was on her breast, squeezing. She thought: Oh yes! All right! And put her arms around him, pressing his head to hers.

9

16TH SIDE:
THE WEDDING FIGHT

†††

Richard Grannam, Lord Brackenhill, had to be helped to his bed by three of his men, who were having difficulty walking in a straight line themselves.

His sister, Mistress Crosar, stood watching, her hands on her hips. She had taken drink herself, mostly wine, and was flushed in the face, perhaps even a little tipsy, but nothing more. Once Lord Brackenhill had been dumped on his bed, his legs asprawl, she said, "Leave him, leave him. I'll see to him."

The men wished her good night and reeled away to find their own beds. Mistress Crosar set about the task of pulling off her brother's boots while he lay flat on the bed.

"Well," she said as, a little out of breath, she threw down the second boot. "Now it's done. I hope it was worth it."

He seemed to be dozing. Setting one knee on the bed beside him, she unbuttoned his doublet and unlaced his sleeves. She shook him hard. "I *said* I hope it was worth it."

"It was. Worth it. It was."

"Sit up—sit up." He floundered and fought to sit up, and she helped him before wrenching the tight-fitting doublet from his shoulders. "Canst ever trust the Sterkarms?"

He made a bleating noise, struggling to put his thoughts in order. "'S much to lose. They got. 'S much to lose. Elves' favor. All that."

"Huh. Treachery is breath to them. They can't help themselves."

"They say . . . they say same about us."

"Huh." Mistress Crosar dragged his jacket off and folded it neatly in her lap. Since she was no longer holding him up, her brother fell back on the bed with a thump.

"I shall miss her," Mistress Crosar said.

Toorkild didn't think much of the bed the Elves had given them. It had no doors to shut him and Isobel in cozy privacy. There were curtains hung around it, but they were flimsy things—you could almost see through them. What was the use of that? Not thick enough to keep out light, or drafts, or prying eyes.

And then the bed was too bouncy, too soft and wallowing. And didn't smell right. He couldn't sleep. More annoying still, his bladder was full. He couldn't keep lying there, pretending it wasn't. Sighing, he pushed aside a bit of flimsy curtaining and hung over the side of the bed, looking underneath.

There was nothing under the bed but the strange Elvish matting. He cursed.

"What's the matter?" Isobel asked, also sleepless, though her mind was full of training her new daughter-in-law—who couldn't help being a Grannam, it shouldn't be held against her—and the grandchildren to come.

"There's no pot. Those damned Elves have no given us a pot!"

Isobel sat up. "It's no their way."

"What dost mean, no their way? They piss!"

"Maybe no," Isobel said. "How would I ken?"

Toorkild, dressed only in his long shirt, threw back the covers and sat with his bare, hairy legs over the edge of the bed. He considered the problem. Did Elves piss? He couldn't say that he had ever, personally, seen one in the act. Sighing, he stood.

"Where art ganning?" Isobel asked.

"Where dost think? To piss, woman!"

Isobel leaned out of the bed. "No in here. Gan out the doors!"

"Ach, why would I gan all the way out the doors?" But, as he scanned around the hall, dimly lit by faintly burning Elf-Lights, Toorkild could see that it was crammed with other beds, and with bedding on the floor, and even with strange, two-tiered beds. There wasn't a quiet, unoccupied corner where a man could piss in peace.

There wasn't even a fireplace, where he could piss up the chimney, out of the way.

Isobel was now kneeling on the bed, her face flushing with annoyance. "Tha'll shame me!" She punched her little fist on the bed. "What's good enough for home will no do here—gan out the doors!"

Toorkild reached out a fond hand and ruffled up her hair. "Tha'rt right, tha'rt right, little woman! To be kind to thee, I'll gan out the doors. I'm ganning, see thee, I'm ganning!" Grumbling and stumbling, barefoot, in his shirt, he made his way to the end of the bed.

"Take a body with thee!" Isobel said. Toorkild groaned. "The place is thick with Grannams!" she said.

"Ach, I'm only stepping out the doors!"

"And it'd take one of they snakes nobbut a second to slit thy throat!"

"Bella, Bella," Toorkild said sadly. "They be family now."

"Aye! Family!" she said. "Guthrun had brothers—and sons!" Guthrun, in the old story, had arranged the deaths of her brothers, and had cooked her own children and served them to their father in a stew.

There was a groan, and a movement in the dimness, as someone nearby climbed out of bed. It was Sweet Milk, who'd heard all their talk. "Toorkild, I'll come wi' thee."

"Good man!" Toorkild said. "We'll see who pisses the highest, eh?" To Isobel, he said, "Happy?"

Settling down, she said, "Hurry back. My feet be cold!"

In the cool dark, Andrea lay with her head on Per's shoulder, breathing in the scent of earth and heather from the moors. His hand repeatedly stroked from her head down to her shoulder, giving her a sense of unutterable peace and rightness. It was, she supposed, happiness.

For there's sweeter rest
On a truelove's breast,
Than any other where.

Per's eyes were closed, as he enjoyed the feeling of his heart and breathing slowing. Under his fingers was the smoothness of Andrea's hair, and the soft roundness and warmth of her shoulder. An Elf-May in his arms. A beautiful, eager, willing Elf-May—she was all that the stories promised.

A Grannam for his wife—for children and land and honor and all those necessary things. But an Elf-May for his lover. For love. And fame. He would be the Sterkarm who had an Elf-May for a mistress.

"Now tha mun gan back to thy wife," Andrea said. She didn't want him to go back to his wife at all. With that statement she was asking a lot of questions.

Per countered with a question of his own. "Now tha mun gan back to Elf-Land."

"Not yet," she said. "I've work to do here."

He said nothing but hugged her tighter, pulling her closer to him. And then the night broke open.

Noise. Bangs and cracks so loud and sudden, they made the flesh jump on her bones. Glaring lights, blue and white, that reeled through the night, swinging across the dark, momentarily, brilliantly, illuminating a tree, a distant rock, then veering away and leaving her blind, until the next flash. Blaring, shrilling, deafening noise—*nah-nah nah-nah nah-nah* . . . Sirens! In the 16th!

She felt Per's body stiffen as he froze in astonishment and fear. Then he scrambled to his feet, buttoning his jeans. Reaching a hand down to her, he pulled her to her feet and yelled, above the din, "Gan!" He shoved her in the direction of the dark moors, away from the camp that was suddenly full of flashing light and din.

She ran, too startled and scared to think about why, though it did come to her that the border country, 16th side, was not a safe place to be. Her feet trod in damp grasses; her long skirt caught on bits of twig and shrub, hindering her. She dragged herself free and ran on, wildly, through the dark and flashes of light, arms, legs, and heart pumping, careless of falling.

She found herself stumbling up a hillside, out of breath, her heart thumping and banging. And then she stepped into a cold little stream, throwing her off balance and bringing her to her knees and her senses. She stayed on her knees for a few moments, panting, with one hand to her heart, which bashed and jumped under her ribs. Then she stood, dragging in a deeper breath. She looked back down the hillside toward the camp just as all the floodlights came on, and she could see everything. . . .

A din, a cannonade, brought Mistress Crosar upright in her bed. Her thoughts, and fright, whirled in her head like disturbed birds in an old barn.

A shrill wailing, like nothing she had ever heard, set her heart skipping and reminded her of the Elf-Woman who screamed in the night before a death. The Elf-Woman screaming before the deaths of Grannams?

Flustered, she looked toward her brother's bed. He was still sleeping! And snoring. But all around the hall people were starting up, faces afraid and alarmed. They were looking to her.

She threw back her covers and ran to her brother's bed, where she shook and shook him. "Joan!" she shouted. "Joan!" She could not help thinking of Joan, alone among the Sterkarms—who knew what was going on or what they'd done to her?

Her brother roused, grunting and coughing. But then—before he could even realize what the strange noises were—in raced Sterkarms, armed and laying about them. Loud, panicked cries added to the din: shrieks, terrified wails from children, cries of pain.

One of the Sterkarms ran at Mistress Crosar. He loomed at her, huge, terrifying, and swinging—a sword, an axe—above his head. She screeched and raised her arms to protect herself, but down the blow came—

Toorkild and Sweet Milk, barefoot and in their shirts, peaceably emptied their bladders in the dark at the side of the Elf-Hall. They shook off the drops.

"Good feast," Sweet Milk said, thinking of the beautiful Elf-May. She wouldn't go with him because she wanted Per—well, Per was prettier. But he was more patient.

"Aye. Good feast," Toorkild agreed, thinking of nothing much but his full belly and general satisfaction.

From the darkness at the edge of camp, carrying over the roofs of the Elf-Hall, cutting through the cool damp air, came the cry of: "Sterk-arm!"

Both Toorkild and Sweet Milk jerked as if stabbed, then reached for their daggers and started through the dark toward the shout. Sweet Milk threw back his head and loosed his own yell—but it was lost in the sudden crack and bang of explosions, so close and loud that they ducked, expecting pistol balls or cannon shot to come hurtling at them. And then the lights, flashing across the sky. And the weird, wild, unearthly wailing.

The two men stopped and half turned back toward the dorm full of women and children . . . but then looked toward the darkness where the rallying cry had been raised. Not to answer a rallying cry was unthinkable. As unthinkable as leaving your women and children to face an attack.

Toorkild turned back for the hall, and Sweet Milk followed. Whoever had shouted for help would have to take his chance. Barefoot, in their shirts, armed with daggers, they rounded the corner of the hall and came in sight of its entrance as all the Elf-Lights came on, lighting everything as bright as day. By that light they saw a troop of men—not Elves, but men—Grannams!—armed Grannams!—running into the hall, yelling murder.

Toorkild and Sweet Milk, together, yelled, "Sterkarm! Sterkarm!" and charged in after them.

Joan sprang up in bed at the first outburst of noise. Cannon? Gunpowder?

The Sterkarms were attacking her family!

She jumped naked from the bed and then halted, hugging herself, realizing that she was alone among enemies, unarmed, and weak. What could she do?

She could find out what was going on. Drawing back the curtain, she crept across the outer room toward the door that opened into the dorm. From outside came an enormous, cracking crash that made her freeze and crouch low, like a frightened partridge. When the hall didn't fall in, she crawled frantically for the door.

Gently she parted the strings of beads, trying not to let them rattle, and peeped through.

Isobel, roused and frightened by the din, was out of bed and scrambling along its side, yelling for everyone to rise and arm, when the Grannams ran in. Some, mostly women and children, were tumbling from their blankets, half dressed, half asleep, and three parts drunk. The men, who had drunk more, were harder to wake, though some were blearily staring about.

A man, big and angry, grabbed Isobel by her long, loosened hair, yanking her sidelong. She screamed with the pain of hair roots tearing from her scalp. He shoved her back and swiped at her, catching her a blow with something that made her head resound with noise and pain. On the man ran.

Toorkild, running in at the door, was in time to see his wife struck with a club, saw her fall. His vision narrowed to that man with the club, whom he was going to kill.

The Grannams ran around the dorm. They punched women. They kicked children out of the way. Where a man drunkenly tried to rise, they clubbed him on the head and shoved him down again. They leaped over beds and trod on the half-awake to evade Sweet Milk and Toorkild. All the while the night outside was ripped with bangs and crashes and wailing. When half a dozen Sterkarm men had staggered to their feet and groped around for weapons; and when several women had taken up lamps and swords and axes— why then all the Grannams ran out in a troop, just as they'd run in. They ran out laughing.

Toorkild ran to his own bed, where he'd seen Isobel fall. He found her sitting on the floor, her face white and streaked with streams of blood.

"I'm well, I'm well," she said as he crouched beside her. "Nobbut a ding on the head." She caught at his wrist as he made to rise. "Thy jakke, thy–"

"Away!" Toorkild said, and pulled himself free. His sword and belt hung at the end of the bed. As he slung it on, he yelled, "Sterkarm!" and gestured for all those on their feet–men, women, it didn't matter–to follow him. He and Sweet Milk led the way to the door. Why worry about armor when you had none with you? They'd come to a wedding, not to a fight. Their helmets, their jakkes, were at home. More fool them, for trusting Grannams.

Isobel, grasping a post of her bed, hauled herself up. If her husband was going to hunt Grannams in his shirt, then she would find some kind of weapon–a spoon, if that was all there was–and join him. But as she stood, she sickened, and reeled, and fell on the bed.

Outside, the banshee screamed, heralding death.

Joan's courage left her. Her glimpse through the curtain had shown her the Sterkarms being attacked. Was it a raid by another family– by the Beales or the Nixies? Dropping the beaded curtain, she ran back to her wedding bed, jumped into it, and, ridiculously, pretended to be asleep. Pulling the covers over her head, she curled into a ball and shook. She had no weapon, nothing with which to defend herself, and who would defend her? Not the Sterkarms.

Andrea, standing on the dark, cold hillside under the barrage of noise, watched appalled as the people, struggling, running, howling, filled the spaces between the shacks and buildings. There didn't seem to be anything she could do except watch. How had this started? Had the Sterkarms–oh, she hoped not, but had they lived up to their reputation for treachery?

She caught a glimpse of Toorkild, standing head and shoulders above the crowd–standing on something. He was too far away for her to see his face with any clarity–she recognized him more by his shock of hair and beard and his movements.

Somewhere behind her–somewhere quite close–someone

dragged a stick along a railing. She jumped, and looked over her shoulder into the darkness, where there was nothing to be seen except darkness. When she turned again, Toorkild was no longer standing head and shoulders above the melee, and was nowhere to be seen among the scrum.

Quickly she realized two things. One, someone was behind her on the hillside, in the dark, dragging a stick along railings. Two, there were no railings for anyone to drag a stick along.

She ran down the hillside toward the illuminated skirmish below. Better to be in danger in company than alone.

In and among the Elf-Hall people were milling, running, shouting. People half dressed, yet armed; people staggering and reeling drunkenly, shoving, falling. Light wheeled and flashed over them until, like a silent and lasting lightning flash, all the great Elf-Lamps came on. The wailing, the bangs, the shrills and explosions made the frightened, angry yelling of the people small and faint.

Per struggled among them, shoving through, jumping to see over heads, fending off hands that grabbed at him or aimed blows. He was yelling but paying no attention to what he yelled. And then he glimpsed his father. Toorkild had climbed up on something, was standing above the crowd and was pointing, yelling, his face red, his teeth white, his dark hair and beard making a wild, hairy halo around his head. Another halo appeared, briefly, around Toorkild's head, and Toorkild dropped out of sight. Just dropped.

Like a swimmer, Per dived into the crowd.

Windsor stood in the back of an open MPV, with men in camouflage fatigues. He said, "Right. Let the bastards have it."

10

16TH SIDE:
AFTER THE FIGHT

†††

Per struggled toward where he'd seen his father fall. Panicked people shoved by, yelling, bashing into him, sending him staggering. Hands grabbed at him, pushed him. Angry, frightened men lunged at him drunkenly. He was aware, remotely, of his eyes stinging, as if smoke had got into them. He seized a man by the scruff of his shirt and his hair, trying to heave him out of his way, and his eyes gushed tears, blinding him. Letting the man go, he put his hands to his eyes, to wipe them, but the tears were a flood stream. Light dazzled and starred, his eyes closed. However hard he tried to keep them open, they smarted and closed. Breathing was harder. His chest and throat tightened. Choked and blinded, his heart pounding with fear of attack while blind, he groped around him, touching hair, touching skin. Was this Elf-Work? His hand closed on air, then smacked against other groping arms. He struck out at them, angry and afraid, and the arms struck back. But Per hadn't the breath for fighting. Bent double, eyes sore, he waited for the next blow from his unseen opponent, but none came. The noise around him had changed. Instead of cries of alarm and anger, now there was a confused groaning and sobbing. Forcing himself to stand upright, he tried to raise the rallying cry but couldn't draw the breath.

Andrea, rounding the corner of the Sterkarm dormitory, saw that the brightly lit area in front of the inflatable was full of people, half dressed, half awake, half drunk, running about and beckoning others on. She hurried toward the entrance of the building but saw something that made her stop dead and raise fists to her face. A man wearing camouflage fatigues and a large, face-covering helmet and carrying some sort of gun—he was unmistakably a 21st sider—darted across the open space in front of the dorm, dodging the confused people. Near the entrance he dropped to one knee, raised his weapon, and fired into the inflatable building.

Andrea shouted, "No!" but couldn't move. Cringing, she waited, horrified, for the dorm to explode, to burst into flames.

Isobel hauled herself upright again and stood, clutching a bedpost. She shook her head and cursed herself for being weak.

The dorm, when she looked about, was almost empty, except for a few very small children cowering on a bed against the wall while a row of women stood in front of them, armed with candlesticks and knives. Isobel let go of the bedpost and determinedly set herself to cross the room and join them.

Something flew through the beaded curtain and landed, smoking, on the floor.

The women cried out in anger and shock, and two of them ran forward and swiped at the thing—it was a canister—with their candlesticks. And then they dropped their weapons and put their hands to their faces.

Isobel took another two steps toward them and found herself blinded.

And Joan, having pulled on her shift and nerved herself to find courage, for the sake of the Grannams' reputation, edged through the bead curtain from her bridal suite, to see her mother-in-law crawling on the floor, sobbing. She halted, appalled, and saw a group of other Sterkarm women twisting and writhing as they turned their faces this way and that, and mopped at their eyes with sleeves and skirts. A heap of children squealed and sobbed on a bed.

Joan drew back into her suite, unable to understand what was wrong with the women. As she stood there, bewildered, her own eyes smarted and flooded.

* * *

Everyone Andrea could see was doubling up, clutching at their faces—but the dorm didn't explode or burn. Something arced over the heads of the people. It looked like a large tin can, trailing smoke. The can was lost to view as it fell among the people—but another and another came arcing into view.

She stopped again, thinking: What are they? Grenades? Shells? She didn't know whether to run forward, shouting warnings, or to run away. As she hesitated, her eyes spurted tears. Putting her hands to her face, she found water streaming from her eyes and felt them smarting. She couldn't open her eyes. They were closed with tears, gummed shut with a barrier of water she couldn't see through. The air had thickened, or her throat narrowed. It was harder to breathe.

Tear gas! She'd seen film of it being used to break up riots—she even had a friend who'd been in a crowd at a demonstration when the police had fired tear gas among them. Her first reaction was gratitude. This would end the fight between the Sterkarms and the Grannams, which would certainly have resulted in murder. It had to be Windsor's doing. Good for him! For once. There'd be some sore eyes among the 16th siders and some coughs, but no one would be hurt.

Her gratitude changed to fear when she felt a hand close around her arm and someone pulled at her. She reached out wildly with one hand, groping, and connected with something hard and rounded—a helmet.

A man's voice, rather muffled and indistinct, said, "It's all right, miss. I only want to take you to the truck. Get you out of here."

The gruff politeness calmed her considerably, and she allowed herself to be towed along, too breathless to talk. At first, bodies bumped against her and staggered away—obviously they were picking their way through people as blind as herself. But then there was more space, and the man beside her said, "Here we are, then, miss. You'll be okay here." The guiding hand left her arm, and she felt lonely and helpless. There were other people nearby—she could hear them moving, and she could hear a car engine. There was also still a lot of shouting and moaning going on. Putting out a hand, she felt cold metal. Feeling around, she decided that she was standing next to some kind of vehicle.

"Andrea!" said a voice she knew, despite its muffled sound. "Silly girl! What did you do with your gas mask?"

Windsor. She couldn't tell exactly where he was, and that made her feel oddly insecure. She wanted to say, angrily, that she didn't have a gas mask, and hadn't known she would need a gas mask, but she could only cough and gasp.

"Couldn't wait to get your hands on young Sterkarm, could you?" Windsor said. "I saw you running out of the tent with him. Indecent haste, I call it."

Andrea coughed again. It was the only sound she could manage.

"If you'd only waited, you could have done it in much more comfort. But you hot-blooded barmaids . . . Never mind! Out of here soon. When we've finished the roundup."

She managed to croak, "What?"

A confused sound of grunting and panting came from close by, and someone—Windsor, she supposed—pulled her out of the way. There were clanging noises, as of something being thrown into a van, sounds of dragging and shoving and shouted, muffled orders.

"We're all off to have tea at Sterkarm Tower," Windsor said. "Oh, girls! *Isn't* this fun?"

II

16TH SIDE:
ELF-RESCUE

†††

In the Elf-Palace that had been the Grannam dormitory, bedding had been dragged from beds. Curtains and wreaths and twinkling lights had been torn down, trampled, smashed.

Richard Grannam, Lord Brackenhill, lay on a bed near the center of the hall. His pillow and the sheet below him were scarlet, soaked with blood. His head was shattered. Other beds, near him, were occupied by people wounded or drunk. Children were clustered around them, sitting on the beds, huddled on the floor.

The able-bodied and almost sober—men, women, and youths—stood or sat around the edges of the hall, holding clubs, knives, swords, heavy ladles, cooking spits—anything that had come to hand as a weapon.

Mistress Crosar sat on a stool near the entrance. Among the men who stood in a half circle behind and near her was Gareth Phillips, in his Elvish jeans and fleece. He held a large kitchen cleaver that someone had brought back from the cooking shacks so it shouldn't be stolen. His hand slipped sweatily on the wooden handle, and he had no idea what he would do with it if a Sterkarm attack came. Throw it at someone, perhaps. What is going on out there? he thought. Somebody might let me know. His throat was tight and his heart beat steadily a beat or two faster than normal, while his nerves were tightened up by uncertainty and anxiety, to the point of snapping. He still didn't think he could actually hit anyone with the sharp blade. The flesh would part, the blood would run out—Horrible. He just couldn't do it.

I can smell blood, he thought. I can *smell* it. This is worse than anybody ever told me it was going to be. I should be paid double for this. There was a woman with a broken jaw. Her jawbone actually broken by a blow. Mistress Crosar had tipped wine down the woman's throat and tied her jaw up. Now she lay on a bed, moaning in a nerve-scraping way.

I'm from the 21st, Gareth thought. This isn't my scene. If asked, he'd have said he was cool about violence, lived with it all the time. It was on TV every day—the knife attack in the city center, the shooting outside a club, and the wars everywhere, the terrorist bombs. You have to have wars, James Windsor said. You don't win freedom or right wrongs by thinking positive thoughts or talking about it. You have to get off your arse and fight. But Gareth had never fought, apart from a few shoves and thumps in the playground. "A woman had her jaw broken" sounded so inconsequential when you didn't have to see the misshapen face or listen to the woman sobbing and moaning in pain for hours. "A man suffered head injuries" didn't sound much when you didn't have to smell the blood and watch it soaking into a bed. He hadn't known that merely seeing, hearing, and smelling these things would make his own body tremble and shudder.

What was happening out there, now that the Grannams and the Sterkarms were all riled up? Why doesn't somebody let me know? They're supposed to keep me informed. This was going in a memo when he got back—failure of communication. His belly was suddenly gripped by a cold spasm, as it occurred to him that he might never see the 21st again. If things—as he half feared—had gone badly wrong, he could be killed. He could really be killed. For a second he thought he might throw up, or piss himself, but the moment passed. It's okay, he told himself. You could get a call any moment. And if things looked as if they were getting really bad—well, the Tube wasn't so far away. He could run for it.

Running away would mean getting fired. Or at least loss of promotion. No house of his own, no beautiful car, no *success*. Well, success would be postponed—and what chance would he have of running for it if a gang of armed Sterkarms came pounding through that door, yelling murder? . . . Keep calm, hang on a bit longer, see what happens.

"It will be light soon," Mistress Crosar said.

Gareth looked at her. She had pulled on her gown but hadn't bothered to have it laced and pinned about her properly, so it hung in strange bags and folds. She hadn't put on her cap, and her fair, graying hair hung down about her shoulders. But, he had to admit, she'd been magnificent. In the attack she'd been knocked down, and it had obviously unnerved her—he remembered how her voice had shaken—but on finding her brother's head smashed, and he beyond rousing, she hadn't panicked or even merely wept. If she had, Gareth wouldn't have blamed her, an aging, bereft woman. Instead, she'd drawn her brother's sword and—well, rallied her troops. She'd cried out to everyone to arm themselves. Some men had run out of the hall in pursuit of the retreating Sterkarms, and she'd run to the entrance and screamed at them to come back. "They trick you, they trick you!" she'd screeched.

Some had persisted in the chase, and God knew what had happened to them, but most had returned. "We mun be ready for them," Mistress Crosar had said. "Stand around the walls. If they cut through the walls, be ready. Guard the door, in case they come again."

"They'll burn the hall over our heads," a man had said.

"No," Gareth had told them. "It won't burn. Elf-Work." Thank God for 21st-century building regulations.

Noticing him for the first time, Mistress Crosar said, "Are you with us, Master Elf? Well come. Arm yourself."

So someone had given him the cleaver. Mistress Crosar herself sat on her stool, guarding the hall's entrance, with her brother's sword, naked, across her skirted knees. Gareth doubted whether she'd ever used a sword, even in a game, but her example was doing wonders for her men. They kept looking at her and then almost preening. "Good old lass," they whispered among themselves—after all, if Grannam women were so brave and hardy, how much braver and hardier were they, the men?

The beaded curtain at the hall's entrance had been looped and fastened back, and through the opening she and her men watched the night fade into gray. It was then, at last, that the walkie-talkie stitched into Gareth's fleece buzzed. Eagerly, he put the little speaker into his ear.

"White Mouse? Come in, White Mouse."

"Here!" he said, too loudly, and startled the Grannams near him. He listened, his face breaking into a big, relieved grin. "Okay! Okay! Will do! Mistress Grannam! Good news from the Elves!"

She was looking at him attentively, as was everyone near her.

"It's over—the fighting's all over. They're sending Elf-Carts to take you all safely back to your tower."

Mistress Crosar remained seated, the sword across her knees, her face tired and baffled. The man who stood by her stepped forward, and Gareth groaned to himself. He'd been expecting this man to stick his oar in all night, and now he was going to. Davy Grannam, the leader of the Grannams' garrison, a man who always stared down Gareth, and even Windsor, with a hard, dark, glittering eye, who never seemed quite able to hide his suspicion of the Elves. You may fool others, his manner and his look always said, but I ken well you mean no good. At this moment he was half dressed in a long, limp shirt, but he wore a helmet and carried an unsheathed sword in his hand, and despite his disarray he seemed, to Gareth, as hard and menacing as ever. A tall, bony man—big, knobby bones, like stones, beneath his eyes, and at wrists, knuckles, and collar. His skin was weathered to brown leather. Beneath his helmet he was bald, but his beard was thick and black. He made Gareth nervous, always had. "How dost ken?" he said.

Gareth waved a hand as he listened to the buzzing in his ear. "The Elves stopped the fighting. They—used Elf-Work. Now they've rounded the Sterkarms up and driven them away in Elf-Carts. And they're sending more Elf-Carts to carry you and the wounded back to your tower."

As he spoke, they heard the grinding sound of Elf-Carts approaching the hall.

Davy's dark eyes glittered—with fear, but also with fierceness. "The Elves said we would be safe at the wedding."

"We didna ken what would happen," Gareth said. "There's nothing to fear now. I swear."

There was a silence in the hall as most of the Grannams waited to hear what their leaders would decide; but there was fear in the air. From outside came the sound of engines dying and the shouts of men. Davy bared his teeth in a grin that had no amusement in it.

Mistress Crosar got stiffly to her feet. Limping a little, cramped from having sat so long, she moved toward the entrance. Davy immediately held out an arm to block her way, but she pushed it aside, saying, "Someone mun look. Master Elf! Come with me."

Several of her men started forward, following her closely, ready to defend her if need be. Gareth had to dodge them and push past them to be beside Mistress Crosar when she reached the entrance. With relief he saw the big Elf-Carts outside and the men getting out of them. One, seeing him, gave him a sort of salute, raising one finger to his cap.

Cautiously Mistress Crosar peered to either side of the hall's entrance. Seeing nothing but Elf-Carts and Elves—no sign of any Sterkarms—she ventured a step outside. Men, armed with clubs and axes, followed her.

The great Elf-Hall loomed about them. Most of the Elf-Lamps still burned, though dimly now full daylight was near. Color was just coming into the grass, and into the shining metal of the Elf-Carts. Clothing lay scattered about—fallen or lost helmets, dropped weapons, lost boots—as well as trampled food and broken wreaths. At a distance a man lay, so still that he was probably dead. Everything was quiet. No one seemed to be fighting anymore. Despite the presence of the Elves the camp felt deserted.

Mistress Crosar raised her voice, shouting to the Elf-Man standing beside the cart. "Truly, have the Sterkarms ganned?"

Gareth quickly translated what she said. The man waved an arm at the hills and moor emerging from darkness. "All cleared off."

"Taking their loot with them," Mistress Crosar said, when Gareth told her. "And my niece." Her men were silent. They were half afraid of her, because she had such cause for grief and yet seemed so calm.

"Filthy, backbiting animals!" she said. "All their fine words and smiles as empty as air! Treachery the very beat of their hearts. They sweat and piss treachery!"

"Aye," said Davy. "But what do we do, Lady? Do we trust the Elves?"

She was shocked to be asked. He knew, surely, far better than she what they ought to be doing. But Davy was her brother's man, and her brother was dead, or near death. She was their leader for now. Davy had to be seen to ask her what they should do, even if he had already decided.

She felt helpless. I want my brother to be alive, she thought, to tell us what to do—though she had often argued with him when he had been alive. But then the orders and the blame had been his, not hers. Now if she gave the wrong orders, she alone would be to blame.

It would be easy to tell Davy to do as he thought best—but no. Clasping her hands before her, she tried to think clearly, without being distracted by thoughts of the terrified children and the wounded. I want my niece back safe, she thought. I want the Sterkarms dead—but no, no. What should they do *now*?

"I think—" she began, and then stopped herself. These anxious people didn't want to hear her doubts. They wanted to be told, without doubt, what to do. Her own fears told her that. Lifting her head, she said, "Master Elf! What is to be done here?"

"Why—only that we put as many people as we can into the carts, and then we take them back to the tower, where they'll be safe."

Davy gave a brief laugh. "You think the Sterkarms'll leave us be now?"

"That's why we mun get you back to the tower," Gareth said.

Davy turned from him in disgust.

"We have many wounded," Mistress Crosar said. "Put them in the carts and the bairns. They gan slowly, these carts—Davy, thou'll walk beside them."

"Aye," he said.

"I shall walk too," said Mistress Crosar.

"Nay—"

"I shall walk," she repeated. "I am not hurt. Give my place to someone who needs it." She turned and went back into the hall. Gareth hurried after her.

"We gan home," she said, to everyone, looking around. "In Elf-Carts."

Everyone stared, and no one spoke. "Make the children ready." Stooping to a child near her, she said firmly, "Thou mun no be feared. The Elves are friends. And thou mun be quiet as we gan, dost understand?" The child shrank back behind its mother. "Everybody mun be quiet." She looked around at the women. They waited for whatever she would say next. "Gan now—take the bairns to the carts." They looked at one another to see who would make the first move. Mistress Crosar clapped her hands sharply. "Gan now! Gan!" She waved her hand at the nearest woman, who guiltily and hastily grabbed a child's hands and started for the doorway. The others all moved after her.

Gareth found, with a start, that Mistress Crosar was looking at him. "Master Elf. Will you come with us, or will you stay?"

"Ah." Tempting thoughts of the Tube's nearness came to him again, but he stifled them. He had a job to do. "I'll come with you. If I may." Maybe the worst was over. Maybe it would be okay from now on. He tried to put thoughts of angry, marauding bands of Sterkarms out of his head.

Mistress Crosar nodded her head graciously and walked past him to the bloodied bed where her brother lay. She stood looking down at him. Tears stung and pressed behind her eyes, but she refused to let them fall. Tears softened. Keeping them within fed the grief and the rage. Before she wept for her brother, she would laugh over the bodies of the Sterkarms.

Per's eyes flooded with tears. Tears poured down his face as if he'd emptied a helmet of water over his head. His lashes were glued together with sticky tears. When he tried to see, he was peering through water, and his eyes burned and smarted. Against his will, they closed and poured more water, while his breath came harder and harder.

He was shoved and staggered by pressing, moaning people who were also blind and breathless, reaching out and grabbing with their hands. He didn't know if they were friends or Grannams, and he couldn't see where his father had been standing before he'd fallen. He couldn't tell if he was still heading that way or if he'd been turned around in his blindness. He wanted to yell with frustration but couldn't find the breath.

Hands grasped his upper arms, hauling him upright. He lashed out with the dagger in his hand, kicked, tried to strike his attackers with his head—but they could evidently see him, and he couldn't see them. His arm was pinioned and the dagger taken from his hand. "*Olla rikti*—all right," a man's voice, rather muffled, yelled at him in the accent of the Elves. But he didn't trust any he couldn't see and kicked again, weakly, because he was breathless and his chest was so tight, it hurt to breathe. He was hauled along so rapidly that his feet dragged over the rough ground, and he couldn't get them under him.

There was a growling, purring noise that he recognized as the sound of an Elf-Cart, and the stink that was distinctive of them. He was shoved against the cart—he could feel its vibration and its hard metal edges. He heard others near him, sobbing and wheezing. Were they Sterkarms or Grannams or Elves?

"Up! Up!" Elf-Voices were saying, and shoving at him, and pulling at his arms from above. Eventually, just so they'd stop pestering him, he made the effort to haul himself into the cart, though his lungs felt as if they would burst. He was pushed into a seat, and someone else thumped against him as they were pushed down next to him.

All Per could do was mop at the ceaseless tears that ran from his eyes, gasp for breath, and bide his time.

More and more people were shoved and hauled into the cart.

Elves yelled through bangs and crashes. Bright lights flashed across the darkness of his closed and swollen eyes.

The Elf-Cart moved, lurching and swaying over the rough ground. Per, gripping the edges of his seat, felt panic—where was he being taken, and why and by whom? He tried to draw breath, to demand to know these things, but it was like trying to breathe with lungs of wood.

Bouncing, swaying, the Elf-Cart drew away from the noise of the fight. Cool silence deepened around him, the cries of disturbed birds were clearer, and his breathing eased. As soon as he could, Per demanded, "Who's there?" His hand found a knee next to him. "Who is this?"

He was answered by rough gasps, coughs, and splutters—but then a woman's voice, croaking, said, "Per? Per?"

"Mammy! Th'art safe?"

Isobel drew a harsh breath and, despite her cut and aching head, said, "I'm hale. Thy daddy?"

It was lucky that Per's breath still came hard. He was about to blurt out that he'd seen his father fall, but breathlessness forced on him time to think. Why tell his mother that, when he still didn't know for sure what had happened to his father? "I've no seen him—hast thou?"

"Nay, nay," Isobel gasped.

"Who's here?" Per asked again. "Who's Sterkarm?"

From different places in the Elf-Cart came coughs and grunts and whispers of: "Sterkarm—Sterkarm—Sterkarm." There seemed a good few of them, and if there were any Grannams in the cart, they weren't admitting it.

A woman's voice said, apologetically, "I'm an Elf. Andrea Mitchell."

Per was puzzled for a moment, and then remembered—the Elf-May, Elf-Windsor's wedding gift. When the Grannams had attacked—just before he'd seen his father fall—he'd been with her. The memory gave him an unpleasant sensation, like eating something bad.

"Don't fret about your eyes," Andrea said. Her own eyes were still sore and watering, but her breathing was easier, and she spoke as loudly as she could, for everyone in the car to hear. "The Elves put something in the air that blinded our eyes." She spoke as if she wasn't an Elf herself. "But it will pass. It will pass soon. Then we'll see just as well as before."

"Truly?" Per's voice asked. He was sitting opposite her.

"Truly," she said. "On my honor." She raised her voice again. "Keep your hands from your eyes, rub them not, and I promise, the tears and soreness will soon pass. You will see again, all of you. The Elves blinded you—and the Grannams—they blinded everyone—to stop the fight. They didn't want any to be killed or hurt. So they blinded everyone, and they brought you away in Elf-Carts. But the blindness will pass, very soon now."

"The Grannams attacked us!" Per said. Everyone knew they were treacherous, but the depth of their treachery still astonished him. Treachery was so engrained in them, so bred in the bone and blood, that not even self-interest could hold them back from a cowardly attack while their victims slept. "Where's my father?" he shouted. "Daddy! Toorkild!"

Andrea felt the people stirring near her, alarmed. She reached to where she thought Per was, touching a knee she hoped was his. "He's safe, Per, I'm sure he's safe. He may be in another cart."

"Where? I want to see him!"

Andrea leaned forward, to where she knew the driver of the car would be sitting. Her sight was clearing, though still blurred. She could see the headlights flashing through the darkness, and could make out something of the figures in the front seats. "Do you know how Toorkild Sterkarm is?" she asked. "People are pretty anxious about him."

The figure in the passenger seat turned toward her. "Is that what all the noise's about?" It was Windsor. "He's in one of the other trucks. So's the bride—in case you're worried about her, Andrea."

"Is he okay?" she asked.

"He's being looked after. Collected a bang on the head as far as

I know. Tell them not to worry."

Andrea had a sudden clear memory of looking down from the hillside into the floodlit space around the inflatables and seeing Toorkild standing above the crowd—and then she'd been distracted, and when she'd looked again, Toorkild had gone. She turned back to the body of the car and said, "All is right! Toorkild is in another Elf-Cart. He's been hurt—" There was an immediate outcry, with Per and Isobel's voices loud. "Not badly! He's being looked after. He's in one of the carts behind."

"Stay!" Per said. "Stay the cart! Let us see him!"

"Per—I don't know—"

"Stay! Stay now!" Her sight was clearing rapidly, and in the light of the following cars' headlights, she saw Per stand, a figure of darks and grays. He snatched by luck at a stanchion as the car lurched and threw him to one side. He seized the stanchion with his other hand and made to shake it, as if he could stop the MPV by main force.

Others joined the cry. "Aye, stay, stay!" They obviously weren't going to be calmed by anything Andrea could say. Leaning forward again, she said urgently, to Windsor, "Can we stop? They want to see Toorkild."

"We'll stop when we get to the tower."

"They want to see him now!"

Windsor glanced around. "Tough shit," he said.

The car ground on, traveling at little more than walking pace, inching and growling up horribly steep slopes, swaying and jolting as it struck ruts, creeping down slopes with its brakes on. The frightened, angry people in the car pulled at Andrea's clothes and jabbered at her. Why didn't they stop? Where was Toorkild? Where were their other friends, brothers, sons, sisters, daughters? When were they going to stop, when were they going to be able to see them?

Andrea tried to explain, trying to shout above the noise of the engine and voices. "Be so good, stay seated. You'll fall out, else." She could hear someone being sick. "Be so good, be calm. We'll reach the tower soon. There's nothing to be done until we reach the tower." She had no idea how close they were to the tower, or even in which direction it lay. She didn't have the sense of direction that had been trained into the 16th siders.

Per's eyes were still swollen and sore, but he could see now. He stood in the back of the Elf-Cart, clinging to the stanchion, feeling the cart's power vibrate through him. But despite its power, it was slow. A man could walk faster. Why were they obeying these Elves, tamely staying in these slow carts? Why was he obeying Elves when his father was missing? He saw another man standing in the back of the following cart. It was Sweet Milk, he was sure. He waved, and Sweet Milk waved back.

The Elf-Cart slowed even more, to negotiate steep, rocky ground, and Per stepped over the side. Andrea cried out and reached for him but was too late. Landing in a crouch on the turf, Per sprang up, waving his arm and yelling, "Sterkarm!"

It was all the encouragement the Sterkarms needed. Half of the people in Andrea's car struggled to their feet and jumped over the side too. Looking back, she saw still others, and even some women, scrambling from the following cars and running forward to join Per. She felt a little like laughing. So much for Windsor's orders! So much for his "tough shit."

Per ran forward, his men running after him. Even though the Elf-Work had left him still a little breathless, it wasn't hard to overtake the slow-moving car. Turning in front of it, in the light of its lamps, Per spread his arms. "Stay!"

The driver braked hard and stopped. Behind, the other cars stopped too, and more people jumped down. Even Andrea jumped down.

Windsor, furious, stood in the passenger seat. "Go around them," he said to his driver. "Go around!" But there was no road, just a rough track made by horses. To go around the people would mean taking the car off the track, and there was no telling what boulders, ditches, or hollows were hidden by the ferns.

While the driver hesitated, Per came to his side. With his left hand he put a dagger to the driver's throat, and with his right hand he took the key from the ignition. At first he couldn't get the key to come out of its place, but in Elf-Land he'd seen Windsor put the key in to make the cart go, and take it out. He knew that the key must come out, and he knew that the cart wouldn't go without it. After a few seconds of angry tugging and twisting, he found the knack, and the key came free. The cart's growling and shuddering stopped. Per tossed the key into the air, caught it, and then handed it to Sweet Milk, who was at his shoulder.

The next car in line was quickly surrounded by Sterkarms, who let Per through to do his trick with the key again. Windsor, watching, leaned against the window and sighed. "Andrea. Keep an eye on the keys, for God's sake. We don't want them lost down some rabbit hole." As Andrea joined the Sterkarms, Windsor stayed in the car. He felt safer surrounded by 21st steel.

Many people, men and women, but all 16th siders, were clustered around the second car. As Andrea hurried toward it, she could see people climbing into the back and obviously being very careful where they put their feet. They were looking down at something on the car's floor. Standing very upright in front of the car's cab was a woman. By the headlights of the third car, Andrea saw that it was Joan. Her face was tight with fear.

Shoving into the crowd, Andrea pushed her way to the car's side and looked down. There was someone lying on the floor between the seats. The light from the headlights didn't reach there, and the faint, gray daylight wasn't yet strong enough for her to be able to see who it was.

Per had climbed into the car. He was crouching awkwardly in the little space he had, feeling at the chest of whoever lay on the floor. "Is it Toorkild?" Andrea asked.

Per glanced up and saw that it was the Elf-May. The one he'd been with when his father had been hurt. Without giving her any kind of answer, he turned to Sweet Milk, who was beside him. "Lift him out."

"Don't!" Andrea said. "Tha knows not how he's hurt!"

Per hesitated. The Elves, after all, knew about healing. But looking again at the way his father lay in the narrow well of the cart's back, he said, "We canna help him here." He edged himself behind his father so that he could lift up his shoulders, while Sweet Milk went to Toorkild's feet.

As they lowered the injured man, awkwardly, from the Elf-Cart, the Elf-May was busying herself again. Pushing past people, she ran to a spot behind the cart, which was lit by the lamps of the third car. "Put him down here, in the light. Has anybody got anything to lay him on?"

But people had dashed out of the Elf-Palace half dressed, and had then been chivvied into the Elf-Carts. They were all cold and had nothing to spare for Toorkild. So he was laid on the turf. Per wrenched off his Elf-Jacket and spread it over him, but it was short and of little use. The people gathered around, staring, but the Elf-May pushed them back. "Keep out of the light!"

Toorkild wore nothing but his shirt. His splayed, bare, hairy legs looked comical and very sad. Isobel came to his side and knelt. "Toorkild?" She smoothed his hair and called his name again, as if he was asleep and she needed to wake him. She lifted one of his hands to her face. "He's cold," she said.

In brushing back his hair from his brow, she saw a spot of dirt just above one eyebrow and rubbed it away. It stayed. She rubbed again, then looked at Per. "A hole."

Per, kneeling at his father's other side, bent low to look. His heart seemed to squeeze tight at the first touch of a greater fear. It seemed to him that his father's head lay a little oddly on the ground. He slipped his hand beneath his father's head, as if to lift it—and instead of meeting a round, hard skull, his hand sank into warm mush. Knowledge too swift for thought sent a spasm through him, holding him frozen and breathless for an eye's blink. Then he withdrew his hand and looked at it. In the gray light from the cart's lamps, his hand was black and glistening.

The spasms shook him again, pulling his belly up under his ribs, shaking him with long, silent sobs. He felt cold all through. He felt that the tower had collapsed, leaving him shelterless and alone on the wet, cold hillside.

He lifted the hand that had been behind his father's head into the light of the Elf-Lamps, so everyone could see it.

From the people gathered around came a deep groan. Isobel looked up. She stared at the blood and matter on her son's hand, and said, "Aaa-aaaa-aaaa . . ." It was a horrible sound, despairing and stricken. It seemed to trickle from her mouth unheeded, and it went on and on.

12

16TH SIDE: RETURN TO THE TOWER

†††

P er's hand was covered in blood, clots of blood, and brains. He made to wipe his hand on the turf but stopped himself. The matter covering his hand was his father. It would be disrespectful and unloving to wipe it away.

He knelt there, by the body, holding his bloodied hand up and away from himself. Toorkild was dead, he knew that. The back of his father's head was crushed, gone. No man could survive that. Not even the Elves could heal it.

The women, gathering around, raised a keen: long, wailing cries that carried far through the cold air. The moorland wind blew past, chill where it touched the skin and damp. His mother's broken-hearted, unbelieving moan went on and on, and his father's body lay on the ground before him. Per, though he heard and felt and saw it all, was almost unknowing of it. His father was dead. He knew that, and his mind circled around it. His father was dead. Was dead. Nothing followed from that—there seemed nothing else to know or think.

Andrea was slower to believe. Not until she'd touched Toorkild's hand and felt how cold it was—damply, chillingly cold, clay cold—did she begin to believe it. And not until she'd felt at both of Toorkild's wrists, and at his throat, and put her ear to his chest, did she actually believe it.

Even then she said, "He might—if we can keep him warm—if we—"

Per turned his head and looked at her, with a force that made her draw her head back, as if she'd been slapped. In the bright light of the headlamps, his eyes were silver. He held out his hand to her, the hand that was clotted with thick, dark blood. He said, "His brains are in my hand."

Andrea dropped back on her heels, feeling winded with shock. How could he *say* that? But he was a 16th sider, far more inured to death than a 21st sider like herself. Her head crowded with thoughts of Toorkild as she had known him in another time—a big, cheerful man, capable of such kindness that she had always easily forgotten the violence and cruelty of which he was also capable. And while she'd been assuring them that he was safe, Toorkild had been snuffed out. Sorrow overpowered her and tears ran down her face. She scrambled around the body's feet, to reach Per and embrace him, to try and let him know that, if she could, she would take some of his pain from him, and that she grieved for Toorkild too. But as she reached him, he held her off with an outstretched hand and got to his feet. His other hand, his bloodied hand, he still held in the air, away from himself. She felt it as a rebuff, and it hurt.

On his feet, Per looked around. Day was coming, and the birds were calling over the moors. Crowded around him were the people from the tower—his people now—half dressed and shivering, their faces shocked and scared. At his feet lay his father's body, his mother kneeling beside it. There were the Elf-Carts, blockish lumps of metal, gleaming in the early-morning light. He saw Sweet Milk's broad face, both anxious and angry. Sweet Milk said, "Grannams."

Aye, the Grannams. They were standing here, on the open moors, without shelter or defense, and none of them knew how close behind their enemies were. His father would never have let them hang around here. They had to reach the tower. And at the tower, they could wake his father's body and give it burial, keep it safe from the crows and foxes.

Stooping, he wiped his hand on the wet grass, wiping it clean of his father's brains and blood. "Mother!" She was still rocking and keening, and he spoke more sharply than he usually spoke to her. "We mun back to the tower. Up!" And he gave her his hand, pulled her to her feet.

Sweet Milk yelled, "Into the carts! Now! Move!" Everyone—men, women, and children—moved toward the carts. They were used to Sweet Milk giving orders, whether they were farming or fighting.

Per lifted his father's shoulders, his clothes becoming more stained with blood. Sweet Milk took Toorkild's feet, and other men came to help lift the corpse into the second cart in the line—the cart where Joan was huddled in a corner.

Andrea, wiping her face, went to Per and said, "Give me the keys for the carts—the keys that make them go!"

Per reached into the pockets of his Elvish jeans and took out the ignition keys. Carrying them, Andrea walked from car to car, returning the keys to the drivers. It occurred to her then that none of the other Elves had left their places in the cars. Not even Windsor. And when she handed the key to his driver, Windsor didn't ask how Toorkild was. He just said, "Oh—can we go now?"

Andrea said nothing but hurried back to the car that now carried Toorkild's body—the car that also carried Per, and Isobel, and Joan. She climbed aboard.

Joan had watched as the men heaved and hauled Toorkild's body on board, knowing that she had missed her chance to run. She shrank into the corner, trying to make herself unnoticeable, but the Sterkarms knew she was there. She kept catching looks from them: long, hard stares.

During the whole time the cart had been at a standstill, she'd been planning an escape. Jump down, she told herself, and run! Two or three times she had actually made a move to do it, with her heart pounding and skipping, but then had sunk back. How could she cross miles of moorland, barefoot, in her wedding shift? And this was Sterkarm country. She didn't know it.

The dead man's head, lying crookedly because of his shattered skull, was laid at her very feet, and in the growing light, she could see his blood on the cart's floor. His face, within his ring of dark hair and beard, was bleached to the off-white of tallow. His teeth showed between whitened lips, and his eyelids sagged. Joan looked away, at the ground.

Her husband, Per Sterkarm, and his mother climbed into the cart and sat with their feet almost on the body. The beautiful Elf-Maid climbed in after everyone else and made people move up to make room for her. And why did she shove herself into this cart, of all the carts? Because she had her eyes on Per Sterkarm—and welcome she was to him! But after one quick glance, Joan kept her eyes down. If she didn't look at anyone, perhaps she wouldn't make them angry.

As the car lurched away, Isobel suddenly threw up her head and unleashed a long cry that startled Andrea so, she felt pinned to her seat. It was a whoop, a hunting call: "A, a, a, a, a, a, a! My man's a-gone! A, a, a, a, a, a, a aaaaa! My man's gone!"

In the other cars, Andrea saw heads jerk up. Among the men walking beside the cars too. She felt the shock and anger roused by Isobel's cry fizzing among the Sterkarms like electricity. Oh, God, she thought: There's going to be trouble. But she was too slow in foreseeing where the trouble was to come from.

Per's hand shot out, grasped Joan's hair, and dragged her head down toward the corpse with one strong pull that made Joan scream with pain and fear.

"See what thy kind's done, tha bitch. I promise thee there'll not be as much left of *thy* father!"

He shook the girl's head by the hair and shoved her face toward the corpse's. Joan's hands scrabbled at his, and she screamed with pain and horror.

Andrea was too appalled at first to react, not only by the violence but because this was *Per*—Per, who had never been anything but gentle and loving with her. She said, "Stop it! Per! Leave her!" He didn't even look around. Andrea got clumsily to her feet in the lurching car and reached over people, falling onto them as she grabbed Per's arm. "No! Stop it!"

"I'll slit the bitch's throat!"

"Be so kind!" Andrea pulled at his fingers, trying to dislodge his hands from Joan's hair. She knew she had no hope of it: His hands were far stronger than hers. "Per, Per, be so good, be kind! She's a bairn." Giving up trying to loosen his hands, she gripped his shoulders and said into his face, "She didn't kill thy father! She can't help what her kin did! Per, I thought better of thee—" Desperation inspired her. "I didn't think thee a man to revenge thy slights on a girl-bairn instead of the man who struck the blow!"

His face changed. He'd understood her. For a moment she thought his rage would turn on her—he was white with anger. Then, breathing hard, he let Joan go. She collapsed back into her seat, clutching at her head and crying.

Thinking to protect the girl for a longer time, Andrea said, "She could be carrying thy bairn!"

"I'll hack it out of the bitch!" he said, sending Joan a look that made her cower more. "I'll never breed a bairn on that!"

Andrea rose to her feet. Clinging to the stanchions, she tried to see how she was going to get past Per to sit beside Joan. There was hardly space to move, and Toorkild's corpse was underfoot—and his blood and brains. She shrank from treading in them—but staying where she was meant leaving Joan exposed to further assault. "Shift!" she said to various Sterkarms, who obeyed her because she was an Elf and a guest. She struggled past them to squeeze into the space beside Joan. She tried to put her arms around the girl, but Joan cringed from her. Still, she hoped she could offer her some protection. To Per and Isobel, Andrea said, "It wasn't any of her doing."

They looked away. The cart lurched on, crawling forward, over the moor, toward the Sterkarm tower in Bedesdale.

Hours later, in full daylight, they came in view of the tower. Andrea could hardly bear it. There it was, on the hillside above the valley, built of reddish-gray gritstone, surrounded by its fifteen-foot wall. So many times, after she'd first been separated from Per, she'd imagined returning here. In dreams she'd walked through it, climbing its narrow stairs, looking for Per. She'd visited it in her own time and seen it in ruins; but never had she imagined returning to it with Toorkild's body at her feet. Or with Per's bruised, frightened wife.

The car moved slowly over the rough ground with many people

walking beside it and behind it, keeping pace. Most of them, men and women, were weeping. The toughest of the Sterkarm men weren't ashamed to be seen in tears—they thought it obvious that a man easily moved to righteous anger would also be easily moved to tears. Catching sight of the tower, one of the women called out, "What will we tell them?"

A deep sob came from a man; and keening rose afresh from the women. Andrea looked at Per and saw his mouth set hard in a white face. Isobel's face, too, was white and hard, while her tears poured down. Andrea didn't know what to say to them.

It took the cars a long time to find a safe way down into the valley and then to crawl across it, and some of the Sterkarms went before them, to take the news to the tower. By the time the MPVs stopped beneath the steep climb up to the tower, Sterkarms were descending from it, bringing horses.

People gathered around the car, peering over its sides to see the body, and men pushed forward, offering to help lift it down. While Isobel, Andrea, and Joan sat still, Per bent to raise his father's shoulders. The body had become rigid, like a heavy plank of wood, and it proved easier to push it along the floor of the cart to the people waiting at the cart's tail. They lifted it like a log and carried it away.

Isobel rose then. Standing above them, she said, "Mistress Elf, you see that this is an unlucky day with us. I hope you will forgive us if we do not welcome you as we should welcome a guest."

"Don't think of it," Andrea said.

Isobel then turned, looked down at Joan, and said, "Thou art well come to thy new home, daughter-in-law. Thou'd best stay by my side."

And Joan, with none of the hauteur she had shown earlier, looked grateful, and hurried to follow Isobel. Sweet Milk lifted Isobel down and afterward reached his hand to Andrea. Joan he ignored, except for one hard look, and she had to slip down from the back of the cart by herself. She kept close to Isobel, walking just behind her, at her shoulder.

Isobel crossed to where Toorkild's body had been set down. As she passed, Sterkarms looked at her with respectful pity and murmured that they were sorry. At Andrea they looked with curiosity, recognizing her as an Elf by her clothes, but she saw them glowering at Joan, and she saw Joan's shoulders hunch and her head duck lower with every step.

Andrea stepped to Joan's side, putting a hand on her shoulder. "All will be well," she said quietly. As she spoke, she stared the nearest Sterkarms in the eye until they turned away, perhaps afraid of her Elf-Eye.

At her touch, Joan flinched and looked up at her in terror. When she recognized Andrea, her mouth twisted with distaste, and she jerked her shoulder away from Andrea's hand.

Please yourself, Andrea thought. Silly little girl. You're going to need friends.

There was an argument going on about how the body was to be transported up the steep hillside track to the tower.

"Too stiff to go on a horse," someone said.

Per said angrily, "My father is not to be slung over a horse like a sack of grain."

Isobel, stepping among them, said, "You will make a stretcher and carry him up."

There was voluble agreement from those who had brought lances and blankets down from the tower for that very purpose—indeed, the stretcher was almost made.

"I'll take one pole," Per said.

"I another." That was Sweet Milk.

"Where's Gobby?" someone asked. Gobby, as Toorkild's brother, would want to help carry his body.

"Haven't seen him," Sweet Milk said. "Is he here?"

No one had seen him at the tower. Gobby—and, for that matter, his three sons—had last been seen at the Elf-Palace, before the attack by the Grannams.

"Gobby can look after himself," people assured Per and Isobel. "He'll turn up."

Toorkild's stiff corpse was lifted onto the stretcher, and Per and

Sweet Milk took their places at the front poles. Other men jostled for places, and the stretcher was lifted and carried away.

Isobel was following when a man stepped in front of her, blocking her way. It was Windsor. No one else there would have done it. Though looking at Isobel, he said, "Andrea, translate for me. Offer Mrs. Sterkarm my condolences—you know the sort of thing to say. Make it good."

"Why *are* you here?" Andrea asked him.

"Andrea. Neither the time nor the place. Do as I ask, please."

Detestable man, Andrea thought. But she said, "Mistress Sterkarm, Elf-Windsor wishes to say how deeply sad he is for the death of your husband. He is grieved for the loss of so valuable and honorable an ally."

"Thanks shall you have," Isobel said to Windsor, with a nod of her head, and tried to pass him by.

"Tell her," Windsor said, "that if there's anything I can do to help her or her family, I'll be happy to do it."

Andrea, thinking it a conventional phrase, translated it.

"Thanks shall you have," Isobel repeated. "Forgive me, Master Elf, but I have to follow my husband home." And she walked past him to follow the stretcher, with Joan clinging close to her side. Andrea translated her words as quickly as she could, and followed. Windsor, she supposed, would now get back into his car and drive back to the Tube.

Andrea caught up with Isobel just as Isobel beckoned to one of the tower women and said, "Go on ahead. Build a bed in the guest bower nearest the tower." Isobel spoke clearly and calmly. "Take the best guest sheets and make it up." She nodded toward the stretcher. "That's where we'll lay him."

The woman stared at her. "The best sheets, mistress? They'll be ruined."

"Do I care for ruined sheets?" Isobel said. "Do as I say."

The woman hurried away, followed by three others, striving to overtake the stretcher party and reach the tower before them.

It was a hard climb, made in silence and a little breathlessly.

Joan, looking ahead, saw the tower come into view. It was small compared to her home, a small, poor tower. To her, once inside its walls, it wouldn't be a shelter but a prison. Her unwillingly moving feet came to a halt, and she stood still, letting Isobel and the Elf-Maid get ahead of her. Other Sterkarms came up behind her and passed her by. They looked at her, and someone said, low, "Grannam bitch!" A shoulder hit her, staggering her. Someone blundered into her from the other side, almost knocking her over, so that she had to touch her fingers to the earth to keep her balance, dirtying her hand. Joan ran a few steps, hurrying up the path to Isobel's side again, regretting, despite herself, that she had strayed away from her mother-in-law. Even the company of that flaunting Elf-May would have given her a little protection. People laughed at her, jeeringly, as she went by.

They reached the tower and passed through its low, narrow gatehouse, where puddles of green water lay on the floor, and emerged into the muddy, mucky courtyard, shadowed by the crowding together of many buildings: storehouses with sleeping quarters above, a kitchen, a smithy, stables, kennels. It was a place of narrow, awkward, stinking muddy alleys with the tower, a squat, ugly building, in the midst of it all. Andrea loved the place. When she'd lived there—in that other world—she'd often been annoyed and frustrated with its inconveniences; but when she'd returned to her own time, she'd missed it. And now, even though Toorkild was dead, there was a certain comfort in being there again.

The Sterkarms were gathered around the guest bower nearest the tower, where Isobel had ordered that Toorkild should be laid out. The guest bowers were small bastle houses—that is, they had a ground floor built of stone, with neither door nor windows. The upper story might also be of stone, but was more usually of wood. On this floor there were small windows and a small, narrow door with a ladder which could be pulled up into the room at night. This upper story might be furnished as a bedroom for a guest—which meant no more than a bed, some pegs to hang clothes against the wall, and perhaps a couple of chests. Or it might have been turned into something like a small bed-sitting-room for someone who lived at the tower. A trapdoor in the floor led down into the stone room below, which was almost always used for storage.

The crowd gathered around the bower was watching Toorkild's body being lifted to the upper story by ropes tied around the stretcher poles. Per and Sweet Milk, standing in the doorway above, hauled it up, while men underneath supported the weight and pushed.

Isobel, as she stood watching, gave a start, remembering her duties. Looking around, she saw her daughter-in-law and the Elf-May and, behind them, an even more important guest—Elf-Windsor, with his Elf-Guards.

"Forgive me," she said. "I must make your sleeping places ready. I'll show you to a fire and see that you have meat and drink."

"Don't worry—" Andrea began, and then saw Isobel's white, set face.

"Be so kind," Isobel said. "Follow me." She turned and led the way toward the tower. The crowd parted before her.

Andrea, catching Windsor's eye, followed her. Hospitality was important to the Sterkarms. Guests should always be warmed and offered dry clothes, if they were needed, and food and drink before they were asked a single question. A guest should always be given the best. Nothing excused a hostess from this duty, not even the violent death of her husband. Isobel must be feeling ashamed that she had so far forgotten herself and, Andrea guessed, would be happier if they allowed her to be hospitable now.

Joan hurried to walk a little behind Isobel and a little before Andrea, because she could feel—and see—Sterkarms staring at her with contempt and hatred from all sides. She felt safer when she was close by the Elves.

As they approached the tower, they passed a single-story building of mud walls and overhanging thatch. Heat breathed from its door, and a smell of cooking. Metallic bangs and clatters came from within. A woman came to the door to throw out a bowl of water—catching sight of Isobel just in time to stop herself flinging the water all over her. She gaped at the sight of her mistress in little more than her shift, and stood still, hugging her bowl and listening to Isobel's rapid orders. Warm water and towels were to be brought to the hall right away; and bread and ale, the best they had. Butter, too, and cheese—"It is for guests," Isobel added significantly. The cook would know, from that, the kind of effort he was to make.

The tower had no windows in its ground story, but there was a small, squat door of thick wood, with a grid of iron behind it. Andrea followed Isobel eagerly through the door, into the dim, barrel-vaulted ground room. As always, it stank of the horses and cattle that had been penned there.

A narrow, winding stair, guarded by another iron grid, led up within the thickness of the wall, and Isobel started up it. Andrea, close behind her, found her feet and fingers remembering every little hollow of the steps and wall, and the way the light fell through the slit windows. She loved it.

Joan, behind Andrea, was longing for her own home as she had never longed for it before. There the family quarters were entirely separate from those for the animals. They did not have to tread through dung to enter their house.

Isobel led them into the tower's hall, which took up most of the second floor. It was a large, high room. Smoke hung thickly in the air—thick, harsh, throat-catching smoke—and had blackened the upper walls and the great wooden beams of the ceiling, from which hung hams, strings of flatbread, smoked and dried fish, onions. Drafts from the unglazed windows pierced and shifted the smoke and chilled the backs of their necks.

The hall was almost empty of furniture and, at that hour, of people. One old woman crouched on a stool by the hearth. The trestle tables had been cleared and stacked against the walls, and on the hearth there were only a couple of settles.

The hearth was huge. A fire burned in it, and on the hood above was carved the Sterkarms' badge, a black shield bearing a red, upraised arm holding a dagger. Their enemies called it "The Sterkarm Handshake," and Joan's father had always said that the

Sterkarms, being mere farmers and thieves, had no right to any badge. The sight of it was particularly bitter to Joan at that moment, seeming to boast of the Sterkarms' murderous treachery. But she dared not say anything or even let her feelings show on her face.

"Be so kind, sit," Isobel said, leading them to the settle. As she watched them seating themselves, she went over in her mind what she had ordered and wondered if there was anything else she needed to do. She realized, suddenly, that her daughter-in-law was wearing nothing but muddy nightclothes—as she was herself. A dart of hatred went through her, and her first thought was: Good. Let her freeze. But the girl was her guest—and her other guests, the Elves, were witnesses to the Sterkarms' manners.

"Daughter-in-law," Isobel said, "come with me. I shall find you clothes." Beckoning, she turned to leave the hall.

Joan jumped up from the settle where she had sat but looked terrified.

"I'll come with you," Andrea said, rising. "I can help you dress."

This Elf-May was a pushy madam, considering the putdown Joan had given her earlier, but this time Joan smiled weakly, though despising herself. She felt safer with Andrea's company. Isobel led them out of the hall and up the staircase to the floor above, which was the private room she had shared with Toorkild. There was a small fireplace, a bed, a settle, a stool, a big chest, and a cupboard that also served as a table. Isobel froze for a moment, looking at the bed. No longer would it be hers. No longer would she be kept warm in bed by Toorkild snoring beside her.

She turned away from the bed, went to the chest, and knelt before it, leaving Andrea and Joan standing in the middle of the room. Unlocking the chest with a key from her belt, Isobel sorted through the things inside, occasionally tossing some item of clothing toward the bed. Andrea picked up those things that fell short.

Isobel closed the chest again and locked it. "Help me dress, daughter-in-law. And then I'll help you dress."

Joan was shocked. She had never helped anyone dress. Her maid had helped her. But remembering that it would be safer for her to please her new mother, she hastily went forward.

Andrea offered her help, too, in lacing skirts at the back, lacing up bodices, lacing on sleeves. Isobel didn't want to accept her help, because she was a guest, but soon found that Andrea was handier than Joan. "I am shamed to put you to this trouble, Mistress Elf. Thanks shall you have."

"It gladdens me to be of help," Andrea said. It saddened her to hear Isobel speak to her so formally.

Once dressed, Isobel was eager to be gone. "Be so kind, Mistress Elf–help my daughter-in-law to dress. I would not ask, but–"

"The day is a troubled day," Andrea said, and moved behind Joan to lace up the skirt the girl had already pulled on.

"Forgive me," Isobel said, and ran away down the stairs.

Joan was silent as they worked together to dress her, and Andrea couldn't think of anything to say. As soon as Joan was dressed, she sat on the bed, clasped her hands in her lap, and looked at the floor.

"I think we should go down," Andrea said. "There'll be food. You must be hungry."

The girl didn't move or speak.

"Did you ken about the attack?" Andrea asked.

Joan lifted her head and stared her in the face. "The Sterkarms attacked us! Did my–my *husband* ken it would happen?"

Andrea sat beside her, at a little distance. "The Sterkarms attacked?"

The girl gave her another angry look. "My father would never be so treacherous!"

Andrea said nothing. She knew that the Sterkarms never considered themselves treacherous either, even when, to anyone else's way of thinking, they plainly were. "Let's gan down and have something to eat. I ken you're scared, but–"

"I am not scared!" Another glare.

Andrea paused before saying, "We–the Elves–will help. I think you should gan home as soon as–"

"Stupid Elf!" Joan said. "I can never gan home!"

Andrea sat silent for a moment. The girl might be right. She had been married to Per, and her relatives and neighbors would assume that the marriage had been consummated, even if it hadn't. And it probably had. There was no divorce in the 16th. To her own family she would be a disgrace and an unmarriageable burden. To the Sterkarms she was one of the people who had murdered Toorkild. Andrea didn't envy her.

"I'm ganning down," Andrea said, and left the girl sitting on the bed. She supposed that, if Joan hadn't come down after a short while, she would be foolish enough to take some food up to her.

In the hall downstairs Windsor was sitting alone on one settle, and his drivers and bodyguard were sitting or standing around the other. They were all hungry, and there didn't seem to be much left of the food and drink for either Joan or Andrea.

There was nowhere for Andrea to sit except on Windsor's settle. She sat at the other end from him and took a slice of bread. Looking at him, she said, "What are you doing here?"

"Andrea, you haven't been paying attention. You see, there's this company called FUP, and—"

"Okay, you stopped the fight. Thanks a bunch. Now why haven't you gone back to the Tube? Why are you still here?"

"I wanted to see that everyone was safe, and to offer my condolences. Where's the little beauty? Gone to bed?"

"Do you mean Joan Sterkarm? Do you realize how much danger she's in? She should be got out of here quickly."

"Oh, you do fuss," Windsor said. "But don't you worry. I'll look after little Miss Joan. We can't have her coming to any harm. In fact, next time you're having a girlie talk, you might put in a word for me. Tell her that I'm looking out for her."

Andrea turned her shoulder to him. "Don't speak to me," she said, "unless you have to. I can't stand the sight or sound of you."

"Oh, Andrea," he said. "Don't be jealous." Several of his men sniggered. Could he be any more hateful? Andrea gathered up what little was left of the food and drink and carried it up the stairs to Joan, infinitely preferring Joan's bad-tempered company to Windsor's.

A bed, brought in pieces from the storeroom below, had been knocked together in the upper room, or bower. A mattress, thickly stuffed with straw, was placed on the heather ropes tightly stretched across the bed's frame, and covered with one of Isobel's best linen sheets. Then four men lifted the rigid corpse like a log of wood and placed it on the bed.

From outside came a loud clanging: a din as if a huge metal ladle was being bashed on a large metal pot. The clumsy bell on the roof of the tower, usually used for sounding the alarm when a ride was sighted, was being tolled in slow rhythm to mark Toorkild's death. People on the hillsides around, people up and down Bedesdale who heard that slow, tolling bell, would know it was rung for a death. They would send messengers asking: For whom is the bell tolled?

Isobel climbed the ladder and entered the room, carrying clothing in her arms, which she set down on a chest before going to the bed and stooping to unfasten the sword belt at Toorkild's waist. She had to tug it free from beneath the body. "Oh, my poor, poor mannie." For years now, whenever Toorkild had ridden away to reive, she had feared this end. Now it had happened. At his son's wedding. She need fear it no more, but she must live with it. The tears she had been holding back burst through, and she sobbed and let them run down her face and drip onto her dead husband's face.

Her very last words to him had been ill-tempered and quarrelsome—and he had answered them forbearingly, humorously. It pained her to remember that she had not wanted to marry him—wouldn't have, if she'd had her way. And yet, now, she thought that she could not have been happier with any other man. She squeezed water from her eyes with her knuckles, because she had to be able to see to undress him, and wash him.

Per came to help his mother undress his father's corpse. It was a hard job, a struggle, because the body would not bend, and its skin was cold to touch. After they had sweated over it awhile, Per signaled to his mother to stand back, and drew his dagger. He cut the shirt from his father's arms, and slit it down the front, so it could be dragged from under the body. It was another sad aspect of Toorkild's death that he'd been surprised, in the middle of the night, in his shirt and nothing else. It was partly this lack of dignity that made Per cry. His father had been a good, brave man, and he shouldn't have died like this, bare legged and bare arsed.

When the body was naked, a woman came forward silently, holding out to Isobel a bowl of water and some washrags. Isobel soaked a rag, wrung it out, and washed the corpse's face, wiping away all dirt and blood.

Per said, "Daddy, they'll pay! They'll pay!"

From all the others gathered in the room rose a loud murmur of agreement. Isobel, stooping over the corpse, said only, "We'll make thee look brave: oh, so fine and handsome. . . ." At her belt, on small chains, hung an assortment of household tools: a needle case, scissors, a knife. From among them she selected a comb, unhooked it, and combed Toorkild's hair and beard, teasing out the clots of blood as best she could. But the head wouldn't lie right on the mattress. After a while of trying to set it right, Isobel wadded together the wet washrags and made a pad of them to set behind the shattered head, to prop it in a better position. It didn't work well. Bloodied water spread from the rags across the sheet. It hardly mattered. The body was going to lie there for three days. Its death sweat would soak into the mattress and sheets, ruining them anyway.

Isobel combed the hair over his brow, to hide the hole in his temple where the Grannam pistol ball had gone in. People coming to see him would make the old joke, made at all wakes: "He looks better now than he ever did alive!" She tried to close his gaping mouth, but, stiff in death, the jaw wouldn't move. "Per?"

By force Per closed his father's mouth, and Isobel tied a strip of cloth under his chin, to hold it in place. Turning to the chest behind her, she took up the cloth she'd put there earlier and shook it out. It was a shroud of thin, gray wool. She had always kept some ready, in her chests. "Be so kind . . ." she said, to everyone in the room.

Several people came forward to lift the stiff, heavy body—undoing all Isobel's work with the washrags—while Isobel spread the shroud beneath it. With the body resting on the bed again, the shroud was folded around it. Isobel tied the knot above the head, and Per—as well as he could, being blinded with tears—tied the knot at the feet. Isobel then opened her needle case, threaded a needle, and sewed the shroud together from head to foot, leaving an opening at the face, so that Toorkild's people could take their last look at his features and try to seal them in their memories.

"Bring the chests here and set them either side of the bed," Isobel said when she had finished. Standing aside, she watched the men move the chests as she'd directed. "Bring me candles," she said to whoever cared to obey the order. "And water. If I'm wanted, I shall be here."

A couple of women pushed their way to the door and climbed down the ladder, to fetch the things she asked for. Per seated himself on one of the chests beside the bed. Isobel sat on the other. "A grave must be dug," she said. "Is Sweet Milk here? Find Sweet Milk and ask him to see to the digging of the grave."

Sweet Milk was standing at the foot of the bed. He said, quietly, "It's being done." He took no offense at the idea that he couldn't foresee the need for a grave himself. The lady was not herself.

Per's thoughts, circling drearily yet again around the fact that his father was dead, came up short on the knowledge that now he was the owner of the tower. He was the one who must see that it was kept in repair, that its walls were sound, that the work was done and there was money to pay for it. He was the one who must keep order within its walls and defend its lands—and his heart beat quicker as he realized that he had not done all that he should. His father would have—but his father could never be angry with him again. He must decide what had to be done himself, and remember to carry it out, and bear the blame if he was wrong.

What must he do? Think! The Grannams had attacked—what

would the Grannams be doing? Think! He rose abruptly from the chest. "I want men on watch!"

Sweet Milk, standing at the bed's foot with folded arms, said, "There are men on watch."

Per shook his head impatiently. "Not on the tower only! I want men at the passes. The Grannams–"

"I've sent men to the passes," Sweet Milk said. "I've sent men to the other towers. If the Grannams come, we'll ken."

Per put his hands to Sweet Milk's arms and lowered his head to his foster father's shoulder. "I should have given those orders."

Sweet Milk put a hand on his back but said nothing.

Per raised his head. "Get the smithy going–get weapons out of store. Round up horses from pasture."

"It'll be done," Sweet Milk said. "Stay thee with tha daddy." Sweet Milk's own father had been killed by reivers long, long before, when he'd been younger than Per. He remembered the grief, but he hardly remembered his father.

Isobel bowed forward over her knees and wept. "Oh my man, my poor, poor man, my mannie."

The sound of her weeping lit, in Per's heart, a smarting pain like a small fire, and it burned and burned.

13

16TH SIDE:
A BURIAL AND A WAKE

††††

areth, cold, and wet with rain and sweat, huddled in his Elf-Coat as he stood beside Mistress Crosar and watched the straggling line of Grannams struggle past, clambering on up the hill, carrying children on their backs or in their arms, or hauling along exhausted elders. The Elf-Carts, loaded with the dead and wounded, or those still too drunk or infirm to walk, had gone by a lower, more negotiable track. Those on foot had, for hours, and at a brisk pace, been climbing steep, slippery hillside paths, jumping streams or splashing through the cold water, stumbling and sliding down steep banks, laboring in thickets.

His feet ached, but it was good to be standing still for a moment. The spot was sheltered by a hill spur, and for once he was out of the blustery, damp, chill wind that buffeted his ears. He was as eager as any of them to reach the Grannam tower, though not because he wanted to go there. God knew, he didn't. But at least this tedious hurrying over steep and difficult ground would be ended. And perhaps the worst part of his job would be over. Or nearly over.

"Set one foot in front of the other, and we'll get there," Mistress Crosar called. A little party of three youths came trudging by, obviously tired. "Will," Mistress Crosar said, and one of them came to her, respectfully taking off his cap. The other two halted close behind him, taking off their caps too. "I haven't seen Old Marie," Mistress Crosar said. "Nor Cal, either. Tha kens how they be—too stubborn to ride in the Elf-Carts." Shyly the boys nodded and smiled, flattered to be invited to join in a little mockery of their elders. "They must have fallen behind." She paused, waiting.

The first lad seemed puzzled, then brightened suddenly. "Will I find 'em?"

"If tha'd be so kind. Find 'em for me, and see they get home. Tell 'em I shall shut the tower gates against 'em if they're not home afore me! That'll keep 'em moving!"

The boys grinned and turned back on their way, dodging the people trudging onward.

"Master Elf!" Mistress Crosar said suddenly, making Gareth start. She turned and looked at him, her graying hair falling loose onto the dark cloak she hugged about her. "This is what comes of trusting the Sterkarms."

Gareth sighed. "I think you may be right, mistress."

"They're celebrating now. Laughing, cheering, dancing, because they have Joan Grannam and murdered her father. What might they have done to her!"

"Mistress—" Looking past her, Gareth saw Captain Davy approaching, leading a horse. He wished there was somewhere he could hide, out of Davy's way. "It could be that Lady Joan is with the Elves, and safe."

"Can you no ask Elf-Windsor with your far-hear?"

"I've tried, mistress." He pulled the little headphones from his inside pocket and, pointlessly, showed them to her. "I don't get any answer." He put the headphones away. "I think we might be too far away. But the Elves will make sure your niece is safe, if they can." He hoped that his words were true.

"We will pray you are right." Hearing the closeness of the horse, Mistress Crosar turned to greet Davy. The man gave Gareth a long, sharp look but spoke to his lady. "Mistress, you ken they'll attack again, and soon."

Gareth edged closer to Mistress Crosar and ducked his head, listening closely. He wished the wind didn't dunt against his ears with such a din—he might miss something.

"Will they sell my niece back to us, thinkst?"

Davy shook his head. Joan, he thought, was as good as dead. The Sterkarms would cut her throat before they returned her. It was time to forget Joan and prepare to defend what they could still defend. "They'll no give us rest now. They dare not. We mun be ready for them."

Mistress Crosar, trudging on, nodded. "Th'art right," she said, and swallowed. "Thou mun tell me what to do, Davy. I ken little of fighting."

"Fire the beacon, ring the bell. Drive the kine behind the walls. And I'll take all the men I can arm to meet the Sterkarms."

Mistress Crosar looked at the tired people ahead of her and thought of those struggling along behind. "The tower will no hold us all." The tower housed a sizeable community of kitchen maids and men-at-arms, but many of the Grannams who had come to the wedding had trudged there from the little farms and villages scattered about the Grannam country.

"The women and bairns mun away into the hills," Davy said.

"Oh, let them rest!" Mistress Crosar cried, herself eagerly anticipating lying down on her bed and letting the aches pass from her legs and hips and back.

"If the Sterkarms find 'em," Davy said, "they'll have a long rest."

Mistress Crosar, as she pushed her tired bones on, thought of the women and children trudging all the way to the tower, and beyond, and then going on, without pause, to climb into the cold, wet hills, carrying with them what food they could. She thought of herself, locked up in the tower, waiting for the arrival of murderous men, and her mind spun. Was there food enough in store? How long would the fighting last this time? Should she ration the food?

"Davy," she said, "lay thy ambushes well, and kill the Sterkarms. Kill them all."

He grinned. "I mean to, Lady." And he strode off ahead, threading through the straggling people.

Gareth dropped back, letting Mistress Crosar go ahead. The path was sunken, and he scrambled to the top of the bank beside it and onto the moor. The noise of the people's feet and murmuring voices, contained by the hollow of the path, hushed. He seemed alone in a wilderness of heather, blueberry, and sky.

He didn't have to go far. Everyone would think he'd gone to take a shit or a piss. They would have simply squatted down in full view of everyone, but they knew the Elves were shrinking and modest in their ways, and wouldn't wonder at him.

The sound of engines reached him, faint and thin in the open air, and he glimpsed the MPVs, making their slow, clumsy way across the moor below him. He squatted, on a guilty impulse, unwilling to be seen by the people in the cars. He took out his headphones and fitted them to his head. He pressed the button inside his jacket. "White Mouse to Eagle. White Mouse to Eagle." The call signs had been Windsor's idea, of course. "Eagle, come in. Eagle, come in?"

He tried for several minutes, but what he'd told Mistress Crosar turned out to be true. Useless things, the walkie-talkies. They only worked over distances you could shout anyway. Oh, for the 21st and cell phones. But there were no satellites orbiting the 16th's skies, and no telephone poles. Sighing, he went back to the path and rejoined the weary people slogging toward the tower.

The stone walls leaned over the corner where the grave was dug, sheltering them from the wind drumming against the stone and roaring at the tower's corners. Candlelight from the lanterns made small patches of golden light, flickering against the cold, wet darkness. Gareth hugged his hands in his armpits. Alongside him was Mistress Crosar, and almost the whole population of the tower, and a few Elves, all crowding close, trying to see.

"I shall not leave my brother to rot like a dead rat in a corner," Mistress Crosar had said, as soon as they had labored into the tower's yard. "Later, maybe, there will be time to give him the proper rites."

The people on foot, surprisingly—well, it had surprised Gareth— had reached the tower first. They'd trudged through the small village of turf and sod huts, shouting and hammering on doors, to give the alarm. The people had scrambled to pack what food, warm clothes, and bedding they had—little enough. The Elves might stifle the Sterkarm attack with magic, and drive the Sterkarms away in Elf-Carts, but the Grannams had known the Sterkarms for centuries, and knew that wouldn't be an end of it. The Sterkarms, having begun such a treacherous attack, *had* to finish it before the Grannams could rally and retaliate. The Elves might watch them, but there were many Sterkarm towers and bastle houses, and miles of hills for Sterkarm rides to hide in. The Sterkarms were, even now, riding their way, and they would be safer in the hills, as far from the tower as they could get.

Even before the Elf-Carts had ground their way as close to the tower as they could come, Davy had sent men from the garrison to round up as many of the cattle as they could find and bring them within the tower gates. He ordered the beacon lit and the bell sounded. Soon there could be no one in the valley unaware that they were in danger. Armed men would come riding from the other Grannam towers and bastles.

There was little rest for anyone, despite the fact that they'd had no sleep and had spent the day walking over the hills from the Elf-Palace. Mistress Crosar ordered the fires built up in the kitchens. Porridge was to be prepared for all. They would eat it when they could. A couple of men must be found—old men, of no use to Davy—who could dig a grave for Lord Brackenhill, and the lord's body must be carried upstairs to his hall, where it was laid out on a table. "Bring me water," Mistress Crosar said. "I shall wash him and dress him. He has a long way to go."

The people from the Elf-Carts arrived, struggling the last distance from where the carts had been left, and Gareth earned Brownie points by volunteering a couple of the Elves for the grave digging. The tower was filled with the din of hammering and grinding. The smithy was working, sharpening weapons taken out of store and repairing old ones. Gareth thought that he should be at work too. He searched through the tower for Davy. Don't let him intimidate you, he told himself. He's just an ignorant, dirty, 16th-side thug. You're a thousand times smarter. And you know what soap is for.

The tower wasn't that big a place, but its small area was crowded with buildings–kitchens, stables, armories, kennels, and all the many storerooms that had sleeping quarters above. Between them were narrow, muddy little alleys that were, that night, busy places, lit by shifting candlelight from the lanterns people carried. The clamor of the smithy resounded over all. Men led horses, or ran, carrying several jakkes.

The ladders were in place against every building, blocking the ways, and men and women were hard at it, scrambling up and down, heaving sacks, lowering strings of dried fish and flatbread, throwing bundled blankets.

In the courtyard before the tower, women harnessed ponies and packed panniers. Men flung down clashing bags of pistol balls and stacked lances like wigwam poles. Everywhere Gareth turned, he was in someone's way.

He found Davy in the open-sided smithy, talking to a filthy, sweating blacksmith. They realized he was there within seconds but pretended they hadn't noticed him, as they talked about iron in store and lance heads. Stubbornly, Gareth stood at Davy's side, determined to stay there until the man had to notice him.

"Master Elf?" Davy said eventually, in a tone that meant: Go away.

"I'm here to offer any help I can," Gareth said. "I can't fight. I've never been trained to it. But whatever I can do–" He spread his hands in a shrug.

Davy studied him a moment. "Go home to the Elves, Master Elf. Or help the women. You're no use to me."

Gareth had known he was no use–had been glad to know that he couldn't really be asked to fight, up close, with the equivalent of heavy razors–but it was still a little bruising to be told so bluntly that he wasn't wanted. "There must be something I can do. I can hold the horses."

It had been meant to be a small joke. Neither man laughed. Davy gazed at him with calm contempt. "Can you ride?"

"Ah. No," Gareth admitted, and the blacksmith laughed. To these people a grown man who couldn't ride was laughable.

"You're no use to me," Davy repeated. "Stay here with the women. Though I doubt they have any use for you either." The blacksmith laughed again.

Gareth felt his face flush slightly, and quickly pressed down his temper. *Don't get mad, get even,* Windsor always said. "Where are you going?"

Davy continued to stare at him without any change of expression, but Gareth could almost feel his boots smoldering. The look said: Do you honestly imagine I'm going to tell you? Finally Davy said, "To kill Sterkarms."

"I suppose," Gareth said, "you're going to lay ambushes?"

Davy stared silently and then turned his shoulder to Gareth with finality. The Elves might call themselves friends and hand out magic pills that took away pain, but it would take many more years of solid, faithful friendship before Davy told them where he was going to lay his ambushes. The blacksmith laughed and hefted a huge hammer. "Ask no questions, Master Elf—be told no lies."

And then the priest went by, carrying his Bible and ringing a hand bell. Davy said, "They're burying the lord." The blacksmith laid down his hammer, and he and Davy followed the priest. Gareth trailed after them. At every corner, in every alley, they gathered more followers.

The grave, not deep, had been scraped in the trodden, hardened earth in a corner of the tower yard. The walls of outbuildings crowded close—there was hardly room. Richard Grannam's body, wrapped in a sheet, a miserable bundle by the lanterns' light, was laid in the scraping by stooping men. The priest stood at the grave's edge, the long scarf around his neck shining silkily in the candle-light, its gold embroidery glittering. He held a small, thick, leather-bound Bible and read words in Latin, his voice resounding from the walls. People peered from the mouths of narrow alley-ways or crowded in the small yard, standing very still, even the children, listening in silence. Gareth didn't understand a word. He wondered if any of them did.

The priest closed his book, stooped, and took up a handful of earth. He scattered it, and it rattled as it fell on the sheeted body. Mistress Crosar stepped forward, took up earth, and sprinkled it the length of her brother's body. "I'm sad for this, Richie. If we live, I'll do better by thee. But now I mun look to thy people."

Davy threw a handful of earth onto the corpse, and people pressed forward to do the same, but Mistress Crosar clapped her hands. "To work! My lord will forgive us—he kens we mun work now." And back everyone went to their work, while two men shoveled earth over the body.

Gareth, still looking for something to do, attached himself to a party of men who were carrying oil and peat up the tower's steep, narrow stairs. Taking up one of the baskets of turfs, he followed them, up and up, around and around, all the way to the roof. It was for the beacon fire, the man in front of him on the narrow stairs told him. The fire had to be kept burning until all fear of attack had passed.

"How long will that be?" Gareth asked.

The man laughed. "Davy'll have a few words with the Sterkarms, and they'll all gan home."

From farther up the steps another man called, "They'll slit tha weasand soon as look at thee, but a sheep's got more wit."

They ducked through the low door onto the roof. The wind was strong, damp, and cold up there, and even though the beacon fire was sheltered, in its iron bowl, the flames were tossed by the wind, and flared, hissed, crackled, and threw off showers of red and golden sparks. The light flared and glowed across the peaked slates of the roof, on the stone pathway around it, and on the walls. Outside the reach of the flames' light, the darkness seemed deep.

As they stacked the fuel in the corners of the roof, Gareth said, "I've heard they're clever at laying ambushes."

The men scoffed and, as they worked, told him tales of ambushes laid by the Grannams—many of them against the Sterkarms. Gareth expressed amazement and pleasure at the Grannams' wit, and they told him more.

One of the men, looking down from the tower, said, "There they go! Davy! Davy!"

The other men joined him, and cheered. Below them, Grannam riders were leaving the tower, faintly lit from above by the beacon's fire, each man with a rolled blanket slung at his back and carrying a lance. The sound of the horses' clopping hooves and rattling harnesses rose to them, but the horsemen were vague, indistinct shapes in the near darkness. Their helmets and lance points had been blackened with soot or covered with sheepskin, so they reflected no gleam of light.

The men stayed at watch on top of the tower, and Gareth stayed with them. It was bloody cold away from the fire, and too hot near it, but at least these men were talking to him. Slowly light came, and color seeped into the landscape. One of the men pointed, with a thick brown forefinger, at a small movement on a distant hillside. "There they go. They've split. Davy's going for Urwin's Gap."

"Aye," his companion agreed. "And Jock'll be going by way of Lang Stane."

"Urwin's what?" Gareth asked, and got them to repeat the names several times. They were the names of ways and paths through the hills, they explained, some of the ways through to Sterkarm country. Not the easiest ways, or even the quickest, but the best ways when you wanted to go quietly, without much chance of being seen.

"That's the way the Sterkarms'll be coming, tha can lay money."

"And when they do, Davy and Jock'll be waiting."

When he thought he had the names, Gareth excused himself. He needed a piss, he said, and they laughed and sympathized.

Gareth hurried down the steps into the yard, which wasn't as busy as it had been, though there were women stooping over bundles and pulling knots tight. The Elves, they told him, were in the tower's hall, so he had to climb the steps again. There were the drivers of the MPVs, next to the fire, drinking ale and eyeing the women.

"Here's the boss man," one said. "What we doing, mate?"

"We're leaving," Gareth said. "Where are the cars?"

"Bottom of the hill, below the village."

"Village! Bloody dump," said another Elf.

"Yeah, well, lucky we're leaving then, isn't it?" Gareth said. "Come on."

They rose, draining their cups. One said, "Aren't you going to say good-bye and thanks for having us to the old biddy?"

"Is she here?" Gareth asked. "No. Come on, we're in a hurry."

They followed him down the steps. "We going back 21st side?"

"Not straightaway." There were some disappointed groans.

A couple of women seemed to be guarding the gates, which were locked. "I have to get back to the Elves," Gareth said. "Tha mun open the gates."

One of the women, arms folded, shook her head.

He tried to get past her to open the gate himself, but she blocked him and yelled, "Fetch the mistress!"

They had to wait until Mistress Crosar came out into the yard, walking stiffly, almost limping, and looking very tired. A little crowd of women and children followed her and stood listening.

"Tatty-bye and thanks for having us!" one of Gareth's men said. Mistress Crosar glanced at him but ignored him and looked, instead, at Gareth.

"I am so sad that you've been bothered, Mistress Crosar," he said. "I mun gan to my Elf-Carts—I want to gan and fetch help from the Elves."

She looked at him seriously. "I can no send anybody with you, Master Elf."

"I have my own men, mistress, with Elf-Weapons."

"What if the Sterkarms find you?"

"We are Elves," he said. "They'll no touch us."

She pulled a wry face. "I'd no be so sure of that, Master Elf. They've shown you scant respect. But I can give you no orders: If you will go, you shall. Thanks shall you have if you bring us help." She nodded to the people around her. "Open the gate for him."

"Thank you, mistress."

"Give me no thanks," she said. "You may live to rue this."

Turning her back, she limped away.

Gareth led his small party of Elves through the gate and out into the deserted village. Behind him the gate was shut and barred.

"No sign of them?" Per said. "Nothing?"

Behind him, on the bed and never quite out of his thoughts, his father's body lay, sewn into its shroud. It was the second day of the wake, and a faint smell hung in the room. Isobel sat on a chest beside the bed, breathing it in, showing no sign of discomfort. Several others stood near the bed. People had been coming all day, and the day before. Some, having been scattered over the moors, had just found their way back, tired and bruised, from the wedding and had been met with the terrible news that Old Toorkild was dead. Others had come riding in from other Bedesdale towers and bastle houses, either because messengers had reached them or to ask for whom the bell was tolling.

"We are sad for this, Mistress Isobel," one was saying. "Toorkild wasn't old!"

"He was a fine man," someone else murmured. "Years of life left to him!"

"It took the Grannams to cut him short!"

"They killed him because they'd none like him, and that's the truth!"

"They'll pay for it, Isobel," someone else said, and a hum of agreement filled the room.

"They'll be sorry for this day, I promise thee."

"Thanks shall you have," Isobel said. "Thanks, friends, thanks."

Per was near the guest room's door with Sweet Milk and the men who had come back from watch on the hills. "Tha saw no sign, no sign at all?"

"These be good men," Sweet Milk said. "They kept good watch."

"I kept my eyes open for my wife and children's sake," one of the men said. "I missed nothing."

"Where be they?" Per said. The Grannams had attacked, treacherously, in the middle of the night and had been thwarted, but they wouldn't leave it at that. They couldn't. When you've aroused and angered an enemy, you have to finish him. "Why do they no come?" He was thinking: Have I remembered everything? Is there something I should have ordered done that I haven't? Are the Grannams getting the better of me?

Sweet Milk, his arms folded, shrugged.

"They be crafty," one of the watchmen said. "They want you to think they're no coming, and then they'll come."

"They want you to be burying your daddy and no thinking o' them—and then they'll come," said another. Sweet Milk grunted, not agreeing nor disagreeing.

"Where will they come?" Per said. "By Clow's Top? Mossy Fell? Where else? Where else?"

Sweet Milk and the watchmen thought it over, sucking on their cheeks and pulling their lips. An angry voice from near the bed cried, "We ought to kill 'em all, wipe 'em out like rats!" Grumbling voices agreed.

"I'd ken thee'd be watching Clow's Top and Mossy Fell," Sweet Milk said slowly. "So I might try and come fast by—"

"By Scarshopsfoot!" Per said.

Sweet Milk nodded. "I sent men there. On watch."

Per sighed and put up his hand to rub at his hair. "It seems tha'm the lord of this tower."

Sweet Milk made a contemptuous sound. One of the other men said, "He's no burying his daddy."

"Buried him long since!" said another.

Per reached out and touched Sweet Milk's arm. "Thanks shalt thou have. And you," he said to the other men. "You must be wanting food and your beds. There'll be food in the kitchens."

The men, who knew a dismissal when they heard it, took themselves off, dropping down the ladder to squelch in the muddy alley below. Per drew Sweet Milk farther into the room, into a corner, away from the door and away from the people gathered around the bed. Quietly Per said, "Be the grave dug?"

Sweet Milk nodded.

Per looked past him, toward the bed, but could see only the backs of those standing around it. Sweet Milk knew, from his face, what he was thinking. Instead of waking the body for another day and then spending a day in burying it—while at any moment during those days the Grannams might come in force—they could bury the body now and be ready to fight.

It would be seen by many—perhaps even by Isobel—as disrespectful. They would speak of "throwing Toorkild into his grave," and of sons who were overeager to snatch their inheritance from their father's still-warm hands. Per knew that, which was why he was reluctant to put his thoughts into words—and yet no one who had known Per and Toorkild could doubt that they had loved each other. And that Per loved his father still. It was anxiety to fill his father's place well, to make no mistakes, that pushed him to think of burying Toorkild after only two days of watching. There was, after all, no doubt that Toorkild was dead. As Sweet Milk breathed, he could smell the body. The death sweat could be seen, soaking into the shroud and sheets.

Per's gaze returned to Sweet Milk's face.

"They'll no take us unaware," Sweet Milk promised. He heard some more people climbing the ladder from the alley, clumping onto the floorboards of the room and interrupting the light from the door, but he didn't look to see who it was. "Wake thy daddy for another day. Thy mammy'll like that well."

Per nodded and relaxed a little. He turned toward the bed as a man's angry voice repeated, "We should kill them all, kill them all!" An angry muttering of agreement followed, and then a man's voice rose above it—but this time, it spoke in Elvish. The last people who had climbed into the room, Sweet Milk saw, were Elves: the Elvish laird, Windsor, and some of his men, and the bonny Elf-May.

It was the Elf-May who spoke next, in English. "If you would be so kind, Mistress Sterkarm, Elf-Windsor wishes to speak to you and your son about the Grannams."

"Thanks shall you have for your courtesy, Mistress Elf," Isobel said, "but it's my son you must speak with."

"I am here," Per said. People made way for him, to let him come and stand beside the bed. Sweet Milk followed, at his shoulder. The Elf-May stood at the foot of the bed, her Elf-Laird behind her, and Sweet Milk saw her face when she looked at Per. It was full of pity, full of warmth. What it was, Sweet Milk thought, to be young and pretty, not old and with a face that had been used as a grindstone.

"Elf-Windsor is sad for your loss, and sad, unco sad that he made this match. He had no thought the Grannams were so treacherous."

That struck the right note, and the room was filled with outcry against the Grannams. While she waited for it to die down, Andrea glanced up at Windsor to see how he was doing. He looked a little sick, and was struggling to keep his face from showing how he felt about the smell in the room. She felt queasy herself. It wasn't that the smell was so bad, as yet, though it was pervasive. It was knowing the source of the smell—and having known Toorkild—that made it hard to bear. She had to fight with herself to keep her hands from her nose.

"It is odd," Isobel said, when the muttering had died away, "that the Elves trusted the Grannams, when we told them plain, many times, that they were no to be trusted." The mutter of agreement rose again.

"What you say is true, Mistress Sterkarm," Andrea said. "We, the Elves, were trusting and foolish. But we have gained wisdom. Elf-Windsor kens now that you are in danger, and blames himself." She paused, but the Sterkarms stared back at her and made no polite denial. "He offers you the help of the Elves."

Per looked across the bed at his mother, and turned to Sweet Milk. All around the room, Sterkarms looked at one another. The general reaction seemed to be: That's more like it!

The offer had puzzled Andrea. Earlier, in the tower, when Windsor had outlined to her roughly what he wanted her to say, she'd asked him, "What help, exactly, are you offering?" He hadn't given her a clear answer—"Oh, you know, accurate maps, tracking devices, walkie-talkies, that sort of thing."

She'd never known the Sterkarms to need maps—they knew their country in the dark—and she wasn't sure how tracking devices would work in a world without satellites, but Windsor had said, "Oh, you're a technological genius all of a sudden, are you?" She'd had to admit she didn't know that much about the technology. And Windsor had been giving her a chance to see Per, and speak to him. Joan, she'd figured, was fairly safe on the top floor of the tower, the family's room. She didn't think anyone would actually hurt her. "Elf-Windsor asks that you come outside and let him show you the help the Elves will give."

The thought of leaving his father's body was painful to Per. It showed disrespect. But he also showed respect for his father by filling his place. Looking at Elf-Windsor, he said, "You will help us to break the Grannams, to finish them?"

Andrea quickly translated this for Windsor, and then said, "The Grannams have broken faith with the Elves, as well as with the Sterkarms. The Elves want peace. We thought to get it by making a peace between the Grannams and the Sterkarms. But if the Grannams will no keep their word, then we must get peace by breaking the Grannams." She didn't feel happy about saying this, though somehow it had seemed more reasonable when Windsor had explained it in the tower. Now the words she spoke seemed to bounce about inside her head, as if she was a hollow pottery figure through which the words were being broadcast. How were the Grannams to be broken? In the tower it had seemed to mean something to do with hard bargaining and diplomatic pressure. Now she wasn't sure.

"Mammy?" Per said, and then made his way around the bed to her. People shuffled out of his way. Reaching his mother, he knelt and bowed his head toward her lap. "I mun gan and see what the Elves will show me. Forgive me."

She bent down and kissed his head. "There's nowt to forgive. Tha mun gan. I'll watch thy daddy. Bring me back ten Grannam heads."

He looked up at her. "I will." He rose and made for the door, looking and beckoning for Sweet Milk. "Come one, come all. Let's see what the Elves can show us."

14

16TH SIDE:
SO BRAW A MAN

††††

Per and Sweet Milk crouched to examine the hole at the base of the dry-stone wall. The shell, or bomb, or missile, or whatever it was called—Andrea really didn't know—had struck at the wall's base, digging into the earth and partially undermining it. Some stones had been smashed, some cracked and chipped, some displaced. Others were falling into the hole. The wall was still standing, but toppling.

The Sterkarms looked at each other, awe on their faces. To achieve a similar result they would have needed heavy, cumbersome cannon, with teams of horses to drag them into position, and more horse teams and carts to bring up the barrels of gunpowder and the heavy iron balls. In the Sterkarms' hilly, broken, almost trackless country, where everything was carried on the backs of pack ponies, this wasn't possible. Indeed, if the kings of England and Scotland had been able to drag cannon over the hills to ding down their towers, their homes would have been rubble long before.

But they had just watched one Elf-Man hold something like a tube on his shoulder and, with a shocking, cracking boom, fire from it a small object that had dug a hole in the earth and all but brought down a wall.

The man who had fired the missile was named Patterson: a thickset man with a red face that seemed made of slabs of meat. His dark hair was shaved close to his skull, its dark shadow matching the shadow around his jaws. With a smile he said to Andrea, "Another shot and I'd have that wall down." His manner was affable. How could he, she thought, be affable and yet be willing to do what he was doing?

She told the Sterkarms what he'd said. Per sprang upright, his face alight with enthusiasm. Her heart ached to see his eagerness.

Patterson swung around and pointed up the hill to the tower. "That'd take longer. It's solid stone, well built. But a couple of us— give us an hour—we could take that gatehouse out."

Andrea, feeling like a machine, listlessly translated what he'd said while asking herself how she could have been so stupid. Accurate maps and walkie-talkies! What other help would Windsor offer against the Grannams except weaponry? Now, surrounded by excited Sterkarms, she could hardly refuse to translate.

Per was grinning, his eyes shining. With the Elves' help revenge for his father was a sure thing. Sweet Milk's expression, as ever, was harder to read. He stood by, his arms folded. Windsor had his hands in his pockets, watching them all like an indulgent father who was giving everyone a treat.

"Show us the grenates!" Per said, and they walked off together, the Sterkarms and the Elf-Men, walking along the side of Bedes Water.

A small sheepfold had been built, of dry-stone walls, at a distance from the river. In one corner of the fold, withy hurdles had penned a sheep. It wasn't the fat, white, woolly thing that the 21st siders would have called a sheep but a small, skinny creature, about the size of a middling dog, covered in long, straight strands of some- thing more like hair than wool, and blackish brown in color. On its head was a starburst of four curving horns, but it might have been a ram or a ewe. Both sexes had horns. Being far wilder and an even more nervous animal than its 21st-century counterpart, it was already turning, twitching, and bawling inside its tight pen.

"*Olla rigti,*" Patterson said. "Stand back a bit. Bit more." Stooping, he took a grenade from a box at his feet. Twisting out the pin, he lobbed it toward the sheep.

Andrea, sick and almost in tears, turned her back and looked up at the tower on its crag. She knew they would listen to nothing she said, so there was little point in wasting her breath.

There was an explosion—not as loud as she'd expected, though she still jumped—and the sheep screamed. The Sterkarms—Per too—cheered. The sheep bawled on and on, a horrible sound that Andrea would never have guessed could go on so long.

"There's hundreds of razors inside," Patterson said to her in his affable way. "You want to make strawberry Jell-O? Chuck one into a crowd." He laughed at her face.

Per came to her, his face bright and alive. *"Vah sayer han?"*—What says he?

As best she could, with the sheep screaming, she told him. They would have no idea of what Jell-O was, so she said, "It will cut them into ribbons."

Sweet Milk, who had been watching her, left her side suddenly. A moment later the sheep was silent. She turned to see Sweet Milk stepping over the fold's wall, holding a bloodied knife that he wiped on the grass. While the others enthused over the sheep's injuries, he had cut its throat, to spare it further suffering. In a grim sort of way, Sweet Milk was a kind man. As she watched, he straightened and beckoned to some men—16th siders—who came forward eagerly, clambering into the fold. It seemed they'd been promised what was left of the sheep. If it was any use to them, full of shrapnel.

Patterson, so affable and jolly, was still standing behind her, laughing and saying, "You ain't seen nothing yet! Nowt!"

Turning to him, tears in her eyes, Andrea snapped, "It'll be people next, not sheep! Children!"

He stared at her, still smiling, but raising his brows in surprise.

"How can you bear to do what you're doing?" Andrea said.

There were a few sniggers from the other 21st men—possibly nervous sniggers, possibly not. Then Windsor said, "Oh, never mind our Andrea. She's a vegetarian."

That made the 21st siders laugh outright. Andrea turned away, furious.

The show was over and everyone, Elves and Sterkarms together, wandered back toward the tower. Andrea didn't follow but stood looking toward the moorland hills. Sweet Milk was still talking to the men butchering the sheep. She'd walk back with Sweet Milk, she thought. He was a big, calm man. There was nothing, he made you feel, that he couldn't cope with. And no one would dare to lightly accuse *him* of vegtarianism.

Per wanted to run, jump walls, punch things. He had been fearful that he couldn't fill his father's place, fearful that he would not prove to be quick enough, cunning enough, bold enough, to take revenge from the Grannams for his father's murder. But with these Elf-Weapons! His success was certain. The Grannams would go in fear of him. They would hang their heads and humbly apologize for his father's death—and they would mean it, because the revenge it had brought on them would be so terrible.

He thought of the Elf-May and looked around for her. He no longer felt the sick pang of guilt stirred by the thought that he'd been with her when his father had been killed. The certainty and totality of his revenge made him full of energy, almost gleeful. Seeing Andrea still standing near the sheepfold, he turned and ran back toward her. As he came nearer, he saw that she seemed miserable and might even be crying. Running up to her, he hugged her boisterously, almost knocking her over, pressing her head into his shoulder and rubbing her back. "Ah, be no feared, wee fowl! The Grannams shall no hurt thee—they'll no come nigh thee! I shall fetch thee ten Grannam heads of thine own!"

He was dismayed when she started to cry in earnest, pushing him away, spluttering, screwing up her face. "Killed!" was the only word he could understand.

"Tha shalt no be killed! My word on it!"

"Not me! Not me! People will be killed! Lots of people! Children!"

Sweet Milk had come over to them, and Per looked at him to see if he could make sense of it, but Sweet Milk only shrugged. "Daftie!" Per said to Andrea. "Tha canst no fight a battle without killing folk."

Andrea looked up at him. "Why fight? Why kill anyone?"

He frowned. "They killed my daddy." He admired her pretty face: the big, clear gray eyes; the brown hair stuck to her tears. "Come on now." Offering her his hand, he led her over the rough meadow toward the tower on its hill. She went with him, and after a few paces, he let go of her hand and put his arm around her shoulders. She didn't pull away. She was too busy talking.

"The killing just goes on and on," she said. "It never solves anything. It never ends. There's no point to it!"

"Dost say so?" Per said. His tone made Sweet Milk, who was walking beside them, glance sideways at him. The expression on Per's face as he looked down at the Elf-May made Sweet Milk smile, and then lengthen his stride so that he outpaced them and left them behind. He felt something of a pang as he realized that the Elf-May was not going to be his, but unless he was prepared to fall out with his foster son and adopted family, there was nothing to be done about that.

"Revenge has never worked—" Andrea was saying as Per saw that Sweet Milk had put a good distance between them and him and wasn't looking back. The rest of the party was far ahead, climbing the path to the tower—and if there were shepherds and herd girls about, he didn't care about them.

"They kill one of yours, and you kill one of theirs, and it just goes on and—"

Per pulled her backward, jerking her to a halt, and kissed her.

She pushed him away, though she couldn't get out of his hold, and their mouths parted with some difficulty. "What's this?"

He made no answer but kissed her again. Why talk? She hadn't made any fuss about meeting him when he'd come straight from his wife's bed.

Andrea grappled with him again, pulling her head back, though he still held her. She twisted her head, trying to see if the men were still by the sheepfold. "I was *talking.*"

"There are gey better things than talking."

"But thy father—the wake—"

"Oh, Entraya—let's frig." He could remember his father's face all too clearly, peering through its shroud, shrunken and yellowish, as if carved from old tallow. The staring coins on his eyes, and the flies landing on his lips. One day he, too, would be like that—but perhaps there would be no one to wake him, and his body would lie on a hillside, torn by crows and foxes. "Let's frig while we're alive."

Looking into his face, she remembered Toorkild, and the smell in the room where the body lay. "In thy bower, then."

Per's bower was in the upper, wooden story of one of the tower's outbuildings. He had pulled the ladder up after them, locked the door, and closed the shutters.

In the middle of the planking floor was a trapdoor giving access to the store below; above were low beams—low enough to crack your head painfully if you were used to the height of 21st rooms—and a thick heather thatch.

There was almost no furniture. A wooden bed, with a thick straw mattress and a feather-filled quilt. A couple of wooden storage chests, and some wooden pegs on the wall, and that was all. Per's longbow and fishing rod leaned in one corner. From the pegs hung his quiver, filled with arrows and some snares. His clothes were on the floor.

The quilt was on the floor now, too, flung off because they were too hot. They had slapped and scratched each other, laughed, pounded, and almost shaken the joints of the old bed apart. They lay quiet, Per on top of Andrea, his head resting on her shoulder. She thought he was sleeping. Though unable to move for his weight, she was happy to lie there, listening to the stealthy movement of some small creature—a bird or a mouse—in the thatch above, and breathing in the strong, sharp smell of his sweat and the summery, musty smell of old hay from the mattress beneath them. She was, for the moment, content. This was what she'd come back to the 16th for.

With a groan Per raised himself and cast himself down beside her. She raised herself on her elbow and looked him over admiringly, from his suntanned neck and brown, muscled arms, down from his wide shoulders to his white, flat belly. His dark cock and balls nestled among wiry brown hair at the intersection of his long legs. He punched the bed, and it creaked, and a great gust of hay scent rose around them. Andrea pushed her hand through his hair and kissed him. He grimaced, his fists clenched, and he drew a long, hissing breath. "Dead and gone!" he said.

Andrea hugged him tightly, with arms and legs. "I'm sad for it, sad for it." She held him while he cried, sobbed, groaned, punched the bed and the headboard.

"Gone—and they killed him! Murdered him! And they are nothing—nothing!"

After a long time he was quieter. She leaned from the bed and dragged the quilt from the floor to cover them. "Per, sweetheart—when tha kills a Grannam, they feel as thou feels now."

He opened his eyes and looked at her, frowning.

"I ken tha no wants to hear that," she said. "But it's true. They hate Sterkarms, because the Sterkarms have hurt them. The Sterkarms hate the Grannams because the Grannams have hurt them. That's all that 'taking revenge' does. It makes grief, and hatred, and anger. You kill them, they kill you. Everybody suffers, everybody loses—even bairns not born yet. Tha canst see that, no?"

He turned on his back and looked up at her—at her lovely, full face and clear gray eyes, at the brown hair falling over her plump, sleek shoulders, at the white and pink curves of her full, hanging breasts. "Aye," he said. Did she think he was a fool?

"Nobody can ever win a feud."

"Kill them all, tha canst."

"But—even if that were a good thing—tha canst no kill 'em all, ever."

"With Elf-Weapons tha can."

"Per, harken to me." Andrea leaned over him, her warm breasts on his chest, her hair falling over him. "Be so kind, be so good, harken to me. I can't bear it—all the killing, all the grief—thy mammy and all the women who'll mourn like her. All the sons like thee. All the bairns left helpless with nobody to care for 'em—poor lonely bairns like Sweet Milk was." He was startled that she knew so much about Sweet Milk. "I ken," she said. "I be an Elf. Be so kind, Per—stop it. Stop it here and now. Be the man who's brawer than all the rest—be the man who's braw enough to say, 'I'll no take revenge. I'll make peace.'"

"Make peace with the Grannams?" Per said, shoving her aside as he sat. "We made peace with the Grannams, honey. My daddy's dead because we made peace with the Grannams."

There was anger in his tone, and Andrea hesitated to say more. She might lose his love, and her influence over him. And she was just a little scared of that anger.

But—if the killing went ahead, and she hadn't done all she could to stop it . . .

"I understand," she said on a sigh. "If tha said, 'No revenge,' thy mammy would be angry, thy father's brother would be angry—it's too much to ask. No one could be so brave."

Per leaned back on his elbow. "I'd no care for them, if—"

"If what?"

"If I thought it was right."

"How can it be wrong? If tha gan to blood feud, there'll be more murders, and more and more, and more sorrow, and more and more. It'll never end."

"They killed my daddy."

"And how many Grannams have the Sterkarms killed? And robbed, and hurt?"

His face was set, angry. That, she knew he was thinking, was different. The Sterkarms were in the right. The Grannams were in the wrong. The Grannams, of course, thought the opposite.

"Per," she said, and put her arms around him and kissed him. "If tha stopped the feud, I'd think thee so braw, so braw a man."

Angry, he moved away from her, to sit on the bed's edge. "Whisht now. I mun go and watch by my daddy." He rose from the bed and gathered his clothes. She lay in the bed and watched him dress, watched him unlock the door and lift the ladder, ready to drop it down into the alley.

"Per." He turned to look at her. "So braw a man," she said. "So braw a man." And after he'd left, she curled herself up, hugged her pillow, and glowed with the sense of her own power.

15

16TH SIDE:
THE FUNERAL

†††

Toorkild's bier was carried on the shoulders of men chosen for the honor. Per was at the front, with Sweet Milk beside him.

Behind the bier came a piper and a fiddler, playing the slowest, saddest tunes they knew; and behind them a long, straggling procession of people, Isobel at their head. Close beside her walked Joan, keeping her hands clasped before her and her eyes cast down. It was the safest place to be because, although Isobel didn't like her, she hadn't, yet, offered to do her any harm. To raise her eyes, to look in any direction, to look at anyone else, was to know how much the Sterkarms hated her.

The Elves, as honored guests, were close behind Isobel—Andrea, in her clothes borrowed from the Sterkarms, and Windsor in his smart suit; and then his bodyguard in their fatigues. After them the more important of the visiting Sterkarms, and then the long tail of farmers, shepherds, and servants. Only a few remained at the tower, to watch the surrounding countryside and sound an alarm if necessary.

The funeral procession followed a path that wound from the tower out onto the moors. Above them was a wide blue sky; around them miles of heather and bracken and scrub, over which blew a thin, cool, damp wind. The space hushed the fiddle music, and through it sounded the call of the peewit. Behind it was a great silence.

A low stone wall surrounded the graveyard. Outside the boundary was the wild moor; within was a grassy lawn, close mown by the sheep that jumped the wall. The ground was rucked, mounded over new graves and sunken over old ones, but there were no head-stones. The Sterkarms remembered where their dead lay, without stones to mark the place.

"They have a nice day for it, anyway," Windsor said to Andrea, and smiled when she frowned.

A roofless, half-ruined building at the graveyard's center had once been a chapel, but no one among the Sterkarms could remember when it had last been used.

In front of the ruin waited the open grave. Joan remembered her father saying, "There's always room in Sterkarm graveyards. Why? Because only the women and children are buried there!" Why was that? He'd laughed. "Because the men are all buried in Carloel city, where they're hanged as thieves!'

Here's one who won't be buried in Carloel, she thought. She kept her face lowered and expressionless while the thought cackled in her mind. She'd felt much safer in the topmost room of the tower, with the Elf-May for company, than out here, surrounded by Sterkarms. Her fervent wish was to get back to the tower room as soon as possible. Better still, to get away from here altogether and back to her own country.

The procession turned in at the gate in the graveyard wall, the slow music still playing, and walked between the grassy mounds toward the open grave. Andrea saw, with a shock, that beside the loose earth dug from the grave was a neat pile of old bones and skulls. The small graveyard was full, and every digging of a new grave meant disturbing others—but the old bones were simply left there, beside the new grave, for everyone to see. Interesting, she thought: the contrast between 16th and 21st attitudes to death. Then she reminded herself that she was attending the funeral of a man who had been her friend, even if in another dimension. Was the Toorkild in that other dimension experiencing a sudden shiver as, in this one, his body was set down beside his grave?

Sweet Milk and the other men waited, looking to Per, who was staring around at the sky and the moor. This, Per thought, was the last of his father. Once the bundled body was lowered into the hole and the earth thrown in, there was no pretending or hoping. He shook himself slightly. What hope had there ever been, since his father's brains had spilled into his hand? Get the job done. Gritting his teeth, he stooped and uncoiled one of the linen bands looped under the corpse. The other men immediately took up the other bands, and between them they lifted the body up and, stepping awkwardly, carefully about the edge of the grave, brought it over the hole. Hand over hand, the muscles of their arms working, they lowered it in.

More and more people were coming up and gathering around. One fiddler still played. The tune was frail in the wind and hard to pick out, but each note was sharp and sad. Those who had walked at the back of the procession were now coming up and, unable to find a place in the graveyard, climbed on the wall. A gang of boys herded three sheep out through the gate.

Under his breath, Windsor said, "I would have thought they could afford a coffin."

Andrea ignored him. Coffins weren't the custom here, 16th side, but she wouldn't waste an explanation on him. His bodyguard were all taking off their caps and respectfully lowering their heads.

The corpse was in its grave and the fiddler stopped playing—but a lapwing squealed, and a sheep baaed. Andrea had to sniff and wipe her eyes. Many of the Sterkarms were weeping openly, the men as well as the women.

Per jumped down into the grave, at his father's feet. Reaching up, he took from his mother's hands a round loaf of bread and placed it at the corpse's side. Isobel was already reaching down, to hand him a leather bottle. Andrea saw the tears shining on Per's face as he looked up. She wished that she could stand beside him and offer some comfort, but with both his mother and wife beside him at the graveside, it was a little awkward.

Isobel leaned over the grave again, bringing something from beneath her cloak and passing it down to Per, who took it from her and, bending, placed it on the corpse's chest. It was a sheathed sword. Then Per held up his hands to Sweet Milk, who hoisted him out of the grave.

Isobel stooped, took up a handful of loose earth, and scattered it over the bundled corpse of her husband. The soil rattled as it fell on the shroud. "To earth tha've come," she said, and choked. "Fare well, Toorkild."

Fare well, Andrea thought, as fresh tears rose to her eyes and throat. That meant not simply "good-bye" but "go well" or "travel safely." Toorkild had a long, lonely journey ahead of him, and they had provided bread and drink to help him on his way, and a sword to defend himself. I must, she thought, at some time get them to tell me exactly what they do believe about the afterlife.

Per stooped and took up earth. He held his hand above the grave and was about to scatter the earth when a cry went up from outside the graveyard. "Sterkarm! Sterkarm!"

The men about the grave jerked to attention and reached for their weapons. Everyone looked around, eyes and mouths open. The people on the wall turned, and waved and jumped down. A new cry went up. "Little Toorkild! Wat!" People were leaving the graveyard.

Per, his heart thumping, shoved his way through to the graveyard wall, Sweet Milk close behind him. Andrea, leaving Windsor at the graveside, struggled after Per, to be near him. She managed to push her way between two men and get next to the lichen-grown stones of the wall but could still see very little, as there were so many people running excitedly up and down on the path that led to the graveyard. But she could hear the plodding of a pony's hooves on the turf and she saw, between the dodging of the people, a pony—no, two ponies—being led toward the graveyard gate.

The ponies entered the graveyard, and everyone turned and surged toward them. Andrea had to struggle again, to push through the people. She heard Sweet Milk bellow for quiet. Good old Sweet Milk! He'd sort things out.

Joan had been standing pressed against Isobel's side, her head lowered until her chin touched her chest, her hands clasped before her. She was painfully aware of every sound—voices, feet on the ground, birds calling, sheep—the closeness of so many Sterkarms and, especially, the touch of their stares. Now they all moved away from the grave—Isobel too—and she was left alone. She waited, wondering what to do. She was no longer closely surrounded by enemies, but she felt even less safe. Daring to lift her eyes from the ground, she looked about for Isobel but couldn't see her. Slowly, looking about her with quick glances, she moved after the crowd, hoping to find Isobel again.

The people were forming into quieter, more orderly lines, and Andrea was able to reach through to the front. There were two pack ponies, and they'd been led to a spot not far from the grave. Over the back of each pony was slung a man, bare legged, dressed in nothing but a shirt. Andrea recognized the men leading the ponies: Little Toorkild and Wat, Per's older cousins. They were dirty and unshaven, dressed in breeches and boots with torn, blood-stained shirts flapping loose about their knees.

Per, going to meet his cousins, had never seen them look so haggard and grim. Little Toorkild grabbed at him and hugged him hard, saying, "It's true, it's true."

Per didn't need to ask what was true. His father lay behind him, shrouded, in his grave. He couldn't speak: He could only hug Toorkild, and nod against his shoulder. Toorkild released him and went to hug Isobel, while Wat embraced Per. Leaning back from the embrace, Wat said, "I'm sad for it, but—we bring more bad news."

Per could only stare at him, and Wat led him, by the arm, to the pack ponies. Flies were buzzing around the bodies tied to their backs, and they smelled bad. Per looked at them, at the white, naked, hairy legs, the feet turning purplish-blue where the blood had pooled. He felt like a sleepwalker.

Sweet Milk called men from the watching crowd and helped them to loose the knots and lower the bodies to the ground. They flopped, heavy and limp, the death rigor having left them. Flies rose buzzing around them as they worked. Ignoring the flies and the smell, Sweet Milk crouched over the bodies and looked closely at the round holes in their foreheads.

The flies whirled and settled again as Sweet Milk rose and drew back. The faces of the corpses were blackening, swollen with blood from having hung upside down over the ponies. They were not, at first glance, recognizable.

"Our father," said Little Toorkild.

Wat gestured toward the smaller corpse. "Ingram."

Per's uncle, Gobby Per, and his youngest cousin, Ingram.

Per tried to speak, and the sound caught in his throat. "How?" he said eventually.

The brothers were slow to answer. They seemed dazed. Little Toorkild, the elder, said, "Shot. In the head."

"Daddy too," Per said. Their voices were clear in the open air, and everyone around them was as silent as if holding their breaths. It was strange to be so calm. "Daddy has been waked. Is in his grave." He was thinking that, if they held another wake for Gobby Per and Ingram, that would be more delay, and the Grannams could come at any time. And then he was angry with himself for being unwilling to give his uncle and cousin a good funeral.

Little Toorkild said, "We held our wake while we brought them here." He looked at his brother, and Wat nodded, agreeing. "Is the grave wide and deep enough?" Little Toorkild asked. "Be so kind, put our father in with thine."

"They shared a bed when they were boys," Wat said, "and often enough since."

"Put Ingram in with them," Little Toorkild said. "They won't mind. Nor will he."

Tears ran down Per's face. He took one of Little Toorkild's hands and one of Wat's. "If you won't be sad for it after."

"We'll bring Grannam heads and pile them on their grave," Little Toorkild said. "Daddy will be happy with that."

Per saw Sweet Milk looking a question at him, and nodded. "Up with them," Sweet Milk said, and jerked a thumb toward the grave. Men lifted the bodies, and the crowd parted hurriedly to let them through. Little Toorkild and Wat followed, and jumped down into the grave, to take the weight of the bodies as they were lowered, so they shouldn't be thrown in. They laid Gobby Per on the right side of his brother's shrouded body, and Ingram on the left.

Isobel, looking down from the edge of the grave, said, "I've no bread for them. No drink." Though she had so often squabbled with her brother-in-law, she sounded grieved.

"Never mind, Father's Sister," Little Toorkild said. "Big Toorkild will share his." There was some quiet laughter, and the joke was repeated for those who hadn't heard. "They'll be company for each other on the road," Little Toorkild added, and held up his hands. Many hands reached down to haul him and Wat up from the grave.

Per had come to the graveside, standing beside his mother. He looked down and saw the shrouded bundle that was his father and the darkening corpses that were his uncle and young cousin. He didn't move or speak, his arms straight down at his sides, his fists clenched. The last of the laughter died in the farthest corner of the graveyard, but from the moors beyond, the curlews cried. The deaths were of no concern to them.

Joan, knowing that Isobel would once more be at the graveside, had edged and sidled her way through the crowd to reach her. People refused to move from her way, jostled her, glared at her, and muttered, but Joan kept her eyes averted and pushed on, her teeth set and her heart thumping. At last she came to Isobel's side and felt safer. From beneath her brows she peeped at the corpses in the grave and tried not to wrinkle her nose at the smell that rose from them. Best to show no reaction at all, to anything. She wished that she had enough courage to shout that she was glad they were dead and on their way to Hell, to suffer for eternity. But hemmed in by Sterkarms, she was too much of a coward.

Per brought his gaze down from the dazzle of the blue sky and was blind for a blink. His sight cleared, and he saw his wife standing, head lowered, beside his mother. How sweet and meek she looked, the lying bitch. She'd known, when she bedded with him, what her kin were planning. No doubt they'd thought to manage better and kill all the Sterkarms in their beds. And then they'd have taken the Elvish gold and the Sterkarm lands and married their whore of a daughter to another fool.

Filling his lungs, Per bellowed, in a carrying yell that traveled across the hills and disturbed distant sheep, "Sterkarm!"

Andrea, startled, jerked up her head. She saw many others, all around the grave, coming abruptly to attention, their faces—especially those of the men—lighting with fierce interest.

Per was staring at Joan. "All here ken the Grannams bereaved us while we were sleeping and unarmed."

Joan was bending her head even closer to her chest, trying to hide. More and more of the Sterkarms were staring at her. The men bared their teeth and straightened their shoulders. It seemed to Andrea that their hair rose.

"Time out of mind," Per said, "the Grannams have killed our men, reived our cattle, burned our houses, starved our bairns." With a scraping hiss Per, with his left hand, drew his dagger from its scabbard at his belt. He held it up, the Sterkarm badge come to life, and the sunlight flashed on its blade. From the moor a peewit called, shrilly and sadly. "I swear this, I swear it by my father, and my father's brother, and my father's brother's son, that I shall never draw a blade but I redden it with Grannam blood. If I don't keep this vow, let any man here throw it in my teeth."

Andrea was startled by a roar of approval, or agreement, from everyone in the graveyard. It was almost, but not quite, a cheer. And there was a great scraping of metal as daggers and swords were drawn, to flash in the sunlight. She looked at the cringing Joan and, afraid herself, could only imagine how the girl felt, alone among her enemies.

"Kill them!" came a shout.

"Kill them all!"

A hubbub of yells and shouts rose, from children, from women, and from men.

Per raised his voice again, and although his first words weren't heard, the crowd fell silent to hear him. "We shall kill them. We shall kill them until their country's empty, till the name Grannam is dead and forgotten. And I swear, I swear, that the last Grannam will be sick and sad to the heart for what their name did here. And sick and sorry they'll be that ever they heard the name Sterkarm."

Per reached across his mother, knocking her backward, grasped Joan by the neck of her dress, and yanked her toward him. She toppled on the edge of the grave, cried out, and clutched at Per to save herself. He pulled her to him, pinning her against his chest with his right arm. In his left he held his dagger.

"Leave her!" Andrea shouted, the force of the yell punching from her lungs and throat.

Joan, her back against Per and his arm hard and tight across her chest, saw the blade of his dagger in front of her face and froze, every muscle locked. The sharp edge of the dagger touched her neck. She felt its cold, slicing edge and closed her eyes. Her heart pounded frantically, painfully, and her thoughts scrabbled, scrambled, hunting for escape.

Birds called, the wind blew, but no one in the graveyard moved or made a sound. It was an eager silence. They were going to witness the first Grannam death and the fulfilment of Per's vow.

"Per! No!" Andrea made a convulsive step forward but stopped, her hands weakly, uselessly, in the air. She had neither the skill nor the strength to stop Per, and might provoke him. Where were Windsor's bodyguards—where was Patterson? She looked to her right and left, stretching her neck to see around people, and glimpsed them at the other end of the grave. They hadn't a chance, in such a crowd, of reaching Joan. But then—Per wouldn't do it. He wouldn't really do it—not to a girl. It was a joke. A threat. He wouldn't *do* it.

Per's hand, in the very act of pressing the knife home, weakened and couldn't find the strength to pierce the skin. It was a girl he held, and he had never killed a girl before. Cowards killed those smaller and weaker than themselves, who couldn't fight back.

But this was a Grannam girl—a treacherous, lying, backstabbing, murdering Grannam. A female rat was killed so it could breed no

more vermin. The death of this female rat would be small payment–no payment–for his father, his uncle, his cousin. His hand
regained its strength, moved, slashed with the dagger.

Dark blood spilled from Joan's throat. Her eyes glared, staring,
wide. She put up her hands to her neck, gasped, bubbled, choked,
and sagged in Per's hold. Contemptuously, he let her go and
stepped back. She fell, with a thump, into the grave, on top of the
other bodies. Her blood soaked into Toorkild's shroud.

There was, for Andrea, a long moment of suspension when
she couldn't believe. In another world, this wasn't happening.
Perhaps . . . ?

The Sterkarms cheered. They waved knives and cheered and
laughed.

"One less!"

"Kill 'em all! Kill 'em!"

A man's voice yelled out, "A Sterkarm kiss! A Sterkarm kiss for
the bride!"

A great shout of laughter rose from the graveside. People clapped
their hands, repeated the joke, laughed again, cheered. They were
laughing at, and cheering, the murder of a girl. Andrea felt she'd
been punched. Then she was seized with the thought that Joan might
still be alive. Her hands fluttered, calling people to help. "She might
be alive! See if she's alive!" She teetered on the edge of the grave,
actually dangling one foot over the edge, as if to jump down, but
then withdrawing. Jump into a pit of corpses, among the flies and the
stench? But the girl might be alive! Awkwardly she crouched at the
edge, meaning to kneel and lower herself over the edge.

A hand took her arm, gripping hard, pulling her back. "She's
dead," a voice said.

Andrea looked up into the meaty face of Patterson, who had
determinedly forced his way through the crowd. He didn't look
cheerful or affable at that moment. "She's dead," he repeated.
"Come away."

"We don't know," she said. "We don't know. People have sur-
vived–"

He tugged her away from the grave, so that she had to bunny-hop and scramble to keep her footing, dragging her between people who were pushing forward to get a better look into the grave. "Trust me," Patterson said. "She's dead." He pulled her clear of the crowd, and she found herself among the bodyguard, all of them looking edgy and alarmed. She stumbled against someone and saw it was Windsor, looking white and sick.

"Make sure," Andrea said. "We have to make sure. Please."

Patterson looked exasperated, but he let go of her arm and dived into the crowd again. When he reached the edge of the grave, he saw that some of the Sterkarm men had jumped down into it and were heaving Joan's body out. They tossed it onto the ground, among the feet of the people, who hastily stepped back and then came forward again to kick the body.

Andrea heard Per's voice—always loud and carrying. "—no be buried with my family. Cast it over the wall."

Between the crowd of shifting bodies, Andrea glimpsed people bending to take Joan's arms and feet, to carry her away. No, she thought. You can't. You can't just throw a body over the wall and leave it. To rot. Where anyone might come on it. Children. Anyone. That's not—it's not—civilized.

"She's dead." Patterson was at her side again.

"Are you sure? Do you—?" Perhaps, Andrea was thinking, perhaps, when everyone had gone, they could go and find where Joan had been thrown, and—

Patterson was bending to look into her face. "D'you think these characters don't know how to cut a throat? She's dead."

"We don't *know*," Andrea said. Per wouldn't do that. Per wouldn't murder an innocent girl. He wouldn't.

Patterson leaned even closer. "He nearly cut her. Fucking. Head. Off. D'you want to see?" He took her arm, as if he would drag her over to the body.

Andrea pulled away. "No! No." She put her hands to her face.

The Sterkarms were filling in the grave. Everyone was helping. Per, Little Toorkild, and Wat were shoveling in earth. Those who had no spades used their hands. Per worked with such fury that he could have done it alone.

Andrea turned her back on the grave and walked toward the gate in the wall.

"Where are you going?" Windsor called after her.

Without turning, she said, "Away from here!"

16

16TH SIDE:
A TINY HOLE

†††

Gareth was a pretty good driver—well, he couldn't see much about his driving that he needed to improve—but he let McKean drive. He was tired, and driving 16th side was no fun. If someone was going to overturn an MPV, or get it stuck in a bog, or break an axle on a boulder, let it be McKean. Even sitting in the passenger seat on the journey from the Grannams' Brackenhill Tower to the Tube was nervewracking. Bands of armed and angry Grannams or Sterkarms might appear at any moment, and if they did, they hadn't a chance of speeding away from them because the "roads" were nothing more than sheep tracks and horse rides. They climbed or descended with terrifying steepness, or clung to hillsides at a slope, and Gareth gripped the edges of his seat with both hands. They didn't talk much. McKean had to give all his concentration to driving.

He had to guide the vehicle slowly through narrow spaces between boulders—drive it at an extreme slant down slippery, grassy slopes—skirt boggy and marshy hollows, while Gareth held his breath, foreseeing that a wheel would get stuck—and drive through rocky streams and rivers. It had been a huge relief to reach the deserted wedding camp and, a little beyond it, the Tube. The MPVs had all drawn up in the compound, and everyone had piled out, laughing and stretching, and strolled into the office, for coffee and Coke in plastic cups.

"Has Mr. Windsor been through?" Gareth asked the man on duty.

"Still out at the Sterkarm tower, far as I know."

"What?" Gareth said, and the men stopped chatting and started listening. "I've got information for him."

"Better start driving, then," the guard said. This wasn't the reply Gareth had been hoping for.

"Isn't there any other way—?"

"Sure!" said the guard. "Phone him on your cell. Post him a letter. E-mail him, why don't you?"

"You're not being helpful," Gareth said.

"I'm a bugger like that," said the guard, who had no ambition.

Gareth turned to other men. "I need a volunteer." They all looked at the floor and into corners. "Fine," he said. "You go through. I'll drive myself."

The men cheered up immediately. With waves and nods they went out to their MPVs—leaving one for Gareth—and drove up onto the ramp and through the Tube. Back to the blessed 21st. Ah well, Gareth reflected, he was the one with the career instead of a dead-end driving job; he was the one who was going to earn the Brownie points.

He drank a cup of coffee and snatched a nap on the office sofa. When he did get back 21st side, he promised himself, he would fire off loads of memos, reminding his bosses of how bloody useful he'd been, and make it count when his assessment came around. Onward and upward!

Half an hour later he climbed behind the wheel of the MPV and started for the Sterkarm tower. The drive was exasperating and difficult—merely a strain while driving over the high moors, but the steep, rugged descent into Bedesdale, in first gear, was frightening. He seemed to have his jaws clenched tight for hours, and his whole skull ached, but at last, at long last, he was bumping and jolting along the valley floor toward the tower. The Sterkarms had cleared some of the boulder litter, after Windsor had encouraged them to the work with gifts of aspirin, cloth, and Wellington boots.

Gareth didn't attempt to drive the car up the steep path to the tower, though Windsor had once boasted to him that he had. Enough was enough, Gareth thought. It was easier to get out and walk.

He was out of breath by the time he reached the gatehouse, and the strong wind was blowing past his ears. He was surprised to see that the gate was open. There was a guard closely watching his approach, but even so, he'd have thought the Sterkarms would be on red alert, given the circumstances. Before he could approach the gate, he heard voices and footsteps from beside the tower. He looked in that direction and saw Andrea Mitchell come hurrying around the curve of the tower's fifteen-foot wall.

She was half running, her hair flying, and she swiped her hands at her eyes as she came. Gareth got the impression that she wasn't happy. "Hi!" he said, and raised his hand in greeting.

She stopped short and stared at him.

"James Windsor about?" he asked.

She came on toward him. Drawing near, she said, "You liked Joan Grannam, didn't you?"

An odd question, he thought. What had it got to do with any-thing?

"I know you did, I know you liked her," Andrea said. "Well, she's dead."

"Dead?" Gareth said, blankly. How could she be dead? There was a higher mortality rate 16th side, yes, but even so, Joan Grannam was only fifteen or sixteen, and in good health the last time he'd seen her, which was only—he couldn't remember the exact time. A couple of days. Three days. Something like that.

"They nearly cut her fucking head off!" Andrea said.

"What? Are you all right?"

Andrea raised her clenched fists on either side of her head. "*I'm* all right! Joan Grannam's dead!" Her hair flew out about her head.

She's mad, Gareth thought, and was relieved to see Windsor coming up behind her with several other 21st siders. He half waved at Windsor, and would have gone to meet him, except he felt vaguely guilty about leaving Andrea when she was so obviously upset about something.

"Gareth!" Windsor said as he came closer. "I'm certainly glad to see you!"

"I've got some—" Gareth began, but Windsor cut him short.

"I'm out of here, leaving straightaway. You're in charge."

Gareth tried to take this in. Windsor, he realized, wasn't looking quite well. He was pale, and there was a jumpiness about all his movements, a slight shake in his voice.

"I'm coming with you," Andrea said.

Windsor looked at her and calmed a little. "You? No, Andrea. We can't spare you."

"I resign," she said.

"Fine. As soon as I receive your formal, typed letter of resignation on my desk, 21st side, your month's notice will begin."

As Gareth, bemused, looked on, Andrea gave Windsor a long look of pure hatred. "You can't stop me from leaving."

"Who's stopping you?" Windsor said. "But Patterson here needs the vehicles. Can't spare one to be your taxi. Of course, you can walk—if you want to walk from here to the Tube with the Grannams on the warpath."

Andrea looked at Patterson, who stood stolidly beside Windsor. She looked at the other men beside him, and at Gareth, but though scared and angry, she wasn't yet quite desperate enough to ask them for help—especially when she strongly doubted that they would help her.

"Andrea," Windsor said, in a reasonable, soothing tone, "I need you here. Gareth will be off into the hills with Patterson and the Sterkarms."

Gareth was startled to hear this.

"So I need you here, at the tower," Windsor went on, to Andrea. "And you're not in any danger. You're an Elf. Nobody here is going to cut your throat." His voice wavered again.

"I don't *think* they're going to—to kill me!" Andrea said.

"Then what is the matter?" Windsor asked. "Why do you want to leave suddenly? Oh—" He smiled. "Is Per Sterkarm not so cuddly as you thought he was? What a pity. Personally, I wasn't under any misapprehension there." His hand briefly rubbed his stomach.

Voices and footfalls made them look around. The rest of the funeral party was returning from the graveyard. Per Sterkarm, ahead of the rest, raised his arm and called to someone among them—it might have been any of them.

Andrea, knowing it was her, was seized with a sort of panic. She couldn't face Per, couldn't speak to him. Being near him would be like being smeared with blood. Abruptly turning away, she hurried up the rough steps to the tower's gatehouse. If she went inside, she could go to her bower, pull up her ladder, hide.

"Who's my driver?" Windsor asked. "Gareth, make my excuses—lay it on with a trowel."

And Windsor, too, ran away, with his driver, down the steep path that led down the hillside to where the Elf-Carts were parked.

Gareth, exasperated and afraid, was left to greet the Sterkarms. "Mistress Sterkarm—I am sad for your husband's death—er—Master Windsor has been called away. On important, urgent business. He wished to stay longer"—Gareth was half aware of Per Sterkarm leaving the funeral party and running up the steps toward the gatehouse—"but truly he could not. He is needed—in Elf-Land—could not stay."

"We are sad for it, Master Elf," Isobel Sterkarm said. Her face was stiff and rather grim, but she was composed. "Shall you be staying with us?"

"Er—I shall."

"Then I will make you a place to sleep," Isobel said, and went on toward the tower. Most people followed her, though some were peeling off and going to their business in the fields. Gareth fell in with Patterson and the other 21st men.

"What's this about me going with you into the hills?"

They grinned at him.

Per caught up with Andrea as she reached the narrow alleyway that led to her bower. "Wait! I've been calling thee! I—"

"Get away from me!" Andrea said, almost in a panic. She tried to go on.

He darted in front of her, blocking her way. "How stands it with thee? What's wrong?"

"What's—?" Andrea's voice croaked into silence. She could only look at him. There he was, tall, strongly made, good-looking. His sleeve stained with fresh blood, his face flushed and lively, his spirits high. That, she thought, is a killer.

"I'm ganning soon," Per said. "I wanted to see thee afore I gan."

"I thought you understood!" she said to him. "I thought you did. I thought you got it. But you don't—you don't at all. You haven't even tried, you haven't thought about it!"

He was baffled. And she was calling him "you" when he'd thought they were "thou" to each other.

"Joan," she said. "You murdered Joan."

He frowned, annoyed. He didn't like being called a murderer. It had been revenge, not murder. "The Grannams killed my daddy."

"Joan didn't!" she yelled at him. "Joan never hurt anyone! Joan was—was—just a little lass."

"Ach! She was a Grannam!"

"And that's reason enough, is it?"

Per looked angrier. He didn't like being shouted at by a woman, not even an Elf-Woman. Still less did he like being shouted at by a woman he'd lain with, and from whom he'd expected kisses and cuddles and kind words.

"And now what's going to happen? You're going to kill more Grannams—whether or not they had anything to do with killing your father. And they'll kill some of you. And you'll kill some more of them. And they'll kill some more of you—and on and on it'll go!"

"Tha'rt an Elf," Per said. "Tha dinna—"

"Why is it that when you kill Grannams, that's right and fair—but when they kill you, that's wicked and wrong? How do you tell the difference between a good murder and a bad murder?"

Per scowled, looking angrier than she'd ever seen him, in this world or the other. His blue eyes flashed silver, as if a light had lit up behind them. He seized her by both shoulders and shook her. Though she always thought of him as slender, he was tall, and he was very strong. His fingers gripped her arms painfully and, big hefty girl as she was, he shook her until her head bobbed and her teeth clattered. She was dreadfully scared: Her heart pounded, her face flushed, and her breath seemed to be lost somewhere in the shaking. It flashed through her mind that he was going to kill her, as he'd killed Joan—what was to stop him? He could do anything he liked. The Sterkarms would always back him. And so would FUP, because he was worth more to them than she was. They would tell her parents, "Dreadfully sorry—your daughter was killed in an industrial accident. Here's some money." She tried to say, "Be so—kind—" but couldn't form the words for the shaking.

"You ken nowt!" Per said. "Nowt!" He shoved her aside, and she stumbled into the stone wall of a storehouse. "The Elves may for-give and forget and live in peace—but this is no Elf-Land! If we dinna kill the Grannams, they will kill us!" He strode away from her and then turned. "And I *shall* kill them!" With a couple more strides he had turned the corner of the alley and was out of her sight.

Andrea huddled against the wall, shaking, for some minutes before she felt able to climb the ladder to her bower. She felt wobbly as she did it and didn't think she had the strength to pull the ladder up after her, but she did and then felt safer.

She lay on the bed, huddling in the smell of old hay, and cried, from shock and humiliation, because she'd thought she could influ-ence Per, and she couldn't—and perhaps from grief—for Joan, for Per, for everyone who was going to be killed and hurt. . . . She didn't know for sure why she cried.

As the sobbing eased and her brain began to work again, she asked herself what she'd expected. Had she really thought that one short pillow talk would reverse the whole conditioning of Per's life? Behind Per lay centuries of blood feud. He thought murder a lesser crime than leaving his father unavenged.

But he'd killed Joan. She hadn't liked Joan—the girl had been prickly, touchy, and hard to love. . . . But she'd been a girl. A fifteen-year-old girl.

Andrea realized that she wouldn't have been so appalled if Per had cut the throat of a Grannam man in front of her. Shocked, yes. Scared. But–she wouldn't have felt such a personal affront. She wouldn't have been so scared when Per had lost his temper and shaken her. At the bottom of her grief was the fear that if Per could kill Joan so pitilessly, then he might also harm her.

And that knowledge grabbed her by the scruff of the neck and shoved her face into the fact that she'd managed to forget again, the fact that she always managed to duck, no matter how often it was brought to her notice. Per was a killer.

He always was, she thought. When he'd seemed so sweet, when she'd known him before, in another dimension–he'd been a killer then. Raised to it, trained to it. But she'd always managed to overlook it. She'd overlooked it so successfully that she'd kissed him, cuddled him, lain with him. She felt like the mistress of some concentration-camp commander, cooing over him when he came in from a hard day's torturing and murdering–wiping the blood and stink off him, kissing him.

She felt sick. She felt filthy. She didn't know what to do.

"Do you ken," Gareth asked, "places called Lang Stane and Urwin's Gap?"

The expressions on their faces told him that they knew them very well.

"That's where the Grannams are lying in wait for you," he said.

"They're lying in wait for us?" Per looked at Sweet Milk. "They're no coming on the attack?"

"Not as I understood it," Gareth said. "I couldn't ask them directly. I gathered that they expected you to be attacking them–"

"And they've set ambushes," Per said, again to Sweet Milk, "where they think we'll come through the hills! That's why we've seen no sign of them, for all our watching!"

Sweet Milk nodded slowly.

"Show us where they are," Patterson said, nodding to Gareth to translate, "and we'll take 'em out."

Sweet Milk said, "The Elf-Carts," and made a dismissive, wiping gesture. He shook his head.

Gareth opened his mouth to translate, but there was no need. Patterson grinned and said, "Tell him we can still use our legs. We were never planning on using the Elf-Carts."

Gareth translated that. Sweet Milk gave the Elves a sidelong glance of amusement, though his face never shifted into even a glimmer of a smile.

"Can you ride?" Per asked, and mimed riding a horse. Several of the 21st siders laughed, shaking their heads.

"Yes," Patterson said.

"Be ready then," Per said and, swinging around on his heel, drew in a long breath and expelled it in a yell of "Sterkarm!" His carrying bellow rang through the tower and jerked· up the head of every man and woman who heard it—and they passed the alert to everyone who hadn't. They dropped what they were doing and came toward the shout, to be met by Per, shouting, "Horses! We ride."

Gareth turned to Patterson to translate and found that he and his men had gone. They knew what they had to do too.

It was little more than an hour later that Andrea heard the ride leaving. She refused to leave her refuge to see them go but went to her bower's one window, opened the shutter, and leaned out. At the end of the narrow alley in which her bower was built, she could see the horsemen passing, above the heads of those who crowded the alleys to watch them. The little, stocky, barrel-chested horses—almost all of them black—with their shaggy coats and long, uncut manes and tails, clopped by, shaking their heads and rattling their harnesses. The eight-foot lances towering above the riders' heads, but not gleaming, as in storybooks. The Sterkarms didn't want any gleaming, flashing lance heads to announce their coming to any lookouts. The lances had been rubbed with a mixture of grease and soot, both to preserve them from rain and to darken them so they wouldn't catch the light. Their helmets had been treated the same, and the many small metal plates of their jakkes were hidden between two layers of worn leather.

She couldn't catch any sight of the 21st men, though presumably they were going with the Sterkarms. Leaning out the window and listening, she heard the horses, yells of "Sterkarm!" and the shouted good wishes of women and children, but she didn't hear any of the MPVs' engines start.

That meant there would be MPVs at the foot of the hill, and she could drive herself. . . . But that idea soon faded. Each would have a personal key, which could be used only by a specific driver. Even those cars driven by several different people would have a code to be punched in before they could be started. She didn't know the code, and she didn't have a personalized key. Neither did she have the skills needed to start a car without its keys.

For a while she sat on the bed and thought seriously about walking to the Tube. It would be a long, hard trudge across very difficult country, but she'd be doing it to escape, to spite Windsor. She didn't know the way, but there would be a track left by the cars. . . . She didn't have the courage, though. Even supposing the track was clear and she didn't get hopelessly lost, there was no telling what raiding parties were out there. Grannams, and allies of the Grannams, looking for revenge. Sterkarms from outlying districts who had never seen her before. She could perhaps rely on them leaving her alone because she was an Elf, but—there was no law, out there on the 16th-side moors. Angry men need not worry about any retribution. She kept seeing the blood pouring from Joan Grannam's throat—but it was her own throat—and hearing Joan's dying gasps and choking in her own voice. She wasn't going to chance it.

She passed the time by thinking over what a bloody fool she'd been, to leave Mick and come back to this godforsaken time and place. What did you expect? she asked herself again and again, in amazement. If the Per you knew before was good-natured and sweet—or capable, at least, of being good-natured and sweet at times—then it was because his father, his uncle, and his cousin hadn't been murdered. She thumped her head on the pillow and told herself: It's no use grieving over the Per you knew and mourning his loss—he isn't lost. This Per and that Per are one and the same. The Per you knew was just as callous and murderous as this one. He'd just never had reason to show it so close to home.

Hours later and dusk was thickening to dark; her hunger became so sharp that she couldn't bear it. She got up, opened the door, awkwardly dragged her ladder to it, and dropped one end into the alley below. Climbing down, she set off to find herself something to eat. The kitchen would give her some flatbread and cheese, if nothing else.

The kitchen was an outbuilding across the yard from the tower's door. It was built all of wood, so that when it burned down—as kitchens were prone to do—it could be rebuilt quickly and cheaply. A thatch of heather roofed it and hung well over the walls, to carry the rain away from them. The entrance was always muddy where water had been thrown out, and was strewn with peelings and other rubbish. The tower's pigs, chickens, cats, and dogs were usually hanging about the door, since they knew as well as the tower's human occupants where the food was to be found. And there was one of the tower's human occupants, an old lady, sitting on an upturned tub under the eaves, eating from a bowl.

Andrea hopped over the mud, stuck her head into the hot, smoky interior, and asked the nearest woman whether she could have something to eat. "Just something quick. Whatever's to hand."

Her question started a bustle, with women fetching other women and shouting to others, but eventually she was given a broad, flat wooden plate on which was a bowl of groats, a lump of cheese, some shards of flatbread, and some slices of smoked tongue and mutton. She was about to leave with this substantial meal when she heard someone say, "Funniest-looking wounds ever I saw!"

It was the old woman. She took another spoonful from her bowl and swallowed. "I said to 'em, 'Toorkild shot by a ball! Never as I live! I've seen some wounds in my time,' I said, 'but that was never made by a ball! Never in this world!'"

Andrea hesitated. Old people talk to themselves, in the 21st as well as the 16th. If she asked the old woman what she meant, she probably wouldn't get any sense out of her but would have to listen to a long, wandering monologue. She took a step away, to return to her bower, but then turned back. "What dost mean?"

She had to repeat herself before the old woman noticed her, and then she just stared while licking her horn spoon.

"Thou said Toorkild was never shot by a ball," Andrea said. "What dost mean?"

"Them holes!" the old woman said, jabbing at her own head with a forefinger and speaking as if Andrea was stupid. "The ones in Big Toorkild's head, and Gobby's and the lad's! The ones they said was made by pistol balls! They never was!"

It was dry under the overhanging eaves, but the ground was thick with rubbish. Still, Andrea trod through it to stand at the old woman's side. "Why dost think that?"

The old woman jabbed at her forehead again. "Too small! Ever seen a hole made by a ball?"

"Well . . ." Andrea said. She'd thought she had.

"I've laid 'em out," the old woman said. "I've washed 'em. Two of me own, an' all. Seen enough to last me a hundred years." She held up her thumb and forefinger, making a circle. "A ball's a big thing, see thee. Big ball of lead. It hits something hard, it flattens. Pick one up that's hit a wall, and tha'll see." She filled her mouth with groats again.

At the back of Andrea's mind some dreadful knowledge was gathering. She almost wanted to leave before it broke on her.

"One hits somebody's head bone," said the old woman, "it makes a muckle hole. A muckle, rough, jaggedy hole. And a muckler one ganning out."

"It did," Andrea said. "They had no backs left to their heads. It made a gey muckle hole ganning out."

"Ah," said the old woman, wagging her horn spoon, "but a wee hole ganning in. That's what I'm saying, see thee. It made a wee, wee hole ganning in—no bigger than the end of me finger. That was no ball. No ball made that hole. That's what I'm saying."

Andrea's mind was working so fast, she could feel the synapses sparking as the thoughts and memories flashed back and forth, connecting. A tiny hole going in. No large, soft lead ball, then, that would flatten on impact. No—it must have been made by something small, narrow, and very hard, traveling very fast, that would punch through the bone, like—a bullet?

"They'm all busying themselves running after Grannams to kill," the old woman said. "Can't look at what's in front of 'em. Can't see for tears. They want to live a bit longer, and bury two sons, and *then* they'll see what's what."

Andrea had stood on the hillside above the wedding camp. She'd stood on the hillside and seen the floodlights come on, lighting up the melee, as the Sterkarms and the Grannams scuffled. And from behind her, in the darkness, she'd heard a strange sound, like a stick being dragged across railings. A short stretch of railings.

She hadn't known what the sound was then. Now she thought: It was a rifle. A muffled, silenced rifle. There had been a sniper on the hillside behind her, in the dark. With a telescopic night sight. And that sniper had lined Toorkild up in his sights and shot him through the head. With a hard, narrow, high-speed trajectory, 21st-century bullet. Making a small, neat hole as it went in, and blowing off the back of his head as it left.

What Grannam had such a weapon? What Grannam could have used such a weapon, so skillfully, if he'd had it? Surely it would have taken a crack shot, someone who'd practiced with the weapon a thousand times.

Andrea felt as if she was hanging, suspended, in cold, empty space. It hadn't been a Grannam who'd shot Toorkild, Gobby, and Ingram. It had been an Elf. One of the Elves who were now on the ride with Per and Sweet Milk. Which one? The affable Patterson?

She imagined him, on that dark hillside, centering the crosshairs of his sight on Toorkild's head. What a laugh.

And if it had been an Elf who'd fired the shot, it didn't take much thought to work out who'd given the order.

What other orders had he given?

17

16TH SIDE:
THE TOWER

†††

Gareth stumbled yet again, and picked himself up, and scrambled on, because he dared not rest and be left behind, alone, in bandit country. To himself, silently—because he hadn't the breath to swear aloud—he swore that if he got out of this and got home to the blessed 21st, he would never leave his couch again. Ever. He would lie there and watch television, eat chips, and drink Coke, and never, ever again leave the comfort of town. He didn't think he'd ever been so miserable in his life. And he could get killed or maimed, too. Bloody Andrea. Lucky Andrea. All that squawking about equality, and women were still getting out of stuff like this because they were too girlie to go raiding in the dark. Per, Sweet Milk, and even Patterson had been unanimous. No girls.

It hadn't been so bad, to start with. He'd felt quite bucked up to be part of the ride as it left the tower. He hadn't been riding, of course. He'd been walking, with Patterson and the other Elves, along with several Sterkarm footmen—fierce, hairy types, wearing blackened helmets and carrying vicious things that looked like big axes with very long handles. It was a "jeddart axe," one of them told him, adding, "It'd take thy leg off. Shall I show thee?"

Then, at first, it hadn't been so bad following the riders across country. True, it had been rough, with scrambles uphill and rocky streams to ford, but the footing had been firm, and it hadn't really mattered if he trailed behind. They were still in sight of the tower, and it felt safe, though as he panted to keep up, he felt that he should have taken more notice of all those 21st-century admonitions to eat less junk food and go more often to the gym.

The horsemen led them out up the high moors, down into steep, rocky declivities, and up steep, wooded sides where riders had to dismount and duck and twist among branches.

The going got harder and harder—and, he supposed, he got more tired. They climbed hillsides calf deep in heather and bilberry where, every time Gareth lifted his foot, he had no idea whether it would come down sooner than he expected on hard, hidden stone—jolting him and throwing him off balance—or whether it would plunge unexpectedly deep into an unseen hollow—making him stumble and stagger—or whether it would sink into a soft, muddy bog, nearly sucking off his sneaker, soaking and miring him to the knee. It was exhausting, this staggering and toppling and wind-milling for balance. It made walking every mile like walking five, and it was completely different from walking on pavement. Gareth realized that he had never before experienced what it was like to walk "rough country." What he had thought of as rough had been mere parkland.

He fell farther and farther behind. The Sterkarm footmen climbed the hill steadily ahead of him—breathing a little hard and certainly not frisking, but showing no sign of ever tiring, either; and they were wearing heavy tin-pot helmets and carrying long knives and axes. Their legs and lungs, he thought, must be made of steel and leather. Gareth longed fiercely for a rest, even if it meant sitting in the wet grass and heather. Stop, just stop, please. I don't even know what I'm doing here. What do they expect me to do—kill people? Damn Andrea. Bet she was curled up by a fire, drinking cream.

A halt was called eventually. Gareth sank down among the tough, prickly moorland plants, his feet and legs throbbing with weariness. His back ached. Even his face ached. Give me the 21st, he thought. Cars, planes, escalators, elevators—and if you must exercise, you can do it in a nice, warm, dry, clean gym.

Per sat on the ground, his horse's reins looped over his arm, and kicked at the turf with one heel. He spoke to no one, and no one spoke to him. Fowl, his horse, nudged him and nibbled at his ear, but when Per pushed his head away, he cropped grass instead. There was little talk among the men. At last Per said, "Sweet Milk?"

Sweet Milk was sitting beside him, his heavy helmet laid on the ground. He looked up. "Aye?"

"Willst lead?"

"Lead?" Sweet Milk was puzzled.

"Be captain."

Sweet Milk was surprised, and took his time answering. Per was head of the Bedesdale Sterkarms now, and the lord of the Bedesdale Tower. He had always been eager to lead, and no one could challenge his right to lead this ride—not even his uncle, Gobby, had Gobby still been aboveground and breathing. Carefully Sweet Milk said, "Th'art captain."

Per was silent. He could barely think of two or three words to link together, his mind was in such a roil. He could feel the red, banked heat of anger at the back of his eyes, in his belly. Grief gripped him— so much grief that he hardly knew how to feel it. He couldn't get hold of even a small corner of it—it was so unwieldy and heavy that it threatened to flatten him. How could he mourn his father, his father's brother, and a cousin all at once?

And always, creeping just below his awareness, was the insidious, sickly memory of what he'd done. He'd been with the Elf-May when his father had been killed; and he had himself killed Joan Grannam, a girl, his wife.

She was a Grannam! A treacherous bitch, bred of a treacherous family. A slit throat and a quick death had been better than she deserved. She should have been strangled slowly. She should have been shut in a cage and starved.

No matter how he tried to shout it down, back the sickly guilt slithered. She had been helpless, defenseless, a woman, a girl child. He could not have killed her father, old man though he was, so easily, with so little risk to himself. Coward, his thoughts whispered. He heard the Elf-May, Entraya, saying that Joan had not killed his father. Joan had not hurt anyone.

But she would have if she'd been able! His banked rage flared up again, fiercely. Kill one Grannam bitch? He would kill the whole kennel of them! Every bitch and every bitch's get! There would not be a Grannam left breathing. But as his rage rose, tears rose too, as grief bit, as memories of his father, and what he had lost, rushed in. His mind dizzied, his sight blurred, he felt tremors through his whole frame. And a ride needed a clear head to lead it. It needed cool planning. A leader who would turn back, or turn aside, if the risk was too great. One who could, without mistake, choose the best way through the hills for their purpose—not the shortest way, perhaps, nor the easiest, but the best for their purpose. A clear head was needed just to remember all the many unmarked ways, and how the weather would have affected them, and how they connected up with all the other unmarked ways. There were a thousand things to consider, and he could think of nothing except his own anger and grief. Reaching out to grip Sweet Milk's arm, he said, "Thou art captain. I can no—" He shook his head.

Sweet Milk studied him. For an eye's blink he thought of refusing. He didn't grudge Per the tower and flocks he'd inherited; but he did begrudge him the favors of the Elf-May, who had seemed to be willing to dance with Sweet Milk until Per had smiled at her. Let Per lead the ride and make whatever mess he could of it. . . . But Sweet Milk knew that he was the best man there to lead, and that even in better times Per would have looked to him for advice. If he refused, if he sulked, then he endangered every other man. And Per, too. His foster son. Toorkild's son. And was it Per's fault that he was young and pretty?

Sweet Milk nodded. "I'll lead." He stared around, at the sky and hillside. "I'm grieved an' all." He'd seen his own father murdered long ago, when he'd been far younger than Per, and no death since had hit him as hard. Even so, it was hard to see Old Toorkild dead. Toorkild had taken him, a loose man, into his own family and, finding him capable and trustworthy, had made him foreman, and even foster father to his son.

There was a song—he couldn't remember it—*The best of friends will turn his back one day, and take the cold clay for his bed.* . . . Something like that. Friends, wives, children, they all died.

Gareth felt something looming over him and looked up, startled, to see Patterson standing by him in his camouflage fatigues. Grasping Gareth by the arm, he hauled him to his feet. "We need to ask some questions."

Gareth levered his aching body to its feet and limped after Patterson, between horses and men, to Sweet Milk and Per. "Ask them are we near. Do we know where the enemy is?"

Gareth translated. Perhaps he was a little offhand about it because he was so tired. Neither Sweet Milk nor Per answered, but Sweet Milk rose to his feet. The eyes of every man in the party were on him instantly. Leading his horse by the reins, Sweet Milk moved off. Per rose and, leading his own horse, followed him. Every man followed after them.

Oh God, Gareth thought. How much farther? How many more hills? How much longer?

Captain Davy, who called himself a Grannam, sat on the steep hillside, his knees drawn up, and glumly watched the scout who was scrambling sidelong to him along the steep slope. He didn't need to speak to the man. He simply raised his brows and cocked his head.

"No sign nor whiff," said the scout.

Davy sighed, a throaty rasp. Like the rest of the Grannam men lying and crouching on that slope, among the boulders and tall bracken, he was wet, hungry, and bored. Clearing his throat, he spat and said, "Where the frig are they?"

He started to worry again. He had brought his party here, to Urwin's Gap, because if he had been a Sterkarm it would have been the way he'd have chosen to come into Grannam country. But it was a guess, and he'd posted men in other places to watch and listen and bring him warning if they came by another way.

But he knew all too well that the Sterkarms were clever, devious animals, and would guess where he was waiting, and where he'd posted watchers, and could find some way to avoid them all—and he hadn't enough men to watch every hillside and dale. He'd had to leave some ways—those he'd thought most unlikely—unwatched. Were they already past him, and burning and killing in Grannam country? Were they at the tower?

Were they sneaking up on him here? Impossible, he told himself, but still he worried. He'd posted men to watch the approach to his position, and he should hear of the Sterkarms' coming long before they reached him, but . . . Sterkarms could hide behind a grass blade, horse and all.

Had he posted his men at the best places? Should he move them? But that would mean reducing his forces by sending other men after them, to give them his orders. Had he laid his ambushes in the best spots? In his head he flew over the hills, bogs, lakes, and woods like a crow, sending his men first by this way, then by that, fretting, worriting—only to decide, yet again, that he could do no better than he had done.

Come on, come on, he begged the Sterkarms. Let's be done with this.

Mistress Crosar climbed the stone steps within the tower's wall and came out on the tower's top. A stone walkway ran around the peaked, tiled roof at the center, and she followed it around to the corner where the small lookout turret rose, almost like a pulpit, with steps leading up to it. Close by, on the roof, was the dark shape of the beacon, an iron basket holding logs and kindling, with a lid to keep all dry.

She pulled her hood closer around her face, to guard herself from the wind that made her eyes water, and peered at the dark shape of the man on lookout, hunched against the sky. The bell was beside him, its rope close by his hand.

Mistress Crosar did not speak to him. There was no need to ask the only question she wanted to ask. If he saw anything to alarm him, he would ring the bell.

It had been pointless, climbing the steps to grow chilled on the roof. If the Sterkarms came, she would know about it soon enough, whether she was in the yard, the kitchens, or her bed. But when she had started climbing the stairs, it had seemed, somehow, that looking out from the roof would bring some ease to her worry. It had not. So down the stairs she went again, to sit, with clenched teeth and tight lips, beside her fire, where she thought of Joan and hoped the girl was not too badly treated and not too scared.

She had always said that no matter how much gold the Elves promised, no matter how much cloth and white pills they gave as presents, they should not marry Joan to a Sterkarm. "Never shake hands with a Sterkarm"–that was old wisdom.

But there. Her brother had thought he'd known better, as men always did. And now he was dead. You fool! she cried at him in her heart, and pounded her fists on her knees. You fool, you fool! But then she wiped away the small tears that had seeped from her eyes. What profit was there in raging at a dead man? Whatever came next, she must deal with it–and test her own wisdom.

Andrea ducked through the kitchen's low door. It was dark, hot, and smoky inside, and smelled of food cooking and of old food. "Can you tell me," she asked politely, "where I can find Mistress Sterkarm?"

The women working in the smoke, gutting fish and cleaning pots, looked at one another and called out. Where was the mistress? Anybody ken? "In the tower," one answered. "Poor lady."

Andrea left the kitchen and crossed the yard to the tower. The wooden door and the iron gate, or yett, behind it were standing open. The bawling of sheep came from inside, and when she entered, she found that several sheep and cows had been penned up in the low, barrel-ceilinged room. It smelled richly of dung and fleece, and Andrea was careful where she put her feet as she crossed to the iron grid that protected the stairs. She climbed to the first floor and the hall.

There were more people than usual gathered in the tower—almost all women and children—because the tower was expecting an attack. They weren't out in the country round about, as they would normally have been. Andrea stood in the doorway and looked around at the women by the fire and at those crouching on the benches, and she couldn't see Isobel among them.

"Where is Mistress Sterkarm?" she asked.

One woman pointed to the ceiling, where strings of flatbread and onions and legs of smoked mutton hung. "Up above," she said. "Poor lady."

The second floor of the tower was the family's private room: a bed-sitter it would be called in the 21st. Up there Isobel and Toorkild slept—had slept—and ate, and sat in the evening, if they had wanted to be private. Andrea left the hall and climbed again, to the landing outside the topmost room. The wooden door was shut.

Andrea stood outside. She didn't want to go in. Isobel—poor lady indeed—had lost her husband, and her only son was away on a ride in which he, too, might be killed. Isobel, she was sure, wouldn't want to see her.

But who else could help her? She tapped on the door. No response came from within.

She tapped again and waited, screwing up her face and biting her lip. Even if she was invited in, she couldn't think of anything to say that wouldn't be awkward in the extreme. Perhaps she should just go away?

No. She seized the iron ring handle, twisted it, and pushed the heavy door inward.

There was a large table in the center of the room and two armed chairs. Chests stood against the wall. She couldn't see Isobel anywhere.

"Mistress Sterkarm? Are you here?"

No answer. Nervously Andrea took a step or two into the room. The far side was taken up with a large curtained bed, and the curtains were partly drawn. Feeling guilty, Andrea crept over to the bed and peered through the gap in the curtains. Isobel lay on the bed, on her side, hugging a pillow.

"Mistress? May I speak with you?"

Isobel was silent as she struggled with herself. For twenty years she had risen at first light every day and set about the management of the tower. She had made it her business to see that everything was ordered in the kitchen, that the eggs were collected, the chickens and the pigs fed. She had overseen the milking of the cows, and the making of butter, cream, and cheese. She had seen to the storing and rationing of all food, ensuring, as best she could, that it neither went bad and was wasted nor ran out. She had brewed beer, had baked bread. She had seen that clothes and bed linen were laundered, made, repaired, and stored so that the moths did not eat them. She had seen that herbs were gathered and dried, for medicines, and for strewing the floors and scenting stored clothes. She had kilted up her skirts and helped with the driving of cattle to the summer sheilings, and with the harvesting—and had made sure that there were plenty of groats simmering in the kitchens for the harvesters to eat when they returned home tired and hungry. She had kept the tower and outbuildings clean and had kept an eye on the thatch and the walls, so she could nag Toorkild into repairing them.

All this work she had kept up while pregnant, calling her maids to her bed to report to her when she could not rise to do it herself. She had travailed and given Toorkild a son—only one—and she had nursed that son through childhood illnesses while ill herself with the most bitter anxiety. She had bitten her tongue when Toorkild had set the tiny, fragile child on the back of a horse, because she knew that the boy must learn to ride. She had choked back her fears when Sweet Milk had given him a little axe, and a little sword, and had taught him to use them, because she had known he must learn to fight. And after all this, all this, she had thought she might, today, with Toorkild dead and that still dear, still fragile child gone away to avenge him, she had thought that, this once, she might hide in her bed and, by stillness and quietness, attempt to smother all that she felt. She had thought that, this one day, for a little while, the household might go on its own way—the way that she had long established—and leave her in peace. But no. Here was someone come right into her private room, calling, "Mistress Sterkarm?" If it had been one of her maids, she would have made her ear sore, but she had not even so much luck. It was the Elf-May. So Isobel fetched up a deep, groaning sigh and said, in a tight, small voice, "What is it, Mistress Elf?"

Andrea's words stuck in her throat. What could she say? I want to talk about your husband's murder? I want to talk about the bullet wound in his head? And what could Isobel do, anyway? But she had to tell someone, she had to feel that she was doing something, however insignificant, to halt the killing. And Isobel was a resourceful woman. Perhaps she would instantly see something that could be done, while Andrea was bewildered. "I am so sad for your husband, Mistress Sterkarm."

Isobel said nothing. Andrea's eyes, growing used to the darkness within the curtains, saw that the pillow Isobel hugged had been dressed in a man's shirt. Unable to look any more, Andrea withdrew and sat on the edge of the bed, facing the rest of the room. "Mistress Sterkarm. The Elves—have pistols that shoot things they—we—call bullets. Not balls. Bullets."

These words meant hardly anything to Isobel—they were mere ramblings. Why should she care?

"Bullets aren't round," Andrea lectured on, wondering if Isobel was even listening. "They're long and narrow. The end is pointed and quite small, like the end of my finger. They're very hard, and they shoot from the pistol very, very fast, with great force. So when they hit something hard—well, they do flatten, but not nearly so much as a pistol ball made of soft lead. They make quite a small hole. Quite small."

From within the bed came Isobel's voice, soft and gruff. "Mistress Elf, what can I do for you?"

"I am sad," Andrea said, "I am so sad to speak this to you, but Mistress Sterkarm, the hole in Master Sterkarm's head . . . it was very small."

There was a stirring within the bed: a creaking of the wooden frame, a straining of heather ropes. A whiff of old hay and old sweat gusted out from the between the curtains. Isobel had raised herself on one elbow. "The hole in my man's head was big enough, Mistress Elf, big enough."

Andrea made herself go on. "But small. It wasn't made by a pistol ball. It was made by an Elf-Bullet."

The curtains parted with another gust of old hay. Isobel's face looked out. Her large blue eyes were red and sore, and she looked paler and older than usual. "What?"

"Mistress Sterkarm—what I am trying to say is that your husband wasn't shot by the Grannams. He was shot by—I am sad for it!—he was shot by Elves. And so were his brother and his brother's son."

Isobel stared at her. Andrea's words had no meaning for her at all. The Elves had shot Toorkild? There was no sense in it. She had always expected and feared that Toorkild would be killed by his great enemies, the Grannams. Now he had been. That made sense. She had no peace, no strength, no time, to consider anything else. "They were shot by the Grannams," she said.

"But the wounds were no made by pistol balls," Andrea repeated. "They were too small. They were shot by Elf-Pistols, loaded with Elf-Bullets. They were shot by Elves."

"Then the Grannams have Elf-Pistols," Isobel said wearily. "They are thieves. Traitors and liars and thieves. I told Toorkild. I told him."

"But Mistress Sterk—"

"No, no—all he could see was gold! So much gold. But not enough. Not enough."

"*Elf* Gold," Andrea said.

"He knew Grannams are never to be trusted. But all he could see was gold!" She punched and pounded the pillow beside her. "Thou fool! Fool! Thou wouldst no listen and now art killed! Fool!"

"Be so kind, listen," Andrea said.

"Such a fool! And now Per's away, and if he's killed too, I shall lie down and die. What is there for me? They should have buried me an' all—och, but I shall no lie easy until I have a hundred Grannam heads and hearts for my Toorkild!"

Andrea felt sick. Weren't women meant to ban the bomb and march for peace? Even in her own 21st, when they were free to choose whom they married, and to have sex with whomever they chose; when they were educated, and politically informed, and could vote; when they could drink, and smoke, and swear, they were still supposed to teach men how to be gentle, caring, and nurturing. Their fierceness was supposed to be directed toward peace. Isobel's hatred of the Grannams, and her thirst for blood and vengeance, made Andrea profoundly uneasy.

"Mistress Sterkarm, how could the Grannams have used Elf-Weapons?" She was thinking of night sights and silencers. "I am certain that your husband was shot by an Elf, on the orders of—of an Elf." Windsor, she thought, but was somehow shy of saying it aloud.

Isobel frowned. Two fine lines appeared between her large, silvery blue eyes. She was silent and seemed to be thinking long and hard. "The Elves want peace," she said. "They always have. They want no feuding, no riding. That's why they piled up the gold, piled it high, until Richie Grannam and my Toorkild agreed to what they never should have done!"

"I ken," Andrea said, "but—"

"So why would the Elves shoot my Toorkild? How would that bring them peace? How? They ken fine we would kill every last Elf—"

"That," Andrea interrupted, "that is why they wanted you to think the Grannams had done it."

"The Grannams did do it! They've always wanted Toorkild dead! And my Per—and all of us! Why would the Elves bring down all their own plans—why?"

It was a good question, and Andrea felt her heart sinking. "But the hole—"

"The hole! The hole! Some pistols are big and some are small. Some balls are big and some are small. Does that mean the Elves shot my Toorkild? No! Why would they? But a Grannam—och, a Grannam would have shot him in the back, in the dark."

Andrea found herself doubting, and felt foolish. Since when had she been a forensics expert, specializing in ballistics? But she remembered the sound she'd heard on the hillside in the dark . . . and Toorkild, Gobby, and Ingram, all with the same neat hole in the front of their heads. Sniper fire, picking off marked men with night-vision rifle sights. It was too neat, too accurate to be the work of Grannams, even if they had somehow got hold of Elf-Weapons. "It was the Elves," she said.

"But you are an Elf." Isobel had sat up, and her stare was hard. "Why would you, an Elf, betray your own to me?"

Andrea had no answer she could easily put into words. Because what Windsor had done was wicked and sneaky and wrong—simply wrong. Because she hated Windsor. Because she was afraid of what would happen next. She said nothing.

Isobel spoke slowly, as if voicing something she had just realized. "You are an Elf, but you are in the pay of the Grannams."

Andrea, in that other dimension, had liked Isobel—probably because Isobel had liked her—but she had always known that Isobel hated her enemies with intensity, and that she had been capable of spite and malice. Now that hatred was directed at her, and it was frightening.

"If they're waiting for us," Sweet Milk said as Per stood beside him, "they're up there." He pointed ahead and upward, toward the cleft that was just becoming apparent between two peaks. Gray and purple cloud gathered around the peaks. "And they ken we're coming."

Per, stroking the nose of his horse, nodded agreement.

Gareth, weary to his bones, sighed, heaved up his voice from somewhere deep inside him, and translated these words for Patterson and his Elves, though he suspected that they pretty much understood what Sweet Milk had said.

"I'll lead," Per said, and Sweet Milk glanced at him. "Up there." Per nodded toward the pass. "It'll gladden them to see me." There were grunts of amusement from those Sterkarms close enough to hear, though none from Sweet Milk. The Grannams might well recognize Per May, and they would indeed be glad of a chance to kill him.

"No need," Patterson said when Gareth translated. "We'll go in. They won't give us any trouble."

"I'll lead," Per said. It was one thing to give leadership to Sweet Milk where clarity of thought was needed. Here all that was needed was courage: the kind of blind, stupid courage that springs from anger and a need for revenge. "They'll be the more surprised."

"Ask 'em what weapons the Grannams'll have," Patterson said.

Gareth did. Per stared at the heather and scrub, making no attempt to answer. When he saw that answering was left to him, Sweet Milk said, "Axes. Swords. Bows. Clubs. Lances—but it's no a place to use lances. Pikes. Maybe a pistol or two."

Patterson squatted down, his hands clasped in front of him, to think. The pistols could be more or less dismissed. There was no guarantee—there were never any guarantees—that some Grannam with a pistol wouldn't succeed in shooting Per dead, but the 16th-side pistols were accurate only over a short range, often misfired, and were slow to reload. The axes, swords, and clubs would have to be used hand-to-hand, so the Grannams would have to come out of hiding and run down to meet Per and whoever was with him—and in doing that, they would expose themselves to Elf-Fire. The long-bows were another matter. They were really dangerous—or would be, for a short time.

"It's not worth the risk," Patterson said. "Tell him. He could be killed by an arrow before we could come in."

Gareth passed the words on, and Per said something. Patterson raised his brows questioningly. "He says there is no risk. That—er—the road of his death—er, that is—how can I say it?—the *way* he dies—but it's the same, the 'way,' the 'road' . . . they were—ah, foretold—no, fated—long ago. Let's say, '*The road he'll travel to death was fated long ago.*'"

"Bloody hell," Patterson said, impressed by this impromptu poetry, not realizing that Per was quoting from a ballad. "Well, it's his funeral. But tell him to leave his horse here. It'll only get in the way. And tell him to fall flat when I yell, or he'll get caught in our fire."

Gareth translated, and Per nodded. He turned and gave his lance and the reins of his horse to Ecky and then walked forward, climbing the horse trail toward the hilltops. Sweet Milk watched him go, feeling that familiar ache under the heart—but it made no sense for both leaders of the Sterkarms to be killed. Sim and Allie left their horses and followed Per, so that he shouldn't be alone. Patterson gestured his Elves to follow close behind them.

Davy Grannam watched the little straggle of men approach on foot. He felt the man nearest to him tense, like a cat watching a creeping mouse. He felt the same tension himself, and relief and excitement, too. At last, after all the boredom and discomfort of waiting, after all the uncertainty and worry, here were the Sterkarms—and approaching so confidently, so innocently. No need to be scared. It was going to be so easy.

But Davy's suspicions were tickled, and his face twisted into a thoughtful grimace. The Sterkarms, innocent? Trotting so trustingly into an ambush. Something was not right. . . .

"That's the May," said the man near him. "Per May!"

Other voices breathed the name, and Davy knew him too—by his height, his figure, and his walk more than anything, since he had on a helmet. But Per May, Big Toorkild's son, was a man the Grannams looked for, and noted. They would know him on a dark, moonless night. And if they were going to kill Sterkarms in revenge, then Per May's head was worth ten heads of lesser fry.

But why, Davy asked himself, would Per May walk—not ride, but walk—into a place where, being no fool, he might well expect an ambush. Something wrong, something wrong . . . Davy had half a mind to call off the ambush and let the Sterkarms through, because something was very wrong. He turned to the man nearest him and was raising his hand to signal to another a yard away—but his men weren't looking to him, and they waited for no orders. It was impossible to tell which had been the first to move, but someone had strung his bow at the first sight of the Sterkarms, and now stood and loosed an arrow. And there was another, standing, raising his bow, and another. Davy heard the soft throb of the string only from the nearest man, and the arrows were too slender and fast to be seen, but he knew that many were flying, silently, well aimed, toward the men below.

Per could feel the blood pulsing along the center of his bones. He knew that if the Elves were slow, or if the Grannams were lucky, in the next breath an arrow could drive through his throat, or a pistol ball punch through his jaw. The fear of pain and the fear of death tightened his back as he took one step after another. He saw the men come to their feet among the rocks and knew they were archers. He didn't see the arrows loose, but he felt the air shift against his face as one went by. The archer had his range; the next would hit.

"Nether!" Patterson yelled. "Nether!"

Per threw himself down.

On the hillside above, Davy Grannam saw the Sterkarms throw themselves down on the ground—and hadn't begun to wonder why when a sound he'd never heard before took all thought away. It was loud—it deafened. He couldn't have said what made it, or even what direction it came from. He saw his men rise in the air and fly backward. They fell from the air, crashing down on the hard hillside. His body turned cold and heavy with fear.

Other men rose from their hiding places—maybe to attack, maybe to run. Some Sterkarms threw things. Head-cracking bangs, flashes, men screaming—bawling out in fear, shrieking in pain. Their jakkes, their helmets, weren't saving them.

Davy didn't see what landed near him; he hardly heard the cracking bang or saw the flash. But the pain filled him, intense, sudden pain. He fell.

The surviving Grannams broke cover and ran. They ran up the steep slopes. They ran down. The Elves followed; their pistols banged and crackled. The Grannams fell, with smashed legs or bodies ripped open.

The din stopped. There was no one else to run. The Elves waited warily, then relaxed slightly, though they still scanned the hillsides around them. Patterson said, "All yours, lads."

The Sterkarms couldn't have understood what he said, but they knew what he meant. They rose from the ground and went to work. Gareth watched in helpless dismay. Scrambling up the hillsides and among the rocks and bushes, they found the wounded and dying Grannams and finished them. Removing their valuable helmets, they pounded in their heads with clubs. They cut their throats. They hacked off hands and they hacked off heads. They turned what had been living, thinking men into carrion, and they did it in minutes.

Gareth couldn't speak. He sat on a boulder and watched the men coming back together. The Elves were a little muddied; the Sterkarms were bloodied. All about the hillside lay bodies and parts of bodies and pieces of flesh and flesh jellied by close explosions. Just lying there. It would rot. It shouldn't be like that.

Per took little part in the killing. He came loping down the hillside, stopped near Gareth, and cleaned his dagger in the grass and moss. Then he sat down on the rock beside Gareth, who wanted to cringe away from him. Per said nothing and looked furious, and even if Gareth had had anything to say, he would have been scared to speak to him.

Patterson, cradling the great Elf-Pistol in his arms, nodded at Gareth but spoke to Per. "How'd you like them apples?"

Gareth couldn't speak. Per, even if he could have understood Patterson's words, wouldn't have understood their sense, but he spoke anyway, angrily.

"What's he say?" Patterson asked.

Gareth shook his head.

Patterson gave his leg a nudge with his boot. "Wake up! What's he say?"

Gareth made an effort. It was like mouthing clay and ashes. "He says. It's like the autumn killing."

"Eh?"

"They kill most of the animals in the autumn so there's fewer to keep through the winter." It was quite easy to talk about history. "He says it's a job for a butcher."

Patterson stared at Per for a moment, then shrugged. "He wanted 'em dead, they're dead."

Per jumped up and walked a few paces away, turned, walked back, turned again, too furious to keep still. He had thought that killing so many Grannams would bring some relief; but his rage was still there, like a smothered fire: red, sullen, choked. The Elves had done the killing, and left the Sterkarms the butcher's job. How was that revenge?

"Now then," Patterson said. "What next? Do we find the other ambush party, or do we go for the tower? My vote's for the ambushers, because if we leave them, they'll get behind us, and we don't want any bother, do we?" He looked at Gareth and wagged his head toward Per. "Gareth? Do the honors?"

Gareth found himself hearing Patterson's words belatedly, and fear made him hurry to translate them. He didn't want angry Grannams coming up behind him. Especially when they had such reason to be angry.

Per listened to the translation and then said, *"Vi gaw til tur."* We go to the tower.

Patterson didn't need a translation. "Tell him! About 'em getting behind us. Finish the job first, then go to the tower."

Gareth started to translate, but Per cut him short. *"Vi gaw til tur."* The more difficult it was, the more revenge was earned.

Mistress Crosar drearily swept up old rushes—the noise of the stiff broom twigs hushed, hushed against the stone flags, and the rushes whispered—and she told Joan to keep her eyes and her thoughts on her stitching. Joan sat in a chair, stitching, and the blood poured from her pricked fingers all over the chemise she worked on. Mistress Crosar swept on until the insistent sound of the brush on the stone became the hard clang, clang of a bell, and she started up.

Sweeping rushes, she thought. How ridiculous. How long is it since I swept rushes? I should set a maid to do it.

The bell. Her heart tightened, and she got up from her bed where she'd been dozing, fully dressed. Her maid shoved open the door. "Riders, mistress!"

"Theirs or ours?"

The maid grabbed the cloak from the bed and swung it around Mistress Crosar's shoulders. "We can no tell. But riders—riders!"

Mistress Crosar needed no candle on the dark, close stairs, she knew them so well. She stepped from the door at the top into the chill, strong, damp wind and made her way around the roof to the lookout turret, where the man on watch still clanged the bell. He made room for her to join him and, for a moment, stopped his ringing. "There, mistress." He pointed. "D'you see? There?"

Clots of darkness, moving in darkness. When she squinted at them, they formed themselves into something like horses moving, with blobs on their backs that might have been men.

"Who are they?"

"Sterkarms, mistress."

The answer shocked her, even though she'd been expecting it. "How dost ken?"

"They'd be whooping and cheering if they was ourn."

Mistress Crosar stared at the moving blobs, thinking that they might still be Grannam men who didn't feel like whooping and cheering. There might be no reason to fear. She said, "Fire the beacon."

She went back down to the roof and stood aside in a corner, to let the man take the lid from the beacon and fire it with the fire canister he had by him. It took a while to catch but then flared up, casting showers of red sparks and tongues of red and yellow light over the roof. The shadows deepened. Mistress Crosar felt the skin of her face tighten in its heat. She looked out over the dark countryside, imagining the beacon carrying its message. Every Grannam tower and bastle house that saw it would fire its own beacon and pass the message on. Help would come.

Every tower had its beacon and bell, to signal its danger to other towers within sight, and so any party besieging a tower would soon be attacked from the rear by those answering the signal. Raiding parties usually relied on speed, attacking small farms, driving off the cattle, and making a dash for home with their booty before armed men from the towers could retaliate.

So Per felt a fierce, gleeful eagerness to see the Elves fire on the Brackenhill Tower: It spat and crackled in the heat of the rage he still felt. Even now, even as they peered from the walls, the Grannams believed that as long as they stayed locked inside, with the beacon blazing on the roof and the bell clanging, no great harm could come to them. But the laugh was on them, now that the Elves had seen sense. Make peace with the Grannams? The only way to make peace with the Grannams was to kill them all. The Elves had been slow to learn that, but they had learned it at last.

The Sterkarms and Elves had reached the tower as quickly as they could, but even so, the farms they'd passed had been deserted. News had flown over the hills. The people knew that the Grannams and the Sterkarms were killing each other again, and they were on the watch. At the merest suspicion that the riders in the distance were armed with lances, the people had left everything and run. It was Sweet Milk who left their farms standing. Per would have burned them. Sweet Milk said that would waste time.

They left men in the hills to watch for the approach of any party coming to the tower's rescue and then rode to within a good bow-shot of the red-gray walls of the tower, before the gate, and there they dismounted and settled to watch the Elves assembling their cannon, which, though small enough for a man to raise to his shoulder, was yet more destructive and powerful than anything men had. Other Elves stood ready to meet any Grannams with their many-shooting pistol, and their grenates that ripped folk to ribbons.

Elf-Patterson and Elf-Burnett put the cannon together and then knelt, took aim at the tower's gate, and fired. The first two shots fell short, with ear-tearing bangs and blinding flashes, but then they had the range. The third exploded against the stonework, sending chips flying. The fourth squarely hit the wooden gate and, crashing, booming, reduced it to flinders. The Sterkarms cheered, though their yells seemed faint among the wide hills.

The explosion, muffled as it was by the thickness of the stone walls, was the loudest anyone in the tower had ever heard. The tower shook with its impact, carrying the tremor through its stones far from the gate. The people felt the blow reverberate through their bones. Mistress Crosar, on the roof, was shaken by it. "What was that?"

The watchman leaned from his turret but shook his head.

Something fell in the courtyard of the tower. There was a flash and a deep *k-rump!* of sound, cuffing their heads. After the noise there was a moment of dead silence: then the cries broke through—cries of terror, alarm, and pain.

"Fire!" came a woman's shout from below, and that jolted Mistress Crosar back on her heels. The tower's yard was full of thatched buildings, and most of the upper stories were built of wood. If fire took hold, they would be trapped in a furnace. She made for the stairs.

* * *

The Elves sent their rockets again and again against the tower door, splitting and crumbling the stone, reducing the iron yett to a glowing twist. They sent firebombs arcing into the castle. Per had given up cheering with every explosion, but he watched, grinning, jumping with glee. Soon, he saw, it would be time for someone to lead the way through the tower gate. He looked around and then went to one of his footmen.

"Andy—give me thine axe."

Andy frowned, reluctant.

Per put his hand on the axe's shaft. "Give it to me. I'll pay thee. I want to lead us in."

Andy handed over the long-shafted axe then, feeling proud that the May was going to use *his* axe and lead them, the footmen. Whatever chaos was in the tower, however weakened were the Grannams by the Elf-Shot, everyone knew that the first man through the tower's low gate into its yard was likely to be the first Sterkarm killed. "And it was my axe," Andy would be able to say, in the future. "It was my axe in the May's hand when he led us into Brackenhill Tower."

"Milk—bring milk!" Mistress Crosar shouted. Her hair was down, her cloak lost. Sparks and ash were flying around her and smoldering in her skirts. Smoke from the burning thatch was thick and harsh and was filling the narrow alleys, and so was heat. Mistress Crosar could feel sweat on her hot face, beneath her arms and breasts. Women, silent, determined, ducked into the dairy to fetch pans of milk to throw on the fires. Mistress Crosar watched one large pan of milk thrown at a patch of burning thatch. Most of it missed. The liquid that landed spat and sizzled in the flames, sending up more smoke and a stink of burning milk. It quenched one patch of fire, but sparks and tongues of flame jumped free and caught at other thatch and at the wood of the shutters and walls. Seeing it, Mistress Crosar knew, deep within her, that it was hopeless—but she turned and took a bucket of water another woman had lugged from the well. One hand on the handle, the other beneath the pail, she heaved the heavy bucket up with a wrench of her back and threw the water onto a thatch.

Other women were pulling down burning thatch and stamping on it. "Good, good!" Mistress Crosar cried, and took a pitchfork from a woman and herself heaved down a great lump of burning thatch that filled the narrow alleyway. The heat grew fiercer and she was enveloped in smoke. It sizzled, and the smoke thickened as another woman emptied a bucket on the thatch before it could set light to the walls.

But then there was no one nearby with water or milk, and the flames were crackling again on the thatch overhead, and the shutters and a ladder were burning. Through their feet they felt the tremor of another explosion, and a heavy despair settled at Mistress Crosar's heart.

A crack, and a wicked, hissing shearing of metal. Hot, sharp fragments bit deep into the wall nearby, making Mistress Crosar flinch. A woman hurrying up with another bucket gave a great gasp, wailed, and fell. Mistress Crosar dropped her bucket, trampled over the remains of smoldering thatch, and bent over the woman, who was squealing and sobbing in pain and fright. Above them flames leaped up onto the thatch. Mistress Crosar stooped and heaved the woman into her arms, ignoring her cries of pain and struggles, and with another heave dragged her toward the end of the alley. Through the smoke came another woman, who bundled up the injured woman's legs and skirts. Another explosion, more cries of alarm.

They emerged into the small yard area before the tower. Someone running past barged into Mistress Crosar and almost knocked her from her feet. From all around came screams, cries, shouts, and the sounds and stinks of burning. Mistress Crosar was aware, too, of small, smarting, bleeding cuts on her hands and face. A *whumf!*—a sound both loud and soft—made them look up, into a glare of heat and firelight, as a whole thatch went up. Still holding the injured woman in her arms, Mistress Crosar shouted, "Fill more buckets! Fill more—" She realized that, though people were running past, dodging in and out of the smoke, no one was listening to her or noticing her at all. Oh God, she thought, looking at the flames and shifting shadows through clouds of smoke: I may not live through this. Oh God: Receive my soul. Oh God: Have a care for my niece, Joan. She's but a lassie, after all, and not the worst of them.

Per watched the Elf-Shot arcing through the air and falling behind the tower walls. His heart rose with it and beat faster. Smoke rose from the burning, and between the dull blows of explosions shrill cries could be heard. That was fear he was hearing. His body recognized it and responded with its own fear and excitement.

He shifted his hands on the long shaft of the axe; shifted them again and again as they sweated, thinking of his father in his grave, his father's brother and his own cousin bundled in beside him. Deliberately he loosed his rage, and it burned up and burned hot. Opening his mouth, he pulled in deep breaths to fuel it. Soon, he knew, he was going to fight desperate, trapped men.

The Elves ran forward, knelt, and sent one of their shots right through the tower's gate, like a visitor coming to call. Smoke, dust, and noise came pouring out from the opening. "*Gaw noo!*" Patterson yelled. "*Gaw noo!*" Go now!

Per looked around. Everyone was looking at every other man and hanging back. They all knew that, when they went into that narrow space, into the smoke darkness, there would be men waiting with axes, with clubs, with spears. The first man through would be killed, if he was lucky. Maimed if he was not.

Per ran at the gatehouse. If he thought about it, he wouldn't do it. Behind him, men yelled, "Sterkarm!" and followed him.

The broken stones of the gatehouse and the twisted remains of the yett gave out heat as Per ducked into the low opening. His nose was filled with an Elvish reek, his lungs with choking smoke that made him feel he'd been punched in the chest. His hair moved beneath his helmet and his skin prickled with the expectation of an axe in the face. Then he was through the gatehouse's tunnel and into the courtyard, where there was more air, though much smoke, and here was a man, swinging at him.

He sprang sideways, collided with a hard, solid body, which fell. Per fell on top of the man, a yell in his ears. He struggled to rise, bruising himself on the iron plates in his own jakke and the hard bones of the fighting man beneath him. Desperate because he couldn't see what was behind and above him, or to the side, Per hammered at the fallen man with the blunt end of his axe shaft and, when the man stilled, lurched to his feet, turning to glimpse, in the smoke, the dark shape of a man behind him.

"Sterkarm!" it said, in Sweet Milk's voice, and Per fell in with him, both of them peering into the smoke ahead of them. Something moved, and Per lunged at it, feeling a rush in his ears as he sensed his opponent's sharp-edged blow coming at him. His axe blade connected, jarring up the bones of his arms and into his shoulders. He was tugged sideways by the trapped axe as the man he'd hit fell. Per tugged, but the axe didn't come free—it wasn't a weapon he was used to. Behind and around him was a tin-pot clattering, a babble of yells, screams, heavy footfalls, bashes as bodies fell against walls, gasps, coughs, barking of dogs, and screaming of alarmed sheep and pigs.

Per tugged frantically at the axe—while it was trapped, he was weaponless. He staggered as it came free but managed to kick aside the axe blade that was feebly raised against him from the ground. He swung around, but no one was near him. In that few eye blinks he realized that he was in the tower and, as yet, without a scratch. He raised an exultant yell of "Sterkarm!"

The smoke was clearing and he could see Grannam men, their dirty faces set in grins under their helmets, holding axes at the ready. One lay on the ground, screaming in short gasps, but there was no time to give him any attention. The defenders were battered, confused, and scared; they took short steps backward, but still they were there to stop the Sterkarms crossing the paved yard and entering the maze of little alleys and closes where the women and children were fighting fires.

Per sprang forward, swinging his axe in an arc, and the Grannams, unnerved by the Elf-Shot, stumbled back. But they had axes too, and Per halted. Fighting on foot, with an axe, was not what he was trained for, but he knew the long axe was a terrible weapon. If he swung at their legs, they could aim a blow that would take off his head. If he swung at their heads, they could cut him off at the knees.

He swung the axe in a figure eight, going forward, yelling, "Sterkarm!" The Grannams hastily fell back, but then they were at the entrances to the alleys. Their women and children were behind them, and they stopped.

Per stopped. Other men were coming up behind him, footmen who knew how to use the axe. He could send them forward, but—then it wouldn't be his leadership that gained his revenge.

"Mind your backs." Patterson shouldered through, the other Elves shoving behind him. They raised Elf-Pistols. The noise sent the Sterkarms spinning away: a harsh, deafening chatter. The Grannams went down, yelling out, pouring blood. The Elf-Balls punched through jakkes, shattered legs, ripped out chunks of flesh, exploded heads. The Sterkarms fell back and gaped.

The pistols stopped, and the sounds were moans, women's cries, the crackling and roaring of fire, a pig screaming in panic.

Per felt anger at being robbed, then relief at still being alive and unhurt—especially looking at the butcher's shambles before him. Then he felt joy: of being alive, of winning, of revenge. He yelled, "Sterkarm!" and ran into the nearest alley, jumping over, jumping on, the bodies that lay in the way. Behind him he heard running feet and his own cry repeated.

Here, in the alleys, was more smoke and the thick stink of damp, burning thatch. Flames roared, and the air jumped. It was hot. A shadow moved in the smoke, and Per swung his axe at it, chopping it down. Its cry of appalled surprise and pain was a woman's. Per stamped his foot against the fallen body, jerked the axe free, and ran on.

The clothes of the woman at her feet were rapidly soaking with blood, the thatches above were burning, and from nearer the tower's gate came yells and a clattering, then screams and cries of "The Sterkarms! The Sterkarms!"

It was a warning, shouted in panic. The women stopped trying to help those hurt. They stopped trying to put out the fire—instead they ran through the narrow alleys for the tower, jumping or tripping over the wounded, flinching from flames, bumping into one another. Once behind the tower's thick door and iron yett, inside its stone walls, they would be safe.

Mistress Crosar didn't run. She caught at the arms of those passing. "Help—" None wanted to help her carry the wounded woman. There wasn't time. "Wait—"

"Sterkarms!" a woman screamed in her face, and shoved her away.

Mistress Crosar heard a male yell, a roar of wordless anger. She saw figures move in the smoke. She ran for the tower herself. An axe chopped into her back, knocking her flat in the mud and smoldering, fallen thatch. The axe chopped at her head. Then the man trod on her as he ran on to the tower.

The yard of the tower was crowded with storehouses, stables, kennels, smithies, dairies—all of them thatched and most of them with wooden upper stories. Many of them were now well ablaze, and most were somewhere on fire. Smoke was thick in the alleys, and a glaring, shifting light reflected off smoke. It stank and clogged the lungs. Burning thatch was falling into the alleys, and whole walls threatened to come down. The heat was intense.

"Out!" Patterson yelled, and made shooing signals at his men.

The Sterkarms were still hunting through the alleys, yelling and whooping hunting calls, mad to kill and utterly blind to danger.

The Elves made their way back to the gatehouse and ruined gate. Fire made them turn back twice, seeking another way through the alleys. The roar of burning and the heat was constant, and Patterson was sure that he'd left it too late and trapped his men as well as himself. But they found the gatehouse and emerged thankfully on the hillside, where it was relatively free of smoke, and cool, and open. The men he'd left on watch were waiting, and Gareth.

Patterson laid down his gun, and while removing his helmet and wiping his dirty, sweating face, he stood in front of Gareth, looking at the kid's anxious face. He said, "Fuck me. Wind 'em up and let 'em go."

"What?" Gareth said. He kept glancing from Patterson to the smoke and flames rising above the tower walls. He was trying to keep himself from asking if that should be happening.

"Your pals. They're still in there."

"Mad buggers," Atwood said without admiration.

"Place is burning down around their ears," Patterson said, "but they don't want to miss anybody out."

"Women and bloody kids," another man said.

Burnett laughed. "Equal fucking opportunities."

Yes, but they're not real people, Gareth found himself thinking. They're history-book people, not real people. It's only like turning a page in a history book—"Brackenhill Tower was taken by assault."

A woman's yell rose above the noise of the fire—not the operatic scream of a film's soundtrack but the choked, astonished yell of a woman whose voice only reached that pitch and volume because of a terror and desperation that Gareth had never felt in his life—but an impression of it thrilled along his nerves at the sound. All the men looked around and froze at that yell—then realized that there was nothing they could do, and relaxed.

"Happy days," Patterson said.

The Sterkarms came ducking out of the gatehouse, coughing,

gasping, spitting, and ran over to them. Not all of them were there, and as they came nearer, the faces under the helmets were so streaked with blood, sweat, and dirt that they were impossible to recognize. And they were carrying heads. Human heads were dangling from their hands by the hair. They slowed to a walk near the Elves, and they were laughing. They threw the heads down on the hard ground. Thump, they went.

Gareth looked away as soon as he realized what the things were, but then he looked back again, fascinated. He'd never seen a head, cut off, before. He had to know the worst. They looked surprisingly normal. Just heads, but ending at the neck. He felt himself turning cold, shudders running through his flesh. These had been people, alive, full of their own concerns. . . . If this could be done to them, it could be done to him.

Someone slapped his shoulder and made him jerk with shock. It was Patterson, yelling at him. "What?"

"What's he saying?"

The man beside Patterson was Per Sterkarm—Gareth could see that, now he'd wrenched off his helmet. His fair hair stuck up in sweat-fixed spikes. Per pointed back toward the tower and said something urgently. Gareth tried to concentrate, with his eyes straying again toward the heads lying on the ground. One was a *woman's* head. A woman . . .

"What's he bloody say?"

"Ahh . . . he wants you to put a shell—or a rocket, or whatever they are—through the roof of the tower," Gareth said.

"There's only women and kids in there," Burnett said. "We ain't doing that, Skip. Are we?"

Per pointed to the burning tower. "That's a beacon fire. Every Grannam who sees it will light beacons, and they'll come here with as many men as they can raise. And more will come after. Can you kill them all? Even with your Elf-Cannon, can you kill them all?" He paused, to let Gareth translate, but paced up and down and didn't let Gareth finish before adding, "If we leave the tower, they'll use it again—use it against us. Put a bomb through its roof! Do it now!"

Gareth stumbled over the words. He found them turning to dry, clogging earth in his mouth, almost impossible to form or spit out. Never before had his words been directly responsible for killing. But by the time his voice dried altogether, he'd translated enough.

In silence Patterson stooped, took a rocket from the box at his feet, and loaded it into his launcher.

"Skipper—" Burnett said.

"See that?" Patterson nodded toward the heads lying on the ground. "You think we've got nothing to do with that?" He knelt, raising the launcher to his shoulder.

"We're just doing their dirty work," Burnett said.

Another man, Ledbury, took out a rocket and loaded it. "We're being paid to do their dirty work." He loaded and knelt.

Everyone stuck their fingers in their ears and watched as first one rocket, then a second, went arcing up. Mouths agape, they watched the trails of smoke, watched them curve down. The first hit the tower's tiled roof near one corner, at the edge—the second struck an eye blink later, more centrally. The explosions came to them as one blast, blowing high dust, tiles, splintered wood. They watched the dust cloud expand, lose its shape, drift. The Sterkarms cheered. They linked arms, danced, and cheered.

The tower itself was burning now. Gareth looked at it, feeling half stunned as he thought of how those rockets, having pierced the tiled roof, would have blown through the wooden floor beneath and fallen into the hall, probably crowded with women and children. He didn't want to think any further than that, but his mind ran on anyway, showing him pictures of metal shards slicing flesh open, of wooden splinters shot through soft bodies, of bones shattering, veins spilling blood, arms and legs parting company with bodies. . . . Was anyone in the tower still alive?

"Away! Away!" The Sterkarms had gathered up the heads, and they were running away from the tower, back to the moor where they'd left the rest of the horses, and they were whooping and laughing.

Gareth hurried after them, afraid of being left behind, but he was thinking, with misery, of all the way they had to travel back—all those hills, and all those streams and bogs. He could feel all his muscles aching and twanging as he ran. And this is what I think of, he thought, when I've just seen people butchered—I think of my own aches and pains. But then, he was amazed that he could still think at all.

18

16TH SIDE:
THE ELVES' OFFER

††††

Y ou'll no touch me," Andrea said. "You're no locking me up
anywhere—you're no!"

"I'll no leave you to run round," Isobel said. "There's no
telling what you might do."

The two big men—elderly, but still big men—edged farther into the
room. There were also several women—big, strapping border lasses.

"I am no working for the Grannams," Andrea said, and stepped
sharply back, raising her hands, as the men and women moved
closer. "I am an Elf! I am a friend of Elf-Windsor! If you lock me
up—if you touch a hair of my head—you'll answer for it to the Elves!"
That made them halt. Andrea looked at Isobel. "If you insult me,
there'll be no more white pills. No more favor from the Elves."

Isobel set her hands on her hips, stuck out her lower lip, and
snorted down her nose. "Then you stay here, Mistress Elf! You shall
no go to my kitchens, nor about my storerooms. Here! With a guard."

Isobel was always one to keep her word. So Andrea was sitting in
one of the armed chairs by the fireplace in the tower's topmost, private room—and remembering how she'd been imprisoned there
before. Per had been away fighting then too—but that time he'd
been waylaying Elves, not Grannams. Had that been a different Per,
or not?

It was hard to think about it without confusion. *Would* her Per
have slit the throat of a helpless girl?

No. He wouldn't. He just wouldn't. He'd fought, yes, and probably
killed, in defense of his land, but he hadn't killed women and children. He'd had courage and a kind of honor. . . .

Don't romanticize, Andrea. It's all circumstance. Don't we all change, and sometimes drastically, when our circumstances change?

Better stop philosophizing, she thought, and hope that this Per comes back alive, and that he's enough in lust with you, at least, to save you from Isobel . . . or that Windsor turns up soon and has enough fellow feeling for another Elf to get you out of here. . . .

When they'd first left the ruined and burning Brackenhill Tower, Per's spirits had been soaring with all the exultation of winning and still living. And he'd had his revenge, more than paid the blood debt, and won fame—he was the Sterkarm who'd attacked and destroyed the Brackenhill Tower.

The others had been in good spirits too, and their long way home had been lightened by memories of the Brackenhill Tower, shattered and burning. "Dost mind how the tower went up? *Kaboom!* The way he ran! Nobody's ever mined a tower afore."

They'd taken, as always, a different way home from the one they'd come by, threading their way through the hills, and they'd run into a party of Grannams, maybe one of those coming to see why the tower burned. Instead of riding to meet them, or running from them, or trying to outmaneuver them, they'd simply sent the Elves forward. The Grannams, unsuspecting, had come onto the fight. The Elves had ripped them into pieces without even getting near them. The Sterkarms had laughed and cheered, and ridden over what was left of the bodies, lancing them.

Now, hours later, the hilarity, for Per, had cooled and congealed. He rode glumly, head down. In his mind, again and again, he saw his father's grave in the little graveyard by the roofless chapel. A grave so new, the earth was still bare, ungreened. The glee, the easing of grief that battle and vengeance had brought, were gone, and the chill left behind was deeper, bleaker. At his saddlebow, by his knee, hung the head of Richie Grannam's sister—it had seemed a fitting revenge when he'd hung it there and would satisfy those at home. The killing of his father, father's brother, and cousin had needed a response so fierce . . . but his father was still dead.

He was too tired to feel it strongly, but it came back to him with renewed certainty that every Grannam had to die to pay this debt. Every Grannam man, and every woman, so no more would be bred. Every Grannam child and baby, so no more would reach an age to kill Sterkarms. And everyone who allied themselves to the vermin. It meant a long, weary time of riding ahead, and he was very tired. Head nodding as he rode, he thought of bed: a warm bed . . . and that led him, inevitably, to think of women. It would be very good to lie in bed with a soft, warm woman, and then, after he'd slept, to play with her. The Elf-May came to mind. A very bonny woman. He wondered if she'd still be at the tower.

Gareth had never been more tired—he was almost too exhausted to think. Sooner or later, he kept telling himself, they had to come in sight of the Bedesdale Tower, and then it would be over. Or nearly over. When the tower did come into view, he felt a spurt of pure joy—and then realized that it was still miles away. And felt like crying.

An age later, a weary age of trudging on legs that could hardly feel the ground, one of the riders drew his pistol and fired it in the air, with a blast that made Gareth's flesh leap on his bones. He clutched at his heart in shock. Ahead of him, all the men hollered, waved, and bawled, eager to let the waiting women know what heroes were returning to them. No response came from the tower. The Grannams were roused and riding, so the women stayed behind the walls, until the riders came so close they could recognize them.

Faced with climbing the steep path to the tower, Gareth sat down on the ground. He'd walked so far and climbed so many slopes; he'd fallen and slipped back, and had to cover the same ground again; he'd scrambled over rocks and jumped or splashed through streams. Now his feet were hot and throbbing. He couldn't climb that hill. He didn't care if the Grannams got him. His muscles were too sore to lift his heavy feet for another step.

He was yards behind the last footman, so there was no one to laugh at him. He hung his head down between his knees and luxuriated in not moving.

Maybe he dozed. He was startled by the clop of a hoof close by him and jerked up his head, his heart thumping, half expecting to see a murderous Grannam swinging an axe. Instead he saw the big man with the odd name, Sweet Milk, leading his horse. Unsmiling— he didn't smile much—he held out his hand. Gareth gave him his hand and was hoisted to his feet with one strong pull. Sweet Milk held his horse's head and, with a nod, indicated that Gareth should mount the horse.

"I can no," Gareth said. He knew that his aching legs would never lever him up that high.

Per came out from behind Sweet Milk. Gareth was surprised to see him. To his even greater surprise, Per crouched down and cupped his hands, offering him a boost onto the horse's back. How could he refuse? Though doubtful of actually landing on the horse's back, Gareth took hold of the saddlebow, set his foot in Per's hands, felt himself catapulted into the air, and somehow did land neatly astride the horse. The saddle was hard as stone, and full of uncomfortable ridges. As Gareth settled onto it and tried to put his feet in the stirrups, he saw something furry or hairy hanging by his knee. With a feeling as if icy water was being filtered through him, he realized that it was a head. He shrank back from it—it felt as if the flesh was creeping along his bones to get away from it. Sweet Milk noticed, and while Per tightened the horse's girth and adjusted the stirrup leathers, Sweet Milk quickly unlashed the head. Gareth thought he carried it by its hair, in his hand. He could hardly believe this or grasp that the man carrying the head was being kind, but at least the thing wasn't near him anymore.

"Thanks shall you have," he said to both Per and Sweet Milk, in a voice that shook. They barely glanced at him, both seeming tired and depressed. Sweet Milk led the horse Gareth rode, and Per came behind, leading his own horse. They didn't seem to find climbing the hill difficult, but then they'd ridden part of the way to Grannam country and most of the way back. That also meant the horse he was riding was too tired to give him any trouble, for which he was deeply grateful.

When, after a long, slow climb, they reached the gatehouse of the tower, Isobel was waiting, on tiptoe, craning her neck, looking for Per. With cries of gladness, she retreated before them, through the dark, dank, muddy tunnel of the gatehouse, where the horse's hooves rang out and echoed, into the courtyard. Women were hugging men, horses were being led away with a clattering of hooves, children were dancing and whooping, dogs were running about, jumping up and barking, chickens were fluttering and clucking, and all was a flurry of noise and movement. Per's horse was taken from him and led away, and Isobel threw her arms around him, crying out, "I'm gladdened to have thee back! Oh, I'm glad!"

Sweet Milk helped Gareth down from the horse and was then enveloped by a couple of young women. Gareth, aching in every muscle, stood amid the jostling. No young women bothered Gareth. He felt very lonely, and longed for somewhere to lie down and stretch out.

Through the laughter and babble rose thin, screeching wails that seemed to scrape down Gareth's backbone. Some women were keening. Two men had been lost in the fire, and not even their bodies brought back. The glad chatter hushed gradually, as more and more people turned to comforting the bereaved.

"We killed a sight more of them!" someone said, and one man was holding up a human head before an audience of impressed, appalled, and delighted children.

"There's hot water," Isobel was shouting. "There's food! Oh God, but we're gladdened to see you all back!"

Everyone was heading for the tower and the hall. Gareth dragged himself up the stone stairs, one step at a time, driven on by the promise of food. Yes, he longed to lie down, but it would be good for his belly to have something to occupy itself with while he slept. In the hall, long trestle tables had been set up, and at one end water steamed in wooden tubs. The men stripped off their shirts and washed away sweat, dirt, and blood, while the women handed them towels or even dried them.

At the other end of the table were set out plates of flatbread and butter, cheese, cold meat, cold porridge, and dried fish—a feast. Even before they were dried off, the men wandered down to that end of the table and started eating. Gareth found himself sitting on the hard stone floor amid the straw—it was better than standing—and relishing great mouthfuls of hard flatbread with butter and cold mutton. A woman handed him a cup of ale, and he took a big swig. It was thick, like thin porridge, and rather sweet, but with more alcoholic punch than its taste and appearance led you to expect. It was "festival ale," the first brew, a special treat for returning heroes.

"We blew down the tower!" someone near him was saying.

"Burned it!"

Feet rustled in the straw, disturbing the scent of dried herbs. The peat smoke had a sharp, throat-catching reek. A big dog sloped past him, smelling rankly of smoke and its own dirty coat.

"Not a Brackenhill Grannam left alive!"

It would be many days—maybe weeks or months—before the account was worked up into a coherent story.

"Mammy," Per said, "I'll gan up the stairs and sleep."

"The Elf-May is up there," Isobel said.

Per stretched and said, appreciatively, "Good." Those who heard him laughed.

"I locked her up there," Isobel said crossly. "Leave her bide. She's—she's—a *Grannam.*"

Silence. Those who knew what Isobel meant waited eagerly, to see what would come of this. Those who didn't stared at Isobel and each other.

"She's a traitor," Isobel said. "She's in the pay of the Grannams."

After a pause Per said, as if kindly explaining a difficult concept, "She's an *Elf.*"

"What of that? Is an Elf one of us? She came to me saying that it was no the Grannams that shot thy daddy, but the Elves."

There was another silence as everyone tried to understand this. Gareth stood up, his tired brain at first fumbling after meaning. She'd said what? And then the implications hit him like a brick. Andrea had said *that?* Oh my God. How did she know? He looked around at the room full of armed savages he stood among. Why the hell tell *them*, anyway? Had the woman no sense at all?

"The Elves shot my daddy?" Per said, sounding slightly amused. "Why would the Elves shoot my daddy?"

Gareth's heart leaped when he noticed Per's eyes on him. "It's nonsense!" he said. Weariness was falling away as his sense of danger increased. "The Elves want peace, not war."

Isobel set her fists on her hips. "The limmer's out to start trouble. To lose us our friends and set all against all. So I locked her up. And I ken what I'd do with her."

What? Gareth wondered but didn't dare ask, in case too many people agreed. The Sterkarms were in the habit of punishing wrong-doers in their isolated little community. A public whipping with a birch rod was common, or a few days locked up on bread and water. They might even hang or drown someone whose behavior they found really objectionable.

"What's going on?" Patterson had come to stand beside Gareth. Glancing around, he saw more of the 21st men pushing up behind him. Were they still carrying their weapons, or had they left them out in the yard somewhere? "Something about Andrea?"

"What you must do with her," Gareth said to the Sterkarms, "is hand her over to the Elves. As our prisoner. We'll deal with her."

"Why would she say such a thing?" Per asked.

"Let me go up and speak with her," Gareth said, and held up a hand to silence Patterson.

Sweet Milk, that big, grim-faced man, stood beside Per. "Let's all hear her."

"Let me speak with her first," Gareth said. "I'm an Elf too. I'm sure I can find out what's wrong with her. Maybe it's a jest."

"A jest!" Isobel said. "A killing jest indeed."

Sweet Milk, calmly, quietly, said, "Bring her down here. Let her tell us all what she said, and whyfor. That's best."

Per glowered at Sweet Milk, and at Gareth, a niggling irritation stirring into anger within him. The Grannams hadn't killed his father? Then he had wasted time and effort—and dishonored his name with crime. How could it be true? Why even listen to such trash?

"I'll fetch the may," Isobel said, her cheeks growing a little pink. Let the limmer have her say—then all would know that Isobel spoke the truth. Let the Elf-May condemn herself out of her own mouth, and then let's see what to do with her! She turned toward the stairs, and the Elf-Man, Gareth, actually put his hand on her arm to stop her.

"I'll go up and fetch her," he said, before becoming aware of the sudden stillness around him and a certain tingle in the air. Looking up, sharply, uneasily, he looked into Isobel's astonished and angry face, and saw Per looking at his hand on Isobel's arm. His hand dropped to his side. "Sorry! Sorry—no offense. Just—if you'll allow me to go up and—"

"The Elf is keen to stop the may speaking for herself," Sweet Milk said.

"Aye," another Sterkarm agreed. "Let's hear her word for ourselves."

Per was still looking at Gareth, and his stance was that spread-legged, loose-armed stance that could move quickly into anything. Gareth stepped back a couple of paces, putting a good distance between him and Mistress Sterkarm. "Mother," Per said, though he still looked at Gareth, "fetch the may."

Andrea stood by the tower's small, high window, peering out. She had heard the arrival of the returned ride and had tried to see what she could, constantly moving her head a fraction this way and that— but try as she might, the alleys were too narrow, and there were too many thatched roofs, and too many people crammed in the alleys, for her to glimpse more than bits and pieces of horses and riders as they passed. She'd been looking out for Per but hadn't seen him—or not any recognizable part of him, anyway. So she didn't know if he was still alive. And if he is, she thought, what has he done while he's been away? Has he killed? Whom has he killed? How many?

Behind her the door opened, and startled, she spun around to see Isobel coming in.

"Come down now," Isobel said.

Andrea stayed where she was. "Whyfor?"

"Come down," Isobel said impatiently, and waited by the door.

Andrea knew that she didn't have a choice, and walked toward the door, but she was scared. She didn't know what she was walking into.

Isobel led the way down the narrow stone stairs. Several people were clustered on the landing, looking up with excited faces. As soon as they saw Andrea, they ducked back into the hall, calling out that she was coming.

Uh-oh, Andrea thought.

She stepped in through the doorway of the hall. One of the long trestle tables had been set up, and people were crowded, standing, around it, men to the fore, and women and children behind them. They had been talking before her appearance but now fell silent and stared at her intently. She felt exposed and in danger, and had to set her jaw to keep herself from cringing as she followed Isobel past them and past the long table. People pushed each other back to make way for them, and still they stared. Whispering broke out behind her.

Andrea was led to the hearth, with its big stone chimney hood carved with the Sterkarm badge, the Sterkarm Handshake. There, on a settle, with his big gazehounds at his feet, sat Per, with Sweet Milk beside him. Their helmets and jakkes were on the floor beside them, and they still had on their long riding boots. Their shirts were rumpled and loose. Per's hair stood on end, from pulling his helmet off. He looked tired. I should be glad to see him alive, Andrea thought—and I am. But she could not rely on his support and favor as she'd been able to do in that other world. I must be careful, she thought. More careful than I have been, anyway.

Gareth stood beside the settle, leaning on it. He didn't look good. Exhausted, red eyed, and rather scared. Behind him, and behind the settle, were ranged the other 21st men, all of them unshaven and grimy.

"Good day to you, Mistress Elf," Per said to her, and behind his dry politeness was a memory of the last time they'd seen each other, when they'd lain in bed together. "Tell me, who put my father in his grave?"

Andrea felt the eyes of everyone in the room settle on her, and briefly shut her own. Why don't I just say, "The Grannams"? That was what everyone wanted her to say. But then they would only ask why she'd told Isobel something different. She opened her eyes and looked at Gareth, who, widening his eyes, seemed to be trying to signal something to her. She didn't know what. But he looked even more scared.

"Master Sterkarm," she said, "I believe that Elf-Windsor ordered his Elves to shoot your father. I believe Big Toorkild was shot by an Elf, with an Elf-Pistol—and so were your father's brother and your cousin."

Chatter broke out all around her—whisperings and exclamations that grew louder as everyone tried to be heard. Andrea was most conscious of Per's scowl and Gareth's expression of sick fright. But there was Patterson, too, his face sullen and darkening with blood.

Sweet Milk's quiet, deep voice broke through the chatter. "Whyfor do you believe this, Mistress Elf?"

It gave her a pang to hear Sweet Milk addressing her so formally, so distantly. She took a deep breath and launched into her explanation all over again: the nature of the wounds; the softness and size of lead balls; the narrowness, hardness, and velocity of Elf-Bullets. She even tried—since they were listening—to explain about the sound she'd heard behind her on the hillside, and about silencers and night sights.

Per's face was furious and baffled. Sweet Milk rose from the settle and turned to look at the Elves behind it. "Elf-Patterson—what say you to this?"

Patterson understood that well enough; and Gareth had been whispering a translation of Andrea's words. "It's bullshit. She doesn't know what she's talking about. She's mad."

Andrea sighed. What do men always say—in any time, in any dimension—when women disagree with them? She's mad, she's hysterical, she doesn't know what she's talking about, she's only a woman. A chill touched her. This wasn't the 21st, with its laws against discrimination.

Everyone was looking to Gareth for his translation. For a moment he was oblivious, but then tripped over his tongue to tell them what Patterson had said. Andrea continued to watch Patterson. The man had spoken quite calmly, even with bravado, and he stood at ease now, staring her in the eye—but he'd been just a little too quick to call her mad; and there was something a little too studied about his manner. The eyes of some of his men were scared. They knew all too well—they'd seen—what might happen to them if the Sterkarms believed her. True, they had their Elf-Weapons; but they were also outnumbered.

"It was you, wasn't it?" Andrea said, speaking to Patterson in English. "You were the sniper. You shot Toorkild. In cold blood. Why aren't you translating this?" she asked Gareth.

"I think we'd better have a care here," Gareth said, very conscious that some of the Sterkarms had picked up 21st-century words and phrases. One of the 21st men said, "Mad cow."

Patterson grinned. "Trying to get us all fucking beheaded, girlie?"

Per was looking from one to another, unable to catch enough words to understand what was said. His temper was rising. If the Elves wanted them dead, why had they helped him to take his revenge on the Grannams? Why had they risked Elvish lives to help him? And the Elves wanted peace. "Whyfor speak you these things?" he demanded of Andrea. He remembered how she'd lain with him, and had seemed so gentle and loving—had she been lying to him and working for the Grannams? And when the Grannam men had come to attack him, just before his father had been shot, she'd been with him then—waiting for a chance to stab him in the back? "You Grannam-loving bitch," he said, and made a grab for her hair. She pulled back out of his way.

"Hey, hey." Gareth stepped between them. He was trembling with fright but still found himself stepping between this Sterkarm killer and the object of his anger.

"She wants to make trouble between us and the Elves," Isobel said.

Andrea's pretty, scared face, with its large eyes and soft mouth, reminded Per of the tenderness he'd felt for her; and that sent a fierce pang through his heart and guts. Rage flared up and he drew his dagger. "I'll treat her the same as that Grannam bitch."

Gareth's heart skipped when he saw the dagger. He could feel it tearing into his own flesh. He felt his knees weaken. It would be easy, and so much safer, to stand aside and let Andrea defend herself.

But he'd done that already—he'd stood aside while Grannam women and children were murdered and burned. That had been easier—they'd been history-book people. Andrea was a 21st sider like himself. There'd been nothing he could do to save the Grannams. There was something he could do here. So although his voice squeaked in his tight throat and he felt sick to his stomach, he looked into Per's eyes, which were alight. It was the most frightening thing he'd ever done.

"Mistress Mitchell is an Elf," he said, his voice shaking. "We, the Elves, will arrest her and take her back to Elf-Land. It is for us, the Elves, to punish her, not for you." His belly quailed as he saw a silver flash in Per's eyes. Oh God; he's going to stab me.

"You're going to *arrest* me?" Andrea said incredulously, in 21st-side English. "For *what*? On what authority?"

"Shut up, for God's sake, haven't you said enough?" In Sterkarm English, he said, "If you harm her, we will withdraw our favor. We will give you no more help against the Grannams."

Per stared at him, and Gareth stared back, afraid to do anything else, afraid that even so much as glancing away would trigger Per's attack. He daren't look down, but he knew there was a long, wicked dagger in Per's left hand, somewhere about hip height. Its point would go into his guts. . . .

Then Sweet Milk touched Per's shoulder and spoke in his ear. Per turned his head a little aside to hear it, and relaxed slightly.

Gareth dared to draw a deeper breath. He said, "I have other offers and favors from the Elves to talk over with you—offers that will win you much wealth and fame—but if you harm any of us, that will all be forgotten."

A murmur of curiosity went through all the Sterkarms gathered in the hall. Per lowered his dagger. "The Elves favor traitors?"

Gareth gave Andrea a push, sending her behind the settle to join the other Elves, who didn't look at her with friendliness. "We will punish her," Gareth said, "but we do not allow outsiders to punish our own—any more than do the Sterkarms."

The Sterkarms acknowledged the truth of that, were even flattered by it. Per returned his dagger to its scabbard. "What are these other offers and favors?"

Gareth took another deep breath. The tremors than ran through him were now of relief. He sat down on the settle, feeling shaky. He'd managed well, he thought. He must mention it in his report to Windsor. "How would you like," he asked, "to fight for us in Elf-Land?"

19

16TH SIDE:
PEACE ON THE BORDER

✝✝✝

I n the great hall of the Bedesdale Tower, the trestle table was still
set up. Per sat at one end, in the settle that had been dragged
from the fireside, with Sweet Milk and Isobel on either side of
him. On long benches on either side of the table sat the Elves, as
well as several favored Sterkarm men. Wooden dishes of bread
were set on the table before them, with crocks of butter, cold
mutton, and jugs of small beer. The table was surrounded by lesser
men, standing, and women and youngsters, listening with folded
arms.

"All that you win while fighting for us is yours to keep," Gareth
said. "The Elves will take nothing of it. All we ask is that you win."

There was a cautious murmur of approval from those around the
table, especially those standing. They liked the sound of this, but
they were looking to the head of the table to hear what their leaders
thought before becoming more vocal. However, they'd made their
wishes clear.

Andrea listened in astonishment. There were many questions
she wished to ask—such as Who were the Sterkarms going to fight in
Elf-Land? Windsor had always hated Marketing and Accounts, but
setting the Sterkarms on them was over the top even for Windsor,
surely? Or was the Inland Revenue the target? At that moment,
though, she didn't feel secure enough to ask rude, probing questions
and draw attention to herself again. She had no friends in the room,
not even among the Elves.

Per, inside the hood of the settle, was consulting with Sweet Milk
and Isobel. Leaning forward, he said, "We are at feud with the

Grannams. We need the Elves' help against *them* before we fight battles for the Elves."

"And you shall have it," Gareth said. "I have the power to promise you that. More Elf-Soldiers, more Elf-Weapons. I promise you solemnly that the Sterkarms will be the lords of the border, with no enemies, because they will have no enemies left."

The Sterkarms stirred and whispered. Andrea, looking around, saw glinting eyes and grins that made her hair move. They liked the sound of that, too.

"This help," Gareth said, "will be in part payment for your help in Elf-Land."

"Master Elf," Per said, "I can no take my men and horses to Elf-Land now. Who will fight the Grannams when they come for revenge?"

"You forget that we are Elves," Gareth said. "We will take you into Elf-Land, and we will bring you back here, to Man's-Home, one eye blink after you leave. In that eye blink, in Elf-Land, you might fight for a year—or two, or three, though it won't take that long. But however long it takes, you will be away from home for only one blink of an eye. I swear."

There was a long silence while everyone thought this over; then a gentle murmur as they explained it to one another, to make sure they understood—and then a babble of confusion, delight, amazement, fear.

Andrea sat still and silent in shock. She had almost forgotten that what Gareth proposed was possible, because the Time Tube had always operated with a policy of keeping time in sequence on both sides of the Tube, to avoid problems of "Tube lag." But of course, so long as they were returned to a time *after* they left, it could be fractions of a second later.

"I can also promise you," Gareth said, "that Elves will be left here to guard the tower even for that moment you'll be away—"

"We don't all live in Bedesdale," said one of the Sterkarms seated at the table. Indeed, Sterkarms were scattered thickly over the country, and even across the border, in what was rightly England. There were many Sterkarm towers and bastle houses, all of which needed defending.

"We will send men with—with rockets, to every tower," Gareth said. "And—and—besides this, and besides help in defeating the Grannams once and for all, and besides taking no share of your booty, we will also pay you for fighting for us! We will pay you in Elf-Cloth, and Elf-Clothes, in wee white pills, and whisky, and—"

"Elf-Carts?" Per said. "Rocket shooters?"

"We will talk about that," Gareth said.

A deep silence fell on the hall. Per talked quietly with Sweet Milk as Isobel leaned to listen. Slowly, voices rose around them as everyone discussed what had been said.

Per struck the flat of his hand on the table, making a loud, sharp noise. There was quiet. Looking at Gareth, Per said, "In Elf-Land, whom shall we fight?"

Andrea sat straighter, waiting for Gareth's answer. This was what she was fascinated to know.

"You will not be fighting Elves," Gareth said. "Or—not Elves like us. You won't be fighting Elves with weapons like ours. Don't fear that."

Per looked puzzled. He spoke with Sweet Milk while chatter broke out again. Raising his voice, Per said, "If not Elves like you, then what kind of Elves? How many kinds of Elves be there?"

"There are many different Elf-Lands," Gareth said. "Some of them are like ours, and some of them are like yours. We want you to go into an Elf-Land very like yours and fight our enemies there, who are very like you, and—"

"Oh my God!" Andrea said, as it broke on her what this was all about. People glanced at her but were too interested in what else was being said to pay much attention.

"They have weapons like ours?" Per said.

"Very like yours," Gareth said. "Swords, lances, pistols."

"Whyfor have you need of us?" Per asked. "Your weapons knock down towers."

"Ah," Gareth said, "but we needed you to lead us to the tower.

We needed you to lead us to where the Grannams were in ambush. That is why we need you in Elf-Land. You know the land, you know how to cross it. You can be of priceless help to us."

"We dinna ken the land in Elf-Land," Per said. "It's no our land."

"It's exactly like this land," Gareth said. "The Elves that live there look exactly like you."

Astounded comment and chatter broke out again. Andrea leaned on the table and put her head in her hands. "They look like us?" Per said.

"It's Elf-Work. They will make themselves look like you—to trick you. They are shape-changers. But they're not you. And if you will help us defeat them, we will pay you generously."

An outburst of words broke on them from all sides; but the Sterkarms probably didn't find the proposal as strange as Andrea did. The idea of mortal men being recruited to fight the Elves' battles in Elf-Land was in their folklore—and so too was the notion that Elf-Land—or at least, some Elf-Lands—were identical to their own world and only subtly, magically different, so that people could step into them and never know that they'd left their own world and fate behind. They had many stories of people going into Elf-Land for an hour or a day and finding, on their return, that years had passed, so there was nothing new to them in the idea that time moved at different speeds in different worlds. And, of course, everyone knew that Elves were shape-shifters and could, if they chose, take on all sorts of forms.

Per struck the table again, calling for silence. "We need to talk about this. We'll give you an answer tomorrow, Master Elf."

Gareth nodded. "Shall we withdraw to our bowers? And meet here tomorrow?"

"That would be well."

And the two sides parted, the Elves going out to their sleeping quarters above various storerooms in the courtyard. Andrea, as she went down the tower steps, had no doubt what the answer would be. The Sterkarms, turn down the chance of a fight, the chance of plunder, fame, and wealth? The Devil would turn nun first.

"Gareth," she called as they ducked out of the tower's low door into the courtyard. Her voice was tight. She didn't want to talk to him and knew that he didn't want to talk to her. "I need to talk to you."

He gave her the barest glance over his shoulder. "Tomorrow. I'm exhausted."

"I *need* to talk to you now." She walked at his shoulder. "I want an explanation."

He turned and faced her. "Who are you to demand explanations? You could have got us all killed!"

Patterson and his men were walking ahead, on their way to their own sleeping quarters. Patterson turned back. "Got woman trouble, Gareth?"

The others laughed. "Need rescuing?"

They were all coming back, with jeering laughs and menacing swagger, all of Patterson's men. Andrea found her breath catching in her throat. She knew they were all angry with her. It would be a mistake to let them see she was scared. Looking Patterson in the eye, she said, "On whose orders did you shoot Toorkild?"

That stopped him short for a second, but then he gestured as if knocking away a fly. "Give it a rest, you mad mare."

"Are you saying that you didn't shoot him?" Andrea watched his face. "Why deny it? Ashamed?"

A spark of anger lit in his eye. "I'm not ashamed of anything I've ever done. After all"–he grinned–"I've never fucked you."

The other men sniggered. One clapped Patterson on the back.

Inwardly Andrea trembled with anger and nerves, but she refused to be either humiliated or intimidated. "Then you did do it. On whose orders?"

"I felt like it. Now, come on. Leave Gareth alone, and let's get you locked up in your pigpen for the night."

"Leave her," Gareth said, sounding tired to death. When Patterson still stayed where he was, Gareth snapped, "For God's sake!" He was annoyed with Andrea too, but Patterson's crudity was unbearable.

Patterson shrugged. "Please yourself." He turned and ambled away, his men laughing and sniggering with him, looking back at Gareth and Andrea and laughing again.

Andrea turned away from them and said to Gareth, "You're sending the Sterkarms through to fight—well, the other Sterkarms. That's right, isn't it?"

Gareth sighed. "You've figured it all out. Why ask me? I just want to lie down and sleep." He started walking toward his bower.

Andrea walked at his side. "Why? Why order such a thing? Is it just spite?"

"It's a business decision, as always," Gareth said.

"I suppose blowing people apart, burning people alive—that's all business as usual? Trade by other means?"

Her words brought back to Gareth, with great vividness, some of the things he'd experienced recently. The smell of burning human fat and meat. A woman's severed head. He'd been hoping not to think much of these things ever again. The contempt in Andrea's voice too—a woman's voice—made him feel as if some tender inner part of him was being sandpapered.

"Are you okay?" Andrea asked.

"I just want to lie down. Sleep."

She said nothing more but followed him to his bower and was closely behind him on his ladder. She was in the room with him before he could do or say anything about it. With a groan he unlaced and pulled off his boots and lay down on the bed.

Andrea shut the door and seated herself on a chest against the wall. "Tell me about this business decision."

He groaned and rubbed his hand over his face. "Oh, leave me alone."

"No. I shan't go away and I shan't shut up until you tell me. Come on. Tell me."

Gareth sighed. "It's no big deal. If you have two dimensions open, then you have twice the trade, don't you?"

"But Windsor made a real mess of things in—with—with the other Sterkarms."

"In 16th-side A," Gareth said. "Yeah. We alienated the natives. So when we came here—16th-side B—we went out of our way not to do that. We laid on trips to Elf-Land, clothes, truckloads of aspirin, whisky—we were Mr. Nice Guy, we really were. And James Windsor"—his tone took on an accusing note—"worked harder than anybody. Promoting peace. Fostering an alliance between the Sterkarms and the Grannams."

"I'm not an idiot," Andrea said. "The Sterkarms didn't attack the Grannams, and—"

"No, they'd never do that, would they?" Gareth's voice was sharp.

"*This* time they didn't. And *this time* the Grannams didn't attack the Sterkarms."

Gareth, resting his forehead on his hand, turned his head sidelong and looked at her.

"The men who attacked the Grannams," Andrea said, "were Patterson's men, dressed as 16th siders. The men who attacked the Sterkarms were our men too—21st siders. Weren't they? Both sides thought they were being attacked by the other, but they were being attacked by 21st siders. By us. And when everyone was outside, fighting, all the floodlights went on. And there were snipers on the hillside in the dark, picking off Toorkild. And Richie Grannam. And—all the leaders," she said wonderingly. "Gobby Per. Everyone Per might listen to. . . ." She looked at Gareth. "Why?"

Gareth gave a slight, weary smile. "Promoting peace?"

"By starting a war?"

"Look. You've got the Grannams, and you've got the Sterkarms. There's Beales, too, and—oh, dozens of others. Always at each other's throats, always raiding, always fighting. As I understand it, we already tried asking them nicely, in 16 A—just cut it out and pack it in, we said. They took no notice. How would you have stopped them? Would they have stopped if we'd paid them, do you think?"

Andrea grimaced and shrugged. "No," she admitted. That was what FUP had done, more or less, in what she'd have to learn to call

16 A. The Sterkarms had taken their payments, asked for more, and gone on raiding and feuding anyway.

"And do you really think the wedding alliance would have stopped them for long?"

"Well, yes, it might." Andrea thought about it. "No. Not really."

"The trouble always was, they were too finely balanced. No one family had any superiority over another. So it went on and on and on, in low-grade power struggles. Solution? Make one side overwhelmingly powerful." He saw realization dawn in Andrea's face. "Yeah. Back the Sterkarms against the Grannams. Make the Sterkarms top dog. *That's* how you make peace."

"Peace for FUP to trade," Andrea said.

"And peace," Gareth said. "Eventually. For everyone. A lot of little Sterkarm kids will grow up in peace and prosperity because of this."

"Is that what you tell yourself? A lot of Grannam children won't."

"And wouldn't, either, if we just let this go on," Gareth said irritably.

"The Sterkarms and the Grannams feud all the time anyway. They've been doing it for years–centuries, probably. So why this charade? Why the wedding–why pay out all that gold to persuade them to marry when you know you're going to break it up? I just don't–"

"For God's sake, because we had to know when it would all kick off," Gareth said. "We weren't going to hang around, containing all their raids and shit, and hoping they'd start a feud sometime soon. What if they'd picked a feud with the wrong people? With the Yonnsenns or Dowglasses? We wanted them to feud with the other big powerful family, the Grannams, nobody else. Let the Sterkarms beat the Grannams out of sight, and there's going to be no trouble from the other little families, at least not for a long time. And hopefully, by then, they'll be so used to our rule . . . So. It was all set up. Bring the Sterkarms and the Grannams together, stage a 'treacherous attack,' and then back the Sterkarms.

You've got to admit it's clever."

"Let me guess who thought of this," Andrea said.

"James Windsor," Gareth said.

"It's such a game," Andrea said. "If you don't mind murdering people to further your five-year plan, why not just go to the Sterkarms and say, hey! How about if we massacre the Grannams for you?"

"And what if the Grannams won?"

"What?"

"Well, I've been told that the Sterkarms kicked ass in 16 A. You'd know, you were there. So you've got to be prepared. What if the Grannams won? If they did, and we'd openly declared war on them—well, that would be difficult. But if the Sterkarms treacherously attack them, and then use stolen Elf-Weapons to—" He was going to say "massacre the Grannams" but a memory rose up of exactly what that massacre had entailed. "To massacre the Grannams," he said firmly, "then we're off the hook." This was the hardening he needed, he reminded himself. You had to be able to keep the big picture in view and face up to what had to be done, like an adult.

Andrea was still sitting on the chest, staring into space. "So now you're going to set the Sterkarms on the Sterkarms. I suppose you're going to do the same to—the first Sterkarms—the other Sterkarms—"

"Sterkarms A," Gareth said.

"You're going to do the same to Sterkarms A as you've done to the Grannams. Attack them with rockets and grenades. Wipe them out."

"Impose peace," Gareth said.

It's my Per, Andrea thought, whom peace will be imposed on. And my Toorkild—still alive in 16 A. And my Isobel, and my Sweet Milk, and Ecky and Sim and all the rest.

I can't bear this, she thought. It's surreal. Per killing Per. No.

"Why involve me?" she asked.

Gareth was rubbing his face. "Eh?"

"Why drag me into it? Why give me my old job back, just to drag me into this?"

Gareth sighed. "You were the candy, weren't you?"

"What?"

"Didn't you have an affair with Per Sterkarm in 16 A? I get the impression it was quite intense."

"Ah—well—" Andrea felt her face warming.

"The long and short of it was: Make the Sterkarms top dog, but make sure the Sterkarms are led by somebody *we* can lead by the nose. So knock out all the experienced, older leaders—"

"Knock out?" Andrea said. "You mean murder."

"Okay. Murder all the experienced leaders and set up a puppet leader—somebody young, inexperienced, easy to influence."

"You mean *Per*?"

"Exactly."

"You think Per is easy to influence?"

"Relatively speaking," Gareth said. "Easier than Toorkild or Gobby. And we've been working on him, giving him lots of presents, taking him into Elf-Land, promising him things. Now that he's the leader, we'll be keeping him occupied with lots of shiny toys. You're one of them."

"Come again?"

"Well, that was the plan anyway. You've cocked it up a bit, haven't you? But you were to be one of the presents to keep him sweet. A beautiful Elvish mistress. Windsor knew you were his type."

Andrea was speechless.

"You were just supposed to sit around looking pretty." Gareth sounded dubious about that. "And flirt. You weren't supposed to tell the Sterkarms that we shot Big Toorkild. What were you thinking of? Windsor's going to be furious when he hears about that."

Andrea stood, waving her hands around her head, as if his words were so many buzzing flies. "Okay, I've heard about enough. I'm going." She climbed down the ladder from Gareth's bower to the alley below and picked her way through the mud and muck heaps to her own bower. As she went, her brain hurried and sallied, turning back and venturing again, thinking: How do I get from here to 16 A? How do I warn Per—my Per? How? How?

20

16TH SIDE:
AN AGREEMENT

††††

"We want to speak with Elf-Windsor," Per said.

They were all in the great hall of the tower again. Per sat at the head of the table in the armed chair where his father had once sat. Sweet Milk was next to him, on a bench. Isobel was watchful nearby, on a stool; and as many others as could escape their duties were standing around the table, so they could tell their children and grandchildren that they were there. If they lived that long.

Andrea sat between Gareth and Patterson. She wasn't happy.

"Elf-Windsor is in Elf-Land," Gareth said. After a good night's sleep, he seemed calm and spoke authoritatively. "I am his man here in Man's-Home. He has given me power to deal in his name. If you make an agreement with me, he will honor it, I promise you."

Per conferred with Sweet Milk and some of the other Sterkarms, and glanced at his mother, but Andrea didn't doubt that he would agree. In the Sterkarms' world almost all bargains were agreed on a handshake and a promise. The Sterkarms were notorious, of course, for not keeping their word with other clans, but between themselves they did, and at the moment the Elves seemed to be considered honorary Sterkarms.

"We shall send a ride into Elf-Land," Per said. "The men will be chosen by me from those who wish to come. Some wish to stay here and keep their own land."

Andrea translated what he said, for Patterson and his men, while Gareth nodded his agreement.

Per, his fist clenched on the tabletop, said, "The Elves will send Elf-Men to every tower here, with Elf-Weapons, to fend off the Grannams when they come."

Gareth nodded again. "That was agreed."

"No more than two men to a tower," Patterson said, after listening to Andrea's translation. Gareth translated that, and Per frowned and opened his mouth to argue. Patterson said, "With Elf-Weapons, you won't need any more. We'll have to draw up a list of towers, and we may have to send for reinforcements. That will mean a wait."

Gareth translated. Per muttered things over with the men around him, and then agreed. Andrea sighed. This looked as if it would take ages.

"When we are in Elf-Land, we want Elf-Weapons," Per said.

Gareth leaned across Andrea and conferred with Patterson. Then he said to Per, "There will be Elves with you, with Elf-Weapons. They will be men expert in their use. It would take a long time to train you to use them. You are wanted for your knowledge of–of raiding." That was simpler than trying to translate "local terrain" and "local tactics."

More muttering among Per and his men. Per said, "You could take us into Elf-Land and train us, and then bring us back here–or send us to the other Elf-Land–an eye blink after. No time would be wasted."

Andrea suppressed a smile. Get out of that one, she thought. The Sterkarms had never been stupid, or slow to see where their own advantage lay.

Gareth and Patterson leaned across her and whispered again. Then Gareth said, "The Elf-Weapons are costly, hard to use, and dangerous to those who are not Elves. It will be safer for your men if only Elves use Elf-Weapons."

Per and Sweet Milk rose and went over to the far wall, to talk. One or two other Sterkarms joined them, and for a moment Isobel looked as if she would rise and join them. But although Sterkarm women had plenty to say for themselves, about everything, it was not the done thing for them to publicly discuss men's business, such as war. After an obvious struggle with herself, she remained on her stool.

The men came back to the table and seated themselves again. "We agree," Per said. Andrea thought that they had probably decided to agree for now, for the sake of the promised booty, but the matter of Elf-Weapons would inevitably crop up again in the near future. "Payment," Per went on. "All that we take on the ride is ours to keep?"

"That was agreed," Gareth said.

"And I want wee white pills for every man. Dicket-adicket-adicket for every man—"

An excited whispering and nudging broke out around the table at this scarcely imaginable number. Gareth had to lean to Andrea for a translation, as he'd never quite got to grips with Sterkarm counting.

"A thousand," she said. "Ten times ten times ten."

"For every captain," Per said, "tayn-adicket-adicket-adicket."

"Two thousand," Andrea said, as the awed gasps filled the hall again.

"For me," Per said, "tether-adicket-adicket-adicket."

"Three thousand?" Gareth asked, and Andrea nodded. Per, she supposed, planned to give the pills to his followers as presents, to keep them loyal.

"I agree," Gareth said. In the 21st, generic aspirin cost next to nothing.

Everyone around the table committed the agreement to memory.

"For every man," Per said, "a pair of good, waterproof boots, a pair of jeans, and a good Elf-Coat." He meant the warm, waterproof, windproof 21st-side coats, much coveted by the Sterkarms.

That would be a good deal more expensive, and Gareth dickered. A pair of jeans for every man; the jeans and the coat for the captains; but the boots only for Per.

There was an outcry of annoyance. The Elves were rich. Did they want the Sterkarms to fight for them or not?

Gareth offered to throw in a bolt of cloth for every man—gorgeous, shiny, close-woven Elf-Cloth. It would make a good present for wives and sweethearts.

The Sterkarms were not enthusiastic. Perhaps they were remembering that Joan Grannam's wedding dress had been made of such cloth and considered it an unlucky gift.

"A pair of good Elf-Boots for every man," Per said.

Gareth didn't fancy presenting Windsor with the bill for so many pairs of high-quality walking boots. He offered to increase the amount of aspirins per man.

Per withdrew from the table again with Sweet Milk, and this time they went over to Isobel, to discuss the offer with her. Andrea could hear it being eagerly discussed among the crowd around the table. The Sterkarms were tempted. They had no reliably effective painkillers to combat their toothaches, head pains, rheumatism, arthritis, period cramps, and all their other ills. Aspirin was, to them, magical stuff.

"Two thousand wee white pills for every man," Per said, coming back to the table. "Three thousand for the captains. Five thousand for me."

"Five thousand?" Gareth said, tapping on an electronic notebook.

"Five thousand. And a pair of boots for every man. We'll forgo the breeches and coats." But the Sterkarms weren't going to let go of those boots.

"Come on, agree," Andrea said. She was impatient to see a settlement made. Beside her, Patterson yawned. Since he could understand only a few words, he must have been even more bored. "You'll buy in bulk and get a discount. Be generous and throw in the jeans as well—cheap pairs. Windsor won't care. It isn't his money. He always enjoys a row with Accounts."

Gareth considered, then said, "Right. Two thousand pills—three thousand—five for Per. A pair of jeans for every man, and a pair of boots."

"Agreed," Per said, and there were cheers, and beams on faces.

All those wee white pills! They were all going to be rich!

"Gold," Per said.

"Gold?" Gareth hadn't expected this.

"Five pieces of gold for every man. Ten pieces for the captains. Fifty for me."

The Sterkarms, as ever, were pushing their luck. Andrea turned and whispered to Gareth. "For the men, nothing. For the captains, a gold piece each. For the Sterkarm leader, five pieces."

While Gareth said this aloud, Andrea looked up and saw Per glowering at her resentfully. The sooner she was out of here, the better.

"Thirty for me," Per said. "Eight for the captains. Three for every man." He was driving a hard bargain, probably because Andrea had dared to interfere.

"Agree, agree," she whispered to Gareth. What did she care, after all?

"Ten for you," Gareth said. "Five for the captains. One for every man."

The Sterkarms consulted, and Per said, "Agreed." There was a certain subdued exultation from those around the table. They couldn't repress it. A piece of gold each, in addition to the aspirins, the boots, and the breeches. It made them dizzy.

"Give us your word the gold won't turn to leaves," Per said.

"Or any trash," Sweet Milk added.

"I give you my word," Gareth said. "I will swear on anything you choose. It will be good, solid gold, no magic about it."

"We want a hostage," Per said.

Nonplussed, Gareth turned to Andrea. "A hostage?"

"They want a hostage," she said. "As a guarantee that the Elves will keep their word. It's quite normal in the 16th."

"But—a hostage. What will they do—?"

"The hostage will stay here, in the 16th," Andrea said impatiently. "Whoever it is will be well treated and looked after, but if the Elves break their word—" She raised her brows. He looked blank. "They'll kill the hostage," she said.

He looked aghast. "We can't agree to that!"

"Why? Aren't the Elves going to keep their word? Keep your side of the bargain and everything will be okay."

But Gareth turned away from her and said to Per, "It's not the Elves' custom to give hostages."

Per leaned back in his chair. "Then we'll no ride for the Elves."

Putting her mouth close to Gareth's ear, Andrea said, "Agree to a hostage! Agree! Or we'll get nowhere!"

"Are you volunteering?" Gareth asked.

"Me? No! I–I can't."

"Then you can hardly–" Gareth said.

Per spoke again. "The Elf-May is to be sent back to Elf-Land. She's no welcome here."

Andrea said, "I understand that. I will go as soon as may be. If the Elves were to grant a hostage, who would it be?"

With a nod, Per indicated Gareth. "Elf-Windsor's man."

Furiously, Gareth whispered to Andrea, "I don't want to be a bloody hostage!"

"You'll be staying here anyway, won't you?" Andrea whispered back. "What difference will it make? Or do you know that the Elves aren't going to keep their word?"

Gareth stared at her. "Of course we are!"

"Good. They don't want me here–"

"Lucky you!"

"Send me back 21st side, and I'll take a letter to Windsor. I'll let him know that you're a hostage for his good behavior. You trust him, don't you?"

Gareth's face flushed. "That's not the point–"

"Of course it is. I can also take the shopping list of aspirins, boots, and what nots. Anything you want him to know."

Gareth saw the chance to send a memo, detailing all his successes, bringing himself to the notice of the men who counted. "Well . . ."

"Agree with them," Andrea said. "They won't understand why you're havering over a hostage."

Gareth hesitated a moment longer, but he felt the pressure of all the many Sterkarms, all around the table, all staring at him and waiting. "All right," he said to Per. "I offer myself as hostage. And I will send the Elf-May home."

Per rose from his seat and held out his hand—his right hand, although he was left-handed. Never shake hands with a Sterkarm. "Then we are agreed. We shall ride for you."

Gareth rose, and they shook. The Sterkarms cheered, and Isobel rose from her seat to chivvy her maids into filling cups and passing plates of bread.

21

2 1 S T S I D E :
B A C K A G A I N

†††

The journey from the Bedesdale Tower to the Tube was one of anger and exasperation, and Andrea ended it feeling that her nerves had been rubbed down with sandpaper. The trip was made in an MPV, jolting and lurching over the difficult ground, with Patterson driving and, beside him in the passenger seat, a man Patterson called Plug, who carried some kind of big gun. Andrea thought it was a machine gun of sorts, but guns weren't one of her interests.

"Sent home in disgrace, eh?" was one of the first things Patterson said. "Really blotted your copybook, haven't you, girlie?"

Plug sniggered. He sniggered at anything Patterson said.

Andrea said nothing. All she wanted to do was reach the Tube and go through it. There wasn't any point, that she could see, in arguing with Patterson.

"Old Jimmy Windsor ain't going to be very pleased with you, is he?"

Andrea thought of asking Patterson whether he called Windsor "Old Jimmy" to his face, but she kept quiet, even when Plug looked at her and sniggered.

"I shall be going to see him, soon as we get in." Patterson looked at her in the mirror. "You can come with me. I'll fill him in on how helpful you've been."

Right on cue, Plug sniggered. Andrea almost wished that a party of Grannams would appear, to give him something to snigger about—but then hastily took back even that almost wish. No Grannams appeared anyway, and the MPV ground and shuddered and swayed on its way, and Patterson made his spiteful jibes, and Plug sniggered, until Andrea felt that another minute would force her to lie on the floor and scream.

They came, at long last, to the place where the wedding feast had been held. There were the Elvish inflatables, now limp and deflated. Some of the huts in the shantytown surrounding the Elvish buildings had been pulled down, others burned down. Debris lay scattered over the grass—cushions, torn drapes, food, ropes. There were many bundles of clothing cast down on the grass—until Andrea realized that they were bodies, just left, lying there. Something scuttled away, low to the ground. A fox. She looked away before she saw anything that she wouldn't forget.

Patterson saw her in the mirror and laughed. "The foxes and crows, they think all their Christmases and birthdays have come at once!"

Plug sniggered. She gritted her teeth. They weren't far from the Tube now.

They drove through the electronic gates into the Tube's compound, and saw the Tube's great concrete pipe waiting for them beside the little prefab office on its stilts. Both looked weird against the wild hills behind. Patterson steered the MPV up the ramp that led to the Tube, halted it on the platform, and turned the engine off. Plug wound his window down.

A security guard stepped out of the office, stooped, and looked into the car. Patterson held up his pass. "Fine," said the guard, and went back into the office. Andrea leaned forward until she could see the panel of lights hung above the Tube's entrance. The red one was on. Soon it would turn to green and they would go through. The light changed. Patterson started the engine and the car crept forward. The plastic screening rattled against the windshield, and then they were in the Tube itself. A few seconds and five hundred years later, they drove out of the Tube's other end, in the 21st century.

Patterson halted the car on the platform just outside the Tube. Another guard popped out of the office, checked his pass, and waved them on. Slowly the car drove down the ramp onto 21st-century gravel. Andrea looked out, with admiration, on neat 21st-century lawns, trees, and flower beds.

Patterson drove the car slowly around the grand country house to the parking lot at the front and parked it alongside the other big, square, tall vehicles that were used for driving to the office and supermarket. The only difference between these and the one that had just driven across 16th-century moorland was that theirs was muddier. Andrea could see her own little blue car a few places away.

Patterson switched off the engine, took the gun from Plug, and said to him, "Okay, lose yourself for a few hours—but keep your bloody cell phone switched on!"

Plug sniggered, climbed out of the car, and walked off.

Patterson got out too and put the gun into the car's trunk. Andrea climbed out slowly. She knew what she was going to do next—or what she wanted to do next. The trouble was she had no idea, as yet, of how she was going to do it.

"Come on," Patterson said, and strode off toward the hall's beautiful entrance, with its pillars and steps. Andrea grabbed her rucksack from the car's backseat and followed him. The car, losing contact with the coder in Patterson's pocket, locked itself.

In reception it was all gleaming wood, shining glass, and a scent of polish. Patterson showed his pass to the bored girls behind the desk and said, "Buzz me through." Andrea fumbled in her rucksack and produced her pass. One of the girls pressed a button beneath her desk, a buzzer sounded, and Patterson pushed open the heavy wooden door into the main building, making straight for the elevators.

Patterson said nothing as they rode up in the elevator, but smirked at her in an annoying way when she glanced at him. They left the elevator on the top floor and walked along a wide corridor with a floor of polished wood. Patterson turned through an open door into Windsor's outer office. Windsor's secretary, Beryl, sat behind a small desk, in front of a computer. Andrea stood back as Patterson spoke with the secretary.

"If you'll take a seat," Beryl said, "I'll tell Mr. Windsor. Would you like a cup of coffee or tea?"

Patterson said no, went over to an armchair, and sat down, his boots planted firmly about a foot apart. He didn't pick up a magazine but stared at the wall. "No, thank you," Andrea said, and took a chair at a distance from him. She did pick up a magazine and turned its pages, but her mind was on other things. Beryl calmly finished what she was doing, then rose, knocked on the door of the inner office, and went in.

For a minute or two Andrea could hear voices speaking quietly in the next room; then the door opened again and Windsor came out, dressed in his usual smart dark suit and white shirt, smiling and holding out his hand. "Tom! Come right in, right in!" As Patterson preceded him into his office, Windsor smirked at Andrea. "Be patient for a few minutes longer, Andrea. Perhaps Beryl can rustle you up a few cookies?"

The door of the office closed behind the men, and the murmuring voices began again. Beryl smiled sympathetically at Andrea and returned to her seat. She looked up after a moment. "If you have changed your mind about a drink—?"

Smiling, Andrea said, "I'm fine, thanks."

Then Beryl went back to her work, and Andrea went back to staring blankly at glossy advertisements in the magazine she held. There was a silence, which Andrea felt to be uncomfortable, though Beryl seemed entirely at ease. A clatter startled Andrea, and she looked up. Beryl had started the printer. Now she rose and, in silence, left the office.

Listlessly Andrea turned more pages. She finished the magazine and took up another, in which she was equally uninterested. Still she was alone in the office. A soft rustle made her look across the room. The printed pages had piled up, and were now slithering onto the floor.

That always happens, Andrea thought. And you have to pick them all up and sort them all out. With a fellow feeling for Beryl, who was also fat and plain and sneered at by Windsor, she rose from her chair and went to pick the papers up.

They were authorization passes for going through the Tube. She shuffled through the pages. They all were. Blank forms, all ready to be filled in, issued only from this office. A large party was shortly going to be sent through the Tube. She looked up, staring at the opposite wall, and took a deep breath, deliberately calming herself.

Beryl came back through the office door and, seeing Andrea standing by the printer with her hands full of papers, stopped short and stared. Andrea felt as if a great chord of music had been struck in her head, almost deafening her. "It's okay," she gabbled. "It's okay! I—well—I was just picking these up for you! It's a nuisance, isn't it, how they go all over the floor?" Shuffling the papers together, she put them down on Beryl's desk but picked one off the top. "I'll just be off now. A lot to do. You know how it is—loads!" Darting across to her chair, she grabbed her bag and made for the door.

"Um," Beryl said, turning to watch her go and vaguely pointing at the paper in Andrea's hand.

"Have a nice day!" Andrea said and, gaily waving the paper in farewell, almost ran out into the corridor.

Beryl remained in the center of the room, uncertain of what she ought to do. Andrea certainly shouldn't have taken one of those papers—she really should have minded her own business and not even picked them up from the floor, but—what was Beryl supposed to do? Rugby tackle her? And Andrea was a nice young woman. Conscientious. Polite. She probably didn't mean any harm. When you got to the bottom of it, it was most likely all to do with her anthropological studies—which sounded most interesting—and nothing suspicious at all. Slowly Beryl returned to her seat and continued with her work. She felt uneasy but didn't want to make a fuss. It would cause a lot of trouble and probably only make her look a fool.

The buzzer sounded on the intercom, and Windsor's voice said, "Can you send Miss Mitchell in now, please, Beryl?"

Beryl hesitated, then answered, "Just a moment, Mr. Windsor."

She looked across the office, as if hoping Andrea might be sitting in the armchair, waiting. She wasn't. Sighing, Beryl rose and knocked on the door of Windsor's office, going in immediately.

"Oh—Beryl," Windsor said, looking up from his "cozy corner," where he was sitting with that Patterson man, whom Beryl didn't like at all. Smarmy, she thought him, and under the smarminess aggressive.

"I'm sorry, Mr Windsor: Miss Mitchell has left."

"Left? How can she have left? Where's she gone?"

"She said something about—er—having a lot to do and—errands to run."

Windsor and Patterson looked at each other. "Did Miss Mitchell deign to say when she might be back?" Windsor asked.

"Ah . . ." Tightening her hand on the door handle, Beryl coughed and said, "I think I ought to mention . . . I hope I'm not telling tales or—making a fuss about nothing—"

"Oh, spit it out, Beryl!"

"I—er—left the office for a few moments and—erm—when I came back—well, the printer had spilled some papers on the floor—"

"What are you chuntering on about?"

Beryl felt her face grow slightly hotter. "I was printing off those forms. Passes for the Tube."

"Yes. So?"

"Miss Mitchell picked them up off the floor. When she left, she, er, took one with her."

Both Windsor and Patterson got to their feet. Both came briskly across the office and pushed past her at the door. Windsor looked around the outer office, as if making sure that Beryl had been telling the truth and Andrea had really gone.

Patterson said, "You know where she's gone. Isn't hard to figure."

"Surely not," Windsor said. "Not even Andrea, surely—?" He reached for the telephone on the desk and dialed. "Hello? James Windsor. Can you tell me—has anyone gone through recently? Ah. Thank you." He put the receiver down and looked at Patterson. "She bloody has. Fuck it!"

Beryl quietly returned to her desk and, head down, began typing again.

"So," Patterson said, folding his arms. "We'll get after her."

"She's taken her car through too. The car that I got her."

"Won't do her any good," Patterson said. "We can take our time, get organized, and go through ten minutes before her. We can be waiting for her."

"No," Windsor said.

"She'll run straight into our arms."

"Can't be done," Windsor said. "The time streams. They'd cross, get confused—it'd be a nightmare."

"Okay. Go back a day before her, then. So we sit on our arses for—"

"Are you deaf? Or stupid?"

Patterson scowled.

"It can't be done. But we can go through one second after her."

Patterson grinned. "How far can she run in one second?"

"Not built for running, our Andrea." Windsor glanced at Beryl, took Patterson by the arm, and drew him back into his inner office. Shutting the door after him, he looked at Patterson. "There's going to be a lot of confusion over there."

Patterson nodded.

"So there might be an incident of friendly fire."

Patterson, his arms folded, nodded and smiled. "Right, boss."

22

21ST SIDE: "SEE YOU!"

††††

A ndrea didn't wait for the elevator but ran down the stairs to reception. One of the girls was speaking on the phone. She asked the other, "What's the number of Tube Control, do you know?"

The girl lifted a receiver. "I can get them for you."

"No, no, I need it for later and I've mislaid the number." Looking disappointed, the girl wrote the number down on a sheet of paper.

Andrea forced herself to walk out of reception in a slow, dignified manner, but once on the gravel outside she ran around the corner, thinking: I'm getting away with it! So far—which wasn't very far—anyway. She looked around for approaching security men.

The coder for her car was buried somewhere deep in her rucksack, and the car beeped and unlocked itself as she neared it. With relief she opened the door, threw her rucksack inside, climbed in after it, and locked herself inside. Then she delved in her rucksack until she found her cell phone. After taking a few deep breaths to calm herself, she punched in the number.

"Tube Control," said a woman's voice. "Kylie here. How may I help you?"

"Ah, hello. This is James Windsor's office. We're sending along a Miss Andrea Mitchell very shortly. We want her sent through straightaway, to 16th-side A. That's A for alpha. Would that be possible?"

"To *16 A*? Did you say 16 *A*?"

"Yes, A, alpha. This is urgent. Will it be possible?"

"Just a moment. Will there be a vehicle?"

"Yes."

"And will Miss Mitchell be alone or with a party?"

"Alone." Andrea gulped and hoped it hadn't been audible.

"And she's going through to 16 A–is that correct?"

"Yes!" Andrea snapped. "16 A. I said this is urgent!"

"Just a moment."

Andrea gripped the phone tightly, holding it to her ear and staring through the windshield at the lawns, flower beds, and trees. Come on, come on–

"Hello?"

"Yes? Hello?"

"We're preparing the Tube now. Can Miss Mitchell be here in ten minutes?"

"Oh yes! Thank you. Good-bye."

She clicked the phone off and found it hard to breathe, so stifled was she with excitement, fear, triumph, and many other emotions harder to identify. Another hunt through her rucksack uncovered a pen, and leaning on her steering wheel, she filled in the pass. She scribbled something at the bottom that might pass for an official signature, if no one looked too closely–well, it hardly mattered. If anyone at the Tube looked at this business closely, or double-checked on her, or asked questions, she was caught. She had to rely on them treating it all as routine.

She reached for the ignition button but drew her hand back. No. Don't give them ten minutes to see how nervous you are, and grow suspicious. Turn up in ten minutes' time and rush through, shouting, "Urgent!" She leaned back in her seat. Ten minutes to wait. Ten minutes could seem a long, long time. Oh well. She could phone Mick and ask how he was. She would say she loved him and hang up with "See you!" She wouldn't say "good-bye."

Andrea drove her car up the ramp and braked on the platform in front of the Tube's mouth. Leaning over, she wound down the passenger-side window, and when a security guard came out of the office, she flourished her pass at him. Bending down, he examined it and squinted through the window at her. He looked at the laminated employee pass pinned to her chest and studied her face.

"You're expecting me, I think," she said, trying not to sound as breathless and scared as she felt. "I'm Andrea Mitchell."

He looked at her face again, as if he was memorizing it. Do guards always do this? she wondered. Perhaps I just never noticed before. If he's caught on to me, what happens next? Police? Interviews? I could handle that. But no—Windsor was never going to bring in the police.

"That's fine," the guard said, handing her back the paper. "Wait for the signal and then go through."

"Oh, thanks." Andrea took such a deep breath, from relief, that she felt dizzy. The guard went back into the office, closing the door behind him. The mouth of the Tube towered over her, and she almost panicked. She glanced over her shoulder. No one was running toward her, yelling. For a moment she wished someone would. Someone should stop her. She was going through, on her own, to 16th-side A—the dimension where FUP had angered the natives and had been thrown out. She'd be entirely on her own. No safety net.

The light above her turned green. Her heart thumping under her collarbone, she engaged first gear and drove forward. The nose of the car brushed aside the plastic strips, and still no one shouted.

It was like driving through a tiled underground walkway—except it was eerily clean, without litter or graffiti. The whining hum was loud enough, for a while, to make her wish she could put her fingers in her ears, but the sound soon passed out of hearing. I don't want to do this, she thought; why am I doing this? But she kept driving. Was that the center point? Had the Tube done its stuff—was she in the 16th now? In seconds, she'd reached the other end and was certainly in the 16th. The car brushed aside the screening.

She drove straight down the ramp—she hadn't time to stop and admire the scenery. She knew that even if days passed before it was guessed what she'd done, all the might of FUP could be less than a second behind her. But she glimpsed the wide, wide space of wet green hills and cloud-heavy gray sky. There was even more space than usual, because there was no office here, no compound. This was 16 A, which FUP had largely abandoned.

It was a little tricky at the foot of the ramp, because it didn't meet the ground, since it hadn't been measured and set up for this dimension. There was a drop which, from behind the wheel, looked quite terrifying, though it was probably a foot and a half or less. No matter: She hadn't time to worry about it. These MPVs were tough little things, built like miniature tanks. The car took the drop, crashed, bounced, shook, but then drove on. There was a second, teeth-jarring crash as the rear wheels dropped from the ramp, and Andrea held her breath—but the car jolted on across the rough ground as if nothing much had happened.

She glanced in the rearview mirror. Behind her was hillside and sky. The Tube had vanished. Fear gripped at her heart: She'd never felt so alone. She'd never *been* so alone.

Drive, she ordered herself. Drive fast, and thank God you're alone. She moved up a gear and pressed down on the accelerator. The car bounced and swayed alarmingly. If there are any gods up there, she thought, anybody at all, look after me now, and you can put your order in for as much devotion and kneeling and praying as you like. Just keep me upright and moving forward.

The car jolted onto a broad ride that led across the moor—but though it was more or less flat and grassy, it was still only a track made by horses and sheep, and it was uneven and stony. She started along it as fast as she dared and then saw something move from the corner of her eye. Looking to her left, she saw that the Tube had appeared again, and issuing from its mouth were horses. Men and horses.

She shoved her right foot to the floor, and with a growl, a leap, and a swaying jolt, her car shot forward.

23

16A:
"The Elves Are Back!"

†††

The cattle, black, skinny, half-wild creatures, were constantly, stubbornly turning aside, trying to find some way to escape the men who pestered them. Per, riding Fowl, turned a couple of cows aside and rose in his stirrups to point and shout a warning about a cow and calf that were making a break for the hills. Swart, his gazehound, ran forward, yapped, and ran back to Fowl's heels.

The cattle weren't shy of charging the men, especially those on foot, and the horsemen had to be quick to spur in, perhaps nudging a cow with the butt of a lance, to turn it aside. It was hot work, and Per's shirt hung open, unlaced. Sweat gleamed on his chest.

Elf-Joe, shirtless, was among the men on foot, dodging out of the way of the cattle, roaring at them and clapping hands, clouting them with sticks. The slope, thank God, was leveling out and growing easier, becoming a broader, better-trodden track down into Bedesdale and the winter pastures along Bedes Water.

Children came running toward them from the ford, a noisy, shouting gaggle who made the cattle shake their heads and stomp. Joe was alarmed, but he should have known that Sterkarm bairns were used to cattle. "Elfie, Elfie!" the little voices shrilled. "Elfie-Choe!"

"Mind! Mind!" Joe said, fearful for them, but the bairns dodged the animals and ran up to him, reaching for his hands and grabbing at his knees. He fascinated them, because he'd been in Elf-Land. They thought of him as a sort of friendly monster. "Tell the May!" they said. "Tell him!"

They were all shouting together, and it was hard to understand. "What?"

The oldest of the bairns, a lassie, said, "Tell the May that the Elves have come back!"

"What?" Joe said, incredulously.

They all shouted again. The tall lassie's voice rose above them. "The Elves are on the moor—they've been seen. Tell the May!" They were too shy to approach the May themselves, Per being a shining hero to the small fry of the tower. But Elfie-Choe, he was even more of an outsider than them. He could do it.

Joe ran up the hillside, weaving in and out of men and cattle, yelling, "May! Per May!" Men pointed him in the right direction and added their voices to his, and here came Per, swaying easily on his horse's back, his fair hair standing on end, his face flushed as he wiped it on his sleeve.

"The Elves!" Joe shouted. "The Elves are back the way! They're here!"

"Elves?" Fowl circled Joe. "Is that what tha said—Elves?"

"Aye! Elves! On the moor!"

Per looked astounded—alarmed—enthused. "Where?"

"Ask the bairns," Joe said, and looked around to see the children already on the other side of the ford, racing for the tower.

Per sat his horse, astonished, his mouth open. Into his mind came a woman: tall, wreathed in soft hair, golden brown and falling in heavy waves. She was heavy bosomed, broad hipped. Generous hillside curves and a generous smile. The Elf-May. Entraya.

But Elves, they'd said. Elves. Entraya was rare. Most Elves were men, and not generous but cunning, armed and out for land and booty. What's more, they could be coming only for revenge. Standing in his stirrups, Per yelled the names of various men, all horsemen, who threaded their way toward him. "The Elves are back! Rabbie, Sandy—stay you here. The rest—with me!"

And away the horsemen went, picking their way among the scattering cattle, splashing through the ford, and then kicking into a canter as they made for the tower.

Joe watched them go, an ache in his heart that he couldn't identify—was it fear or longing? He knew that, like the other footmen, he
was supposed to stay with the cattle, but—"Bugger that!" Tired
though he was after the long trek through the hills, he picked up his
feet and ran. If the Elves were back, he had to see. All the other footmen, seeing him go, deserted the cattle too—and Rabbie and Sandy
cantered after them.

The bell was ringing from the tower, a clanging and clattering of
iron on iron that rang out across the fields and called people to it.
Men who had been repairing the stone walls of sheep folds, and
women who had been gleaning in small fields of oats, or tending
vegetable plots, came trudging over the fields, calling to each other.
Why tolled the bell? Hearing a thumping of horses' hooves and a
jingling of harness, they pointed as Per and his company came can-
tering up.

Per reined in as the other riders came around him. "Elves!" he
yelled at the people. "The Elves are back!"

They were astonished by the news, and gaped, and chattered. Per
was about to lose his temper when a lad came to Fowl's shoulder,
blushing but bursting with the importance of his errand. He was to
wait for the May and give him the news. He'd been running the
words over and over in his head, trying to pack much into little.
"Elves!" he said. "On Easter Fell, nigh Aldkirk. Your daddy is
arming. He says gan and see!"

"Canny lad!" Per said, which made the boy blush hotter with
pleasure. Per drove his lance into the turf, dismounted, and took off
Fowl's headgear. Passing it to the boy, he said, "Get me a horse."
The boy ran off, followed by a friend, and Per took off Fowl's
saddle. The other men of his party were unharnessing their horses.
The animals were too tired, after their morning's work, to be ridden
fast into the hills.

While they waited for the boys to bring them loose horses from
among those that grazed all about the valley, they rubbed down the

tired beasts with grass. The boys came back, proudly leading fresh horses by their reins. Per was saddling his fresh mount when Rabbie came trotting up. Elfie-Choe was riding pillion behind him. Before he could ask why they'd disobeyed his orders, Joe slid down from the horse's back and said, "Take me with thee. I want to see the Elves. I can speak Elf!"

"Tha canna ride bareback," Per said. "And tha canna keep up on foot."

"I speak Elf," Joe said. "Tha needs me."

"Rabbie," Per said, "gie Elfie thy saddle and hoss."

Rabbie had already claimed one of the fresh horses as his and wasn't pleased to give it up, but as Per came over to help Joe put on its headgear and saddle, he meekly stood aside and said nothing. Everyone knew that Elfie-Joe was a favorite of Per's.

The horse saddled, Per crouched and held out his hands to give Joe a leg up. Joe didn't hesitate and, in a second, found himself on the horse's back without really knowing how he came there. It was as uncomfortable as ever, and he didn't look forward to the ride. His riding had improved, but it was always a way of getting from place to place, never a pleasure. He doubted that he could keep up with the expert riders around him, but if the Elves were back, he had to try. Per tightened his girth for him and said, "Keep up or be left behind."

Per tightened his own horse's girth, mounted, took his lance from a grinning lad, and kicked his horse forward. All the other mounted men fell in behind him, trotting off across the valley floor, with Joe at the end of the line, gripping a handful of saddlebow, reins, and coarse mane. The watching shepherds and farmers raised a cheer and waved them off, and the clanging of the tower's bell followed them.

Elves! Joe thought, as he rose and fell with the horse's trot, jolting uncomfortably into the saddle. How many? Eight? Ten? Armed? Of course they'd be armed—no Elf in his right mind would come unarmed into Sterkarm country, not after their last meeting. Would the Sterkarms kill them? If he fell behind the ride, would the Elves all be dead by the time he came up? He hoped not. He wanted to talk to them—in English. He didn't know why. He wasn't going back to the 21st, not now, but he did want to hear English again. He had to keep up.

24

16A:

A Truelove's Breast

††ſ

I t had seemed to make sense to send the Sterkarm horsemen
through first–they were the ones who knew the terrain best,
and were the most expendable–but it took ages to coax the
horses into the Tube. They didn't like the look of it, the sound of
it, or the smell of it. They didn't like going into an enclosed space,
and they didn't like the ramp. Some of them had eventually allowed
themselves to be persuaded; others had to be blindfolded. And
then, when they reached the other end of the Tube, the horses
didn't want to leave it. They didn't like the ramp, and the tricky bit
of footwork required from them because the ramp didn't quite meet
the ground. One or two were so obstinate that they had to be led
back through the Tube. It was all delay, and Patterson wasn't happy.

Nor was Per. If everything had gone as he wished, he would have
been first through the Elf-Gate, but Fowl was choosing that day to
be particularly difficult, and Ecky and Sim persuaded their horses
through before him. They cut turfs and packed them beneath the
ramp, and with that difficulty removed, Fowl decided that he liked
the look and smell of the green hills better than the strangeness of
the Elf-Gate and the 21st, and he allowed Per to lead him down
onto firm ground.

They led the horses away from the ramp to make room for others
to come down, stuck their lances into the turf, and looked about as
they soothed the animals. None of them spoke, but they were all
thinking the same thing. These were their hills. The sound of an Elf-
Cart was fading on the air, and they were on the moors above
Bedesdale. Per's tower wasn't far away.

Ecky asked, "This be Elf-Land?" He grinned, but his eyes were wary.

Per, too, was wondering if the Elves were making fools of them. They had been told that this Elf-Land looked just like the real world, and many old stories said the same—but even so, he'd expected some difference. They were to fight here—to fight Elves who looked just like them, in this land just like theirs? He had never felt colder and less like fighting. And then he saw something that made his hair prickle under his helmet.

"Didst hear an Elf-Cart?" he asked.

"Aye," Sim said.

"A blue yin," Ecky said, and pointed. "It made off over the rise, there."

"Look," Per said, pointing to the grassy track. The Elf-Cart had made hardly a mark. In their own world, which they'd left early that morning, the coming and going of Elf-Carts had made deep ruts. It was plain that there had been no traffic of Elf-Carts here.

From behind them came shouts, in Elvish. Turning, they saw men, Elf-Men, coming hurriedly down the ramp, packs on their backs, Elf-Pistols in their hands, to crouch or even lie down in the grass and bilberries. They recognized Elf-Patterson and Elf-Gareth, who were making for them.

Elf-Patterson shouted out something, in an angry tone, and Elf-Gareth told them what he'd said. "He wants to know where is the Elf-Cart that came through just before us?"

Per didn't feel like answering the Elf while he was shouting at him like a servant, but Sim pointed out the way the cart had gone. Elf-Patterson kicked the ground, and turned to watch the men still coming down the ramp. It was obviously going to take a long time, and there were a lot of horses to come through yet.

"Will we gan after it?" Ecky asked Elf-Gareth. "They gan slow."

Gareth passed the offer on to Patterson, who said, "No—no!" Putting his hands on his hips, he yelled, "Hurry up—hurry the fuck up!" Maybe, he thought, he should let a small company of

Sterkarms ride after Andrea. She was an untrained, unfit, fat woman: It wouldn't take Supermen to overtake and overpower her.

But no. She'd got in thick with the Sterkarms; she'd been giving the eye—and more, he guessed—to young Per. Asking them to get rough with her would only cause trouble. As for sending his own men—that would be splitting his forces. He had only a hundred men, and though his advantage in firepower was overwhelming, he needed every one of those hundred men. The mistake FUP had made previously had been to be overconfident. These people he was up against—Sterkarms, Grannams, reivers, whatever you called them—were expert guerrilla fighters. You never knew when they were watching you. Send, say, five men away from the main band and, despite their rifles, that could be five men lost, because the Sterkarms had long-range weapons too. They were called long-bows, and a smart man remembered that they were still every bit as lethal as they'd been seven hundred years ago, despite bulletproof jackets. Bulletproofs wouldn't save you from an arrow through the face or neck, or through the leg.

He watched as more restless, struggling horses were brought down the ramp with agonizing slowness and wondered if he was being overcautious, even cowardly. . . . No—he'd made his decision: Keep his small force together at full strength. Now he had to have the courage to stick by it.

"Come on, for God's sake, come on!"

In the end, some of the men and horses had to be left behind, because the horses just couldn't be persuaded to come through the Tube. Only five, but that was five men less. Bloody horses; bloody useless things. But finally they were all through, and the men were fighting with the beasts, trying to calm them—and all the progress they'd made was undone when the sound of the Tube became audible again. Its high-pitched whine made the horses prance and rear, and they took fright again when the Tube blinked out of sight. The disappearance of the Tube, leaving them on a wide expanse of alien moorland, with no way back until the Tube came on again, didn't do much for the nerves of the men, either.

Patterson came striding over to Per, Ecky, and Sim again, with Gareth hurrying to keep up with him. "Do you know where we are?" Patterson asked. "Ask them, do they know where we are?"

"Yesss," Per said, without waiting for a translation, to put Patterson in his place. "We ken."

"Can they take us to the Bedesdale Tower?" Patterson asked.

Gareth translated and Per, insulted, deliberately looked away. A wee bairn pulled off its mother's tit could have found the way to the tower from here.

"There is a tower here?" Ecky asked Gareth. "Like there is in Man's-Home?"

"This world is exactly like Man's-Home," Gareth told him. "All the hills and rivers and towers are in just the same places." The Sterkarms looked at each other and shook their heads.

"First things," Patterson said. "I want that bloody car and Andrea bloody Mitchell." He waved his men on, and they followed him at a smart pace, picking up the narrow horse ride that crossed the moor in pursuit of the little pale-blue MPV. Patterson scanned the moor and hillsides around. There was a hawk in the sky, but not another living thing could he see, not even a sheep. But if there was somebody watching, some shepherd or bloody milkmaid, then this line of moving men was, he guessed, the kind of thing that would catch their eye. He remembered something he'd read while boning up on the Sterkarms—maybe it had even been written down by Andrea bloody Mitchell: "No one can enter Bedesdale without the Sterkarms' knowledge, and no one leaves Bedesdale unless the Sterkarms allow it."

He noticed the Sterkarms, with some admiration. Some were riding, stooped low over their horses' necks; others were leading their animals, keeping close by the beast's side, so it might be taken for a horse wandering loose by itself. And they had split up, individual riders scattered over the hillside, instinctively keeping away from the skyline and moving into dips of land. Their clothes all being of soft buffs and grays, they blended into the landscape—hard to see, and if you did see them, you might, in the next instant, think you'd been mistaken. Had that been a horsemen on a distant hillside? Or had it been branches stirring in the wind, or a sheep bounding out of sight? He wished he could speak better Sterkarm, or that there'd been more money to spend in training the Sterkarms in modern weapons. He'd stand more chance of success if all his men were Sterkarms.

They made their way up and down several rises and dips, and then there was the little pale-blue MPV. As he'd guessed, bloody Andrea hadn't got far. The vehicle was off the track, such as the track was, with its nose deep in the heather and its rear in the air. The driver's door was open. Its engine was still running. Patterson wasn't surprised. You had to be a good driver to take even an MPV across country like this at speed. Well, it saved a bullet.

Patterson held up his hand to stop the men behind him and then counted off five. "With me." The other men remained where they were, warily looking about the deserted land.

Patterson edged around the car, approaching it cautiously, and his men copied him, even though there could be no one in it except an untrained, unfit, fat woman, and probably badly hurt at that. Patterson looked at the ground near the open door, expecting to see the body lying there in the heather, but there was nothing. Slowly, carefully, he approached nearer, expecting Andrea to be sprawled across the front seats, cut and bloody—but there was no one in the car, and the windshield wasn't broken. They checked thoroughly, poking through the scrub around the car, even opening the trunk.

So, quick decision—to spend time searching for that pain-in-the-arse of a woman or not? Their target was the Sterkarm tower: reach it fast, take it by surprise, destroy it. The more time they hung about searching for Andrea sodding Mitchell, the more chance there was that they'd be seen and reported, and the Sterkarms they'd come to finish would be forewarned. Even if the damn woman was still alive, what were the chances that she'd find her way, alone, across this country before them, with their expert guides?

"Okay, forget the bitch," he said, and looked around. There was

Per Sterkarm, standing by his horse's head, and at his side, usefully, was Gareth. Patterson walked over to them. "Right," he said. "The tower."

Andrea knew she hadn't much time. It was, as she'd suspected, much harder to control the car even than she'd been able to imagine, and the faster she drove, the harder it was. The car bounced, swayed—making her gasp as she remembered how tall, narrow, and unstable it was. She looked in her rearview mirror to see if she was being pursued yet, but all she could see was a crazy blur of sky and hills as the car jolted. She had to assume that whoever had come through the Tube behind her would be after her like grayhounds on a hare. And, of course, they wouldn't necessarily follow tamely along her track. They might get around in front of her. She looked to the side, and the steering went all wrong, the car rocked wildly, and she struggled for a blind, frantic moment before she realized that she was still upright and continuing to lurch across the moor.

If I'm the hare, she thought, I have to go to ground. Hares can't drive cars. Dump the car. Disappear.

The car lifted off the ground as it went over another rise, crashed back to the turf, lurched, swayed, and went on. Andrea braked and looked in the now steady mirror. There was no sign of anyone behind her. She opened the door, kicking it wide. Hurry, hurry— they might be galloping after her now, now, right now.

She grabbed her rucksack from the passenger seat, bunging it into the driver's seat. Leaning into the car—her hair rising on her neck as she imagined someone behind her, reaching for her—she used the rucksack to press down the clutch while she put the car into first gear. She lifted the clutch and the car purred forward. Now she stuffed the rucksack down on the accelerator and jumped back. The car rolled away down the slope of the moorland track without her, its door open.

She snatched one look all around. No one in sight. She ran across the track to the opposite side and plunged downhill, through the heather and the bilberry bushes and briars that scratched her legs and caught at her skirt. No time to care about that, or breathlessness. She had to run and jump, and keep her balance—she fell and rolled some way downhill—never mind, it was all progress.

Coming to a halt, she lay still, listening, and lifted her head slightly to peep above the scrub. A bird had put up near her, calling, but there was no other sound and no sign of anyone. Crouching, keeping low, sometimes even crawling, she continued to move downhill, through harsh scrub, over boulders, through bog holes. Any sound—sometimes sounds she made herself—would make her crouch low and hold her breath while her eyes almost twisted themselves from their sockets in trying to see in all directions at once.

Faint shouts from higher up the hillside. She flattened herself to the turf amid the bracken, screwed shut her eyes, held her breath. Waited. Her heart thumped against the ground beneath her, and she became confused—was it her heartbeat or the earth's? Another faint shout—a spasm of shock went through her, making one foot jump, but the shout was just as distant as the others.

She lay for an age, until she remembered lying in bed as a child, terrified of the wolves who lived in the cupboard, not daring to move or breathe for hours—and then she raised her head. She could hear birds, wind in the scrub, but no sounds that might have been made by men.

I'm going to get up, she thought. I'm going on my way. If I'm caught, I'm caught.

A long while later, muddy, sweaty, dirty, and thirsty, she had reached the bottom of a narrow, V-shaped valley, where a stream ran down among big boulders. What was she going to do now? Which direction was she going to head in, what was she going to eat, what exactly was the plan?

Miles and miles of nothing. Moorland, heather, fern. Deep, deep silence. Hills, steep valleys. A thin, sharp, damp wind. Far off, on a distant ridge, three black blobs—sheep—made their way upward.

Andrea had never had the Sterkarms' ability to tell one bracken-covered hillside with a stream and a sheep from another. Which way to Bedesdale and the tower? Was she even in Sterkarm country?

Was she in the right time window?

Why did you do this mad thing? she asked herself, and found tears of pure fear welling in her eyes. You could have gone back to life in the 21st. You could have gone back to Mick, and he would have been delighted, and you could have lived happily ever after. The only price she would have paid was knowing that, somewhere, on the other side of the air, murder was being done. And that would have been easy to forget about, wouldn't it? She'd ignored and forgotten murder almost every day of her life.

She couldn't stay here in the hope that someone might turn up. It could be weeks before anyone did, and then they might be the wrong family. Was any direction more familiar than another? Even faintly?

Choose a direction, she ordered herself. She decided to follow the narrow valley she was in downhill, toward the larger valley it must, surely, lead into. She started, clambering over large boulders, scrambling around others through thick undergrowth, crossing and recrossing the narrow stream. She knew that she'd be walking for hours, without any sign of having got anywhere. And if she met any of the locals, she might be even sorrier than she was now.

Andrea had walked and walked. Cold streams had wet her skirts, which now clung chillingly to her legs. She climbed and slipped on steep banks, where the grass was wet and slick. She was rained on. When she felt tired and wanted to sit down, she trudged on. She became so absorbed in putting one foot in front of the other that she didn't notice the riders until the sound of hooves reached her.

She looked up and saw a sight both alarming and exhilarating. A horseman on a thickset black horse, its almost ground-length mane riffling in the wind. Above the rider's helmeted head towered a tall lance.

Instinct, and a certain knowledge of the Sterkarms, made her look over her shoulder. She glimpsed another rider, who immediately wheeled away, vanishing behind rocks and scrub. When she turned again, the first rider had gone.

Outriders, she thought, checking on her and this whole area. This country seemed empty, but you never knew when a shepherd or a herding child was watching. Letting her see them had probably been deliberate. They meant to worry her. They did. Were they Sterkarms? If they were, she was safe. Well—maybe. Those horsemen she'd glimpsed coming out of the Tube behind her . . . these horsemen might be those. Her throat felt tight, and she had to swallow hard, as her heart beat faster in a heavy, almost painful way. She could speak their language, and if she talked for her life—and since she was a woman and alone—they probably wouldn't *kill* her. (But was she sure of that?)

What if they were Grannams? She suddenly felt as soft and squishy as a snail without its shell, as small and weak as a mouse: entirely unable to defend her body against sharp edges and points. Against rape. She was so scared, it felt as if she was being stifled. You didn't think this through, Andrea.

She turned in a small circle, looking all around. There was nothing to see except the thick, flowered turf and heather, rocks, scrub, and, far above, gray sky. *"God dag!"* she called out, feeling intensely foolish even as her voice shook. *"Vordan staw day?* How stands it with you? *Yi air ayn Erlf!* I am an Elf!"

A curlew called, somewhere off to her left, in all that space. She could smell something scented and spicy in the air—thyme perhaps. And then, so faint, the jingle of a bridle. They were still near!

"I am the Elf-May, Entraya! Do you mind me? Hello!"

Joe had been bumping along at the rear of the ride for a miserable age. He'd long ago lost any sense of where they were or where they were going. He was wet with both rain and sweat, though his hands, on the reins, were cold, and his nose was cold and dripping. He could only be thankful that his horse was a plodder, and be glad to still be on its back. When the ride halted at last and showed no sign of moving on, he tutted to his horse and nudged it, persuading it to move forward. Some of the other horses stamped or shifted a little as his horse came near, making him nervous, but the horses were herd mates and had been trained to stand quietly when in harness. He brought his horse up close to Per's and was relieved and glad when he saw Per looking for him, smiling when he recognized him.

Then the woman's voice called, and Joe felt his hair prickle. "I am the Elf-May, Entraya!" If only it was true! He felt, in that moment, that he loved, adored, Andrea. Another Elf! To talk again with another Elf!

He looked at Per and had never seen anyone so thunderstruck. In the next instant he thought he'd never seen Per look so afraid.

"Is it her?" Per said. Ever since word had been brought of the Elves sighted on the moor, he'd been hoping that Andrea was with them, and then sternly denying to himself that it was at all likely, for fear of disappointment, for fear of a trick. And now, hearing her voice, it was almost as much of a shock as if he'd had no knowledge of the Elves' return.

Joe opened his mouth to shout and found that the words of the 21st century no longer came readily to his tongue. He had to pause, and think, before shouting, "Andrea? Who is this?" His own voice, using those words, sounded like a stranger's to him.

There was a long pause. Silence settled back among the hills.

And then the woman's voice. "Joe?" It grew more excited. "Is that you, Joe? Joe Sterkarm, from Carloel? *Air day thu, Joe?*"

A creak of leather, a thump of weighty hooves, and Per was gone from Joe's side—and the rest of the ride moved forward, creaking and tinking, the slender ends of the lances whiffling in the air.

Per came around some boulder litter, and there stood a woman, with light-brown hair blown around her head and shoulders. She was dressed like an Elf, swathed in a large coat, but he knew the generous figure that lay hidden beneath the clothes.

He had meant to be cautious, to ask her what had been his last words to her, to test her, but as his horse picked its way closer to her, he saw more and more clearly: her anxious little face, with its clear pink skin and plump cheeks, the full mouth and the gray eyes with their scared stare. And he knew. He knew it was her, and she was alone, and had changed her mind, and given up the luxuries of Elf-Land for him. There was no need for tests or questions.

He cast down his lance and swung from his horse, letting its reins hang. He went to her, and she came to him, and as her warm solidity filled his arms and her head fitted, as if made for it, into his shoulder, tears came to his eyes.

When Andrea saw this Per swing down from his horse and come to her with his arms spread and that smile on his face, she knew. She knew this was *her* Per, could only be her Per. No one else had ever looked at her like that.

She was clenched hard against the iron plates of his jakke and enveloped in his thick smell of horses, sheep, dogs, peat smoke, and sweat. She tightened her arms around him, and who cared if the metal plates hurt? Hug him tight, press him right into her forever, and never mind if it hurts.

But there was a message she had to give. Struggling to lift her head against his hand, she said, "Per–"

His mouth pressed her lips against her teeth, his growth of stubble sandpapered her skin, the brim of his helmet bumped her head. Behind him, the Sterkarms jeered, laughed, and cheered.

When he broke the kiss, it was to press her head into his shoulder with his gloved hand and to hug her even tighter with his other arm. She was quite unable to speak. The warning could wait a minute more. She leaned on him and closed her eyes.

For there's sweeter rest
On a truelove's breast
Than any other where.